Stranded in Paradise

Steamy days, hot passionate nights!

Stranded in Paradise

OUTBACK MAN
by
Miranda Lee

THE RELUCTANT FIANCÉE
by
Jacqueline Baird

PRISONER OF THE HEART
by
Liz Fielding

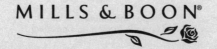

MILLS & BOON®

*MILLS & BOON and MILLS & BOON with the Rose Device
are registered trademarks of the publisher.*
Harlequin Mills & Boon Limited,
Eton House, 18-24 Paradise Road, Richmond, Surrey, TW9 1SR

STRANDED IN PARADISE
© by Harlequin Enterprises II B.V., 2001

Outback Man, The Reluctant Fiancée and *Prisoner of the Heart*
were first published in Great Britain by Harlequin Mills & Boon Limited
in separate, single volumes.

Outback Man © Miranda Lee 1991
The Reluctant Fiancée © Jacqueline Baird 1997
Prisoner of the Heart © Liz Fielding 1995

ISBN 0 263 82777 1

05-0901

*Printed and bound in Spain
by Litografia Rosés S.A., Barcelona*

Miranda Lee is Australian, living near Sydney. Born and raised in the bush, she was boarding-school educated and briefly pursued a classical music career before moving to Sydney and embracing the world of computers. Happily married, with three daughters, she began writing when family commitments kept her at home. She likes to create stories that are believable, modern, fast-paced and sexy. Her interests include reading meaty sagas, doing word puzzles, gambling and going to the movies.

Look out for
A SECRET VENGEANCE by Miranda Lee
In Modern Romance™, February 2002.

OUTBACK MAN

by

Miranda Lee

CHAPTER ONE

THE small red and white Cessna 172 was poised for take-off at the end of the runway, the lone woman pilot waving away the ground attendant. His job completed, the man glanced up and gave her one last long, admiring look.

He had watched her earlier, striding over to the plane, her slender but shapely figure stylishly dressed in a beige trouser suit and a bright yellow blouse. A man wouldn't have been a man if he hadn't been struck by her beauty. Even from a distance, the perfection of her profile was evident, as was the lustrous quality of the white-blonde hair that fell in gentle waves to her shoulders.

Now that he could see her face close up and full on he stared openly at her equally attractive features—the delicate uptilted nose, the sexy, bow-shaped mouth, the very expressive and lovely grey eyes. Eyes which glared at him with definite irritation before their owner masked their expression behind a pair of opaque sunglasses.

The groundsman moved off, muttering. Women couldn't have it both ways, he reckoned. If they did themselves up to attract male attention then they should be prepared to get it!

Adrianna Winslow took a deep, steadying breath, the man already forgotten. She was thinking with some annoyance that she didn't really want to go to Ayers Rock. Sightseeing was not her objective in going flying that afternoon. She was quite happy to just fly.

But red tape demanded a definite flight plan. So she

had given them one. Alice Springs to Ayers Rock to the Olgas, then back to Alice Springs.

Simple.

Only things weren't quite that simple, Adrianna admitted as she stared distractedly through the cockpit windscreen down the length of the runway. Nothing seemed simple to her any more.

Alan's proposal of marriage the previous evening had completely thrown her off balance. She needed time to think about it. Time alone, with nothing but empty sky around her. Time to work out just why she was even considering saying yes, when she had vowed years before *never* to get married, *never* to give a man that sort of power over her life!

She frowned as she recalled her first reaction to Alan's question. Heavens, she had been too stunned to speak. He had to be joking, she'd thought. After all, he was already married. To his business!

But then she had seen that he was serious…

Why, she began puzzling, had he asked her now, three years after they had become lovers? There had to be a reason. Alan always had a reason for everything he did.

She could still remember the night when their platonic friendship had abruptly changed into something more intimate. He had taken her out to dinner for her birthday and later, instead of giving her his usual goodnight peck at the door, he had asked to come in.

Looking back, she had the feeling his seduction of her was deliberately planned. And while she could have resisted—her mind and body had *not* been rendered useless with passion—she had sensed a desperation and need beneath his actions that moved her.

Adrianna had never found out what had been behind it all. Perhaps just normal male frustration. But, because their feelings for each other were based on true respect and affection, she had responded to his need and had quite consciously allowed him to carry her off to bed. She had expected nothing really in return, not even physical satisfaction, her one and only other sexual experience having been disappointing, to say the least.

But, surprisingly, sex with Alan had turned out quite well, his skilful lovemaking showing her how clumsy and ignorant her first lover had been. And while her eventual release had hardly been cataclysmic in intensity, it had been pleasant and satisfying.

There seemed to be no way of turning back after that, and Alan had become her lover, visiting her at least once a week. It had proved a comfortable, if somewhat lukewarm affair which Adrianna had never envisaged becoming anything else. Yet now, all of sudden, he wanted to marry her! Why?

Adrianna gave herself a mental shake. Did there have to be a reason, other than one human being's need for the company of another, a need not satisfied by an occasional meeting of bodies in bed? At twenty-eight Adrianna had been living on her own for ten years, and though she had relished her privacy at first there were times now when she ached for someone to just *be* there on a more permanent basis. Couldn't Alan be feeling the same way?

Yes, she decided, he could. And at least, she argued silently, he didn't want children. He had said so.

She closed her eyes, a shudder running through her as the thought of having children evoked memories from the past, memories which she preferred not to think about, memories which still had the power to upset her terribly.

'Miss Winslow! You've already been cleared for take-off,' a male voice ground out impatiently through the radio.

Adrianna snapped back to the present, pride in her normally efficient piloting taking a nosedive. She stiffened her spine and set the Cessna in motion, annoyed with herself for daydreaming at such a time. It wasn't like her to be so easily distracted. Not like her at all.

But then, she admitted ruefully as she accelerated the neat craft down the runway and scooped up into the wide blue yonder, she hadn't been her usual self since Alan had popped the question. She had been confused and disturbed and oddly depressed.

Yet within seconds of leaving the ground she felt a lift in her spirits, an exhilaration. That was how it always affected her, this initial soaring upwards into the air, this moment when the so-called security of terra firma was left behind, exchanged for the nebulous support of air currents rushing over seemingly fragile wings.

Was it the element of danger, she wondered, that caused the addiction to flying, that had made her pursue an amateur pilot's licence after her first joy flight four years before? Was she, underneath her supposedly cool, hard-headed businesswoman façade, really a thrill-seeker?

Unlikely. She hated taking risks in her life, hated the feeling of not being in control.

What Adrianna liked most about flying was not that first rush of adrenalin, but the feelings she experienced later, after the world on the ground had receded from her conscious mind and she was faced with nothing but wide open spaces and endless blue sky. Then she would be enveloped by a mental and spiritual peace that nothing could equal.

It was this mental and spiritual peace she desperately needed today…

She angled the small single-engined plane away from the airport and into a wide sweeping circle, deciding to take in an aerial view of Alice Springs before heading over the mountains to the south and across the desert to Ayers Rock.

She leant sidewards and peered down at the township below, and slowly shook her head. Alice Springs wasn't at all like she'd expected. She had pictured a harsh frontier town, choked with heat and dust, not this green, tree-dotted replica of Sydney suburbia. It was hard to believe that the ordered settlement below was smack dab in the dead centre of Australia.

Apparently they had had a bumper year with regard to rainfall, the normally dry Todd River actually over-flowing its banks several times. The town wasn't usually so lush, the locals said. So Adrianna conceded that she wasn't seeing the real Alice Springs at all. Though Alan had been right in his assessment of the tourist situation, judging by the number of motels she had spotted that morning during her drive around the town.

'There's plenty of money passing through the Alice,' he had told her over dinner last Friday in Sydney. 'Plenty of money to buy your Adrianna brand of exclusive Australian fashions. I'm flying out myself on Monday to tie up a site for one of my own stores. Why don't you come along and have a look, see if you can find a suitable spot for one of your upmarket boutiques?'

So Adrianna had flown to Alice Springs with Alan, confident that he would never advise her badly. He had his finger on the fashion pulse, his record for success impeccable during the years she had known him. At the relatively young age of thirty-one he already owned and controlled a flourishing rag trade business, not to men-

tion a chain of quality menswear shops in every main
city and large town in Australia.

He had helped her select a boutique site yesterday—
in a small but central arcade—and she had tied up the
lease then and there. Then Alan had successfully nego-
tiated his deal. Adrianna recalled glancing across the table at him as he studied the menu last night, and thinking
how much alike they were, how much in common they
had. He had looked up suddenly, seen her watching him,
and smiled.

Had the same thoughts struck him too? Had his proposal of marriage been a spur-of-the-moment decision?

Adrianna didn't think so. Alan was not a spur-of-the-
moment sort of person.

With a jolt she realised she had been holding the plane
in a continuous circling pattern for ages. She flushed as
pride in her powers of concentration dropped another
peg. Anyone watching her from the ground would be
thinking she was mad! Which perhaps she was, to even
be mulling over the matter. Marriage was not for her,
no matter how much she and Alan had in common!

She quickly straightened the highly manoeuvrable
craft and set a south-westerly course, resolving to forget
about Alan's proposal for the next few hours and just
try to enjoy herself. She had committed herself to going
to Ayers Rock, and it was, after all, supposed to be worth
seeing.

But to say that Adrianna enjoyed her flight to the
Rock was a long way from the truth. She had flown into
Alice Springs at night, so she hadn't really seen the surrounding countryside. With Alice Springs so green she
had expected the desert to have sprung to life as well.
So as she gazed at the landscape unfolding before her
eyes she was quite shocked by what she was seeing.

Apparently the rain hadn't reached this far south, or if so its effects had been quickly swallowed up by the hot sands, for she was being confronted by the most awesome, endless expanse of flat, dry, hot, red, wretched land she had ever seen. Not a speck of appreciable grass in sight. Not a decent tree, a river, a house. A forbidding, frightening frontier.

She dragged in a deep breath, then let it out with a ragged sigh. 'Heavens,' she muttered. 'What am I doing, flying over this godforsaken place?'

She tried a laugh, but it came out sounding like a nervous squeak. She swallowed, but there was a tight constriction in her throat, a fluttering in her stomach that wouldn't go away. This unfamiliar feeling of fear soon brought a countering rebellious surge, and she clenched her teeth hard in her jaw.

Don't be ridiculous, she told herself. You're no more at risk here than you are anywhere else in the air. Besides, you've paid good money for this flight. Make the most of it!

Her self-lecturing over, Adrianna did settle down slightly, even to almost appreciating the primeval power of the land below her. There was no denying its overwhelming size, its brutal beauty, its ancient grandeur. But she doubted she would ever feel entirely comfortable with putting herself within grabbing distance of its pitiless bony hands. How could one survive, she wondered, if abandoned to such an environment? Death, she felt sure, would come slowly, and very painfully.

So she tended to keep her eyes straight ahead, finding comfort from the familiarity of the sky. Though even the sky was different from what she was used to, the darker blue having a brittle-bright harshness that pierced her sunglasses and made her look down every now and then.

Oh, the joy, the relief, when on one of these occasions she saw a bus streaking along what she supposed was a road, red clouds of dust billowing out behind it. She wasn't alone at all!

The eventual sighting of Ayers Rock in the distance was the final distraction from any further feelings of fear.

'Wow! That's really something!' Adrianna exclaimed aloud.

And something it certainly was. The world's largest monolith, the last remnant of what had once, billions of years before, been a mountain chain, it rose from the desert, majestic and incredibly solid, mute testimony to the incomprehensible dimensions of time and the incorruptible forces of nature.

Adrianna had no idea how big it looked from the ground, but as she drew nearer its enormity awed her. As did its colour—a glittering bronze on top, deepening to a burnished red on the sides.

The strangest sort of feeling washed through her as she approached the Rock. It was humbling, but at the same time uplifting. Adrianna didn't find it surprising that people came from the four corners of the earth to look at this wonder, this concrete reminder of the permanency of their planet.

She waggled her wings as she flew over, waving to the many tourists struggling to climb up the formidable incline. They all stopped, smiled and waved back, and she felt a brief but startlingly intense burst of happiness. It surprised her at first, till she accepted what lay behind it: that, much as a person could take pleasure in something by him or herself, the pleasure was much greater when that something was shared.

The word 'shared' lit up like a headline in her brain. Wasn't this what she had had been missing in her life?

Wasn't this the one part of marriage that definitely appealed to her? How satisfying it would be to have Alan always there to share things with, her troubles as well as her successes. Already they shared a good deal. Why not the rest?

It made sense—solid sense. Adrianna decided then and there. She would accept Alan's proposal. She would marry him!

With the weight of indecision lifting from her shoulders, she instantly felt better. Only then did she realise that this was what had been depressing her—her uncharacteristic lack of direction. It was good to feel in control again, to know where she was heading.

A light laugh bubbled up through her nicely shaped mouth. I'll tell you where you're heading, her newly happy self said. To the next wonder of the world!

And with a relaxed smile and the automatic skill of a pilot who had over five hundred hours' flying to her credit, she swung the Cessna away and set her course for the Olgas, the smaller sisters to Ayers Rock. She could see them in the distance, looking like a handful of lavender-coloured marbles, though she knew from reading her tourist brochure that up close they would look much larger and assume an orange-red or yellowish glow, depending on the time of day.

Adrianna was over the huge rounded boulders within minutes, and they were just as fascinating, though not quite as impressive, as Ayers Rock. She circled over them a couple of times, half reluctant now to turn the plane for the flight back to Alice Springs. She had technically chartered the plane for the whole afternoon, a tankful of fuel giving her a range of over six hundred miles. If she went straight back, she would be throwing away three hundred miles' worth of pleasure, just because she felt slightly nervous of the territory she was flying over. Which was pretty pathetic, she decided, never having been one to give in to irrational fears.

So she set a northerly course, resolving to fly a hundred and fifty miles that way before heading for home. She could see a mountain range in the dim distance, which she reasoned was probably the Macdonnell ranges that led right into Alice Springs. They would do for a turning point.

But she came to the mountain range so quickly she decided they couldn't be the Macdonnells, a decision backed up by the sighting of some more peaks on the horizon. She headed their way, enjoying the terrain more now that there was the light and shade of frequent ridges and hills, and the occasional tree and smattering of green on the plains. The sun was beginning to sink in the sky, and a glance at her watch told her it was after three. Once over the ranges she would turn east and head for Alice Springs. She soared over their relatively low height with ease, and was glancing back over her shoulder at them when disaster struck.

What actually happened she had no idea. One second she was flying happily along, the next there was this awful reverberating thud. The back dipped first, then shot up as the nose dropped, the plane plummeting downwards in a deadly spin, its front propeller pointed straight at the ground.

Panic came quickly, and stayed, joined by a wild surge of adrenalin that had Adrianna searching frantically for some way, some hidden skill that would let her escape the certain death she was facing. Those long-forgotten hours of acrobatic flying that were compulsory for all learner pilots came back to her in a jumble. She struggled with the controls, fighting to get the nose up, the wings steady. But her hands were shaking uncontrollably, her stomach in her throat, a burning in her chest. The only plus in the horrendous situation was that the mountains were now behind her, giving her another precious thousand feet with which to avoid the seemingly unavoidable.

Then without warning, without knowing how she had done the impossible, the nose limped upwards, the wings shuddering to a semblance of being level. She was still going down, still going to crash. But she had a chance, with the ground rushing towards her looking blessedly flat.

It wasn't.

The front wheels hit a hump in the sand within seconds of touching down and ricocheted upwards. Adrianna's heart and stomach went with it. 'God help me,' she prayed.

The plane had somehow spun round and was charging towards the base of the mountains she had just passed. It bucked and leapt a crazy path with the brakes virtually useless. The wheels were never on the ground long enough to grip. The crazed craft was gradually losing speed. But not quickly enough.

A cliff face loomed up in front of the windscreen, a head-on collision inevitable. The impact was bone-shattering, but only lasted a couple of seconds before everything went black.

It was dark when Adrianna came round. Dark dark. She couldn't even see her hands before her eyes. But even without seeing them she knew they were trembling. Her whole body started trembling. Her worst fears had materialised. Not only had she crashed, but she had crashed somewhere in that ghastly decrepit desert without anyone in authority knowing exactly where.

Bile rose into the back of her throat and she bent forward, sure she was going to be sick. But she forced her nausea back down, calling on that emergency supply of courage people sometimes found in moments of crisis. Panic and hysteria hovered around the edges of her mind, but she pushed them to one side, telling herself that it couldn't be time for her to die just yet. If it was, then she would have perished in the crash.

She said a little prayer of thanks and set about examining herself for damage. Her hands still shook, but she slowly and methodically felt over her face. No blood, no swelling, just a small lump behind her left eyebrow. She had a headache, though. A bad one.

But one didn't die from a headache, did one?

She stayed where she was, moving first one bit of her body, then the next. There were some parts which, if she could see, were probably bruised, since they were sore. But she didn't think there were any bones broken. It was at this point that she remembered the cockpit light and the radio. Shock had robbed her of her brains, she decided. Cursing herself for her stupidity, she groped forward till she found the light switch.

It didn't work.

She controlled her disappointment with difficulty and groped further, and with a rapidly sinking heart tried the radio. Tried and tried and tried. But there wasn't even a bleep, or some static to give her hope. It was dead. As dead as the plane was, as dead as she should have been.

So be thankful for small mercies, she told herself firmly when panic and despair raised their ugly heads again. They would know by now back at Alice Springs that you haven't returned, she reasoned. Planes will be out searching at first light. And a wrecked plane should stand out like a sore thumb in a desert.

Sure it should, a brutal inner voice piped up. If the rescue planes knew where to look, you blithering idiot!

Adrianna groaned her dismay. Why, oh, why hadn't she radioed in her flight detour? It was pointless to argue that most joy-riding pilots didn't bother with what seemed an officious air-safety rule. The fact was, she had made a fatal mistake which could cost her her life.

But surely, she argued shakily, they would still eventually find her?

Yet even as she kept soothing her fears with logic— Alan was a wealthy man; even if the authorities gave up he would hire all the planes, all the helicopters he could find—a dark feeling of despair took possession of her and her eyes filled with tears. She dashed them away impatiently, only then realising that her sunglasses were no longer in place. She supposed they must have fallen on the floor somewhere. Not that it mattered. Nothing mattered any more…

She started crying with violent, bone-wrenching sobs. This time she didn't try to stop, or tell herself to be brave. It felt good to cry, to let out all the shock and terror that had been building up in her ever since she had come back to consciousness. And by the time the sobs had subsided she did feel better. Stronger. More able to cope with the problems ahead.

A shiver ran through her, reminding her that her most immediate problem was the cold. It was only newly spring, and, while the days were nicely hot in the desert, the nights were freezing. Adrianna shivered again as she reached for her linen jacket on the empty co-pilot's seat, dragging it over stiffening shoulders. She thought about trying to get out of the plane—since nature was calling—but in the end decided to try to hang on till dawn.

It would be crazy of her to fall over and hurt herself in the dark after surviving such a horrific crash.

The dawn came with agonising slowness, worry, muscular cramps and a bursting bladder making real sleep impossible and the wait sheer hell. Around five there was sufficient light for Adrianna to struggle out and relieve herself. But she was appalled to see exactly where the plane had finished up, jammed under a ledge, with a surprisingly leafy tree growing out of the cliff above and completely overshadowing it. From the sky the little Cessna wouldn't be visible at all.

She groaned, her despair intense as her eyes travelled wearily along the body of the plane till it reached the tail. Or at least, where the tail should have been. Her gasp echoed up the empty grey hills behind her. Goodness, what had happened to the *tail*? Surely it couldn't have fallen off through metal fatigue. It looked like a fairly new craft. She must have collided with another plane in mid-air, even though she hadn't seen one. Perhaps the other plane hadn't been damaged and had flown on to tell the authorities what had happened, and where? If so then they would know where to look for her after all.

These thoughts lifted her spirits. Till she gazed around properly for the first time. 'Oh, my God!' she cried softly.

A pale pre-dawn light was streaking the cliffs behind her with an eerie misty blue. But it wasn't this that filled her with dread, but the terrible ocean of sand that stretched ahead of her as far as the eye could see. What if she were wrong? What if there had been no other plane? What if no one ever found her?

She turned away, her eyes brimming. She blundered over to the plane and sagged against it, her head dropping into her arms. But within minutes she had straightened, resolving to spend her energies, not on panic and futile tears, but in finding ways and means to help her survival till rescue came.

First she searched the plane, and was greatly relieved to find a two-gallon can of water, two apples, a thick checked rug and a small tin of cream biscuits tucked under the passenger seat. That, combined with the orange drink, banana and packet of mints she had in her straw carry-all, would at least stop her from dying of thirst and starvation till she could be rescued. She was glad too that she had brought a hat with her, even if it was a rather impractically elegant straw creation which sported a jungle-print chiffon scarf around the crown. With some orange juice and a banana in her stomach and the hat on her head, she set about collecting rocks to make a large SOS out in the open.

The sun lifted higher, a hot ball of heat that sapped her strength and dehydrated her body. And while she was hellishly hot she kept her jacket on so that her arms wouldn't burn. She wished her sunglasses hadn't been totally obliterated in the crash, for the glare was horrendous. The flies were a bother too, making her regret she'd left her insect repellent back at the motel. Perfume and hair spray, she had found, didn't work.

But creature comforts were hardly important at this point in time, she thought, and kept carting more and more stones into place. She had already completed the letters, but she continued making them more definite, thinking that any activity was better than none. She was afraid that sitting around worrying would quickly bring on the hysteria she felt lurking just beneath her surface composure. Twice she heard planes. Depressingly, though, they didn't come near enough to see her distress signal or her frantic hat-waving.

The third time she picked up a sound Adrianna scrambled up on to a high rock ledge. Her gaze searched the pitiless blue sky, but she couldn't see any plane. Gradually, the sound she was hearing became clearer and louder, but it wasn't anything like the drone of an engine. It wasn't coming from the sky either, but from somewhere out on the desert plains ahead.

She shaded her eyes with her hands and peered out into the distance where the escalating heat had turned the sands into what looked like a shimmering lake. It was the first mirage she had actually seen, and she could imagine how they would have fooled many a man dying of thirst.

The sound was coming closer, becoming a definite clang-clang as regular as a pulsebeat. But still she couldn't see anything.

And then she did, her hands dropping from her eyes, her mouth gasping wide as a camel and rider appeared through the haze. They were moving at a quick trot, a swinging cow-bell under the camel's neck responsible for the noise she was hearing. A pack-camel followed behind, strung to the leading animal by a rope, its neck stretched forward with obvious reluctance at being hauled along at such a speed.

Amazement soon gave way to an overwhelming relief, and Adrianna found herself leaping down from the ledge and dashing across the hot red sand towards her rescuer. Her hat flew off on the way, but she didn't care. 'Here! Here!' she screamed. 'I'm over here!'

Her heart pounded as her feet stumbled over half-hidden rocks. But she didn't seem to notice the scrapes to her sandalled feet. The man on the camel had seen her—she was sure he had. She was safe, she was safe. She wasn't going to die after all!

CHAPTER TWO

THE man riding the camel looked startled by her hysterical approach, and reined his animal in with a loud 'whoa!' It responded immediately, skidding to an ungainly halt not a metre from Adrianna, but the camel behind blundered on, cannoning into its leader's backside and almost dislodging its rider from the enormous bedouin-style saddle.

Adrianna stared up at her unlikely knight in shining armour on his equally unlikely steed, unashamed tears of relief welling up in her eyes. But the man wasn't looking down at her. He was glaring back over his shoulder and slowly shaking his head.

'For Pete's sake, Dumbo,' he chided, 'are you deaf as well as stupid? I said *whoa*, not *go!*'

The camel hung its head, glancing up at its master so sheepishly that Adrianna found herself laughing.

The man swung his gaze back to peer down at her. He lifted one large leg over the saddle and slid down to the ground with a surprisingly light landing. 'You have an unusual sense of humour, little lady,' he drawled.

Now not many people called Adrianna *little*, her five feet nine inches being considered quite tall for a woman. Admittedly, she *was* lightly boned and the well-designed trouser suit and yellow silk shirt didn't add any bulk to her curvy figure. But not in anyone's wildest imagination could Adrianna be considered petite. Still, next to this man, any woman might have seemed little. Not only was he excessively tall—six four or five at least—but he was broad and muscular as well.

Very muscular, she judged, mentally stripping him of his bushman's clothes of khaki shirt and faded blue jeans. Her eyes ran down two long powerful legs, then up, till they reached a ruggedly handsome, tanned face and the bluest of blue eyes she had ever seen, eyes that were surveying her from underneath the dusty brown Akubra hat with an equal and rather unnerving candour.

'I take it you're the only survivor?' he asked.

'Yes,' she croaked.

The man sighed. 'So the pilot *was* killed. Poor devil!'

'No, no, you've got it all wrong.'

His frown showed confusion. 'He *wasn't* killed?'

'No…he wasn't… I mean…' Adrianna dragged in a steadying breath. 'I'm the pilot,' she stated. And waited resignedly for the usual male reaction.

It didn't come. There was a slight lifting of his left eyebrow and a muttered, 'Well, well,' as his eyes swept over her again in a swift reassessment. But all in all his reaction was less chauvinistic than one might have expected of an outback man.

'Passengers?' he asked, clearly a man of few words.

'None,' she answered just as succinctly.

A flash of relief crossed his eyes, and she wondered why.

'And you're not hurt?' he went on in that lazily attractive voice of his.

'A few bumps and bruises,' she admitted. 'And my shoulders are a bit stiff.'

'Mine too,' he said, and sucking in a deep breath, stretched his arms wide.

My, but he had a big chest, Adrianna thought, seeing the buttons on his shirt almost pop out when his lungs expanded. Big chest, big shoulders, big hands. Big all over, she fancied.

A flush crept up her neck as she realised where her eyes had strayed. She whipped her gaze back upwards, relieved to find that her rescuer hadn't noticed her potentially embarrassing appraisal. His blue eyes were fixed over her shoulder, staring at the wreck of the plane.

Adrianna felt quite irritated with herself, not to mention startled. It wasn't like her to ogle a man physically. She knew a lot of women did, but she never had. Alan was a strikingly handsome man, tall and lean and well-proportioned, but his physical attractions hadn't figured greatly in Adrianna's relationship with him. It was his quick decisive mind, his strong driving ambition that she found the most appealing part of his person.

Now here she was, being unexpectedly impressed by a brawny individual who probably had little more brain power than the camels he rode. As for drive and ambition... It was hard to see this hulk of male machismo having any measurable quantity of either. He talked slow, moved slow, and by his escalating silence even thought slow. She decided he probably made love with the same lack of energy and enthusiasm.

His eyes swung back to hers, with Adrianna still rattled by this last thought. For a woman whose mind rarely dwelt on sexual matters, her thoughts since encountering this desert cowboy were definitely getting out of hand. So he was a good-looking guy with a great body. So what? she thought dismissively. The only thing about him that should matter to her was his ability to conduct her safely back to civilisation, or to stay with her till the cavalry came.

'You certainly are one lucky lady,' he said with a wry shake of his head. 'When I saw your plane go down like a stone, I thought you were a goner. But after I didn't see any signs of fire I began to wonder. I knew I couldn't make it this far yesterday afternoon before dark, so I came over at first light this morning.'

'Came over from where?' she asked, hoping and praying that he meant a nearby cattle station. Though from the look of the surrounding desert-like countryside she couldn't imagine any animals grazing over it with any success. Still, she had read that there were cattle stations in very remote areas now since the advent of artesian bores and other new management ideas.

'I'm camped about twenty miles away. That way…' He pointed back towards the shimmering horizon. 'I left most of my supplies behind in case I needed Dumbo here for someone to ride. It's just as well I did, and it's also just as well there's only one of you.'

'*Me*? Ride *Dumbo*?' On hearing his name said so loudly, Dumbo reefed backwards and almost fell over. Adrianna's face showed horror. 'For twenty *miles*?' she squeaked, aghast. Heavens, she had never even been on a horse, let alone a camel of such obvious waywardness!

The man's face held a sardonic amusement. 'Twenty miles will seem like nothing by the time I get you back home. We're a long way from anywhere here. But don't worry, Dumbo's a lamb. And I'm an expert instructor. Look, I'll go tie the camels up under that tree for a couple of hours' rest while we have lunch and a siesta, then I'll give you some riding lessons and we can start back.'

He began walking towards the cliffs and the plane, dragging the camels behind him. Adrianna stood where she was for a couple of seconds in shock, then raced to catch up. 'But wouldn't it be wiser to stay here with the plane?' she said frantically. 'It's only a matter of time till I'm found. I know the plane's camouflaged by that tree overhanging it, but I've made an SOS out there in the open with rocks.'

'No one's likely to see it,' he said.

'Why do you say that?'

'Firstly, you're not under any usual flight path. Secondly, you obviously didn't have time to send out a proper Mayday call and give your location, or a rescue helicopter would be here by now. They've had all morning. And by the look of that wreck, your radio's busted as well.'

'Yes…yes, it is,' she confessed, surprised by his intuitive and deductive reasoning.

'Want me to make another guess?' he went on drily. 'You took a slight sightseeing detour and didn't radio in your change of flight plans, right?'

'Right,' she admitted unhappily.

His sigh carried exasperation. 'You do realise that's a cardinal sin out here in the outback? People die when they make stupid mistakes like that.'

Adrianna bristled.

'Still,' he continued before she could bite out a fitting retort, 'we're all guilty of taking our safety in the sky for granted every once in a while, me included.'

'You can fly?' she almost gasped, then realised how condescending that sounded. 'I mean…' Her voice trailed away in embarrassment.

His expression betrayed definite irritation. 'Flying in the outback is almost as common as driving in a city,' he pointed out sharply. 'I take it you *are* a city girl?' he added, giving her an impatient glance.

'Well, yes, but… Oh, you must be psychic or something! How could you possible know I'm from the city?'

Those startling blue eyes raked over her from head to toe.

'Aside from your making a basic error no outback pilot ever would,' came his laconic observation, 'not too many country girls tog themselves out in pure linen and silk when flying.'

Adrianna stared over at him. He recognised pure linen and silk at a glance? Who *was* this man? She could hardly imagine some roving jackaroo, or drover, or camel trainer, or whatever he was, having such an eye for fashion fabrics. But then he was constantly surprising her, wasn't he?

They reached the back end of the wrecked plane and the man paused, lifting his hat and scratching his head as he stared at the jagged edges of metal where the tail had been. Adrianna stared too, but not at the plane. Her eyes were on the man's well-shaped head, which was covered with attractive thick brown hair cut very short all over. It was not a style she normally liked, but on this man it looked very attractive in a rough-and-tough Army sergeant fashion. Here was a man you just knew you didn't cross swords with, his deceptive slowness probably hiding reflexes that could be as quick as his mind had proved to be.

'Have you got any idea what caused this?' he asked, clearly puzzled.

She shook her head. 'Not really. I thought I might have collided with another plane, but…'

'There wasn't any other plane,' he interrupted firmly. 'I watched you crash through my telescope and there wasn't another aircraft in sight.'

'There wasn't?' She was mulling over what else might have caused her to crash when she suddenly realised what he had said about a telescope. 'Oh! Oh, I see,

you're an astronomer!' she exclaimed, pleased at con-
firming her growing suspicion that her rescuer couldn't
possibly be a country yokel.

His laugh was deep and drily amused. 'Sorry to disappoint you. I simply like knowing where I'm going
while I'm on walkabout in the desert. I do confess to an
occasional study of the stars at night, but I wouldn't
know one heavenly body from another. At least...' a
slow but wickedly knowing smile captured his strong,
wide mouth '...none that are beyond reach.'

Adrianna stiffened, his suddenly admiring eyes sending a warning shiver up and down her spine. 'I thought
only Aboriginals went walkabout,' she said in a cold
voice, intent on making sure this outback Lothario didn't
get the wrong idea where she was concerned. She should
have realised that a man as good-looking as this would
fancy himself a lady-killer.

He eyed her thoughtfully before speaking. 'In the
main, I guess that's so,' he admitted, 'but you can't live
out here for as long as I have and not pick up some of
their ways. Look, I think we'd best cut the chit-chat short
and get out of this heat. You don't have anything on
your head, and you'd be surprised how quickly one can
get sunstroke.'

With that he took her elbow and urged her to sit down
under the shade thrown by the body of the plane. The
bush flies immediately surged on to her still body, making her swat from side to side in the great Australian
salute.

'Little devils, aren't they?' he observed. 'You'll be
pleased to know I have a roll-on insect repellent back at
my camp. Plus some other mod cons.'

'Such as?' she threw after him as he strode away, the
two camels in tow.

'Toilet paper,' he returned with a laugh.

Adrianna cringed. This was going to be a nightmare! She sighed and watched wearily as her intrepid bushman led his trusty transports up on to the rock ledge and settled them down under the tree before returning to squat beside her.

'How much water have you got?' he asked, pushing the brim of his hat back so that it was perched on the back of his head. It gave her a clear and close view of his face, of the strong bones and planes that fashioned its rugged attractiveness. The lines around his mouth and eyes could have been premature ageing from the sun, she reasoned, or the natural result of his being about the thirty years he looked.

She went to ask him how he knew she had any water, but stopped herself in time. She wasn't sure yet if he was a genuinely intelligent being, or merely possessed of a canny sense of logic and survival. But in either case she instinctively knew he would have a valid reason behind any conclusion he came to. And she wasn't going to humiliate herself further by amusing him with her pathetic questions.

'There was a two-gallon can in the plane,' she told him.

'What about food?'

'I've got two apples, a tin of biscuits and a packet of mints. I had some orange juice and a banana for breakfast.'

He glanced at his watch. 'Half-past eleven... If we leave around one, we should make it back to my camp before dusk. But we can't afford to dawdle across that particular stretch. It's mostly salt-pan and there's no water at all along the way.'

Adrianna digested all this for a few seconds without

saying anything. It bothered her that she felt so helpless and ignorant. Also that she had to depend on the judgement of a virtual stranger. She had never trusted her future to another human being, and it worried her to have to do so now. 'But isn't your camp due west?' she questioned. 'Wouldn't we be more likely to come across a road and people sooner if we go east?'

'Yes.'

'Then why don't we?'

'Because I'm not sure of the way,' he explained curtly. 'Because I only brought limited supplies with me. And because my dog is waiting for me back at my camp.'

'Oh…' She could hardly suggest he abandon his dog, or strike out across unknown territory.

'We'll leave a note behind in case a search plane sights your SOS. Though unless they see it soon, the rocks will quickly be covered by blowing sand. Don't look so worried,' he added. 'I've got plenty of provisions. I was expecting to be out here for two weeks yet, but I'll get you home safe and sound in less than a week.'

'A *week*!' she gasped.

He shrugged at her shock. 'It'll take about six days to get back to Dover Downs. But there's a plane there that can take you to whatever city you live in.'

'Sydney,' she told him, frowning. 'Dover Downs… I've never heard of it. Is it a town?'

'No, a cattle station, south-east of the Kimberleys, not far from the border between Western Australia and the Northern Territory.'

'You work there, do you?' When he hesitated she added somewhat caustically, 'When you're not on walkabout, that is.'

His left eyebrow lifted slightly again, and she wished she hadn't used that sarcastic tone. She wasn't sure why she had, except that this man was rattling her as no man had ever done before. Cold sarcasm had often proved an effective weapon for her in the past, when she felt sexually threatened by a man. The difference here was that it was her own sexual awareness that was worrying her, not the man's! Really, except for that one remark about heavenly bodies her rescuer hadn't shown any male-female interest in her at all.

He sat down on the rocky ground next at her, his expression one of total indifference. 'You could always stay here by yourself,' he said, 'and keep brushing the sand off your SOS. They might widen the search for you after a day or two. Are you important enough for them to?'

'My fiancé might think so,' she countered, stung that this man didn't seem to care what she did one way or the other.

His glance went to her conspicuously ringless left hand.

'I... We only decided to get married two nights ago,' she elaborated hastily, an embarrassing heat zooming into her cheeks at this light stretching of the truth. It wasn't really a lie, she excused herself. She would say 'yes' as soon as she got back to Sydney.

Her present companion didn't make any comment, however, and Adrianna got the impression he didn't give a damn whether she was engaged or not anyway. His gaze had returned to the smashed tail of the plane and he was staring at it, frowning.

Adrianna tried to ignore the pique she felt at such obvious uninterest, but it was impossible. She kept thinking what a mess she must look and began fingering down her fringe, smoothing and turning the ends of her hair under in a rough semblance of its normally sleek, well-groomed state. She groaned inwardly at the thought of her face. Every vestige of yesterday's make-up would have melted off long ago, probably leaving streaks and smudges. She didn't carry a mirror or make-up in her bag, having always hated women who primped and preened all the time.

This thought brought her up with a jolt. What am I doing, trying to look attractive for this man? she thought. I'm an engaged woman. Well…almost!

She lowered her hands and clenched them tightly in her lap, then stared agitatedly out at the desert. 'Alan won't let a stone remain unturned till he finds me,' she insisted.

'Right!' The man beside her stood up. 'In that case, what say I give you what supplies I can spare and leave you to it?'

Adrianna jumped to her feet. 'But…but…I'll die here if no one ever finds me!' she protested.

'True,' he said without a flicker.

She was appalled by his apparently indifferent attitude. 'Don't you *care*?' she asked accusingly.

'Of course I care,' he said in a maddeningly phlegmatic tone. 'But I'm not in the habit of forcing people to do things they don't want to do. I gather from your response to my earlier reference to your delectable female body that you're afraid I'm some sort of wandering sex maniac who's going to ravish you in the desert sands.'

She tried to keep a straight face, tried not to let any sort of guilt show. Little did he know that what she feared most was that she might *want* him to ravish her!

'Let me assure you, lady,' he added with a dry laugh,

'that making love is not high on my agenda of activities for desert crossings. Firstly, the sand is hot enough to burn one's butt off. Then there's a few other hazards such as flies, ants, scorpions, lizards and snakes. Not to mention spikes and prickles. Rolling into a spot of spinifex would dampen even the most determined Casanova, believe me. I don't know about you, but I like my sex between cool sheets, with a freshly showered partner beside me. I also prefer my women definitely unattached, being single myself. So I'm afraid that at the moment, despite your undeniable attractions and a certain lingering dash of French perfume, you just don't qualify.'

Adrianna gaped at him. She wasn't shocked by what he had just said—she was a modern woman, after all—but she hated the feelings of fluster this man kept engendering in her. She was used to being on top of situations, particularly in her relationships with the opposite sex. Now here she was, being thoroughly thrown by this…this *farm-hand*!

She felt the urge to explode into a most uncustomary tantrum, telling him she didn't appreciate such talk; that her sex life was her own business; and that his uncouth self would be the last person on earth she would entertain the thought of cohabiting with—even between those aforementioned cool sheets.

'Well, what do you say?' he went on brusquely. 'Are you coming with me or not?'

Her mouth snapped shut, and she kept it that way while she battled to control her rampant emotions. Finally she lifted her chin and eyed him with a type of cool reproach. 'It seems I have no other viable alternative,' she said coldly.

'It seems so,' he agreed, an answering hardness steeling those beautiful blue eyes.

Three hours later, Adrianna was regretting her decision to go with him, thinking privately that risking death was preferable to what she was going through. Her head was aching; her shoulders were aching; her bottom was aching; her thighs were aching. Sweat was pouring down her face, her neck, her back, soaking her clothes and making them stick to her in the most uncomfortable fashion. Flies crawled around her eyes, up her nose, into the corners of her mouth. She decided she hated camels, hated the desert, hated the heat; and, above all, hated the man riding the camel in front of her.

Riding lessons, he had said. Huh! He'd virtually plonked her on to the highly uncomfortable saddle, showed her how to hold the reins, shouted 'Up, up!' to the camel, and they were on their way. The only consolation she had was that by the time twenty miles of this torture was completed it wouldn't matter that dumb Dumbo didn't know the difference between 'whoa' and 'go'. They would both sink to the ground in an exhausted, shattered heap.

She glared at the man ahead, amazed that she could have for a moment found him attractive. He was nothing but a bully-boy with no consideration for others, a typically high-handed male egotist who didn't think he had to explain anything to a woman. Within minutes of her agreeing to go with him, he had virtually reduced her to the role of weak, helpless, dependent female, telling her what she could eat, how much she could drink, how long she could rest, what she should wear, etc, etc, etc, without giving the slightest concession to her own intelligence or initiative.

The trouble was that under the circumstances she could do little but acquiesce, or seem like a fool. So she smiled on the surface, and seethed inside. And if she betrayed her underlying resentment occasionally, he pretended not to notice, except perhaps during the incident over her hat. She would never forgive him for that. Never!

It had been so unnecessary to rip two holes in the brim to stuff the scarf through in order to tie the hat on to her head. But he had done so without consulting her. When she had pointed out with sweet sarcasm that the same result could have been achieved by taking the long scarf *over* the brim his face had hardened and he'd said gruffly, 'Not as much shade that way. Nor as firm.'

Then he proceeded to demonstrate by ramming it down on her head and tying it so tight it must have made her look ridiculous. She had fumed under the feeling of impotence that raged within her, unable to stop the fury from showing through in her cold-eyed glare. For a second he had glared back at her, and she could have sworn was about to say something, but at the last moment he had whirled away and stalked off. It had given her a vengeful sense of satisfaction to see that he could be stirred from his annoyingly self-contained persona.

But he had quickly resumed his calm, composed I-know-better-than-you attitude, leaving her feeling just as powerless as before. He was the omnipotent boss in this situation and he knew it. *She* knew it. But it didn't make it any easier to bear, resentment burning through her entire being. Perhaps he sensed the hate-filled glare boring into his back as they plodded along, for suddenly he whirled around in the saddle. 'You OK back there, Adrianna?' he asked.

'Fine,' she smiled through gritted teeth. She refused

to call him Bryce, though they had exchanged Christian names back at the plane. She refused to acknowledge that he would ever be anything more to her than a nameless itinerant station worker with whom fate had forced her to spend an unfortunate span of time.

'I want you to grip the front of your saddle,' he shouted back over his shoulder. 'I'm going to break Jumbo here into a trot, and Dumbo will naturally follow. OK?'

'Fine.'

She did as he told her and braced herself for further horrors. Walking had been bad enough, the rolling, rocking gait constantly reminding her of every bruise in her poor battered body. But when the beast below her lurched into the faster motion Adrianna almost died. Her bottom bounced up and down, up and down, till every bone from her pelvis upwards was being jarred with the most excruciating pain. She clenched her jaw hard and held on grimly, determined that not a word of complaint was going to come from her lips. Not a single word! She glared ahead at her tormentor, vowing she would never give him a solitary reason for making her feel more weak and helpless than she was already feeling.

They trotted across the flat, seemingly never-ending plain for over an hour, the salt surface finally giving way to clay, then sand. It felt like a year to Adrianna. She would never have believed she could endure such torment. As she looked dazedly around her at the dry, red parchment of earth, stretching on and on to the depressingly flat horizon, her mind began to wander. She started fantasising about her beautiful home unit back in Sydney, with its wide cool balcony overlooking the crystalline blue waters of Sydney Harbour.

Oh, to be there now, sipping a gin and tonic, relaxing

on her favourite lounger, wearing nothing but her silk kimono, her naked flesh feeling refreshed after a cooling shower.

Dumbo stumbled and Adrianna's mind was jerked back to the present, a scream bursting from cracked lips as she began to lose her balance and slip sideways. The enemy was beside her in an instant, pushing her back into the saddle. 'You all right?' he asked gruffly.

'Of course I'm not damned well all right!' she snapped, all her patience worn to a frazzle. 'There isn't a single part of my body that isn't either stiff, sore or sorry. I'm dying of the heat. I've got a rotten headache. And I'm tired and thirsty.' She placed her hands on her aching hips and glared daggers at him. 'I want nothing more than to lie back in a soothing bath full of Radox and have someone bring me a long cool drink!'

A reluctant smile twitched at the corners of his mouth. 'Sorry, can't manage that at the moment.'

Adrianna sagged in the saddle, all the fire gone out of her with her outburst and his understated reaction. Why, oh, why couldn't he at least do her a favour and lose his temper, really lose his temper! She wanted to see for once that he was as human as she was.

Her tired eyes washed over him. He looked too good to be true, his body seemingly immune to the conditions around him. Even the flies let him alone. But of course, he had probably lathered himself with insect repellent that morning, she thought ruefully.

Now his smile had widened, and he was shaking his head at her.

'What?' she snarled.

'You won't want to hear it,' he said, sardonic amusement in his voice.

She lifted her arms wide to encompass her surroundings and herself. 'Could anything be worse than it is? For pity's sake satisfy my curiosity, if nothing else.'

His eyes betrayed a momentary surprise, and Adrianna realised what she had just said. 'I didn't mean it that way,' she groaned.

His laugh was very dry. 'No, I don't suppose you did. But it does make my confession slightly more awkward. I wouldn't want you to get the wrong idea.' He swung his camel and urged it back into the lead, where he stopped and twisted round to look back at her. 'I think I can tell you from the relative safety of this distance.'

'Oh, good grief, what is it?' she demanded impatiently.

The corner of his mouth lifted in a rueful smile. 'At the risk of sounding terribly banal, I was going to say how beautiful you look when you're angry.'

She stared at him as an undermining wave of pleasure flooded through her. But hard on the heels of the pleasure came the disturbing acceptance of her vulnerability to this man. A smile and a tossed-off compliment, and she melted.

But only inside, where no one could see.

'Really?' she said with a cold sniff, and saw the smile instantly fade.

'God, woman,' he scowled, 'you don't know how to take a genuine compliment!'

'Pardon me if I find it hard to believe I look beautiful when I'm dying.'

He made a scoffing sound. 'You haven't begun to die yet.' He went to say something further when a dark frown swept across his face. 'Damn,' he muttered, glaring at something behind her. 'Hold on tight, Adrianna. We have a slight problem.'

And with that he kicked Jumbo into a gallop,

Dumbo's subsequent leap into action immediately distracting her from any other thought but stopping herself from falling off.

CHAPTER THREE

ADRIANNA hung on like grim death, her stomach heaving, her mind whirling. What had he seen behind them that had brought such a swift look of panic?

No, not panic, she conceded. A man like Bryce wouldn't panic. Concern and a degree of annoyance was more like it. But over *what*?

If only she dared look behind her.

But she did not. She was having enough trouble keeping her balance with her eyes glued straight ahead.

They were really travelling, each galloping stride of the camels' long gangly legs covering enormous ground. Suddenly the horizon wasn't flat any more, a ridge of sandhills was looming up before Adrianna's eyes.

They hit the soft sand so abruptly that even Jumbo almost lost his footing. Bryce shouted 'Whoa!' but dopey Dumbo hadn't mastered that command yet and careered on. Fortunately Bryce leant over and grabbed the reins, reefing them out of Adrianna's sweat-soaked hands and jerking the animal to a bone-crunching halt.

She gripped the front of the saddle as her body lunged forward, then whiplashed backwards. She closed her eyes and grunted with the pain, though curiosity had her soon twisting around to see what they had been fleeing from.

'Oh, my God,' she croaked. 'Is it a sandstorm?' Her grey eyes widened with horror at the swirling, whirling mass of red dust whooshing towards them.

'Not quite—more a willy-willy. If we can get over

40

this ridge—and the next—we might leave it behind.
Sometimes they go back towards the saltpan.'

She steeled herself and sent Bryce a resigned look.
'Then what are we waiting for? Let's head for the hills!'

He looked taken aback for a second, then grinned and
kicked Jumbo in the flanks, 'up-upping' both the camels
into immediate torturous action.

Luckily, though, he was right. The willy-willy stayed
on the salt-pan. But they didn't stop galloping till they
were approaching a second line of dunes, these steeper
than the last. Only then did the camels slow to a walk,
Adrianna sagging across the saddle as the exhausted animals struggled up the incline.

Bryce reined Jumbo in on the crest and waited for
Dumbo to draw alongside. 'Almost there now,' he said,
and pointed.

Her eyes followed the direction of his finger to land
on a most incredible sight. For not more than half a mile
away, nestled within a rocky outcrop of low hills, was
a small lagoon, fringed by white sands, eucalyptus trees
and the greenest of green grasses.

'Why, it's an oasis!' she exclaimed.

'A very temporary one,' he informed her.

She frowned at him. 'Temporary?'

'I don't mean it's going to disappear overnight, but
give it a month or two of this heat and the billabong
will dry up. It's fed by a creek bed that only runs when
it floods up in the north as it did this winter. Twice. We
don't have many wet winters like that, though.'

'Well, thank the lord you did this year,' she sighed
wearily.

'Poor Adrianna, you must be done in. Sorry I had to
push, but you can see why. The salt-pan is no place to
linger.'

His unexpectedly gentle tone was more her undoing than all the compliments in the world. Her heart turned over, her stomach contracted, and, worst of all, tears welled up in her eyes.

'Come on, city girl,' he sighed, and took Dumbo's reins, leaving her nothing to do but hold on to the saddle while he led her slowly and quietly down the sandhill. They didn't speak, the silence oddly soothing to Adrianna's shattered nerves.

He wasn't such an ogre, she decided as she blinked away the tears. Not really…

Not at all, she finally admitted. Back at the plane she had asked for his exasperation, what with her patronising him and her prickly, ungrateful, argumentative attitude. Yet, except for the business with the hat, he had remained remarkably patient with her. She was the one who was the ogre, not him.

She shook her head wearily, a silent groan welling up within her. If only he didn't affect her physically the way he did. Heavens, he only had to smile at her and she was all mush inside. It was crazy really. He wasn't her type at all!

The only thing she could think of was that it had something to do with the situation she was caught up in. She had read of prisoners imagining they had fallen in love with their captors, their emotions confused by feelings of total dependence and vulnerability. Was that what this was? Had the crash and the desert stripped her of all her usual confidence in herself, making her susceptible to Bryce's autocratic personality in a way she would never be in her normal life? Or had there always been within her that ghastly feminine weakness she abhorred, the one that made a woman want to surrender her will, her body, and sometimes her whole life, to quite often the most unsuitable male, all in the name of what the female sex foolishly called romance?

A shudder rippled through her at this last thought. It couldn't be, she decided. She wouldn't *let* it be! Alan was the man for her. Alan, who never threatened her peace of mind, who never tried to run her life, who wanted only as much as she was prepared to give, if not less!

'Romance,' she muttered scornfully.

Bryce twisted round and frowned at her. 'Did you say something?'

The blood raced to her cheeks, making her almost glad that her hat was pulled down as it was, for it hid her crazed fluster.

'Not really,' she said curtly. 'I was just giving the flies a piece of my mind.' And she swatted them away all the more vigorously.

'Glad I'm not a fly.'

Again he gave her one of those drily amused smiles and again something deep inside responded, making her feel almost sick. She clenched her jaw hard to stop a returning smile from bursting from her lips, her expression retaining its brittle façade with great difficulty. She was almost relieved when she saw Bryce's eyes darken with exasperation, even more relieved when his total attention was claimed by a black and white dog streaking towards them across the red plain.

'Here, Bully!' he shouted, dropping the reins and leaning to one side, his arms open.

Adrianna was just thinking that no dog could leap that high when the mad animal propelled itself upwards, was caught, and gathered in, its adoration of its master evident in the frantic, feverish licking of his face. Bryce was laughing. 'Good dog, good dog,' he praised, lavishly hugging and rubbing his pet.

Adrianna's stomach contracted as she watched them, her reaction distressing her immensely. Surely she couldn't be jealous of a man's love for his dog, could she?

But then she realised her feelings hadn't sunk to anything quite so low. It was jealousy all right, but more of Bryce's capacity to show his affection so openly, so un-inhibitedly. She could never imagine herself doing anything similar, either to man or beast, and it suddenly bothered her. Oh, how she wished she could throw off all the inhibiting controls under which she lived her life. All her fears.

Fears?

She stiffened her spine, her lips pursing together. Now that was carrying self-recrimination a bit far. She had never been a cowardly person! All she did was guard against things happening that could ruin her life, things she knew she couldn't cope with. She wasn't really hard-hearted or cold. Underneath, she was just like anyone else, wanting someone to care about, someone to care about her.

But she had known many years ago that she wouldn't fall in love and enter into a normal marriage. She just wasn't capable of surrendering herself and her life to a man in so total a way, not after all she had seen and been through. Marriage to Alan was different. He wouldn't ask her to shelve her career or abandon her independence. He wouldn't demand that she change or make unfair sacrifices.

Adrianna darted a rueful sidewards glance over at Bryce. She couldn't say the same for the likes of *this* fellow. Any woman in *his* life would have to be a meek, slave-like creature capable of enduring his long absences without a whimper, content to be waiting for him if and when he deigned to return to them. Marriage with a man like that, even without children, didn't bear thinking about!

Yet even as Adrianna's intelligence rejected such a notion she was staring at him, at his wide laughing mouth, at his strong powerful thighs gripping the sides of the camel, at his large male hands hugging the dog. And she was consumed with an insatiable hunger to have that mouth, those thighs and hands on and around and over her hot, tingling flesh.

She shook her head, such crazy, uncontrollable feelings filling her with incredible dismay. Why was she being plagued by this overpowering sexual attraction for this man? *Why*?

'Don't you like dogs?' he asked, giving her a sharp look before letting the wriggling animal slip back down to the ground.

'Why do you ask that?' she managed in a husky voice.

'You were shaking your head and giving poor Bully one of your disapproving glares.'

'Oh...' A type of guilt pricked her conscience. How many disapproving glares had she subjected Bryce to so far? 'Not at all,' she explained in what she hoped was a softer tone. 'I wasn't really looking at your dog. My mind was a million miles away.'

'With some not very nice thoughts, by the look on your face.'

Adrianna swallowed. 'Yes, I...' She hesitated, but he said nothing, obviously waiting for her to explain further. She felt impelled to apologise, but there was a part of her that found such a prospect not only difficult, but vaguely unnerving. Why, she wasn't sure. Perhaps it was because she didn't want to show any weakness in front of this man who was so incredibly strong in every way.

'I…I was thinking how rotten and ungrateful I must have seemed to you back at the plane,' she said tautly. 'And since.'

His eyes showed surprise. But still he said nothing.

'I…I'm sorry,' she managed at last.

Yet he merely shrugged off her apology. 'Don't give it another thought. You were in shock. You're probably not usually so difficult.'

She fell silent at that. It made her feel small to think she had made him suffer for something that wasn't his fault, especially after all he had done for her. He couldn't help being attractive. Or having to contend with a woman who for some reason had unexpectedly turned into a raving nymphomaniac. It was up to her to keep her unfortunate feelings in check.

And totally hidden.

Adrianna conceded that while Bryce might not be the sort of man to force himself on a woman, it could be a different story if she let him know how vulnerable she was to him. He was, after all, a very virile-looking man who she suspected wouldn't be easy to ward off once aroused. And who knew how long he had been in this desert?

Adrianna decided not to ask him, though. Instead she adopted a friendly expression and said, 'What did you call your dog just now?'

'Bully.'

'And is he one?' she asked, smiling.

He gave her another look of surprise, as though he didn't think her capable of smiling. She wished he wouldn't keep staring at her mouth so. It was making her feel uncomfortably aware of him again, which was the last thing she wanted.

She almost sighed with relief when he looked away and down at his dog, who was dancing excitably around the camels' legs. 'He's not any more,' he gruffed, then added more gently, 'Are you, old boy?'

Bully responded with another burst of barking before dashing off in the direction of the oasis. He stopped after fifty yards or so, spinning around and barking demandingly.

'He's very excitable,' Adrianna remarked, grateful for any distraction from her increasingly disturbing feelings.

'Yes... It's his breeding.'

She had no idea what his breed was. He was a medium-sized dog, with a stocky body, a long thick nose, small pointed ears, and a weird black and white patched coat. 'What is he?' she asked.

'Half kelpie, half bull terrier.' Bryce chuckled. 'He spent the first six months of his life not knowing if he should muster cows or kill them!'

Bully's strident bark sounded impatient. 'We'd better keep moving before he has a nervous breakdown,' Bryce advised, and resumed leading Dumbo along, talking as he went. 'A chap came through Dover Downs a couple of years ago making a documentary about the outback. He had this mad white bull terrier with him which was the most fearless dog I've ever seen. He terrified the life out of everybody, but one of the station dogs—a lovely black kelpie bitch—thought he was just the ant's pants. She had a litter of six pups a couple of months after the film team moved on, five of them exact replicas of the mother...and Bully. My God, the bedlam that pup caused, fighting and scrapping with everything that moved! He was going to be put down till I gave him a reprieve and took him on walkabout last year.'

'And?' Adrianna prodded, intrigued by the story. Or was it the man telling it?

Bryce shrugged his huge shoulders. 'I bonded him to me.'

'How?'

His backward glance slid over her and a shiver rippled down her spine. 'It's amazing what some time in the desert can do to one's personality,' he drawled. 'It takes out all the anger, all the aggression. It makes one look within oneself and find out what one's real priorities are... Bully finally calmed down enough to find out it was better to be friends with me than fight. After all, there was no one else to relate to, and dogs, like people, need love and companionship. We've been mates ever since.' Again those blue eyes found hers, locking briefly before swinging slowly back to the front.

Adrianna's throat had gone dry. Had there been some sort of message in that penetrating look?

A sardonic gurgle almost broke from her lips as her brutal sense of honesty took over.

Adrianna Winslow, you're becoming far too fanciful for words! she told herself. This desert must really be getting to you. Why should there be any underlying message? The thought that Bryce might be thinking of taming *you*, making *you* his mate, is ludicrous! My God, the man almost left you behind, that's how much he fancies you! For goodness' sake get hold of yourself and stop acting and thinking like some over-sexed adolescent fool! Of course he isn't going to use your enforced time together to try to bond you to him! Of course he isn't planning to seduce you like some lecherous sheikh! He was merely recounting a tale about his dog. Good grief, get a hold of yourself!

All this heated mental arguing did have one desirable result. It took Adrianna's mind totally off her physical discomfort, which had by now reached mammoth proportions. She covered the last few hundred yards of their trek, totally distracted from her various aches and pains, from the flies and the heat, not to mention the gritty dryness of her throat, and the rumblings in her stomach. She was all bitter self-recrimination and grim resolve, so much so that it was Dumbo's sudden stooping of his neck that made her realise they had actually arrived at the edge of the billabong.

'Do you need help getting down?' Bryce asked, slipping down to the ground beside Jumbo. Bully was frolicking in the water around the camels' heads. 'I want to let the camels have a long drink.'

'I can manage,' she said.

But the words were hardly out of her dry swollen lips before every bone, every muscle in her creaking body screamed her mistake. She tried to lift one leg over the saddle as she had seen Bryce do so easily, but she could barely move it a couple of inches.

'Here,' he ordered, extending outspread hands up towards her. 'Just lean to one side and let yourself go. I'll catch you.'

She had little option but to do as Bryce suggested and have her shattered body caught up by his strong male grip. He settled her on to very unsteady feet. When he went to let her go she groaned and sagged.

'Bad, huh?' he asked, holding her upright against him.

'Mmm,' was all she could say.

'I've got an idea.' Abruptly, he undid the scarf under her chin and took her hat off, throwing it to one side before sweeping her up into his arms. She gaped up at him as he held her close and tight.

'What…what are you doing?' she gasped, trying not to notice that his hard ribcage was pressing into the soft side of one breast, or that one of his arms was wrapped around her waist, the other curled around her thighs.

'Wait and see,' he grinned, and began striding around the edge of the billabong along the surprisingly white sand that edged it. Adrianna had frozen in his arms, her hands clenched tightly together across her chest, every muscle in her body taut with excruciating tension.

'Relax,' he drawled. 'I won't drop you.'

Drop her? She wasn't worried about him *dropping* her! Her worries lay entirely in another direction. She held her gaze steadfastly upwards, staring with wide eyes through the dappling shade of the river ghost-gums to the darkening blue sky.

Perhaps he sensed her confusion and fear, for he looked down at her with a sardonic sparkle in his eyes. 'There's a sandbank out here,' he explained, and began to wade into the water. 'It'll be shallow and warm. You can lie there and soak those stiff muscles of yours while I get you a drink.'

She closed her eyes and gave a little moan when he lowered her gently into the surprisingly warm water and let her go.

'I know it's bad,' he soothed, thinking that physical pain had brought the sound from her throat. 'But this should help. Here…let me help you out of your jacket. It looks uncomfortable. There, that's better, isn't it? I'll be back shortly.'

Her eyes followed him as he left the water, followed him every step of the way as he walked back to the camels and his camp. And as she watched him she thought she had never seen so big a man move with such smooth grace. There was no side-to-side rolling of his shoulders, no clumsy swagger. Just a long, easy athletic stride that flowed from his narrow hips and compact buttocks, his broad shoulders held square but not tensely, his long arms swinging comfortably.

He walked straight past the drinking camels, past his camp-site, where he tossed her jacket aside, and around to the far side of the billabong down where the water looked much deeper. There he astonished Adrianna by suddenly tugging off his boots, throwing off his hat and plunging in, disappearing completely under the water. Bully danced around on the bank, barking excitedly.

She gasped to a sitting position when Bryce didn't surface immediately. Seconds ticked away, terror holding her frozen. Then suddenly a hand broke the surface, holding a wine bottle aloft like the Lady of the Lake with Excalibur, followed by a triumphant Bryce. 'Success!' he shouted.

He emerged from the water, his wet clothes outlining his impressive body with startling clarity. Perhaps Adrianna should have looked away then, but she couldn't, and when he glanced over at her she was still sitting up, staring at him. 'Now lie back down in your bath like a good girl,' he admonished her across the water, 'and I'll bring you a sample of some perfectly chilled Chardonnay.'

She closed her eyes and sank back into the warmth, willing her body to relax. Her muscles were doing so quite nicely, but her mind—and her imagination—had definite ideas of its own. Her eyes kept flickering open and darting to find Bryce as he returned to his camp and went about opening the wine bottle. Finally, with the

bottle and two tin mugs in his hand, he began striding
her way.

A definite lump formed in her throat at the sight of
him coming towards her through the water, his damp
shirt clinging to the broad muscles of his chest, the beginnings of an amused smile pulling at his mouth.

'And what do you find so funny?' she demanded, her
inner susceptibility making her terse.

'You have a very dirty face,' he grinned, and reached
out to touch her nose with a spare fingertip.

She splashed her face with the warm water, rubbing
it vigorously before glaring up at him, her skin shiny
and clean. 'Better?' she snapped.

'Much better,' he said, and settled himself down to
waist-level in the water beside her. 'Now all you need
is half a bottle of this inside you and you'll start feeling
human again.' He poured a generous swig into one of
the mugs and held it out to her. 'It might help your sense
of humour as well.'

She took it with a grudging, 'Thank you,' and downed
the whole lot in one swallow without so much as a splut-
ter or a hiccup.

'Ah,' he drawled, 'I see I'm in the company of an
experienced drinker! Don't worry, there's plenty more
where this came from.' He waggled the bottle at her. 'I
buried half a dozen bottles in the sand last year.' He
poured himself a healthy mugful and proceeded to sa-
vour it with considerable sounds of appreciation.
'Hmm… Marvellous… I can see I've found a most efficient natural cellar. Here, have some more.'

'I don't think…'

'Good idea—*don't*!' he cut in firmly. 'Thinking is the
bane of the human race. It causes untold misery. Now

drink up, but not so quickly this time. It might not sit too well on an empty stomach.'

Yes, it wouldn't do to get drunk, she thought ruefully. The last thing she needed was to let down her guard with this man. So she lifted the mug carefully to her lips and let the cool wine slide more slowly down her parched throat.

Nevertheless, in next to no time the alcohol hit her system, making her head swim. Initially, Adrianna was instilled with a sharp sense of danger, but the effect of the wine was insidious, gradually pervading her whole body, dulling her conscience and making every part of her feel wonderfully liquid and melting. Any remaining muscular pain receded, her thoughts now of nothing but her immediate surroundings—the beautiful billabong, the warm water suffusing her skin, the man next to her.

Her slightly blurred gaze was drawn to his large, confident hands as he topped up his drink. She watched him lift the mug, watched those strong male lips curl over the rim, watched the wine wash over his tongue and disappear into the dark, moist depths of his mouth. Gradually everything went out of focus for her except that mouth. She saw his tonguetip flick out to capture a drop of wine from the corner of his mouth, and it felt as if it had flicked over her entire body.

Her heart began to pound, her head spinning, her body gripped by the most amazingly intense, incredibly compulsive need. To have this man kiss her, touch her, right here, right now, was not only imperative but essential. She lifted her eyes to his, uncaring that her hungry gaze would betray her desires. This need had no pride, no shame. It drove her to want him to recognise what she was feeling, and respond to it.

Her eyes didn't find his, however, for those deep blue

pools were busy with an occupation of their own, staring
with narrow-eyed intent over the rim of his mug straight
at her chest. Taken aback, she looked down at where her
wet blouse was stuck to her breasts like a second skin,
the well-rounded bra-less mounds as good as naked before his gaze. As were the rock-hard nipples, jutting
through the damp silk like twin spear points.

Oddly enough, his blatant staring at her aroused body
had the opposite effect to what one might have imagined. It sobered her immediately, making her realise
what a monumentally stupid thing she had been about
to do. Alcohol had temporarily sent this crazy sexual
attraction spiralling out of control. Of course she didn't
want him to make love to her out here like some sort of
wild animal. My God, among other things she could
quite easily become pregnant. Whatever had possessed
her!

With a half gasp, half groan she sank down to neck
level in the water, the action sending Bryce's eyes snapping up to hers.

It shocked her to see the lingering lights of a naked
desire blazing in them. Shocked her even more to realise
that a moment ago, it was what she had *wanted* to see.

But Bryce wasn't shocked. He wasn't even apologetic
as he regained control over himself, his smouldering
gaze quickly cooling to an icy blue. He even gave an
offhand shrug. 'You have a desirable body, Adrianna,'
he said. 'Don't expect me not to look. I'm very much a
normal male, not one of those effete excuses for men
who grace your city offices. I know who and what *I*
like.'

He poured the last of the wine into his mug and
drained it, then gave her an uncompromising look. 'But
don't worry, I'll keep my hands off. Much as I happen

to find city women very sexy, I'm not that hard up that I have to force myself on one who's already spoken for. Though to be honest, dear lady…' he darted her a hard, dry glance '…if you want to credibly keep up that air of cold aloofness where I'm concerned I suggest you don't look at me as you did a moment ago.'

Adrianna sucked in a startled breath. So he *had* seen her lustful gaze. Oh, how could she have put herself into such a humiliating position!

There was only one means of escape, one way to salvage some of her damaged pride and avoid a potentially dangerous situation from developing. But it would take every vestige of composure and cool she could muster.

She sat up in the water and lifted her left eyebrow in a sarcastic arch, letting her eyes slide over him in a bold scrutiny. 'You have a highly desirable body too, Bryce,' she returned in kind. 'So don't expect *me* not to look. I'm very much a normal female, not one of those horsey excuses for women who stomp across your cattle-yards. But don't worry, I'll keep my hands off. Much as I find your macho body quite sexy, I happen to prefer my men with a little more spit and polish.' Her nose tilted up with what she considered just the right amount of disdain. 'And I certainly haven't forgotten that I'm an engaged woman. I realise that there are some people who have no loyalty, and who indulge every passing fancy they have, but I'm not one of them!'

For a few seconds there was an electric silence, with Bryce's eyes boring into hers. But then, just when Adrianna was experiencing a prickle of fear—had she gone too far?—he threw back his head and roared with laughter.

She could only stare at him in astonishment. Her

clever counter-speech, her cool sarcasm had been utterly futile in putting this man in his place.

Bryce stood up, still laughing, and the water cascaded down off his huge shoulders. 'I'll say one thing for you, Adrianna, you're not boring!' He reached out and took her empty mug, then whirled and began to surge towards the nearby bank with powerful strides, leaving her staring open-mouthed after him. Once on the sand he bent to pat the ever-waiting Bully, then turned back to face her.

'I have to get on with unpacking and making a camp-fire before it gets dark,' he stated matter-of-factly. 'Stay in your bath, by all means. You wouldn't be much use anyway. By the time I explained to you what to do I could have done it several times over.'

Adrianna was still reeling with shock and a sorely damaged ego. To be told now that she was useless, and without initiative, was too much! 'I'll have you know that I…that I…' she began, spluttering as she tried to get to her feet and failed, her waterlogged clothes and exhausted limbs working against her.

He threw an exasperated glare at her across the water. 'Put a lid on it, will you?' His voice had a harsh, impatient tone he had not used on her before. 'You might be queen bee where you come from, honey, but out here you're nothing but a decorative distraction and a right pain in the neck. So do yourself and me a favour. Just do as you're told from here on in, without argument, and definitely without any of your smart-mouthed retorts, and we'll get along fine. Right?'

'Right!' she ground out through gritted teeth. She folded her arms and sat there, glaring back at him with steely grey eyes.

His grin showed her she was a maiden in the insolence

stakes. 'Glad to see you're a quick learner. You never know, once you get off that high horse of yours, we might even become friends.'

He strode off then, leaving Adrianna seething with hostility and humiliation. But at least the scene had totally obliterated any attraction she had been feeling for the man. How she could desire him even for a second she could scarcely believe! He was worse than she had first thought. An egotistical, domineering, typically bossy chauvinist of the worst kind! And he called *her* high-handed. Good God, he left her for dead in that regard!

She watched him go about his chores with the vain hope that he would do something stupid, or clumsy. But no! Everything he did went swiftly and smoothly. The camels were unpacked and turned out to graze. The camp-fire was made, a billy boiled, food prepared. Even the excitable Bully was settled with a large can of dog-food.

A mere half-hour later, with everything apparently done, Bryce returned to stand on the bank opposite her, holding the checked blanket she had found in the plane. 'You'd better get out of those wet clothes,' he advised, 'and wrap this around you.' He dropped the rug on the sand. 'They'll dry in no time near the fire. And before you say it, no, I won't watch. Not unless,' he added drily, 'you want me to.'

Adrianna controlled her temper with difficulty. 'I think I'll bypass that pleasure this once,' she said tartly, and began to dog-paddle towards shore.

He waded into the shallows and met her, holding out his hand to help her stand up. She took it and was hauled upwards, her clothes plastering around her entire body from top to toe as the water streamed downwards. She might as well have been naked, for there wasn't a curve or crevice that couldn't be clearly seen.

She heard his swiftly indrawn breath, felt his fingers tighten around her hand. Her eyes flew to his, but those blue pools were already waiting for her, glittering and unrepentant.

'OK, I looked again,' he ground out, 'and this time it turned me on. What am I supposed to do? Apologise for being a normal male?'

'You…you said I could trust you…'

For the first time she saw real anger in his face. 'You can,' was his snarled reply.

'But…'

'Look, darlin', if a man tried to rape every woman who unintentionally turned him on, this world would be in a right old pickle, wouldn't it? Of course…' his eyes latched on to the colour flooding into her cheeks, and the way her breasts were rising and falling in a rapid, syncopated dance '…some women prefer the decision to be taken out of their hands…'

It was just as well, she realised later, that that was the moment a herd of wild camels chose to arrive.

CHAPTER FOUR

THEY came out of the desert, swooping down from the sandhills with red dust flying from their hooves, their leader a huge bull camel making loud snorting noises from his flaring nostrils.

'Bloody hell,' muttered Bryce, a dark frown wiping everything but worry from his face. He abandoned Adrianna and made a dash for Dumbo and Jumbo, who were skittering around under a nearby gum-tree. Grabbing their reins, he tied them securely to the trunk before racing over towards the camp-fire and snatching up a rifle.

'Get out of here, you mongrels!' he shouted, lifting the nose of the barrel and firing a warning shot just over the leader's head. 'Watch yourself, Bully,' he directed to the dog as it flew past. 'That first fellow is mean. Adrianna, for Pete's sake get back into the water!'

But she couldn't seem to move, frozen with shock as Bryce and his crazy dog raced out towards the massive camel. Bully didn't hesitate, charging in and giving the animal a nasty nip on the heels. A large bony leg lashed out in anger, but missed. Bully charged again, and again, till the camel had had enough and retreated a little. The rest of the herd followed and they stood at the camp's edge, tense with thirst and fear. The big bull was swaying from side to side and stamping his feet, seemingly trying to make up his mind if it was worth the risk to try for another drink regardless of the dog and the man.

'Get off with you!' yelled Bryce, firing the rifle one

more time. 'There's plenty of water around. Find your own place!' He ran at them and this time the herd bolted.

By the time Bryce turned and walked back to the camp, Adrianna's frozen state had thawed to one of uncontrollable trembling. He found her still standing at the edge of the water, shivering with both reaction and the gathering cold. The sun had well and truly set while all this was going on, and the chill and blackness of night was descending with astonishing speed.

Bryce stood looking down at her, one hand on his left hip, the smoking rifle in the other. His face carried both exasperation and concern. 'Just look at you, standing here freezing to death! Why didn't you get back into the water? At least then you'd have been safe *and* warm.'

'I... I...' was all she could get out between chattering teeth.

'God!' He threw the rifle down, snatched up the checked blanket and wrapped it around her shoulders. 'Come on, let's get you over to some warmth,' he growled, and guided her stiffening limbs over to the camp-fire. 'Here...sit on my bedroll, then you won't get your clothes dirty again. Don't worry about taking them off,' he added abruptly. 'They'll dry in the end. Mine did.'

She sank down to sit on the thick grey blanket, hunching her knees up and leaning towards the heat. She stared blankly into the flames, unmoving, unthinking. The trembling soon stopped, but both her mind and body seemed to have seized up, the incident with the camels having compounded with all the other emotional upheavals of the day to bring about total shut-down.

Bryce crouched down beside her and looped a wet strand of hair over her right ear. A shiver reverberated all through her.

'What you need,' he said firmly, 'is a mug of hot billy tea. I'll just let the camels loose and get you one.'

When he brought it several minutes later she cupped the battered enamel mug in her hands and drank like a robot, without even thinking to thank him.

But Bryce was right. The hot drink did make her feel better. Not good, but better.

The reviving caffeine and the heat of the fire finally forced her mind into gear and her tongue to work, and she looked across at where he was sitting down on a log not far from her, drinking his own tea. He was leaning forward, elbows on knees, looking bleak and oddly troubled. She caught his eye and without thinking what she was doing, smiled. 'Thank you,' she said simply.

His blue eyes were surprisingly hard as they fastened on that smile. 'Don't tell me I'm to be forgiven,' he said caustically.

'There's nothing much to forgive,' she said truthfully. After all, what had he done, except respond to a blatantly exposed female body like any normal virile male? It was her own dark desires that had made the incident seem more dangerous than it was, dark desires that she was determined to conquer. 'I overreacted,' she apologised. 'I'm sorry.'

There was a momentary flicker in his gaze that was almost irritation. It perplexed her. Didn't he want her apology? Didn't he want them to try to be friends, at least on the surface? His eyes dropped to the fire, his handsome face marred by a most uncharacteristic scowl.

A silence descended between them that quickly got on her nerves. She searched her mind for a safe topic of conversation and decided on the wild camels. 'Does that sort of thing happen very often out here?' she asked.

His head jerked up. 'For God's sake!' he said sharply.

But when he saw her surprised look his frustrated expression cleared to one of dry amusement. 'Oh...you mean the camel business.'

Only then did Adrianna realise what he had first thought.

'No...not really,' he went on in that lazy drawl of his. 'But the outback has more wildlife than most people suspect, and some of it isn't friendly. You always have to be on your guard.'

'How did those camels get to be here in the first place? I mean...they're not native to Australia, are they?'

Bryce lifted the lids on the two iron pots that were sitting virtually in the fire and stirred while he talked. 'No, they were brought in from Afghanistan last century as pack animals, taking food and supplies to the men building the telegraph and railway systems across the desert. Ironic thing is, by doing so they eventually did themselves out of a job. Once the railway was finished they were no longer needed, so rather than go to the expense of shipping them back to their homeland, their owners let them go. Same thing happened with horses and donkeys. There are plenty of those running loose as well. The camels are the biggest problem, however. Last I heard they numbered over thirty thousand.'

'Thirty thousand!' Adrianna shook her head in astonishment. 'That's an awful lot!'

'Mmm. They're not too popular with some of the cattle men, I can assure you.'

'But you don't seem to mind them?' she pointed out, nodding towards Dumbo and Jumbo, who were grazing contentedly nearby.

'Can't stand those wild ones,' Bryce answered. 'Not only do they devastate the grazing land, but they're totally unpredictable. The bulls are particularly mean at the end of the mating season. Jumbo and Dumbo aren't the same at all. They're domesticated, and trained. Well...*almost* trained. Dumbo's only young. Besides, they're both gelded, so they don't present a problem with their sexual urges. Not like that crazy mongrel you just saw.' He glanced over at her with a self-mocking smile. 'I meant the bull camel, not myself.'

Adrianna saw the funny side of it and laughed.

'You wouldn't find it so funny if you were a man,' he said darkly. 'You women have it easy. You seem to be able to turn your physical feelings on and off like a tap.'

She gulped down the involuntary tightening in her chest. Little did he know...

His sigh was heavy. 'Where was I?' he growled. 'Ah yes...dinner.' He left the stirring and turned to pick up two pale blue enamel dinner plates and two large forks.

'What have you been cooking?' she asked, resolving to get the conversation back on to a less dangerous track.

'A rare couple of dishes! Madam has a choice,' Bryce said drily. 'She can have either beans and wonderfully tasteless dehydrated vegetables. Or wonderfully tasteless dehydrated vegetables and beans. Feel free to take your time with your selection, but be assured that either will tantalise your taste buds as no other culinary delights you're likely to encounter in the Great Sandy Desert.'

It was no use. Even while being sarcastic the man had an incorrigible charm that totally undermined Adrianna's intention to keep him at arm's length. She started to giggle, then laughed outright.

'That's the first time I've ever heard you laugh,' he said, almost accusingly.

'Is it?' She chuckled some more. 'I can't help it. You made me.'

His glance was sardonic. 'One point to me, then.' He handed her a steaming dinner plate and a fork. 'I wouldn't think there'd be too many men who could make you do *anything*, my dear Adrianna.' He cocked his head to one side, and the firelight struck the sculptured planes of his face. 'Adrianna what?' he asked, his beautiful blue eyes softening.

For a second she stared back at him, astonished by the pleasure his warm look evoked in her. Finally she had to drop her eyes lest she betray her feelings, clearing her throat and poking at her food. 'Winslow,' she answered. 'And you?' she added, risking a brief upwards glance.

'McLean.'

'Bryce McLean,' she murmured. 'Nice…'

'I'm a nice man. As you're basically a nice woman.'

Adrianna's eyes snapped up to his face then, startled by this rather backhanded compliment. For what seemed a long time they just looked at each other. It was not a particularly sexual gaze, Adrianna thought, more a slow steady assessment, a discovery of each other as people. There was interest in the blue eyes looking back at her. Interest and warmth. And yes…a most likeable quality of openness.

Adrianna was the first to look away, a host of butterflies in her stomach. God, she liked this man, really *liked* him! It was a disturbing realisation, for it gave her earlier desire for him a different connotation, one that terrified the life out of her. Lust alone she could probably cope with, ignore, control.

But lusting combined with liking was a different kettle of fish entirely. This was unknown territory for her, and far too close to the concept of romantic love for comfort. It perhaps explained why already she'd had trouble keeping her physical feelings in check. The thought that she could become prey to such an unstable and potentially destructive state of mind sent her into a genuine panic. Falling in love was not part of her plans for her life, and she had no intention of doing it. Not now. Not ever!

She dragged in a deep breath and raised decidedly steely eyes. He was still looking at her, his food untouched on his lap, his expressive face betraying definite disappointment at her change of mood.

'I think,' she stated matter-of-factly, 'that once I've finished this I should get some sleep. I'm very tired.'

He gave her a long, unwavering look, then nodded. Slowly. Wryly.

'How soon will we have to be on our way in the morning?' she asked.

'I think we'll just play it by ear, don't you?' he said offhandedly.

This lackadaisical attitude went against her grain, for she had not achieved all she had achieved in life by playing things by ear. 'Can't you give me a time?' she demanded impatiently.

'After breakfast?' he suggested with a lazy grin.

'Oh, for heaven's sake!'

His smile faded to a pitying look. 'I think a few days' trekking in the desert will do you a world of good, Adrianna. You're far too uptight.'

'And you're far too sloppy,' she shot back. 'We can't all go through life on walkabout, you know.'

'Pity.'

She made an impatient sound, but underneath she was feeling a lot better for her outburst. She had been getting too cosy with Bryce for comfort. Maybe her lightweight feminine side was stirred by his macho body and laid-back charm, but that part of her brain which directed all her important decisions kept reminding her there was a lot about him she found downright irritating. He was domineering, chauvinistic, typically male. Not to mention lacking in ambition. Oh, she conceded, he seemed intelligent enough, but he obviously refused to use it. No way could she fall in love with someone like that. No way!

A wave of relief flooded through her. It was as though she had safely put him into a box, all packaged and labelled. *Bum*, it said. With a soothing sigh she began spooning the beans into her own mouth, only then realising how hungry she was. She started eating quite ravenously till Bryce stopped her with a question.

'Do you argue with your fiancé all the time?' he asked unexpectedly.

Startled, Adrianna blinked over at him, her fork hovering midway between her plate and her mouth. 'Of course not,' she retorted. 'Alan and I never argue.'

Bryce raised an eyebrow and lowered his own fork to his plate. '*What*? Lovers who don't squabble? Now that's an odd kind of love, I say.'

'Really?' She successfully captured a cool, faintly caustic tone, though behind the controlled mask she was being stirred up again. Who did this man think he was, questioning her relationship with Alan? 'I would have thought such a love had far more chance of lasting than one where people throw things at each other.'

And oddly enough, that was what she wanted to do all of a sudden, throw something at him. Her fingers fairly itched around the dinner plate. So much for having put him into a safe little box!

Bryce's face adopted an innocent pose. 'Whoever said anything about violence? I was merely saying that if there isn't any passion at the beginning of a relationship, then…' He broke off and shrugged carelessly.

'There's plenty of passion between Alan and me,' she lied fiercely.

Bryce forked a mouthful of food into his large mouth and sent a sceptical look her way. 'If you say so.'

She clenched her jaw in an effort to get control of herself, at the same time wanting quite desperately to lash out, to rant and rave at him, to even reach out and slap his smug, handsome face. Maybe then she could assuage that combination of needs which was bubbling up inside her—to both touch and hurt him.

With an enormous effort she copied one of his offhand shrugs. 'If you knew Alan then you wouldn't be making such ridiculous statements. He's the most handsome, charming, sexy man. Why, there must be hundreds of women who'd give anything to be in my shoes! Being asked to be Mrs Alan Carstairs is not a put-down, be-lieve me!'

Adrianna was feeling so pleased with her little speech that it took some time before she realised Bryce was staring at her with eyes filled with true shock.

'Bryce… What is it? What did I say?'

'Mrs Alan Carstairs,' he repeated in a stunned voice. 'Alan Carstairs? Good God…'

'You…you *know* Alan?' Now she was the one who was shocked.

Bryce was shaking his head. 'If he's the same Alan Carstairs who lives at Vaucluse and owns all those Men About Town stores, then yes, I know him.'

'But…but how?' Adrianna gasped.

Bryce's glance was close to savage. 'Must you continually sound surprised over things about me? I'm not a total Philistine, dear lady. Neither have I spent my entire life in the nether regions. I lived in Sydney for a while when I was younger with relatives who were neighbours of your charming fiancé. In fact, I dated his secretary for a short time. Only he wasn't so charming in those days. He was an out-and-out bastard!'

Adrianna had to close her mouth before she could protest, but by this time Bryce was in full swing again.

'Oh, don't get me wrong,' he laughed mockingly. 'He wasn't a bastard with the ladies. From what I gathered, there *weren't* any ladies in his life. All he had time for was work, work, work, twenty-four hours a day, seven days a week. And heaven help any of his employees who didn't fancy doing the same!'

Adrianna found her voice at last. 'There's nothing wrong with being ambitious!'

'There certainly is,' Bryce retorted, 'if it's to the exclusion of everything else. My God, he didn't even take the day off to go to his father's funeral!'

'But that was at least ten years ago,' she defended hotly, though in reality she was shocked by Bryce's revelation. Even *she* had gone to her own father's funeral, and she doubted anyone had ever had less reason to.

'So it is,' Bryce admitted, the high colour in his face fading as he got control over his burst of temper. It was only then that Adrianna wondered why he had reacted so strongly to her news, anyway. What was it to him who she was marrying? In less than a week they would go their separate ways and never set eyes on each other again.

'I'm sure the Alan you knew has changed,' she stated categorically.

Those penetrating blue eyes gave her a slow onceover. 'Yes… I can see he must have.'

The implication shouldn't have annoyed her. But it did. 'Not that it's any of your business,' she pointed out coldly.

A muscle twitched along his jawline. 'No, I suppose it's not.'

'Then let's drop the subject, shall we?'

'By all means.'

A tense silence reigned as they both returned to finishing their meals, after which Bryce took her empty plate and began washing up in a plastic dish filled with billabong water.

'You should have let me do that,' Adrianna reproached.

His expression was totally unreadable as he turned his face her way. 'Why? Because it's traditionally women's work? I would have thought a liberated female like yourself would be pleased to see a man washing up.'

Her sigh was weary. 'I merely wanted to do something to help, and that was one thing you wouldn't be able to say I couldn't do as efficiently as you.'

'Well, it's done now,' came his curt answer, as he dried the last plate on a tea-towel and hung the damp cloth on the triangular iron construction that sat astride the fire.

The flames had by this time died down to hot embers, sending a golden glow over everything within a couple of metres. Bully lay sleeping in the sand a short distance away, his white flanks taking on an almost orange hue.

'Time for bed,' Bryce announced once he had tossed the dishwater away and put the empty tin with a stack of other equipment. He picked up the checked rug that had ended up lying in a heap at Adrianna's feet and

began spreading it out on the sand near the dog. 'You
can take my swag,' he told her. 'I'll sleep here.' He
scooped the sand into a type of pillow beneath the blanket and stretched out, his hands coming up to rest behind
his head, his eyes closing. He looked instantly as comfortable as though he were lying on the softest sofa.

Adrianna looked ruefully down at the rough sleeping
bag she was sitting on. It consisted of two heavy blan-
kets sewn together on three sides, with a rough-looking
pillow attached. A queen-sized sleepmaker bed it was
not! 'Er—I hate to disturb you, but could you get me
my carry-all bag?' she asked, unstrapping her still damp
leather sandals and putting them neatly beside the fire.
'I'd like to brush my hair before going to sleep. If I
don't, it'll be impossible in the morning.'

He opened his eyes and looked at her as though such
female attentions were totally unnecessary, given the situation, but fetched the bag as asked, and handed it over
without a word of comment. She extracted the hairbrush
and began to work her way through the mass of tangled
knots, wondering idly what Bryce would say if he saw
what she usually did before going to bed. It was like a
royal ritual, the taking off her make-up with special re-
mover, then the applying of various lotions and creams
to the different parts of her face and body. Not that she
was obsessed by her looks, but she was sensible enough
to know that a well-groomed and attractive appearance
was important in the business world.

She stopped brushing for a moment and ran her fingertips over her forehead and cheeks. Her skin felt very
dehydrated and her lips were rough and dry. Another
day of this and they'd crack right open.

'You look fine,' Bryce startled her by saying sharply.
She glanced over to where he was watching her from

the checked blanket. 'My lips are terribly dry. Heaven knows what they'll be like after five more days of this!'

'I have some cream you could use on them,' he volunteered, much to her surprise, and promptly got up once again, striding over to search through one of his many canvas packs. He returned with a small white tube in one hand.

'What is it?' she asked as he dropped to his knees next to her, unscrewed the cap and squeezed a dob on to his first two fingers of his right hand.

'Lanolin.'

'I… I can do that,' she choked out when he went to spread it on her lips himself.

'You'll get your fingers sticky if you do. It's no trouble.'

Adrianna literally held her breath as his creamed fingers made contact with her mouth. It was all she could do not to suck in a gasping breath when he began rubbing and massaging the cream into her lips with slow, circular motions. As it was, her stomach twisted into knots and she started mentally counting to ten, assuring herself that by then it would be over.

But the ten seconds came and went and still the erotic torture went on and on. Just as she was sure he was finished his fingertips returned to dab lightly at her top lip, then the lower, then deep into the corners, after which he began moving them round and round her mouth as though tracing a circle. She felt the blood race to her lips, making them swell and tingle.

'Haven't you finished?' she said at last in a strangled voice. Her eyes were beginning to feel oddly heavy and she looked up through half-closed lashes at his.

His returning look was equally heavy-lidded, and she knew then, knew with a startling stab of shock deep inside her, that he was deliberately prolonging doing what he was doing, was indeed becoming as turned on by it as she was.

'I think that's enough,' she said breathlessly.

His gaze dropped to her parted lips, then lifted back to her eyes. 'No,' he said in a voice thick with arousal. 'No, Adrianna... It's not nearly enough...'

Any desire she was secretly harbouring was swamped by panic in the face of his fierce and passionate resolve. It tore deep, warning her that if she let him make love to her he would take far more than her body. 'Bryce, no!' she rasped.

He ignored her feeble protest, a single fingertip returning to trace her mouth again, more slowly this time, very seductively, his eyes glazing as they followed its sensual path. A tiny moan whimpered deep in her throat, her stunned and terrified mind fighting a desperate battle with the temptation to part her quivering lips even wider, to suck his flesh into her mouth.

She struck his hand away with a sob and jerked her head back. 'I said *no!*' she cried.

The almost incoherent expression on his face cleared as he focused on her wide eyes. 'You want me to,' he said, so calmly that it was doubly shocking.

She gaped at him. 'I don't!'

'Yes, you do,' he repeated. 'You want me to make love to you. Here... Now...'

For a few horrified seconds she just stared at him, drugged by the sensual power of his deep, sexy voice. But then she was shaking her head—wildly, frantically. 'That's not true!' she cried.

Her denial seemed to galvinise him into action. He grabbed her by the shoulders and shook her. 'Yes, it is! Why don't you admit it, damn you? It's there...between

us…has been all day. That's why we've ended up snip-
ing at each other tonight. It's called desire, Adrianna.
Desire… Stop being such a little hypocrite and admit it!'
His eyes were challenging, taunting. Arrogantly certain.

Something exploded in her head, something equally
forceful and certain. No man pushed her into a corner,
either emotionally or physically. No man! 'All *right!*'
she screamed at him. 'All *right*! I want you to make love
to me! OK?'

She yanked away from him and stood up, throwing
her hands in the air in an angry, dismissive gesture.
'Does that make you happy? Does it boost your insuf-
ferably large male ego to know you attract me against
all the dictates of common sense and decency?'

She glared down at him with blisteringly cold eyes.
'Because I don't *want* to want you, Bryce McLean. Even
if I wasn't committed to someone else, your sort of man
is not for me, not even for a one-night stand! You country cowboys have no real respect for women. Oh, sure,
you like them in your bed every now and then, but that's
where it ends. Then it's back to your animals and your
mates and your drinking binges down at the pub. Believe
me, I've seen your type in action. So just *wanting* you
is as far as I intend going. I have no intention of putting
that want into action, of letting you use this unfortunate
weakness of mine to satisfy your own animalistic urges.
And please, for pity's sake don't have the gall to call it
making love! With you it would only be having sex,
nothing more. Men like you know as much about love
as Dumbo there knows about *whoa*! At least Alan knows
how to treat a woman. Oh, yes, sneer all you like, but
he makes love like a dream and I care for him dearly,
and I wouldn't dream of being unfaithful to him.'

Those blue eyes blazed up at her with an anger that

looked like outstripping hers. He slowly got to his feet, looming over her like an avenging angel. Only this angel was straight out of hell, all fire and brimstone and dark menace. Adrianna backed away from him, but he followed, pulling her to a shaking halt with an iron grip on her upper arms.

'Bulldust!' he snarled down into her wide grey eyes. 'You don't love Carstairs—no woman could love that cold computer of a man. At least, not the woman I've seen you to be. You're an intelligent, proud, spirited lady, Adrianna. You couldn't give your heart, your soul, to a man like that!'

His mouth twisted into an ugly grimace. 'I'm not saying you haven't given him your body, or that he wouldn't know how to push the right buttons. He probably had all the correct moves programmed into his silicon chip brain the second he passed puberty. But Adrianna…'

He yanked her against him, his fierce embrace punching the breath from her lungs. His hands dropped to cup her buttocks, lifting and kneading them before using his bruising hold to pull her breathtakingly close. 'If *I* made love to you,' he promised huskily, 'you'd know the difference. Say what you will about the sort of man you think I am, but at least I am that—a *man*, not a sleek-suited masquerade who's more concerned with his perfectly orchestrated technique than the woman he's with. My God, when I take you, my hot-blooded harridan, you'll *know* you've been taken, I can assure you!'

A moan escaped her lips as he pressed her even closer, moulding her soft stomach around the evidence of his claim. She tried to fight the hot tide of desire that washed up through her, her stunned mind hardly believing what was happening to her. It was a nightmare all right. Not the nightmare she had thought this trip would be, but a nightmare all the same. This man was making her forget everything she had just said. Her lifelong resolutions...her opinion of him... Alan... Everything!

All she wanted was to lose herself in the orgy of sensuality that was invading every pore of her body. It had already taken over her imagination, evoking startlingly clear fantasies to further tantalise her senses. Herself and Bryce naked; his doing incredible things to her; and herself, doing all the things she had never done or ever really wanted to do with a man.

Her pulse-rate took off and the blood began to pound in her veins, her temples, her head.

With a weird sense of fate closing in she tipped her head back and lifted her chin in readiness for the possession of his mouth. He stared down at her, blue eyes smouldering like hot ice. Her lips parted. Not just for him to kiss them but to offer her total capitulation in the plainest, most shocking words. 'Bryce...'

But no sooner had his name left her lips than a memory, stark and vivid, leapt into her brain. That of a woman, sitting at a battered kitchen table, her head in her hands, crying, saying she was pregnant—*again*—letting out all her despair and misery to the only person who would listen. Her ten-year-old daughter. And the daughter, unhappy, helpless, wondering why her mother kept making babies with a man who didn't give a hoot about her or his never-ending brood, who didn't support them, didn't love them, didn't even bother to come home most nights. But all the woman could say was that she loved him.

The memory burnt a path into Adrianna's brain, obliterating her desire as swiftly as a winter storm destroys the last remnants of autumn. Fear swept in instead, a fear that made her strike out blindly.

She lifted her knee and rammed it upwards between Bryce's thighs, then staggered backwards to watch, wide-eyed, as pain destroyed his arousal as effectively as the past had destroyed hers. He doubled over in sheer agony, his hands clutching his groin, his sharp inward breath more revealing than the loudest moan.

But when his eyes lifted to hers, his pain-filled, bewildered, accusing eyes, Adrianna was immediately consumed with an overwhelming remorse. 'Oh, Bryce!' she cried piteously, and stumbled forward to try to help him.

He repelled her with a vicious glance.

Bully, woken by the incident, came to his master's side and whimpered. With a grimace Bryce bent down and lightly touched the dog's ear. 'I'll be OK in a minute, boy,' he muttered between tightly drawn lips. 'Don't worry.'

Tears welled up into Adrianna's eyes. 'Oh, Bryce, I'm so sorry...'

'So am I,' he groaned.

'I didn't realise...'

'God!'

'Please forgive me.'

'Not bloody likely!'

She blinked. 'Oh...' She wasn't used to having an apology thrown back in her face.

He was finally able to straighten, though he was obviously still hurting. 'Don't look so petrified,' he grated through clenched teeth. 'I have more respect for my private parts than to come near you again. God...' He dragged in another deep sigh and let it out raggedly.

'Oh, Bryce, I... I...'

'For Pete's sake, don't you have any idea when to shut up, woman? Go to bed!'

She scrambled into the rough sleeping bag and just lay there, a shattered emotional wreck. One part of her kept saying she had done the right thing, the only thing. But still...

Eventually she risked a glimpse over at where Bryce was still standing, staring across at her, a black look of deep puzzlement on his face.

'What...what is it?' she asked nervously.

Bryce didn't answer her question, giving her a dismissive shrug and turning his back on her, leaving Adrianna with the impression that he would like to turn his back on her in more ways than one.

Not that she blamed him. No doubt he was now bitterly regretting his noble action in going to rescue her. He was probably wishing that he'd never set eyes on her, or that he had left her to the mercy of the desert.

Adrianna's mind whirled on and on, making her toss and turn in the rough bed. But finally sleep stole across her troubled soul, bringing with it a soothing blanket of oblivion. It was just as well, perhaps, that Adrianna couldn't see what the morrow would bring. Otherwise she might not have slept at all.

CHAPTER FIVE

ADRIANNA was dragged from a deep sleep quite abruptly, her eyelids propelled open by a cacophony of raucous birdcalls. She blinked volubly at the stark brightness of daylight before staring upwards into the towering pink branches of the river-gums under which Bryce had made his camp.

A flock of black cockatoos, their flamboyant orange tail-feathers flashing in the morning light, were jumping from branch to branch and screeching their strident music. Adrianna put her hands over her ears, but continued to watch them, awed by the birds' undeniable beauty. Large and glossy, they had a proud carriage and a wild, wicked beauty, looking like winged devils as they darted this way and that, their ebony coats the colour of Hades, their flaming tails a glimpse of hell-fire. All in all, magnificent, breathtaking.

But the *noise* they made! Adrianna rolled to one side, closing her eyes against the glare, and it was then that the memory of what had happened the night before finally filtered in.

Oh God! she groaned silently, and closed her eyes even tighter.

Thank the lord her back was to Bryce's bed! She couldn't look at him, couldn't face him. The reality that there were still five days of his sole companionship to go loomed large and fearful in her mind.

It wasn't that she didn't trust him. If he'd been going to do anything to her, he would have last night, when his blood and temper were up. But he hadn't. In fact, he'd shown an astounding amount of restraint, considering. Some men would have struck back at her quite violently.

It was herself she didn't trust. Or at least, that part of herself she seemed unable to control where Bryce was concerned. She still couldn't believe the intensity of her physical reaction to him. Though at least now she doubted if he would continue in that light, almost flirtatious manner he adopted sometimes. Neither, she suspected, would he be smiling and joking all the time.

This would provide her with some relief, she decided with a sigh. A few scowls and frowns were infinitely preferable to the way his eyes lit up so attractively whenever that irrepressible grin split his handsome face. Yes... If he kept his distance and treated her with cold wariness, or even downright contempt, perhaps she would survive this nightmare.

Perhaps...

It was an infinitely depressing realisation that if she hadn't had that vivid memory of her mother's misery she'd have let Bryce make love to her. By now he would have left her bare of more than her clothes. He would have also stripped her of her pride and self-respect, as her father had stripped her mother. What that man had done to that poor sweet woman didn't bear thinking about!

At least her mother's life now was a lot easier and happier, Adrianna reassured herself. The generous cheque she sent every month allowed her to rent a nice place with plenty left over for herself. Of course she probably gave some of it to those rotten ungrateful sons of hers, but there wasn't much Adrianna could do about that. She could hardly put conditions on the money. But by God, she wouldn't voluntarily give those brothers of hers a cent. Not a single cent! They were as lazy and useless and selfish as her father had been.

A deep sigh wafted from Adrianna's lips. She didn't want to think about her family, didn't want to think of all those years she had spent, having to come home from school and do everything most mothers would normally have already done. Except that *her* mother had had to go out and work long hours as a cleaner to bring *some* money in to feed and clothe their ever-expanding family. Adrianna had two older brothers and five younger ones before her mother stopped getting pregnant.

In Adrianna's view it would have been fair if all the children had bogged in and helped around the house—not to mention her perennially unemployed father—but because she was a girl, and her father was the chauvinist to beat all chauvinists, it had fallen to her alone to do all the housework and cooking and minding of the younger ones.

Adrianna's teenage years had gone by in an endless round of dirty nappies and screaming kids and never-ending baby-sitting. There had been moments when she had wanted to wring her baby brothers' necks—*literally*—her feelings sometimes so violent and resentful that even now she could not remember them without feeling guilty. Obviously she wasn't the self-sacrificing maternal type.

Though it seemed unfair to condemn herself too strongly after what she had had to put up with. But either way, the thought of having a husband who expected her to stay home and have baby after baby sent shivers up and down her spine.

Which brought her to another mind-blowing thought where Bryce was concerned. Last night, before she'd woken up to herself, she hadn't given a single thought to pregnancy! It just showed you how irrational a female could get when her hormones were working overtime.

Quite automatically her mind started ticking over dates. It was mildly consoling to realise that she was unlikely to conceive at this time of the month. What wasn't so consoling was that she still thought she might need this reassurance. It was as though, down deep, she believed she might still encourage Bryce to make love to her, which was so self-destructive she had to be crazy.

What about Alan? she berated herself. Don't you have any loyalty to him?

Not enough, apparently, to ward off this overwhelming desire. Which upset Adrianna considerably. For she was by nature a loyal and true person, and Alan was not at all the unfeeling bastard Bryce had tried to paint him to be last night. He might be hardworking and ambitious, but underneath he was a good man. And he *did* put aside time for things other than work these days.

There was his relationship with her, for instance, and just recently she had found out that he had a ward he was responsible for, the young daughter of good friends of his who'd drowned in a ferry accident three years previously. Adrianna had seen her photo in his wallet and asked him about her.

Apparently the girl had been fifteen and in a boarding school when the tragedy had happened and he had been named as executor in her parents' will. Ebony was her name—Ebony Theroux. It seemed Alan visited her occasionally at the boarding school, taking her parents' roles at speech nights and concerts and such. The girl also came to his home during her holidays, where she was a warm favourite with his widowed mother. She

would live there permanently, it appeared, after she left
school at the end of the year.

Thinking of Alan's home brought another thought to
Adrianna's mind. Where, she wondered, would she and
Alan live after they were married? Surely not with his
mother and his young ward...

A frown puckered her brow as she lay there, chewing
away on her thoughts, and gradually she became aware
that everything was very quiet around her. She peeped
a look over her shoulder and upwards, and saw that the
cockatoos had left. The silky green leaves were still and
silent, not even a breeze rustling through them. But it
surprised her that Bryce wasn't up yet, poking around,
rattling the billy or loading up the camels. And what
about Bully? Shouldn't she have heard a bark or two?

Apprehension struck fast and furious and she was instantly on the move, rolling over and jerking upright as
if a bomb had gone off at her feet. Her eyes darted here,
there, everywhere!

Bryce's blanket was coldly empty. There were no
camels grazing in the lush surrounds of the billabong.
And Bully, like his master, was nowhere in sight.

Shock was a sick turning over in her stomach. He's
gone and left me, she thought. Left me to die...

But then her brain clicked fully into gear. She saw
that all his packs were still here, piled up nearby. Even
his hat. Surely he would have taken his *hat* if he didn't
mean to come back? She searched for some reason for
his absence. Perhaps he was out for an early morning
ride!

The idea seemed ludicrous to Adrianna that anyone
would ride camels for pleasure as though they were
horses. But she clung to the notion, for she could think
of nothing else. And if she didn't have some explana-

tion—however stupid—to soothe her growing fears, she would have gone mad.

The silent empty minutes ticked away as she waited for Bryce to reappear. After half an hour, she busied herself finding some firewood from under the trees and getting the campfire going again, the dry dead branches catching alight quickly from the still glowing embers. She even boiled a billy, found some tea-bags and made herself some tea.

But that was as far as she went, her agitation making her continually walk out to where the green grass finished and the sands began. Shading her eyes with her hands, she scanned the distant dunes, willing Bryce to suddenly appear.

He didn't.

After nearly an hour of this torturous waiting, she slumped down next to the campfire and dissolved into tears. And it was while she was crying that she heard the most wonderful sound she had ever heard—Jumbo's cowbell.

Her relief was like a huge tidal wave, washing through her, her tears instantly dry, adrenalin firing her veins with life-giving energy. Ignoring the still protesting stiffness in her muscles, she jumped up and ran towards the sound, her fair hair flying out behind her, her feet unshod, a joyous smile breaking over her face.

She was halfway to the sandhills when she spied them, coming over the crest, Bryce on foot, leading the camels, Bully padding along beside him, tongue lolling out of the side of his mouth. If Adrianna had been approaching more slowly and with any degree of observation, she would have seen that Bryce looked tired and disgruntled, his appearance unkempt with bloodshot eyes and a beard-roughened chin. He was hardly in a receptive mood for the way she flew at him, throwing her arms madly around his neck.

'Oh, Bryce, Bryce, thank heaven!' she cried, her chest heaving against his. 'I was so worried. I…'

She froze when she saw the look in his eyes. It would have killed a cobra at ten feet. Before she could react, he dropped the reins, lifted his hands, grabbed her wrists and unpeeled her arms from his neck, depositing them back by her side and pushing her aside as though she were a contaminated person who had broken quarantine. 'Do you *mind*?' he said in a voice dipped in lemon.

Adrianna now felt sick in a totally different way. She had thought she would welcome his contempt, his coldness. But the reality was far, far different. Something shrivelled up inside her, making her want to crumple up and burst into tears again. She longed for one of his smiles, one of his light remarks. Even a casual civility would be better than this ghastly scorn.

'I would have thought you'd have a bit more sense, Adrianna,' he bit out with another savage look, 'than to throw your bra-less breasts against me like that. I would appreciate it if you would keep your distance, in future. And perhaps your jacket on? That way I might get out of this desert intact!'

Her cheeks flushed bright with guilt and shame. And indignation. She was perfectly decently dressed, if a little crumpled. 'I wasn't throwing myself at you in that way,' she argued, tossing her hair back from her face in a defiant gesture. 'I was just so happy and relieved to see you. Surely you must realise how worried I was when I woke to find you and the camels gone?'

His eyebrows lifted as he realised what she must have thought. 'Am I so low in your opinion that you believed I would resort to murder?'

She couldn't think what to say to that.

'Not that you don't *deserve* murdering,' he added testily.

Again she said nothing.

'Not very communicative this morning, are we?' he went on. 'What a pleasant change!' He picked up the reins and brushed past her, striding back towards the camp.

Adrianna ran after him till she was level with his shoulder. 'Where…where *were* you?' she asked breathlessly.

'Finding the rotten damned camels, of course! The mongrels took off in the night.'

'But you said they were tame!'

'Not *that* tame,' he snapped, then added in a dark mutter, 'I should have hobbled them before I went to bed. I usually do.'

'Then why didn't you?' she asked. Hobbling must mean tying up or staking out, she frowned to herself.

His sideways glance was blistering. 'I had other things on my mind!'

She bit her bottom lip.

'Besides,' he growled, 'I didn't really think they'd wander, with all that lush feed and water virtually at their feet. Perhaps that mad bull came back skulking around in the night and spooked them. The stupid fools were heading back for the salt-pan when I found them. If it hadn't been for Bully, I wouldn't have even considered looking that way.'

'Thank heaven for Bully, then,' she put in.

'You're not wrong there. I wouldn't like to walk my way from here, I can tell you. And speaking of walking, I think, Adrianna,' Bryce pointed out curtly, 'that you'd be advised to wear your sandals. That is if you want those delicate little feet of yours to last the distance.'

Despite the sarcasm in Bryce's voice, Adrianna detected a reluctant compliment in his words. She glanced down at her feet, acknowledging that she *did* have attractively dainty feet, with small slender toes and nicely shaped toenails. Yet Alan had never remarked on them, or even noticed them, for that matter. A shiver of pleasure rippled over her skin that Bryce was still so aware of her.

There quickly followed a black wave of self-disgust. All that self-lecturing and I'm no closer to controlling my feelings for this man, she thought. Even with his obvious derision, I'm looking for signs that he still fancies me. Because the truth is, I want him to still fancy me, I want him to fancy me so damned much that he'll somehow ignore what happened last night. I want him to use his male strength and natural sexual aggression to force me to admit these underlying feelings, to force me to…to what?

The possibilities made her throat go dry, made her heart pound madly within her breast.

She slanted him a quick sideways glance, glimpsing the stubborn set of his jaw as he marched along, a hint of suppressed violence in the way his lips were pressed together in a thin line. Perhaps she should be grateful for his hostility towards her, she thought bleakly. It might be the best protection she would ever have. She certainly couldn't rely on her own self-restraint!

They reached the camp, where Bryce led the camels over to give them a drink of water while he held the reins, leaving Adrianna standing beside the fire like a shag on a rock. She decided to get Bryce a cup of tea whether he wanted her to or not, carrying it over to him.

He was clearly startled as she pressed it into his hand,
his eyes betraying a reluctant flash of pleasure. But it
was quickly gone as a stony expression took its place.
'Thanks,' he muttered, and lifted the mug to drink.

'I… I'd make you some breakfast too,' she said, 'but
I don't know what supplies are in what bag. If you'd
just show me…' Her voice broke off when he made
some scowling sound and she sighed. 'Please, Bryce…
I said I was sorry… Can't we forget about last night?'

His glance was long and hard. 'Can *you*?'

She stiffened. 'I'd like to try.'

Bryce gave a tired, mocking laugh.

'OK, so you hate me now,' she said softly. 'Fair
enough. But we're stuck with each other for a while yet
and it's far better all round if we try to get along, at least
on the surface. Don't you agree?'

His eyes were fixed on her face, narrowed unreadable
eyes. Oh, how she wished she knew what he was thinking!

'Very well,' he said curtly. 'I'm not an unreasonable
man.'

Adrianna smiled with relief, but the smile faded
quickly when his face tightened at the sight of it. Clearly
their truce was not supposed to extend to smiles. And if
she were honest with herself, Adrianna knew that was a
good idea. Smiles were hardly the way to keep a man
at bay. Or a woman, for that matter.

'One thing especially,' she went on in a more matter-
of-fact voice. 'I'd like to help more, Bryce. I'm not stupid, really I'm not.'

There was the faintest twitch at the corner of his grim
mouth. 'All right.'

He was as good as his word. First of all, he showed
her all his supplies, which were extensive, even includ-

ing a battery-operated razor which quickly returned his
stubbly chin to its former clean-shaven state, after which
they breakfasted on tinned peaches and muesli, topped
with reconstituted powdered milk. More tea followed,
then an apple each. Then he gave her some basic chores
to do like washing up, filling the water bags and covering the fire with sand while he packed and loaded the
camels, sharing the load between Dumbo and Jumbo.

One thing she noticed, though, was Bryce's reluctance
to look straight at her, or touch her in any way. There
was certainly no hint of his offering to apply either the
sunscreen or insect repellent he gave her. Even their ac-
cidental brushing against each other resulted in his either
moving himself further away, or actually flinching.
Adrianna thought he was overdoing it a bit, and in the
end she said so, which brought a ghost of a smile to his
lips.

'Better to be safe than sorry, I say,' was his answering
remark.

But he was a fraction more relaxed after that, and
actually touched her thigh while getting her saddled up
without looking as if he'd encountered a leper. Adrianna
wasn't sure what to think about his behaviour. She
couldn't believe he was actually afraid of her assaulting
him. Which left a possibility that she found both disturbing and tantalising at the same time. He might hate
her, but he also might still desire her. Far too much,
obviously, for his peace of mind...

Two hours after Bryce's return they were on their
way. By noon they had covered several miles, moving
along at a steady walk, following the path of a dry creek
bed which Bryce said had intermittent waterholes. He
was right, and they rested at one for nearly two hours
over lunch, but encountered nothing that day as large

and lovely as the lagoon they'd just left. Nevertheless, it was a far pleasanter route to travel along than the desert and dunes, shade from the river-gums providing a cooling respite from the fierce heat. It was great too that the flies no longer bothered her. In fact, by late in the afternoon, although tired, Adrianna felt quite relaxed.

Bryce was right about the desert, she thought. It had a way of emptying one's mind—a bit like flying. It also played tricks with time. Several times she thought an hour had passed, but then she'd find out only several minutes had gone by. This effect, combined with the drugging heat, meant that one's whole being was lulled into a type of drowsy trance which was oddly soothing. Her body soon learnt to move with the rock and sway of the camel without tension, without strain, and as they ambled along late in the afternoon her eyelids grew heavier, and heavier, and heavier…

'You're not going to sleep sitting up, are you?'

Her eyes shot open to see Bryce alongside her. Dumbo, she noticed with a jolt, had stopped walking.

She blinked. 'You know what? I think I was,' she said, surprise in her voice.

Bryce laughed.

A warmth rushed into Adrianna's heart. It was good to hear him laugh again. And she smiled at him.

Immediately his laughter stopped and he jerked his head away. 'We'll camp here for the night,' he announced abruptly. 'This is as good a waterhole as we're going to get along this part of the journey.'

'Oh…' She looked at the small, slightly muddy pond in front of them, trying valiantly not to let his return to sharpness bother her.

'Well? Are you going to sit there dreaming all day?' Bryce asked impatiently. 'You said you wanted to help!'

'Oh yes…yes…' She gave him a flustered glance, but he was already looking away from her.

The evening passed eventually, but not pleasantly. Bryce did a good imitation of a sulky Marlon Brando, only opening his lips to mutter some instruction to her, or growl at Bully, who seemed to have the devil in him and was taking pleasure in antagonising the camels. After a severe scolding the dog skulked over and sat next to Adrianna, something he hadn't done before. But when she stretched her hand out to pat him he snapped at it.

Like master, like dog, she thought ruefully.

The ground wasn't as soft as the sand around the lagoon either, but when she mentioned this fact Bryce gave her a scathing look.

'Must you complain all the time?' he growled. 'This isn't the Ritz, you know.'

'But I don't complain all the time,' she defended, stung by his accusation. 'I… Oh, to *hell* with you, Bryce McLean!' she snapped suddenly. 'Just because you're in a filthy mood don't think you can take it out on me. I'm not a *dog*, you know!'

'No,' he flung back at her, 'you're a silly damned bitch!'

Silence fell over them like a sodden blanket. Bryce made another scowling noise and stalked off into the night.

Adrianna had never felt so hurt in all her life.

Tears sprang to her eyes and she threw herself down on the bedroll, burying her face in the lumpy pillow and sobbing noisily.

In typical female fashion she half expected him to hear her, to return and comfort her. But he didn't, leaving her to her misery and bewilderment. She found it both disconcerting and perplexing that the worse he treated her, the more she wanted him. It was crazy in the extreme, and very distressing, mostly because it went against all that she considered both logical and normal. Shouldn't a woman be attracted to gentleness and kindness and consideration, not macho displays of rudeness and total disregard for her feelings?

She took a long time to get to sleep, a long, long time. Long enough to decide that she was a damned fool, that Bryce was a nasty bit of goods and that she would never speak to him again as long as she lived!

It was a resolution that lasted till morning. After all, it was hard not to speak to the man after he'd saved her life.

CHAPTER SIX

SHE was lying on her back when she woke slowly the next morning just before the dawn, and became gradually aware of an unnatural weight on the blanket, across her thighs. Could it be Bully? was her first thought. Probably, she decided.

Yet somehow she couldn't bring herself to take a look and tiny shivers kept running up and down her spine. The reasoning behind her nervous reaction finally slotted into her sleep-slowed brain. The weight wasn't heavy enough for such a solid, nuggety dog...

In that case, what was it?

Her breathing began coming in short, shallow pants as she tried to gather up the courage to look. Slowly she started to lift her head from the pillow, her heart hammering painfully against her ribs.

'Don't move,' came the low, husky warning form the direction of Bryce's blanket.

Her heart jumped into her throat, but she lowered her head with excruciating slowness back down again. 'What is it?' she rasped back, not daring to even twist her head to one side so that she could see where Bryce was.

'Just...don't...move,' he repeated, each word low and emphasised.

'Oh, God...'

There was only thing it could be, of course. A snake. A *big* snake, by the feel of it.

Adrianna abhorred snakes. Even a picture of a snake

92

made her skin crawl. The thought that one was lying in her lap, with only a blanket between its deadly fangs and herself, made her feel ill. Perspiration broke out on her forehead as the seconds ticked away.

'Where are you? What are you going to do?' she whispered urgently.

'Will you shut up?' hissed Bryce, his voice this time coming from nearby.

She could see him now, crouching near her head, bending over her. Slowly, ever so slowly, he slid his hands under her armpits and took a firm grip on her upper body. 'On the count of three,' he told her quietly and steadily, 'I'm going to yank you out. OK?'

'OK,' she agreed, terrified.

'One…two…*three*!'

She shot out of the rough sleeping bag like a cannon-ball out of a cannon, her whole body landing on Bryce's with a resounding thud. But he was instantly rolling away from under her, snatching up his rifle and firing. Whatever had been on that blanket was now sorry it chose that place to sleep, Adrianna thought dazedly.

When Bryce returned to gather her body up into his arms she began to shake. 'What…what kind of snake was it?' she asked.

He held her away from him briefly and gave her a wry smile. 'And how did you know it was a snake, Miss Smarty-pants?'

'You're…you're not the only one who can make a l-logical con-conclusion. Bryce…why am I sh-shaking so?'

'Shock. You'll be all right in a little while. Want to look at the body?'

A shudder reverberated through her as she glanced

reluctantly down at the huge, ugly mass of reptilian remains.

'Just as well Bully's off chasing an early morning rabbit,' he told her, 'or he'd have dived on this fellow for sure, and God knows what would have happened then. It was a King Brown,' he added. 'Deadly as hell.'

Adrianna went weak at the knees, but Bryce propped her up again. 'I think what you need is a slug of brandy,' he said, then led her over and settled her on the log. She slumped down like a sack of potatoes.

Bryce squeezed her shoulder before walking over to the supplies. 'I have a medicinal quantity here somewhere...' He rummaged through one of his personal bags. 'Ah, here it is.' And he produced a small flask.

He came back, unscrewing the cap on the way, and handing it over without a glass. 'Just take a swig,' he suggested. 'I'll risk your germs.'

She did as she was told, coughing slightly as she swallowed too much too quickly. 'You're always getting me reviving drinks,' she said.

'You're always needing them,' he chuckled, taking the flask from her and rescrewing the lid.

She smiled up at him. 'True... But I can't help it if my body's not immune to all these dramas the way yours is.'

His face darkened, and she wondered what she had said or done wrong now. What Adrianna hadn't realised was that when she had smiled up at Bryce her eyes had sparkled flirtatiously as a woman's did when she was as aware of a man as she was of him. It wasn't a deliberate thing, her throwing out of a sexual challenge, but it was there all the same.

'My body isn't immune to anything,' he said coldly,

'as I'm sure you are well aware. It's as vulnerable and mortal as the next man's.'

There was no hiding the surprise in her eyes at his about-turn, and he shook his head in exasperation. 'I wish you'd make up your mind,' he went on irritably, 'what you want of me.'

'Want of you?' she repeated blankly, stunned by the swift change in both his mood and the situation. Suddenly all was tense and electric between them.

'Look, I'm not going to beat around the bush any longer,' Bryce ground out. 'I'm not into playing the sophisticated sexual games you city folk indulge in. I call a spade a spade and to hell with it! I want you, Adrianna. I've wanted you from the first second I laid eyes on you, running towards me.'

Adrianna gaped. He'd wanted her all along? But he'd given her no indication. No indication at all! Not till the lagoon...

'I didn't think it was the right time or place to come on strong straight away,' Bryce continued. 'And then you dropped your bombshell about being engaged. Damn it, I thought. She's out of bounds. OK, laugh it off. Make light of it. It's nothing anyway but a physical thing. An ache, like a headache. Take a cold swim every night. But then all of a sudden, the status quo changed. You wanted me back. I saw it, in your eyes, in the lagoon. Then, to top it all off, I found out that the man you were engaged to wasn't worth spitting on! I figured there wasn't any reason why I shouldn't go after you, no reason why I shouldn't just do what your eyes kept telling me you wanted of me. So when the opportunity presented itself—with the lip cream—I began taking it. With unfortunate and rather painful results, however.'

'Bryce, I...'

'Be quiet and hear me out!'

Her mouth snapped shut.

'I know you said you were sorry,' he bit out. 'But that doesn't wash away your reasons for suddenly going cold on me last night and almost damaging me for life! Don't think I don't know why you did it, because I *do*! And lady, I don't take kindly to that sort of thing. Not kindly at all!'

He glared at her with bitter resentment which only increased her confusion. How could he possibly know about her background, about her sudden vision of her mother?

'Don't bother putting that innocently bewildered look into those beautiful grey eyes of yours, Adrianna. You're about as innocent as a politician! You and I know exactly why you got cold feet last night. At the last moment you couldn't lower yourself to actually let a man like me put his grubby hands on you, could you? You don't think I'm good enough for you, which is why now, no matter what you say or do, no matter how often you go hot and cold, I have no intention of touching you.'

He set wintry eyes on her wide-eyed face. 'You judged me, madam, without even knowing me. You slotted me into the ne'er-do-well category and closed the file! But that's all right, because I'm returning you the favour. I'm slotting you into the category of snobbish, mercenary career bitch who wants her cake and wants to eat it too; a super-suave millionaire to satisfy her need for money and social position, and a bit of rough stuff on the side to satisfy her libido. How am I going? Am I close? After all, you *have* finally got over your qualms at dirtying your hands, haven't you?' His laughter grated over her nerves like chalk on a blackboard. 'That's why you're being nice to me all of a sudden, isn't it?'

He flung this last derisive remark at her, a taunting glint in his eyes that demanded a reaction. It brought a reaction all right, but one she didn't give him the satisfaction of seeing. The half-truths behind what he'd just said evoked undermining elements of guilt and shame, but this last accusation was so patently false and unjust, so cruel and nasty, that she refused to concede anything to him.

Adrianna squared her shoulders and lifted her chin, her eyes almost as chilling as his as they flashed across the space between them. 'I would say your skill with a rifle is far more accurate than your assessment of me and my motives,' she grated, her words like chipped ice. 'As I said once before, Bryce, I was briefly—*very* briefly—attracted to you. Please put it down to an aberration after the plane crash, a reaction to the gratitude I felt for your Lawrence of Arabia rescue. I was quickly over it. It seems to me that you must have an over-inflated opinion of your sex appeal if you think that every woman who's pleasant to you wants to rip your clothes off. There again, perhaps you judge everyone else by your own urges, which seem to quickly get out of hand. After all, you've just confessed to desiring a woman you dislike. I find that a contradiction in terms. I know I certainly couldn't continue to desire a man I disliked.'

Her shrug was most convincingly indifferent. 'Anyway, it's a comfort to know that you'll play at being a gentleman for the rest of the trip, though may I suggest, by way of precaution, that you keep having a cold swim every night!'

Her words shocked him, she could see. Or was it her manner—her confident, commanding, coldly caustic manner? Little did he know that inside she was weeping,

weeping for the messed-up future that lay ahead of her. For how could she marry Alan now? How could she go into his bed every night, wishing he were someone else…

'My God,' Bryce muttered, his bottom lip curling over in disgust. 'You're more of a bitch than I thought!'

Adrianna closed her heart to his derision. 'Think what you like. The fact of the matter is that all this will be irrelevant in a few days' time. We won't ever see each other again. So let's try to be civil, shall we? Or is that too much to ask for a macho outback man like you?'

Adrianna knew straight away that she shouldn't have used such a goading, inflammatory tone. But it was too late now to take it all back. He would only scorn any attempt at an apology.

A smile slowly came to Bryce's mouth, a wickedly cruel smile that struck dread into her soul. 'You'd be surprised how civilised I can be, Adrianna,' he said in a voice like silk. Or was it like a snake?

Apprehension rippled over the surface of her skin. If he dared touch her she would have him arrested for rape! 'I'm glad to hear it,' she said, her throat clamping tight in an effort to control her shaking voice. It made her words come out curtly, as though coated with contempt. 'Now, do you think we could get on with things? Perhaps if we can make really good time we might be back to that cattle station of yours in two days instead of three.'

'Cattle station of mine?' he repeated archly.

'You know what I mean… The place where you work. Dover Downs or whatever it's called.'

'Ah yes, Dover Downs, the place where I work… Well, if you're prepared to spend long hours in the saddle I think we might manage it in two days, if that's what you really want.'

'That's what I want,' she said stiffly.

'Be it on your own head,' he muttered.

It wasn't just on her head. It was also on her bottom, her poor stiff, aching bottom. Not to mention the rest of her. But by heaven they covered some ground that day, the camels barely able to pick up their feet when they were still being pushed along the creek bed as the sun finally set. 'Bryce,' she said at last, her voice quavering with exhaustion, 'I can't go on. I...'

'Can't go on?' he scoffed. 'Why not? It was what you wanted, wasn't it?'

'Because...because...' In the end she didn't have to give him a reason, for she slithered sideways off the saddle and on to the sandy ground in a dead faint.

When she came to, it was cold, the sky was pitch dark and she was in the bedroll. Bryce was a couple of metres away from her, crouched down, holding a match to a pile of dry kindling that would eventually become a camp-fire. Adrianna tried to sit upright, but slumped back as a wave of dizziness claimed her, a moan escaping her lips.

Bully came over and nuzzled her hand.

Bryce walked over and handed her a flask, his face in darkness with his back towards the flickering flames. 'Here, sip this water... I have to get this fire going properly, before we freeze. Will you be all right to lie there a bit longer?'

'Yes,' she said weakly.

But he didn't leave. He just stood there and stared down at her. 'You collapsed,' he said simply.

'I know.'

'It was all too much for you.'

'Probably.'

There was a short sharp silence.

'I'm sorry, Adrianna.'

'I am too,' she managed, a lump in her throat, tears scalding her eyes. Suddenly it was all too much for her and she began to cry, deep racking sobs that tore through her tired, aching body.

'Don't!' groaned Bryce. 'Please don't...'

'It's all right,' she gasped out between sobs. 'You don't have to do anything. Just leave me be... Go back to the fire...'

For a second he hesitated, as though unsure what to do. Then he shrugged unhappily and went back to do as she said.

Oddly enough, she fell back to sleep almost immediately, waking some time later to find the fire roaring, and the smell of food cooking. Bryce was sitting in the dirt, idly stirring the iron pots, the light from the flames touching first one side of his face, then the other. He had changed his clothes, she noticed, into a fresh blue shirt and darker jeans. His hair was damp, as though he had been swimming, yet a quick searching glance revealed no nearby waterhole. Not that she could see very far, the glow from the camp-fire only providing a meagre circle of light in the pitch-black dark of a desert night.

Bryce was obviously unaware of her silent scrutiny, for he continued to stare into the fire, his blank bleak gaze showing his mind was far away in another world.

Where? she wondered. With some woman he had left behind? Some country girl who liked and respected him for what he was, who wouldn't hurt him both physically and emotionally as *she* had done? For Adrianna could not deny that the Bryce who had driven them both so mercilessly all day had been deeply hurt by her stupid and unfathomable behaviour. OK, so his anger was probably based on injured male pride—or an intense sexual frustration—but that didn't make her actions any less excusable. She had been playing with the man's feelings, one moment wanting him, the next rejecting him, and shame was a heavy load on her heart. It was hardly the way to treat a man who had saved her life, not once, but twice!

Looking over at his grimly hunched figure, she resolved to do everything in her power not to annoy or upset him for the rest of the trip. She would not only be civil, but she would be decent and pleasant, show him that she didn't look down on him at all, that she appreciated what he had done for her.

Her sense of guilt increased when she realised she had not once asked him about himself and his life, that she had indeed prejudged him. Not to mention patronised him. Adrianna groaned as she recalled the wide-eyed surprise she had displayed when he showed himself for the intelligent man he really was. Not only intelligent, but clever and self-sufficient and strong and caring and...

Adrianna brought herself up sharp. Now stop that! You're making him sound like a cross between Mother Teresa and St Francis of Assisi. He's not that much of a saint! Why, he's done a spot of prejudging himself, hasn't he? And he couldn't have made a nastier accusation about you if he'd tried, virtually calling you a two-timing tramp.

Ah, yes, but...that inner voice of conscience inserted softly. There was more than a spot of truth in that accusation, wasn't there? Alan hasn't exactly been figuring too largely in your thoughts lately, has he?

'Oh, shut up,' she muttered under her breath, and propped herself up on one elbow, all the more determined to act decently. 'Bryce,' she said, wincing slightly when his head jerked round to set hard eyes upon her, 'I…er…I'm awake.'

'So I see,' was his dry reply.

Her sigh carried genuine regret. 'Let's not be nasty to each other any more, Bryce. I'm sorry for the things I've said. I'm sorry for everything…'

He made an exasperated sound, but a wry smile was tugging at his lips. 'My God, let me jot this momentous occasion down in my diary! Adrianna Winslow, saying she was wrong about something!'

'Oh, I didn't say I was wrong,' she countered with a smile of her own. 'I merely said I was sorry I said what I said. After all, look what it got me. A backside that probably won't be able to sit down for a week, let alone ride Humpty-Dumpty!'

It was surprisingly good to hear Bryce laugh again. He tipped back his head and let the happy sounds roll from his throat. They echoed back in the still of the night, bringing some startled barking from Bully. His eyes pricked up when he heard the echo of his own barking and he raced off into the darkness to see where the other dog was.

'That dog of yours is almost as dumb as your camels,' she chuckled.

'But not nearly as dumb as his master,' Bryce said with obviously cryptic intent. Adrianna wisely decided to make no comment.

'At least I was right. We're not too far from the gorge,' he went on. 'There has to be more than sandhills and creek beds to make an echo.'

'What gorge is that?' she asked.

'Just a gorge. It's got an Aboriginal name, but I can't recall what it is. It's too remote and uninspiring to warrant attention for tourists, so it hasn't acquired an English name. An old Abo showed it to me years ago, because he said it was a reliable waterhole. Even in a drought the water doesn't dry up, because it's fed by an underground spring. This year, with the added run-off from the rain, the lagoon will be brimming.'

'You look as if you've already had a swim. Is there a waterhole near here?'

'Unfortunately no, but I thought we weren't far from the gorge, so I used up some of our water supply having a good wash.'

'I wish I had a change of clothes,' Adrianna said with an unhappy glance down at herself. Her linen pants and silk blouse were grimy and dusty, with caught threads and dirty smudges all over them.

'You can wash and dry them at the gorge tomorrow. We'll camp there for the day, if you like; give you a chance to recover.'

'Yes…yes, I think we'll have to,' she said thoughtfully. No use pretending she was in a physical state to keep going. As it was, she would have to walk the rest of the way to the gorge. Riding was out of the question.

'Ready for some dinner yet?' he asked.

'Definitely.'

'You'll be pleased to know there's a change of menu. Pasta and tinned sauce, followed by fruit salad splashed with some of that brandy and long-life cream.'

'Mmm,' she sighed. 'Sounds marvellous!'

Bryce brought a steaming plateful of the Italian-smelling dish over and she pulled herself upright to sit on the relative softness of the lumpy pillow, having to bite her tongue to stop a groan from escaping. She must have looked pained, however.

'I'll give you some horse liniment later,' he offered as he handed over the plate. 'Rub it in wherever it hurts.'

'In that case I hope you've got a bucketful!'

His downward glance held reluctant amusement. 'You know, Adrianna, you can be really nice when you want to be.'

'Goodness, let me jot this momentous occasion down in my diary,' she retorted, in a parody of what he'd said earlier. 'Bryce McLean, saying something nice about me!'

He laughed. 'You're too smart for your own good, do you know that?'

'Yes,' she said with a rueful dryness. It was exactly what her father had said when she'd gained a really good pass in the Higher School Certificate, despite having missed countless days.

'I can't stand smart women,' Bryce added, still smiling.

'I don't wonder,' she returned.

His eyes flashed and there was a split second when the situation might have got sticky. But Bryce quickly relaxed into a grin. 'I've been wondering,' he drawled, 'just what you do for a living. Now I think I know. You're one of those lady lawyers who go into a courtroom, oozing sweet smiles and ultra-feminine glamour, just to instil the opposite side with a false sense of confidence, then, when the defendant is in the box, whammo! That acid tongue and steel-trap mind of yours goes to work and the poor bastard gets so mixed up he ends up dobbing himself in.'

Adrianna giggled and shook her head.

'No? Let's see…what else is there? Public relations? Super-secretary?'

Again she smiled and shook her head.

'If you tell me you're a check-out chick I won't believe it!'

Now she laughed outright. 'Actually, I was a check-out chick for three years while I was going through college.'

'If so then I bet all the other girls in the supermarket hated you. I'll bet you scanned all those items so fast you made them look like they were standing still.'

He was right, actually. In the end, she had learnt not to be so efficient, rather than endure the vicious looks and jealous comments from the other women.

'Well?' he prompted. 'Are you going to tell me what you did at college?'

'I will, *after* I've eaten this delicious food.'

'I'll keep you to that,' he warned, and walked off to hobble the camels for the night.

Adrianna watched him work while she ate, recalling how she had first thought that hobbling meant tying up—to a tree or something similar. But it wasn't like that at all. Both the camels wore leather cuffs low down on their front legs which Bryce linked together every night with chains. Each chain was only a foot long, which allowed them the freedom to walk and graze but not to wander or run off too far.

After hobbling the camels, Bryce fed Bully, then rejoined her with the promised dessert, settling down on a blanket next to her and doggedly returning to his earlier questioning about what she did for a living.

'I have a fashion business,' she told him. 'I design a range of women's wear under my own personal label, and I own a few boutiques that stock them exclusively.'

He looked surprised. 'I'd never have guessed it. I would have thought you'd do something more intellectual.'

'There's very little money in being intellectual.'

One of Bryce's eyebrows lifted. 'That sounded cynical.'

'I guess I am a bit,' she murmured, and spooned some of the delicious fruit salad and cream into her mouth.

'How does one go about becoming a fashion designer and boutique owner?' Bryce asked after he'd reduced his dessert considerably with a couple of huge mouthfuls.

With some pauses for eating, Adrianna patiently revealed that after leaving school she had taken a textiles and design course at a Sydney college, after which she had secured a job as assistant to the designer in a minor fashion house. Even then she had continued her studies at night, doing a managerial and business administration course. By the time this second diploma was completed, she was twenty-three, and ready to go out on her own.

'I knew I'd never get rich working for wages,' she commented, 'something I learnt from the lady my mother used to do cleaning for. I think I was around fifteen when Mum came home one day and repeated what her employer had said.'

You'll never get anywhere, Flo, working for so much an hour for someone else. You should start a company that supplies cleaners, send other women out on cleaning jobs and collect a commission!

'Mum laughed,' Adrianna explained, 'but I thought the idea brilliant. It came to me then that I would have my own business one day. So once I was properly qualified, and had saved up enough money to back myself, I did just that!'

'And made a success of it, I'll warrant,' came Bryce's comment.

'Well, yes, I have…'

He gave her a long, penetrating look. 'Tell me,' he said at last, 'is it so important for you to be rich?'

She gave the question honest consideration. 'I don't want to be too rich,' was her thoughtful and frowning answer. 'Being too rich means a loss of privacy. But I want to have enough money to be my own person, to not have to depend on any man for my next meal.'

'Then why are you marrying Alan Carstairs?' Bryce asked, frowning.

Adrianna took a deep breath, and battened down the hatches on her sudden rise in blood-pressure. Of course a man like Bryce would equate marriage with a woman giving up her independence. Most men did. Still, she didn't want another slanging match with him, and she resolved to answer carefully.

'Alan and I are friends, Bryce. We like and respect each other. And we both want the same things in life.'

'Which are?'

'A satisfying career and a life partner to share things with but who will still give their respective spouses the right to do and be what they want to be.'

'You didn't say anything about having a family.'

Adrianna stiffened. 'No,' she said tautly, 'I didn't.'

'You don't want children?'

'No.'

'I can understand why Carstairs wouldn't want them—he wouldn't want to be put to the trouble. But why don't you want them, Adrianna?'

She set reproachful eyes on him. 'Will you please stop sneering about Alan? After all, weren't you the person who accused me of prejudice? You don't really know

Alan, you know. Not the man he is now. So you can't say what his reasons are for not wanting children. As for my reasons, I just don't think I'd make a very good mother.'

'Why not?'

'Oh, for heaven's sake!'

'That's what I say. Fancy deciding not to have children for such a silly reason! A lot of women think they won't make good mothers, but after they've actually had a baby, all those suppressed maternal feelings suddenly burst into life.'

'I doubt it,' was her dry comment.

'Why do you say that?'

Adrianna rolled her eyes. 'Will you kindly drop this subject?'

'No.'

She glared at his determined face. 'Because I've been there before and I didn't like it,' she snapped.

He was clearly taken aback. 'You've *had* a baby?'

'No,' she sighed impatiently. 'Oh, good grief, I suppose I'll just have to tell you everything to shut you up.'

He sat perfectly still, looking at her intently as she began telling him as quickly and impersonally as possible all about her growing-up years, about her frustrations and resentments, her near-miss violence with her baby brothers, her contempt for her father, her pity for her mother. Of course she couldn't keep up the cold matter-of-fact tone. After a while her voice started vibrating with emotion and once or twice words caught in her throat.

Yet somehow in the soothing quiet of the desert night, the words kept spilling out, on and on. It was like a catharsis of all those bitter years, a cleansing of her soul.

'I left home immediately after I did my HSC,' she

concluded. 'Dad followed me and demanded that I come back and help support the family. I looked him straight in the eye and told him what I thought of him, that I had no intention of letting him take any of the money *I* earnt for grog and gambling; I told him he was a useless, hopeless rotten excuse for a husband and father and I never wanted to see him again.'

'Wow!' Bryce exclaimed, but his eyes showed respect. 'That temper of yours isn't new, then.'

She gave him a shaky look, her whole being trembling inside with spent emotion. 'No, I guess not...' Yet oddly enough, in the last few years she had kept it well under control. It had only been here, in the desert with Bryce, that it seemed to have reared its ugly head again.

'You did the right thing,' he said with gentle understanding.

She didn't make any comment to that, her chin quivering dangerously as tears pricked her eyes. *Had* she done the right thing? Would she ever get over the guilt of leaving her mother behind? Yet she had begged her mother to come with her, but she wouldn't. Her spirit had been long crushed. Adrianna's only comfort had been that her mother had been set free eventually, by her father's death. Even then her mother had refused to come and live with her, deciding to spend the rest of her life looking after sons who were proving as useless and parasitic as their father.

'Come along, don't cry now and spoil your image,' Bryce warned.

She had to laugh. 'No need to ask what image that is, I suppose.'

'Ask away, I'll tell you.'

She sighed. 'All right, tell me. I can take it.'

He smiled at her. 'That's just it.'

'What?' she asked, confused.

'The fact that you can take it. I'd say you can take an awful lot without cracking. You're a strong and very courageous woman, Adrianna Winslow. A rare woman…'

Adrianna stared at his openly admiring face, then quickly dropped her lashes. 'Don't, Bryce,' she choked out.

'Don't what?'

'Don't like me. And don't make me like you back. I…I can't handle it. I…' Her hand shook violently as she lowered the now empty plate to the blanket. She closed her eyes tightly. 'I love Alan and I'm going to marry him,' she lied.

When she opened her eyes again, it was to find Bryce frowning at her. Gradually the frown cleared and he nodded slowly. 'It's all right, Adrianna,' he said soothingly. 'It's all right. Don't upset yourself so.'

'But it's not all right!' she cried, lifting her hands up to hide her weeping from him. 'I *do* like you. I *do*…'

A silence fell between them—an electric silence. The seconds ticked away as agonisingly as they would during an atom-bomb countdown, with Adrianna petrified that her admission would make Bryce do something foolish, something they would both regret later. If he touched her or kissed her…

Her eyes flew open in a panic when she heard Bryce get to his feet. She stared up at him, her face filled with both fear and an awful excited churning. What was he going to do?

But he merely shook his head. Picking up the blanket, he walked slowly around to the other side of the camp and dropped it to the ground. 'Goodnight, Adrianna,' he

called across the fire, his voice sounding terribly tired.
'Sleep well.'

'Good…goodnight,' she answered weakly.

And oddly enough, she did sleep well, emotional and
physical exhaustion eventually taking their toll. But before her mind was snatched into oblivion it whirled and
whirled, tortured by thoughts that she would rather not
have had.

I wouldn't have stopped him, she kept thinking, if
he'd wanted me.

But the worst realisation was that he hadn't wanted
her. Not any more.

CHAPTER SEVEN

THERE were no disturbing thoughts or feelings, however, when Adrianna woke the next morning. It was hard to concentrate on anything other than pain when one's muscles had set during the night into hard, twisted knots of agony.

She struggled out of the bedroll and tried to straighten, with little success. Hands on hips and teeth gritted, she finally managed it, flexing her shoulderblades back and forth till she had some of the crinks out. But of course it was her lower half that presented the worst of her troubles. Her thighs and bottom, to be precise.

A brisk hand-rub on the latter and a couple of knee bends loosened her up a fraction, then she took a quiet stroll around, careful not to wake Bryce, who was still sound asleep. Bully joined her, his beady black eyes looking up at her every now and then whenever she groaned.

'I'd pat you,' she told the dog, 'if I didn't think you'd bite my hand off.'

Bully gave a low growl as though he agreed with her. They walked along ahead for a while, with Adrianna looking for a sight of the gorge. But the creek-bed twisted and turned, the lining of large leafy eucalyptus trees obscuring any long-distance view, so eventually she turned around and went back to the camp, finding Bryce up and busy with breakfast. He hadn't shaved yet, but the stubbly chin didn't look bad on him. In fact, he looked too damned attractive all over, his chest-hugging shirt and body-moulding jeans leaving little of his impressive male frame to the imagination.

Adrianna tensed up as she drew near, and when Bryce looked over his shoulder and sent her one of his lazy grins, her whole insides did a somersault.

'Feeling better this morning?' he asked, and stood up straight, stretching wide with a yawn.

'Yes,' was her one-word, almost curt reply.

'Still stiff, by the way you were walking. I forgot to give you that liniment—sorry.'

He gave her such a warm, caring look that Adrianna tensed even further. She shouldn't have admitted to liking him or told him so much about herself. Those kinds of revelations broke down barriers between people, barriers she would have preferred to be still firmly in place.

'It doesn't matter,' she said sharply. 'I'll loosen up in the walk to the gorge. Riding is out of the question, I'm afraid.'

'That bad, eh?' he said, apparently thinking her snappy tone was the result of discomfort. 'Oh, well, it's not far.' He bent then and lifted the lid on the large iron pot in the middle of the smouldering fire, and a delicious smell wafted up to hit Adrianna's nostrils. Quite involuntarily she drew in a deep breath and sighed sensuously.

'Fantastic smell, isn't it?' he drawled. 'There's nothing better than damper for breakfast on a crisp desert morning.'

Adrianna's mouth was practically watering as Bryce scooped the circular, bread-like loaf out of the pot on to a large plate.

'It's certainly of bribable quality,' she commented.

His sideways glance had an amused twinkle in it. '*How* bribable?'

'Not *that* bribable!' she shot back.

He laughed. 'You don't know what I was suggesting?'

'It doesn't take a genius to guess.'

He pretended to look offended. 'Oh, Adrianna, I'm wounded.'

'You will be if you try anything,' she snapped.

He held the lid of the iron pot in front of his groin. 'Go ahead,' he teased. 'See if I care!'

A reluctant giggle came to her throat.

'My God, Bully, did you hear that?' Bryce cried in mock horror.

The dog cocked his head on one side, looking so silly that Adrianna burst out laughing.

'Good grief, now she's getting hysterical. It must be hunger. Here, I'd better give her some of this damper, Bully, before she goes over the edge.'

Despite her repeated laughter, Adrianna found breakfast oddly unnerving. When in good humour Bryce was a charming and amusing companion. That and his macho sex appeal were a lethal combination and she found it hard to stop herself looking at him with both affection and desire. However, when on one occasion she caught him staring at her quite speculatively, she quickly fashioned her face into a cool expression and asked whether, if they made their stop at the gorge a brief one, it was possible to reach Dover Downs before nightfall.

Bryce gave her a frowning look. 'In case you haven't noticed, the camels are done in,' he said, his tone puzzled and almost angry. 'They need a rest. I thought you did too.'

Her agitated sigh drew a darker frown from him this time, but he said nothing. 'It was just an idea,' she muttered.

'Is my company so obnoxious to you?' he asked, clearly irritated.

'You know it isn't,' she said unhappily.

'I won't make a pass at you, you know.'

She stiffened. 'I realise that.'

'Is that what's bothering you? That I *won't*?'

Her mouth dropped open, her cheeks flushing guiltily.

He swore and spun away from her. 'Be ready to leave in half an hour,' he snapped over his shoulder. 'We'll reach Dover Downs today if it kills the bloody lot of us!'

It took them less than half an hour of quick walking across the open plain to reach the gorge. Half an hour of incredible heat burning up through the soles of Adrianna's sandals. Half an hour of complaining muscles and gritted teeth and uncomfortable silence.

But she forgot her wretchedness for a moment when the gorge came into view.

It was, quite literally, stunningly beautiful. Not picture-pretty, as the oasis had been, but far more impressive. A large expanse of blue-green water, edged with enormous yellow ochre rocks on two sides, a small sandy beach down the shallow end, and the gorge at the other. Down there, the waters looked very deep, becoming black and crystalline as they flowed through a ravine less than ten feet wide and seemingly endless, red and black cliffs rising sheer out of the water on either side.

'Why, it's magnificent!' she exclaimed.

'It is, isn't it?' Bryce agreed softly.

She swallowed as she looked over at him, his gentle tone catching at her heart-strings. This was another side of him she hadn't really appreciated till now, this softer, gentler side, this lover of animals and nature. It unravelled all her defences, making her feel mixed up inside as she yearned to reach out to him. 'Bryce, I...'

Her words broke off when she saw his eyes harden. 'No,' he snarled. 'No apologies, no making up, no nothing any more! I've had enough, Adrianna. I'm not a puppet who can be pulled this way and that depending how you feel at the moment. I'm a man, and by God, if you don't watch it, I'll give you a memorable demonstration of that fact! And believe me, it won't be rape. We both know that, don't we?'

She watched with chest contracting and heart aflutter as he grabbed both camels' reins and stalked off in the direction of a large acacia tree. Before she could think what to do, he dragged the checked blanket off Dumbo's saddle, let the camels go and stalked back towards her. She just stood there, frozen by the aura of simmering violence in his angry approach. He stopped a couple of yards from her, eyes ablaze.

'We'll start out for Dover Downs after lunch,' he ground out. 'That gives you three hours to rest and wash and dry your clothes. 'Here...' he threw the blanket at her feet '...take this with you so that you can use it as cover till your clothes dry. May I suggest for the sake of all concerned that you keep to one side of the lagoon while I keep to the other, since we'll both be swimming in the raw.'

'I...I'll need some soap,' she said shakily.

'It's in one of the bottom packs,' he growled. 'And for pity's sake don't offer to help me find it. I'll get it for you after I've attended to the camels and cooled off a bit. I suggest you do the same. You look almost as hot as I feel!' He whirled on his heels then and marched off.

She glared after him for a second, furious with him. And herself. She didn't deserve to be treated this way!

And yet she supposed that after all that had happened, any attempt of hers to be nice *might* have looked like some pathetic ploy to seduce him. Muttering her exasperation, she snatched the blanket up and strode off in the direction of the far side of the gorge, thinking that Dover Downs could not come quickly enough.

Though to be honest, she wasn't looking forward to seeing Alan again, to telling him that not only did she not want to marry him, but that she didn't want to continue their affair either. Alan deserved better than a half-hearted wife—or lover—which was what she would be after this experience. It would be a long time before she would get Bryce out of her mind, her heart, and her body.

She finally came to a spot where the rocks were large and smooth, dipping gently down to the water's edge. It was the ideal natural ramp from which to slide into the water, letting the blanket go at the last moment, then scooping it up on exiting.

An agitated glance back in the direction of the camp showed that Bryce's back was to her, so she quickly divested herself of all her clothes and slipped into the water. The unexpected coldness took her breath away and it was several minutes before she got used to it, several minutes of consciously not looking either back at the camp or across at the other side, in case by this time Bryce was there, undressing. Adrianna didn't think that a long-distance view of a man's naked body would disturb her too much, but she wasn't taking any chances. Besides, if Bryce caught her looking at him he would probably accuse her of ogling him on purpose.

Even so, when she actually heard the splash of someone diving into the water a sliver of shocking awareness rippled through her. It was hard not to picture Bryce's nude body slicing through the water, very hard *not* to want to look over at him, even if he was at least a hundred yards away.

She didn't deliberately look his way. But the sound of Bully's barking drew her attention and out of the corner of her eye she was surprised to see Bryce already leaving the water, the dog dancing around his master's dripping legs. She was instantly dry-mouthed as she watched Bryce bend over and pick up his jeans. His actions looked angry as he inserted each leg, then pulled them on over his glistening buttocks. Not glancing back, he scooped up the rest of his clothes and began to stride, bare-chested, back towards the camp.

Dragging her eyes away, Adrianna trod water for a while, trying to control the body responses she was beginning to hate—the quickened heartbeat, the flush of heat, the surge of erotic visions. With her unfortunate feelings and thoughts finally dampened down she had just decided to get out herself when a cramp struck her foot.

Not panicking, she quickly side-stroked over to the rock, only to find it was far easier to get in than to get out, the rock surface under the waterline scooping inwards and being covered in slippery moss. She struggled to find a foothold, but there weren't any. Then she tried spreading her arms wide and digging her elbows downwards in an attempt to lever herself up on to the rock, but in her weakened state she didn't have the strength to overcome the dragging weight of the water.

She was in considerable pain and beginning to feel definite alarm when Bryce's bare feet appeared on the blanket in front of her. An upward glance saw him standing, still disconcertingly bare-chested, looking down at her with black humour in his eyes.

'Having trouble?' he drawled.

'Yes, I…I can't seem to get a foothold.'

'It's quite easy to get out on the other side,' he mocked. 'Swim over there. I'll take this soap and your blanket over for you.' He went to pick up the blanket, but didn't, straightening to give her a knowingly malicious smile. 'Or were you expecting me to help you out?'

'Well, no, but I…I don't think I can make it over there,' she gasped. 'I have cramp.'

His laugh was cold and cruel. 'In that case you'll just have to drown, won't you?'

She grimaced as the cramp worsened, looking over at the other side with a sinking heart. It was too far…

His expression remained ruthless. 'If you think I'm going to haul you out of that water as naked as a jay-bird and then just walk away, you're a fool, Adrianna Winslow! You've been putting me through hell, and I'm not in the mood to be merciful any longer!'

She stared up at where his arousal was clearly outlined against the damp denim of his jeans. Her eyes shot up to his face, only to find his own gaze roving hotly over her bare shoulders. Then lower…

To have him look at her naked breasts that way, even through the distortion of the rippling water, was incredibly exciting.

'It's up to you, Adrianna,' he ground out, and bent forward, throwing the cake of soap behind him and sending a tempting hand downwards. 'You can either take your chances with the water. Or with me. But be warned, I'd choose the water if I were you!'

CHAPTER EIGHT

HER hand shook as she placed it in the large palm, but her eyes were oddly steady, meeting his with a flash of fire. She had decided, even if she had to suffer for it for the rest of her life.

'So!' he said, his surprise quickly replaced by a triumphant smile. His hand slipped past her trembling fingers to close around her wrist and he lifted her as if she was a feather, lifted and deposited her next to him in one fluid movement.

His eyes swept over her dripping nudity with an all-encompassing regard, returning to her face with a look of such passion that it took her breath away. 'I knew you were beautiful,' he rasped, 'but I didn't know how much.'

Adrianna stared back at him, thinking dazedly that she could not say the same in return. To describe him as beautiful would be totally inadequate. He was magnificent, breathtaking. The supreme male animal… As perfectly shaped as a David or an Adonis, but larger, stronger, harder! What had he said to her once? When he took her, she would know she'd been taken by a man! Her throat went dry just thinking about it.

Another spasm in her right foot brought a whimper of pain.

'Do you honestly think that ploy will work?' Bryce snarled. 'I won't have pity on you, you know. It's gone too far for pity!'

She winced again with the pain and lifted her foot

slightly, pressing her toes hard against the rock, trying to unravel the cramp. A slow, wicked smile sliced across his broodingly handsome face and he dropped to one knee, picking the foot up and massaging it with exquisite skill. Adrianna almost overbalanced, putting her hands on to his shoulders so that she didn't tip back into the water.

'You have the sexiest little feet,' he murmured, his thumbs kneading the pain away and sending a thousand electric shivers charging along her nerve-endings.

Adrianna gazed down at him through a type of erotic haze. Quite unbidden, her hands began to slide back and forth across his broad strong shoulders in a journey of sensual satisfaction. A low moan whispered from her lips.

His upward glance was heavy-lidded as he continued to massage the sole of her foot. 'You like that, don't you?' he said thickly.

She blinked down at him, eyes wide, lips falling slightly apart. Never in all her life had she envisaged the sort of feelings this man could make her feel. Anything—even the slightest touch—excited her unbearably, sending her insides twisting into a tight ball of excruciating need.

'Yes,' she breathed. 'Yes…'

'And this?' He placed her foot back down and slid his hands up her legs, caressing the backs of her knees, then sliding upwards to linger on the soft flesh of her thighs.

Adrianna sucked in a deep breath and held it. 'Yes,' she choked out.

'And this…' His feathering fingers found more intimate targets. She gasped aloud, and began to sink downwards.

Somehow they both ended up kneeling, facing each

other on the blanket, Adrianna's chin tipped up so that she could keep looking into his smouldering eyes. It was like a drug to have them staring into hers, holding her while his hands explored and aroused her to fever pitch.

'Tell me what else you like,' he whispered, his hands abandoning their devastating caresses to slide up over her stomach towards her breasts.

'Anything,' she said, her voice shaking as she struggled for breath, her cheeks raging with the heat of excitement and desire.

His hands lifted off her quivering expectant body to cup her face, his mouth smiling as it began to bend. 'That's a very open invitation, Adrianna... Are you sure you mean *anything*?'

It was clearly a rhetorical question, for he cut off any answer with a kiss, an open-mouthed yet oddly gentle kiss that still sent her head spinning. She made a tiny sound of disappointment when the soft sucking of her lips ended.

'More?' he murmured seductively.

She nodded numbly, aware that her heart was beating so fast she thought it would burst.

With his thumbs massaging the corners of her mouth he began by moistening her lips with his tongue, running the tip over them till they were soft and pouting and tingling. The thumbs retreated to her cheeks then, allowing his mouth an unimpeded possession. His lips pressed on to hers, then parted, taking hers with him. Once they were open for him, he sent his tongue forward to play sensuously and slowly with hers, then darted back to his own warm moist cavern so that she ached with the desertion and sent her own tongue forward.

It was a game, a sexy game of foray and retreat that took all Adrianna's attention and left her unknowing that the rest of her body was responding as wildly and fiercely as her mouth. Her breasts were swelling to an engorged sensitivity, her nipples rock-like in readiness for further erotic play. Unbeknown to her fevered brain, the hard points were already brushing against Bryce's chest, sending electric impulses to other parts of her body, other parts which were flooding with a liquid heat.

At long last Bryce stopped kissing her and laid her trembling body back on the blanket, parting her thighs and bending his mouth to where she was already a cauldron of fire. She cried out in some sort of vague protest, groaning as she felt her body rushing towards a climax. Quite abruptly he abandoned her, getting up to stand at her feet, holding her madly dilated eyes with his while he stripped off his jeans. Her eyes grew even wider as she saw him in all his naked glory, wondering if her slender body could encompass such a man.

'Don't look so worried,' he soothed as he stretched out beside her. 'We'll be perfect together. Now…where was I? Ah yes, I remember. Let's try something less stressful, shall we?' And he bent his head and starting licking one of her nipples.

Adrianna had to bite her bottom lip to stop the moans. But when he kept doing it and at the same time slid a hand down between her thighs, she could not contain a convulsive shudder.

'God, you're so hot in there…so hot…'

Adrianna shut her eyes tight, her insides squeezing just as tight against the sensations that were rocketing through her. 'Oh, Bryce!' she cried, her hips lifting to writhe against his devastatingly intimate caress.

'Yes?'

'Please…' Her breath was coming in rapid panting gasps. 'Don't keep doing that. Please…I can't bear it…make love to me…properly…now…I don't want to…to…'

He stopped immediately, taking her hands and surprising her by pulling her to her feet. 'That rock's too hard on your back,' he said thickly. 'Here… When I lift you put your arms tightly around my neck.'

His hands slid down to span her buttocks, lifting her with ease, her thighs falling either side of his hips quite naturally. Her arms went up around his neck, her elbows resting on his shoulders, her fingers splaying up into his damp, spiked hair. For a second he clasped her to him, burying his face into the valley between her breasts, but then he was holding her away, positioning her so that his manhood probed at her soft, moist flesh. Then in a slow sensuous sheathing he pulled her down on to him, the sensation of his filling her to capacity taking her breath away.

It seemed to take his breath away too, for he sank to his knees, gasping and closing his eyes for a few seconds. She wrapped her legs tightly around him and pressed her lips to his right ear. 'Oh, my darling,' she murmured softly. 'My darling…'

He groaned at her endearment and she slid her lips across to cover his mouth. He sank back on his heels and while she was kissing him he began to move her, slowly, easing her away, then pulling her back down on to him till she engulfed every inch of his throbbing manhood once more. It was the most erotic, the most tormenting mating, as he refused to be hurried, even by her groans of impatience. He even stopped once, lifting his mouth from hers and looking deep into her glazed eyes, his own heavy with passion.

'Now you're mine, Adrianna,' he rasped. 'Mine…'

'Yes, my darling, yes,' she agreed, her head tipping back, lips parted with excitement.

He made some sort of sound, then taking the back of her head in a savage grip, he pulled her hungrily back to his mouth, thrusting his tongue inside with a sudden ferocity. Just as abruptly he abandoned the kiss to clasp her hips again, his fingers digging into her soft flesh as the rhythm of his hands rapidly reached a frenzied pitch. Adrianna's low moans became whimpering cries, then gasping groans, her whole being besieged by a wild combination of sensation and tension. The feelings of pleasure and pressure spiralled upwards, totally out of control. It wasn't just him moving her now. She had joined his urgency in a frantic feverish ride.

'Oh, Bryce…Bryce!' she gasped, sensing her body on the knife-edge of ecstasy. And then it was happening, her climax exceeding even her wildest expectations, her fierce contractions convulsing around him and sending his seed spilling into her with a strength that tore a loud cry from deep within his throat. She clasped his shuddering body close, hers still moving, savouring every last erotic nuance of feeling she could experience.

But finally, reluctantly, the heat of passion ebbed from her body, replaced by a swimming sensation of utter satisfaction and contentment. She sighed and slumped downwards, her arms around his chest, her head tucked under his neck. His lips moved lovingly over her hair and she felt his breath like a warm breeze down the back of her neck. They stayed that way for some time, rocking slightly, holding each other, enjoying the moment of total intimacy and tender joy.

Adrianna felt the beginnings of apprehension the second Bryce lifted his head. She just *knew* he was going to say something to spoil the illusion of happiness she had been basking in.

'You can't marry Carstairs now,' he said, almost accusingly.

Adrianna groaned inside. That was it... This was where it would all begin... The demands...the telling her what she could and could not do, all because she had betrayed her love for him with her body.

She sucked in a startled breath, her head snapping up to stare at him. My God, what did I just say to myself? she thought. I can't love him, not really. It has to be just sex. It has to be.

But of course she knew it wasn't.

'No,' she admitted on a shaky sigh, 'I'm not going to marry Alan now.'

She saw the look of triumphant relief flash across Bryce's blue eyes and wondered if he loved her back. But only for a second. Physical men like Bryce didn't *really* love. When they said they loved it usually meant they desired or wanted or needed. They married girls when they thought they loved them, only to have unlimited access to their bodies, but they quickly grew bored and began looking elsewhere for their pleasure. The trouble was, by then a baby had usually made an appearance.

'I won't marry you either, Bryce,' she added before he could say another word. 'We're not right for each other.'

His face darkened. 'You can say that while we are as we are?' he grated, giving her a savage yank to remind her of their extremely intimate position. 'We *love* each other.'

'Don't, Bryce,' she said in a strangled voice.

'Don't what, Adrianna?' His voice was low and taunting. 'Don't mention the word love? Or don't make love to you? Perhaps I should remind you of what you said in the heat of your passion… You said you would be mine, my love. Would you like to tell me in what way you meant that?'

Adrianna refused to say a word.

'You meant just sexually, didn't you?' he snarled. 'That's all you want from me, isn't it? Not my love or anything else I might be able to give you. And the ironic thing is I *can* give you more,' he added in a type of pained desperation. 'Much more than your narrow-minded view of me decided at first sight.' His eyes blazed as they raked over her flushed face. 'God damn you, Adrianna! God damn you!'

She was taken aback and distressed by the depth of his emotion and fury. Perhaps he did really love her, and perhaps he imagined he could somehow make a decent life for her out here in the outback. But if he thought *she* had spoken in the heat of passion, then wasn't he doing the same? What of their future in the cold light of day, when it became obvious that they had nothing in common, that she would not buckle under and become a domestic slave, that the only thing they *did* have together was good sex.

Yet despite her common-sense reasoning, she ached to put her arms around him again, to soothe his anger, to tell him she did love him and she would be his forever. Adrianna shook her head, amazed. A few days ago she would never have dreamt of doing such a thing. Maybe Bryce was right when he'd said the desert changed people. It had certainly changed her, so much so that she was almost hoping she had conceived a child a few minutes ago. Maybe she couldn't come to terms with living in the outback, but somehow the idea of a baby—Bryce's baby—wasn't so abhorrent to her. It was, in fact, very attractive. Which was amazing really…

'And what does that shake of the head mean?' Bryce said coldly.

'Oh, Bryce…Bryce,' she cried softly, slipping her arms around his waist. 'I feel so mixed up.' She lifted unhappy eyes to him and couldn't bear to see the disillusionment and derision in his face. 'I *do* love you…I *do*!' And she hugged him and pressed her lips to his chest, raining kisses over his skin.

She felt him shudder, but when she looked up she wasn't ready for the look in his eyes. It was so…*happy*! He kept gazing down at her, but then a slight wariness slipped into his eyes and he too shook his head. 'You don't know what you want, do you?' he said indulgently.

'I know I want *you*,' she husked. 'But, Bryce, please try to understand. Marriage between us…it…it probably wouldn't work out.'

He stared down at her for a long time and she became faintly worried by the unreadable expression that clouded his normally expressive and open eyes. It was as though he were deliberately hiding his feelings from her. 'I think you're right,' he pronounced carefully at last. 'A marriage between us is doomed to fail.'

'It…it *is*?' she repeated, feeling perversely hurt that he agreed with her, that he wasn't even going to try to persuade her.

'It couldn't work at all,' he went on. 'For one thing you don't want children. Any woman I marry would at least want to have one child.'

'Oh…well, Bryce, I…'

'Not only that, you're a city girl,' he cut in firmly. 'You wouldn't be able to stand life out here. The heat, the dust, the flies, the loneliness, would all get to you after a while. And as for me…I couldn't stand the hustle and bustle of the city. Not permanently. It would be a funny marriage with us living hundreds of miles apart and no children.'

'Yes…I guess so, but…'

'There's no use talking about buts, Adrianna,' he said. 'Facts are facts. The more I think about it, I don't want to marry you, any more than you want to marry me. It's only common sense—I can see that now. Still, there does seem to be one thing we do want from each other, doesn't there?'

And he silenced any further arguments with a kiss, which was just as well, Adrianna thought dazedly, for she'd been about to say that she had changed her mind about all those things; that she would give up her career, she would live wherever he lived, she would have a dozen children by him!

Good lord, what was getting into her? Was she going the same way as her mother, letting the seductive power of physical pleasure colour her thinking? Yet it was so hard to think straight when Bryce was kissing her, when already she could feel his body stirring to arousal again.

Oh God… It wasn't just Bryce who was getting turned on again, Adrianna soon realised. Already the desire to move, to feel his growing hardness, was becoming impossible to ignore. With a sensuous sigh she surrendered to it, lifting her body and sinking back, revelling in the glorious feeling of his rapidly swelling desire. Again she did it. And again.

Bryce groaned, his mouth leaving hers to trail moistly down her throat, then slide back up to blow gently in her ear, making her shiver uncontrollably.

'Let's not talk about the future just now,' he husked. 'Here…at this moment…there's no outside world, no tomorrow. Just you and me, like this. We have something very special together, Adrianna. Let's enjoy that, at least for now. Forget everything else but touching and kissing and making love, over and over and over…'

'Oh, yes, Bryce,' she said with a shudder of wild, wanton delight. 'Yes!'

It was a wonderful, exciting, bewildering day for Adrianna.

Bryce refused to do anything except make love, with the occasional break for refreshments. All thinking and talking was banned, he commanded, except for love talk and banal comments like, 'Isn't the water cold?' and 'What shall we have to drink?'

Adrianna found herself taken to a level of sensuality she hadn't thought existed, each lovemaking session seemingly satisfying her, but leaving her still half aroused and even more heart-stoppingly aware of Bryce. She could not seem to keep her hands off him—nor he off her, for that matter—and they spent countless hours, touching and caressing each other, in the water and out, their hands and mouths seemingly never still as they sought out the many various ways of pleasuring each other.

It was both a revelation and a vague concern to Adrianna that she would find nothing off-putting in forms of erotic play she would have previously shrunk from. If truth be told, she was often more turned on by what she did to Bryce than the other way around. He certainly enjoyed her ministrations too, finding obvious satisfaction when she confessed on one such occasion to never having done such things before.

'Then you're truly mine,' he murmured at this confession, reaching down and running his fingers through her hair till she lifted her face up to look adoringly at him.

The sight of his heavy-lidded, desire-filled eyes brought a sense of pleasure and power that she found incredibly exciting. She continued her highly intimate love-play for several seconds, then glanced up at him again. 'Do you like it when I do that?' she murmured.

He touched her swollen and highly sensitised lips with a loving, possessive touch. 'I love everything you do to me...'

She returned her attentions to his aroused flesh, revelling in his groans of ecstasy, quite deliberately and lovingly choosing to continue till he was totally out of control and there was no turning back.

'You're thinking,' Bryce murmured in an accusing tone.

Adrianna glanced up at him from where she was lying in the crook of his arm, a faint frown marring her otherwise smooth and contented face. 'I can't help it. Today has been incredible, Bryce. But tomorrow will come... And I don't want it to.' She gave a little shiver and put her head back on his arm to stare up at the stars twinkling in the black night sky.

'You're not worried about getting pregnant, are you, Adrianna?' he asked softly.

Her heart skipped a beat. In all honesty she had not given a thought to pregnancy all day. It just showed how an intelligent woman could quite easily fall pregnant when in love. But Bryce's question reminded her that he couldn't have known it was a relatively safe time of the month for her, and she felt slightly uneasy that he hadn't mentioned it earlier. Surely he hadn't been trying to get her pregnant, had he, to force her to marry him? She couldn't get out of her mind the moment when he had closed his thoughts to her, as if he had some secret plan of action he didn't want her to know.

'No,' she said, frowning.

'Sure?' he persisted.

'Positive.'

'How?'

'Trust me,' she almost snapped.

His sigh was telling.

'I…I'm sorry, Bryce. It's just that…'

'It's all right,' he soothed. 'To be honest, I didn't think about it earlier and I should have. It was stupid and thoughtless of me, and I'm sorry. When is your period due?'

Adrianna flinched away from such personal talk—which was silly after what they had both been doing that day. What could have been more personal than that?

'In a few days,' she admitted stiffly.

'Just as well we're getting you back to civilisation, then, isn't it?'

'Yes…yes, I suppose so.'

'You don't sound so sure?'

'I guess I'm not looking forward to seeing Alan again.'

She felt Bryce tense. 'What are you going to tell him?'

Adrianna swallowed. 'The truth.'

'Which is?'

'That I can't marry him, that I've fallen in love with someone else.'

'And?' Bryce grated.

'And what?' she asked, twisting round to look up at him again.

'And you won't be seeing him again. Ever!'

Adrianna sat upright, her anger swift and strong. 'Oh, yes, I will, Bryce McLean. Alan was my friend long

before he became my lover. I won't throw him away just
because I happen to have fallen in love with you!'

Bryce glared back at her, his eyes narrow, his jaw
clenched hard. Then suddenly he seemed to make a conscious effort to relax and pulled her back down to him.
'Fair enough,' he conceded. 'I guess I'll just have to
make pretty frequent trips down to Sydney and make
sure I keep that highly active libido of yours under control.'

'You're…you're going to come down to Sydney to
visit me?' she asked, glancing up again.

His eyes carried reproach, but his grin was very, very
sexy. 'You don't think I'm going to let you get away
from me as easily as that, do you?' He rolled her up and
on to his chest. 'Of course I'm going to come down and
visit you. Just as I expect you to visit me. I'm going to
be your lover, woman, something I can't do by corre-
spondence. Now kiss me, like a good girl. We haven't
made love for at least an hour, and I'm getting mighty
frisky again!'

CHAPTER NINE

BRYCE was all business the following morning, so much so that Adrianna began to wonder if the hot-blooded lover of the day before was a figment of her imagination. They breakfasted and broke camp soon after dawn, with Bryce saying that he wanted to be back at Dover Downs before the heat of the noonday sun.

They were making their way silently and steadily along an hour later, Adrianna having already seen signs of approaching civilisation with their frequent meeting of fences and gates, when she realised she still knew no real details about Bryce's life, his work, his family. She didn't even know his *age*!

She up-upped Dumbo till she drew level with Jumbo, bringing a questioning glance from Bryce. He looked marvellous this morning, she thought, distracted for a moment from her intention. Marvellous... Her eyes roved from his freshly shaven face down his broad chest to his hands and thighs, and she felt a tightening all over her body.

'Yes?' he prompted with a wicked twinkle in his bright blue eyes.

'Oh, I...I was thinking. I don't even know how old you are, or...or anything else about you.'

'*Now* she asks!' he drawled.

Her flush carried a small measure of guilt, and a bucketful of desire. 'Well? How old *are* you?'

'I turn thirty next month. Want to tell me how old you are?' he returned. 'Though I suspect twenty-seven or eight.' When she looked totally exasperated at his accuracy he laughed. 'Remember, you have told me quite a bit about yourself. I just added your college years on to a likely eighteen at leaving school, came up with twenty-four, then added two or three years for a hard-working, ambitious girl like you to make a success of her business.'

'I'm twenty-eight,' she admitted. 'Last May.'

'A Taurus?'

'Yes.'

'It figures,' was his wry comment.

'And what does *that* mean?' she bristled.

Bryce held up his hands in mock defence. 'Nothing, nothing. Taurus ladies are lovely, sweet, amenable females.' His smile was rueful. 'Once every hundred years or so.'

She went to hit him, but he grabbed her wrist and chuckled. 'Naughty, naughty! I can see I'm going to have fun with you, Adrianna. You're just like Bully. Unpredictable, wild…but a good mate, nevertheless!'

Her throat contracted as Bryce turned her palm over and lifted it to his mouth, his moist licking kiss sending hot shivers up and down her spine. But along with the physical pleasure was an appalled realisation of what Bryce had done to her. He had just said it, hadn't he? He *had* bonded her to him in the desert, like his dog. He had made her his pet, one that would grovel at his feet for a pat or a stroke, who would roll over on her back whenever he snapped his fingers. Even now she was quivering with need…

A surge of pride-filled anger and indignation had her wrenching her hand away. But he merely laughed and angled Jumbo closer, reaching over to cup the back of her head in a vice-like grip. 'That won't work any more,

Adrianna. Not even remotely…' And with that he brought his face down to hers, giving her a brief but intimately possessive kiss. 'You see, my darling,' he husked, looking deeply into her eyes, 'you're mine, and there's nothing you can do about it, so stop trying, stop fighting it, stop going against everything that Mother Nature has ordained.' And he kissed her again.

But even as he evoked an inevitably fierce yearning in her there remained a deep core of rebellion that would not totally surrender to this man, *any* man. She jerked her head away and glared up at him. 'You can have my body, Bryce,' she said in a strangled voice, 'but that's where it ends!'

She was rocked by the glint of steely determination that burnt deep in those beautiful blue eyes. 'No, Adrianna,' he corrected strongly, 'that's where it *begins*!'

Then unexpectedly he flashed her a smile and urged Jumbo ahead, breaking the camels into a trot till another gate halted their progress. 'We're almost there now,' he announced quite happily, his manner seemingly unperturbed by their brief altercation. Adrianna was simply more confused than ever.

Suddenly the sound of an engine pricked up everyone's ears, especially Bully's. They all looked towards the horizon, the view unimpeded by the flat, sparsely treed countryside. A motorbike appeared, coming quickly, sending out a dusty cloud behind it. It was almost upon them by the time they had manoeuvred their way through the gate.

'It's Pete,' Bryce informed Adrianna, 'one of the stockmen on Dover Downs. He's probably on his way out to check the bores.'

The noisy motorbike geared down to a rattling halt

beside the well-behaved Jumbo, but Dumbo did his usual crabwards flight of nerves till the engine was cut dead.

'Hi, Pete,' Bryce called down to the grinning Aboriginal lad.

'Hi, boss. Back early?'

'Yep. Picked something up along the way that I needed to bring home.'

The cheeky black face moved across to Adrianna. 'Good-lookin' find, boss.'

'I reckon, Pete.'

'Gotta go, boss. That windmill in the far paddock wasn't workin' too well yesterday. Gotta fix it.'

'Want to take Bully with you?' Bryce suggested. 'You know how he likes riding on the back of the bike.'

'Sure thing, boss. Come on, dog.' Pete patted the seat behind him.

Bully gave a delighted bark and leapt on to the seat. 'See yuh, boss.' The motorbike roared off with Bully perched on the back like the Queen on a royal tour, his tail wagging a regal salute.

Adrianna didn't laugh as she might usually have done because she was busy giving Bryce a frowning look, a sick suspicion in the pit of her stomach. '*Boss*?' she directed at him, accusation in the word.

Bryce shrugged. 'I did try to tell you once.'

'You mean you *manage* Dover Downs?'

'Nope,' he smiled. 'I own it.'

'You…you own it?' she gulped.

''Fraid so.'

Her eyes narrowed. 'And just how large *is* Dover Downs?'

'Give or take an inch, about ten thousand square miles.'

She opened her mouth, then shut it again when a swear-word had been about to escape.

'Shall I say it for you?' teased Bryce, and leant over to whisper a vivid selection in her ear.

Adrianna pushed him away angrily. 'I think you *enjoyed* deceiving me!' she accused.

'You think so?'

'Yes!'

He gave another shrug. 'You could be right.'

'And what other surprises have you in store for me?'

'You'll just have to wait and see, won't you?'

'Oh, you…!'

'Temper, temper, Miss Taurus!'

Adrianna dragged in a steadying breath, determined she would not give him the satisfaction of being surprised or shocked by another single thing!

Which wasn't easy when she came face to face with an airstrip and hangars that boasted several helicopters and a luxurious twin-engined Beech Baron, not to mention the enormous colonial homestead perched on a hill overlooking a river, or the elegant woman in the blue sun-dress who came down from the house to the bottom of the hill to greet them, looking as if she'd just stepped out of an air-conditioned beauty salon.

'My mother,' Bryce murmured as the other woman approached.

She didn't look at all as she would have pictured his mother, Adrianna thought. Her own mother had become shapeless and worn over the years, but this woman was slim and smart, her face showing only a minimum of wrinkles.

'Bryce dear, what are you doing back so soon?' Blue eyes the same as Bryce's peered around at where Dumbo had naturally ducked in behind Jumbo. 'My goodness, and who have we here?'

Bryce had stopped the camels near a group of out-buildings where a flock of happy smiling Aboriginal children seemed to have materialised from nowhere, not to mention a couple of weatherbeaten stock-hands. Now all of them joined Mrs McLean in staring up at Adrianna with avid curiosity.

'This is Adrianna Winslow, Mother,' Bryce explained. 'An intrepid lady pilot whose Cessna crashed not far from where I was camping. She wasn't hurt, but I could hardly leave her in the middle of nowhere, could I?'

The woman gave Adrianna a surprisingly thorough scrutiny, then beamed up at her son. 'So you brought her home.'

'Yes,' Bryce beamed back at her, 'I brought her home.'

Adrianna just knew those smiles held some secret message between them, but quite frankly she was too rattled to even hazard a guess at what it might be. She sighed, her shoulders slumping wearily.

'I think your friend is tired, dear,' Mrs McLean pointed out.

'Yes,' drawled Bryce, 'I imagine she is.'

Adrianna rolled her eyes at his knowing look, but allowed him to help her down and lead her up the for-midable path and steps and into the astonishing cool of the house. Her head shook ruefully as she took in the air-conditioning, the elegant foyer, the spacious rooms leading off the wide central hall. No wonder his mother had looked refreshed!

She was guided into an enormous and very formal sitting area which had a huge mahogany fireplace and elaborately curtained French windows overlooking a

wide verandah. The polished wooden floors were dotted
with Persian rugs and the sofas and chairs were covered
in a subtle green brocade. Gilt-framed oil paintings and
exquisite old photographs hung on the richly papered
walls. A crystal chandelier hung heavily above. It could
easily have been a room out of a society family's mansion.

Adrianna looked around in total confusion. Why had
Bryce kept his wealth a secret? Why…particularly after
they had become lovers?

'I think Adrianna would like a shower and a change
of clothes, Mother. I would too, but first I'll contact the
authorities, let them know she's all right. Have you been
hearing anything about a small plane crash on the news?'

'Now, Bryce, you know I don't listen to the news
when I visit here.'

Bryce nodded, and Adrianna wondered where his
mother usually lived. Obviously not out here on Dover
Downs. Such a big house, she thought, for only one man.

As though her thought had conjured up another person, a very attractive Aboriginal girl suddenly appeared
in the doorway. 'It's time for tea, Mrs McLean,' she said
in a low, husky voice. 'Will the lady want some as
well?' she asked, spotting Adrianna.

'Yes, Helen. And some sandwiches and cake. We
have a *couple* of hungry travellers here.'

'Hello, Helen,' Bryce said from where he was standing, a hand on the curtains of one of the large French
windows.

The girl was startled. 'Oh…Mr McLean! I didn't see
you there.' She blushed very prettily, Adrianna thought,
and jealousy stabbed into her heart.

She looked over to find Bryce's eyes upon her, and
her chin lifted defiantly. His answering smile unnerved

her. What else was she going to find out about this man whom she had taken to her heart? If he thought she was going to share him he had another think coming!

'Make up a tray, Helen,' Bryce suggested. 'Miss Winslow will have it in her room.'

Helen turned and walked away, leaving Adrianna with a clear impression of long brown legs, lovely dark eyes and lush full breasts.

'Good idea,' Mrs McLean agreed. 'I'll show you to your room, Adrianna, then Bryce can tell me all about your adventure.' She led her back out into the hall, turning right towards the back of the house.

'Not that way, Mother,' Bryce called after them sharply. 'Put her in Brett's room.'

Adrianna saw the flicker of surprise in his mother's face, but the woman nodded and took Adrianna the other way. 'Bryce is right,' she said as they walked along. 'The guest wing's too lonely.'

'Who's Brett?' asked Adrianna.

'Bryce's younger brother. There's only the two of them. I didn't have any daughters, though I would have dearly loved one.'

'And Brett doesn't live at home any longer?'

'No. He runs the family's other cattle property, over in the Channel Country. It's called Lowland Downs. Here we are...' She stopped and opened a door on the right and Adrianna stepped into an enormous, decidedly mannish room with heavy dark furniture, a royal blue quilt on the bed and few fripperies. 'I hope this will be all right,' Mrs McLean said uncertainly. She walked over and pushed the curtains back from the French doors, then pointed to an adjoining door. 'The bathroom's in there, but I'm afraid you have to share it with Bryce. His room is on the other side.'

For a second Adrianna stiffened, disturbed that Bryce's intentions had been obvious to his mother. 'It's fine,' she said with an edgy smile. 'I mean, it won't really matter, since Bryce is going to fly me down to Sydney later this afternoon, anyway.'

'*Is* he?' The other woman frowned. 'I would have thought he'd have you stay the night and take you down tomorrow morning.'

Adrianna blushed fiercely. 'Oh…'

The woman's glance was sharp, then softened to one of gentle concern. 'You can talk it over with Bryce when he brings you your tray. Now I'll just get you some fresh towels, a nightie in case you need it and something else to wear. I have some things here that should fit you and shouldn't be too matronly.'

'You're very kind,' Adrianna murmured.

'My dear, I'm only too pleased to do what I can. You must have had a…trying experience.'

A lump was gathering in Adrianna's throat. 'Yes…yes, it's been difficult.'

'We'll talk later, perhaps.'

Adrianna nodded. 'Yes.'

Mrs McLean came back with two cream towels and a négligé set that looked suspiciously like a leftover from a honeymoon—all white silk and see-through lace. Adrianna wondered wryly if Bryce had his mother trained to aid and abet him in his seductions, though the other clothes she left were not at all provocative: a pair of loosely fitting pink cotton trousers and a pink and white striped top. She also thoughtfully supplied her empty-handed guest with a toothbrush and a pair of cotton briefs, both obviously new, still in their plastic packets.

Adrianna moved almost nervously into the bathroom, but was relieved to see she could lock both doors from inside. The bathroom was almost as masculine as the bedroom, with austere brown and white tiles and plain gold taps. Brown bath mats covered the floor and there were no pots of cosmetics or cans of hairspray in sight on the spacious vanity unit. There was, however, a hair-brush and comb in one drawer she could use, and the shelf in the shower had a couple of choices of shampoo and conditioner.

Adrianna luxuriated in a long hot shower, shampooing her hair till it squeaked with cleanliness and revelling in the feel of drying herself with the thick, fluffy towels. A glance in the large vanity mirror showed a tan such as she had never had before, and a blush crept up her neck when she realised she had acquired it frolicking naked all day at the gorge.

She swallowed as she once again remembered how submissive she had been to Bryce's demands. No, not submissive, she amended. Very co-operative would bet-ter describe her behaviour. It still had the power to amaze her, but she knew she would act the same way again, whenever Bryce wanted her to. Such was his sex-ual power over her.

It distressed her to think she had come to this, not much different from her mother. The only thing she could cling to was her determination not to marry the man, or have children by him. Her earlier waffling about having a baby was by now well and truly stifled. And yet…her eyes travelled around the room. The situation had changed somewhat, hadn't it? It wasn't as though Bryce was a poor man. Or lazy. Or mean…

What about unfaithful? her honest side inserted.

Something had transpired between him and that Aboriginal girl—she was sure of it.

Adrianna's chest tightened. Her father had been a handsome man, almost as handsome as Bryce, with a manner not dissimilar, an easy line of patter and a sexy, laid-back charm that women had found irresistible. It hadn't taken him long after he married her mother to begin sampling all that was readily on offer. What guarantee did she have that Bryce would be any different?

None, my dear, the answer came back, as swift and sure as a boomerang. None.

She was a fool to be tempted into thinking of marriage. A fool! Besides, hadn't Bryce decided he didn't want to marry her anyway, that he was content with the role of lover?

But a lover could be unfaithful too, couldn't he?

This thought brought such distress to Adrianna that her hands were shaking as she pulled on the day clothes Bryce's mother had given her. She was back out in the bedroom and brushing her hair with harsh, vigorous strokes when there was a knock on the door.

It would be Bryce, she thought, stomach aflutter.

But it was only Helen, standing there with a tray, her handsome face lit by a pleasant smile. Any relief, however, was short-lived as Bryce came strolling down the hall, taking the tray from the girl and coming into the room. 'Thank you, Helen,' he said without a backward glance.

The girl closed the door quietly, and left.

Adrianna fidgeted with the hairbrush while Bryce placed the tray on top of a large chest of drawers and began pouring her tea. 'I can do that for myself,' she said curtly.

'So you can,' he smiled, putting the teapot down and

walking across the room, where he sat down on the side of the huge double bed. It creaked under his weight. 'I forgot my days of being your lackey were over.'

His words and manner irritated her for some reason, which was silly really. In love or not, she wanted to maintain her role of independent, liberated woman, didn't she? 'Huh!' she snorted. 'You were only my lackey because you didn't think I could do anything properly!'

'True.'

'Must you always sound so smug?' she flung at him.

His eyebrows shot upwards, but she noticed that underneath his reaction he was eyeing her refreshed self with an admiring gaze. She spun away and poured her tea. 'Your mother says you expect me to stay the night,' she said abruptly, replacing the rattling teapot on the tray.

'I would have thought that only sensible. Besides, there's no real reason for you to hurry back today, is there? I've notified the police, who agreed to contact both your family and your business associates. I gave this phone number in case anyone wants to contact you personally.'

'I...I would like to ring my mother myself...and Alan,' Adrianna added with a surge of butterflies in her stomach.

Bryce's mouth tightened. 'If you must.' He stood up and moved slowly towards her. She practically shrank back into the wall as he reached for her, but he only cupped her chin. His eyes carried a dry amusement. 'It's one step forward and two steps backward with you, isn't it, my love?'

'I...I don't know what you mean,' she said huskily.

'Oh, yes, you do... You know darned well what I

mean. But one day, Adrianna, you might get a shock and find out that your preconceived ideas about men don't always apply. Meanwhile, I won't let this hot-and-cold act of yours bother me any more, because it's just an act.' He bent to brush her lips with his own in a tantalising and totally unsatisfactory manner. 'Just an act,' he murmured.

Adrianna clamped her teeth down hard to stop herself from throwing her arms around his neck and dragging his mouth down on hers. Shame at the truth behind his statement brought resentment and anger, but enough common sense remained not to deny what he was saying. It would probably only lead to his setting out to prove to her she was a hypocrite. And the last thing she could cope with at that moment was Bryce reducing her to a quivering, mindless, wanting wreck. Neither was she going to be cowed by his knowledge of her weakness. Her eyes were bold and proud as she glared up at him.

'Have you slept with that girl?' she demanded.

He seemed startled by this abrupt change of tack. 'You mean Helen?' he frowned.

'Of course I mean Helen,' she snapped, colour in her cheeks.

His smile was slow and almost cruel. 'You expect me to answer that?'

'Yes!' she hissed.

'Let me just say that while I'm in your bed, my sweet, I certainly won't be in hers.'

His blunt answer rocked her into silence.

'Is that satisfactory?' he drawled.

'What if I asked you to get rid of her?'

'What if I asked you never to see Alan again?' he countered.

Her mouth fell open, then slowly closed. 'I...see...'

'I hope so,' Bryce ground out in the closest he had come to anger all day. 'There's a phone in the foyer,' he stabbed out. 'Feel free to use it as often and for as long as you like.'

'Alan?'

'Adrianna?' He sounded stunned. 'Is that you?'

'Yes... Haven't the police been in touch with you yet?'

'No, I've just arrived back from Alice Springs. But my God, Adrianna, where are you? Do you realise I've had search planes looking for you for *days*? Are you all right? What happened?'

'It...it's a long story,' she began.

'Then tell me it, dear heart. I want to hear it all!'

Adrianna winced at his loving address and launched into the same nervous, edited version she had just finished telling her equally relieved mother.

'...and so you see, Alan, I'm really all right. Mr McLean brought me back to his property—Dover Downs. I...I'll give you the phone number...'

Alan wrote it down.

'Oddly enough, Adrianna, I think I know that McLean fellow,' he said. 'Is his name Bryce?'

'Yes,' she admitted shakily, 'you do know him. He told me he'd met you a few years back.'

Alan laughed. 'That's a mild way to describe our encounter! He came storming into my office one day demanding that I let my secretary leave because he had a date with her, yet the girl had known full well she might have to work late that day. A very good-looking fellow, as I recall, but too hot-tempered for my liking. Quite a ladies' man too. My secretary was only one in a long line of young women to be squired around Sydney by the handsome young grazier come to town. There were plenty of broken hearts when he had to return home quite suddenly, believe me! Anyway, that hardly matters now. That was years ago, but it's a small world, isn't it?'

'Y-yes.' A ladies' man, Adrianna kept thinking. Just like her father…

'You sound very tired, Adrianna. When are you coming back to Sydney so that I can look after you?'

Oh, God, she thought wretchedly.

'Adrianna? Are you sure you're all right?'

'Yes,' she admitted.

'I know this probably isn't the time, but have you given any thought to that question I asked you?' Alan went on.

'Yes…'

He gave a slightly nervous laugh. 'I don't like the sound of that yes.'

'Alan, I…'

His sigh carried resignation. 'Funny, I really thought you were going to say yes. Well, that's torn it!' he finished irritably.

'Alan, please don't be upset with me,' she begged.

'I'm not upset with you, Adrianna,' he sighed. 'Look, when are you getting back?'

'I'll be flying down to Sydney tomorrow.'

'Do you want me to meet you at the airport?'

'Well, I'm not sure exactly when I'll be arriving,' she hedged, knowing that Bryce was sure to be with her and would insist on taking her home.

'What about dinner, then? Or will you be too tired?'

'Dinner will be fine,' she said. What she had to say to Alan really couldn't wait.

'Seven o'clock?'

'I'll be ready.'

'I'm so glad you're all right, Adrianna. I just knew you would be.'

'Did you?' she laughed weakly.

'Of course. You're indestructible, my dear girl. A veritable tiger when cornered.'

'Oh, dear, I sound horrible!'

'Never. You're delightful.'

An embarrassed blush came to her cheeks, and at that moment Bryce appeared in the doorway opposite the phone table and just looked at her, his expression hard.

'I...I must go, Alan,' she stammered. 'I'll see you tomorrow night.'

Bryce walked over and took the receiver from her hand and hung it up. 'What's all this about tomorrow night, Adrianna?' he said coldly.

She steadied her burst of nerves. 'I'm going out to dinner with Alan, to explain the situation.'

'*Are* you? What's wrong with telling him over the phone?'

'He deserves better than that, Bryce.'

'And what about me? What do I deserve? You do realise that I intended flying you back and staying the night with you.'

She stiffened. '*Did* you?'

'I did.'

'Then I suggest that next time you make plans that involve me, you consult me first. I don't take kindly to people organising my life for me.'

'I'm not people, Adrianna. I'm the man you happen to love.'

'That doesn't mean you can take me for granted, Bryce,' she retorted.

He gave her a long, considering look, then slowly nodded. 'Point taken.'

Adrianna was so astonished by this concession that she was lost for words.

Bryce surveyed her surprise with a lazy smile. 'See? I'm capable of appreciating the arrogance of my sex. And I'm very capable of changing. All you have to do is show me the way.'

'And have you changed since your days in Sydney, Bryce?' she asked, wary of any man who claimed he could change. 'Or are you still a ladies' man?'

His instant anger alarmed her, because it was so controlled. 'Carstairs didn't wait long to put the knife in, did he?' he said bitingly.

Adrianna felt flustered. 'It...it wasn't like that,' she said, almost regretting having mentioned it now.

'Go out to dinner with him,' he ground out. 'But I'll be there waiting up for you when you get back, and God help him if I find out he's tried anything!'

And with blazing eyes, he whirled around and stalked off, leaving her standing there, staring after him, her heart pounding. Much as Adrianna didn't like Bryce being possessive and distrusting of her, she couldn't help being thrilled that he appeared to care about her so violently.

She walked slowly back to her bedroom where she picked up the lace and silk négligé, fingering the transparent lace panels while her mind whirled with her ambivalent feelings. She pressed the silk to her cheek and wondered with a quickened pulse if Bryce would come to her bed that night.

Or whether she would be forced to go to his.

CHAPTER TEN

THE BEECH BARON touched down at Sydney's small-craft airport at Bankstown shortly after two the following afternoon, the flight having been long and, for Adrianna, a strain.

The night before had not gone as expected. She had fallen asleep in the afternoon, not waking till nine in the evening, when Mrs McLean had brought her some supper on another tray. They had talked for a while, with Adrianna finding the woman as intelligent and charming as her son. Apparently she had a house in Adelaide where she now lived, though she often stayed with her two sons at their respective properties, mostly when one of her boys wanted a break for a while, either going to the city or on the occasional overseas holiday.

Bryce, it seemed, always went walkabout to wind down after mustering was completed, so it was a set arrangement that she look after Dover Downs while he was away. When Adrianna expressed surprise that a woman could manage such a big property, Bryce's mother explained that she had always actively helped her husband when he was alive—he had been tragically killed by lightning while out riding nine years before—and was quite capable of taking over the reins whenever needed.

Bryce had finally interrupted their little tête-à-tête, with his mother withdrawing tactfully. But if Adrianna thought he was going to make love to her or spend the night with her she was sorely mistaken. After a token talk and a peck on the forehead he had said goodnight, saying he was very tired and wanted to get an early start the next day. Adrianna had lain in that big lonely bed until the early hours of the morning, tossing and turning, till finally she had succumbed to sheer emotional exhaustion.

The morning found her feeling edgy and strained. It bothered her that her future lay ahead of her as a series of restless, sleepless nights, all because of this awful state she had got herself into over Bryce. Falling in love with as self-destructive as she had always known it would be, she thought unhappily as she got up and stripped off, tossing the wasted négligé on to a chair in frustration.

Breakfast was a trial, with Bryce looking even more disgustingly attractive than ever, his crisply ironed short-sleeved shirt a dazzling white against his tan, and the tight, stone-washed jeans hugging his lean hips and muscular thighs like a second skin.

Adrianna did her best to act naturally, but underneath she was annoyed with him, especially when he kept flashing a blushing Helen those sexy smiles of his. Jealousy was an emotion Adrianna was not used to, or comfortable with. It underlined the way love affected one's life—and not for the better!

It was a partial relief that his mother accompanied them to the airstrip, and that two of the stockmen wanted a ride to Sydney for their yearly holidays, as their presence prevented any intimate conversation between herself and Bryce. Adrianna needed time to get her shrewish thoughts under control.

But as soon as Bryce had her alone in the hire car he had organised to be waiting at the airport for him, he gave voice to her suspicion that she had been making her feelings all too obvious.

'Like to tell me what's eating you?' he demanded.

'Nothing,' she grumped. 'I just don't feel like talking.'

'Suits me,' he shrugged, and fell silent.

This irritating refusal to give her raw nerves the balm of a good argument annoyed Adrianna all the more. She sat there in a brooding silence, watching through the side window while Bryce manoeuvred the nifty Saab through the traffic in the direction of the city, taking back streets and short-cuts with the sureness and expertise of a taxi-driver. It piqued her that she had felt like a fish out of water in the outback, whereas Bryce was as much at home in the city as she was.

'And just how much time *have* you spent in Sydney?' she finally burst out.

He gave her a narrow-eyed look. 'Spit it out, sweet-heart. You've been wanting to since you got up this morning. And it's certainly got nothing to do with my knowing where I'm going. Which, at the moment,' he added cryptically, 'I'm not sure I really do!'

Adrianna found his comment confusing. Bryce never seemed unsure of anything. It was she who was always confused, bewildered, disorientated these days. Here she was about to begin a chapter in her life she had no blue-prints for, and she didn't know what to do, how to act. With Alan she had always been sure.

'Just tell me *why* you didn't stay with me last night?'

she asked wretchedly. 'Why you didn't want to make love to me?'

His eyes showed true astonishment. 'Is that what this is all about? My not spending the night with you?' His laughter was relieved and happy. 'My God, Adrianna, I thought I was doing the right thing! I thought I was being considerate—my mother said you looked tired. I can't win with you, can I? Hell, I paced up and down the room into the early hours for nothing!'

He threw her a smouldering look that allayed any fears she had that he had grown tired of her already.

'Oh, Bryce,' she cried, 'I...I thought you might not want me any more!'

'Just point me in the direction of your unit, my love,' he growled, 'and I'll show precisely how much I want you.'

Adrianna's heartbeat revved up with the car, and by the time she directed Bryce into her allotted car-space under her block of units she was in a high state of excitement. They made their way swiftly to the escalator that would take them up to the tenth floor and her unit. Side by side and silent, they stood together in the lift, the sexual tension between them consuming Adrianna with a wave of hot awareness, making the small space encompassing them seem even smaller, and suffocatingly intimate. She was thinking of holding his hand when the doors whooshed open and camera flashlights began popping off in her face, journalists with notepads pushing forward.

'Miss Winslow, tell us about the crash!'

'Miss Winslow, did you know that your plane was hit by a piece of space debris falling to earth?'

'How does it feel to find yourself lost in the middle of the desert, Miss Winslow?'

'What about the man that rescued you, Miss Winslow? A Mr McLean, wasn't it? I hear you spent some considerable time alone in the outback with him?'

Luckily enough they didn't appear to know that the man with her was the aforementioned Mr McLean. If they did he would have been besieged with questions as well. As it was, after the initial shock, Adrianna handled the situation without too much trouble, telling the media with a firm no-nonsense approach that she was exhausted, that she wanted no publicity other than the report given to the police, and that if they harassed her further the same police would be called and if they didn't leave she would have her bodyguard—this, indicating Bryce with a curt nod—remove them forcibly from the premises.

'Bodyguard?' Bryce repeated wryly once the unit door was closed and locked.

Adrianna noticed for the first time that he was looking peeved. He was also glancing around the smartly furnished unit with a gathering frown as though he didn't like being actually confronted with the evidence of her material success. She could understand his feelings only too well. Being confronted by *his* wealth had been a none too pleasant shock, for it underlined all she didn't know about him, and made a mockery of what she had believed him to be.

Still, she had never hidden her background from him, which made his frowning a puzzle. The feeling that he was withdrawing from her brought true alarm. In the lift they had seemed so close to each other, their mutual desire overriding any other doubts they had. Adrianna refused to let them crowd back, refused to let them spoil what she wanted most at that moment.

Moving quickly to him, she slid her arms up over the hard wall of his broad chest and around his strong neck. 'And a very good bodyguard you'd make too,' she murmured seductively.

But when she went to go up on tiptoe and kiss him, he pulled back.

She stared up at him. 'What's wrong?'

'Most men like to make the first move, Adrianna,' he rebuked.

'But that's silly and old-fashioned,' she said softly, and pressed herself closer. 'I want to make love to you, Bryce…the way I did out at the gorge. Please let me…'

He groaned, and bent his lips to hers with a primitive hunger that took her by surprise, ravaging her mouth with an intensity bordering on violence, his tongue plunging deep, his hands bruising on her back. Then with a single savage movement he tore his mouth from hers, swept her up into his arms and carried her into the bedroom.

Adrianna woke with a long satisfied sigh, her mind filling with erotic memories: Bryce, stripping her quite roughly; semi-brutal hands moving over her naked flesh in an incredibly arousing fashion; their ultimate and very exhausting union.

A large arm slid under her shoulders and pulled her back into him, spoon-fashion. 'You called?' he whispered, his lips feathering over her ear.

A shiver rippled down her spine and her eyes shot

open, making her suddenly aware that there was very little light coming through the bedroom curtains. She sat up abruptly, snapping on the bedside lamp. Her bedside clock showed ten past six. 'Heavens, look at the time! I'd better go and shower and get dressed. Alan said he'd be here at seven, and he's never late.'

'God forbid,' Bryce mocked drily from where he was lying on the bed, his arms tucked behind his head, a sheet half covering his body.

Adrianna got up and walked naked over to the small walk-in wardrobe, where she slipped into her silk kimono, returning to the bedroom to give Bryce a frowning look. 'Why exactly are you so antagonistic towards Alan? Surely you can't still be harbouring a grudge over something that happened years ago? Besides, I think you were hasty in your judgement of him back then. It couldn't have been easy having to run a business at his young age. And it's not as though that secretary was the only young woman in your life. You seem to have been a very busy lad in the romance department!'

Adrianna hadn't meant to put in that last little dig, but once it was said, she refused to back down. She had been wanting to ask Bryce about his time in Sydney for ages.

Bryce's returning look was narrow-eyed and angry. He propped himself up on one elbow and glared at her. 'You're very quick to hop to Carstairs' defence, aren't you? *And* to understand him. How about a bit of understanding for me as well, eh? I was only young too. Barely turned twenty, with a country upbringing that undoubtedly put me years behind my city counterparts. One look at Alan Carstairs told me just how far!'

He made a scoffing sound. 'And believe me, he was running his father's business with an efficiency and ruthlessness that was awesome!'

He tossed back the sheet and sat up, swinging his bare legs over the side of the bed. 'You want to know what I've got against Carstairs besides the obvious?' he growled. 'I'll tell you. It's memories, Adrianna. Memories of a time I'd rather forget, memories of a boy who selfishly wanted to rebel against everything he'd been brought up to be, and a father who was big enough to let him go for a while, even though it probably cost him his life!'

Adrianna's heart turned over as she saw Bryce's shoulders slump and his face grow bleak. He looked so down she came forward and sat beside him placing a comforting hand on his shoulders. 'It wasn't your fault, darling,' she said softly. 'Your mother told me about it. It was an accident…'

His eyes were pained as they met hers. 'Maybe… But I can't help feeling that I should have been there, helping him, not gallivanting around in the city, acting like some adolescent idiot, chasing every bit of skirt that came my way. Poor Dad, I let him down…'

'No, you didn't,' she soothed, replacing her hand with soft lips. 'As you said, you were only a boy. Don't be so hard on yourself…' And of course he *had* been only a boy at the time.

He reached out and curved a gentle hand around her cheek. 'You *do* understand, don't you?' he said. His kiss was warm and tender as he tipped her back across the bed. The hand on her cheek slid down her throat then inside the robe, caressing her breast with light, stroking movements.

'Oh, Bryce!' she moaned, her need for him intense and instant.

He stopped kissing her mouth and pressed his lips to her throat. 'Don't go out to dinner with Carstairs,' he whispered. 'Put him off... Call him.'

Adrianna froze.

The hand on her breast did likewise.

He withdrew it with a sigh and she got up, retying her robe with shaking hands. The thought that Bryce had just tried to manipulate her through sex was churning away inside her as she turned on him. 'Don't you ever do that to me again,' she blazed. '*Ever*!'

'Do what?' he said in a flat, tired voice.

'Try to get your own way by...by... Damn it, Bryce!' She stamped her foot. 'You *know* what I'm talking about!'

Bryce sighed again and leant over to where his clothes were scattered beside the bed. He dressed with remarkable speed, and when he began to walk from the bedroom, Adrianna ran after him, catching at his arm. 'What...where are you going?'

'Home,' was his curt reply.

'But...but...'

His jaw clenched down hard. 'I wasn't trying to manipulate you, Adrianna. Not in the way *you* meant. And if you think I'm going to stay here and watch you doll yourself up to go out with that man, then you must be crazy!'

She blinked up at him, unable to take in this unexpected development quickly enough to know what to say.

'Look,' Bryce ground out, 'I always said I wouldn't play sophisticated games, but that's not strictly true, Adrianna. I have been playing a game. A desperate one.'

'A…a game?' she repeated weakly.

'That's right. I've been pretending I didn't want to marry you. Insane as it is, I *do*. I thought, if I gave you some time, you would eventually come round to my way of thinking. I had some sort of crazy idea, you see, that this problem of yours was a temporary hangover from your upbringing. She'll get over it, I kept telling myself. She'll see I'm not anything like her father. But now I'm not so sure. I don't think you will change, Adrianna—your distrust of men and their motives goes too deep. So I think the best thing I can do is get out of here while I still can!'

When he went to move she clung on tightly, frantically. 'But you can't go, Bryce. You can't!'

'Too damned right I can,' he returned hotly. 'And I'm warning you, don't come after me unless you've changed your mind about marrying me and having my children!' And with that, he walked out, slamming the door behind him.

Adrianna stared at the door for ages, unable to think or move. But then she began to pace up and down, up and down, her emotions churning, her mind arguing frantically with her heart.

Let him go, common sense kept saying. You knew it was hopeless. *Hopeless*! He wants too much. Expects too much! If you marry him you'll be wretched… miserable.

But I'm miserable *now*, her heart cried.

So what? a cynical voice shot back. You'll get over it. In time… So will Bryce. And a damned sight quicker than you, my dear. How long do you think it'll be before he hops into the easy comfort of Helen's bed, eh? Leopards don't change their spots. Once a ladies' man, always a ladies' man!

Adrianna's heart hit rock bottom as this last truth hit home.

She stopped pacing and threw herself down on the sofa, tears flooding into her eyes. The sound of the doorbell ringing made her jump to her feet, her eyes blinking madly. He's come back, was her immediate thought, and against all reason her heart soared. The tears were dashed away as she flew to wrench open the door, her face full of wild hope and happiness.

Alan stood on the doorstep, his smoky blue eyes showing surprise as they took in her wide-eyed expression. He frowned at her state of undress and glanced at his watch. 'It *was* seven we agreed on, wasn't it?'

Adrianna face fell and she did the only possible thing. She burst into tears.

Alan, in true gentlemanly fashion, strode inside, closed the door, then gathered her weeping frame against his elegant grey suit. 'There, there, my love,' he soothed, stroking her hair. 'Was it that bad out in the desert? There, there… It'll be all right now. I'm here…'

She pulled away from his embrace, tears streaming down her face, despair making her strike out blindly. 'No, no, that's not it at all! Don't you see? You can't make anything right. Bryce is the only one who can do that,' she went on in choked, broken words. 'I love

him…and need him, and…and he does love me…I
think. He wants me to marry him, but I won't… I can't!
So he left me and…and… Oh, God,' she sobbed, 'I can't
live without him!'

To give Alan credit, he reacted to her muddled outburst with a remarkable degree of composure, though
there was a definite tightening of muscles along his jawline. 'Ah, now I see! Our Mr McLean did a little more
than just rescue you, didn't he?'

Adrianna slumped down on the sofa, her head dropping into her hands. 'Oh, Alan,' she groaned, 'I'm so
sorry. I didn't mean to blurt it out like that.'

He laid a heavy hand on her shoulder. 'Never mind,
my love. Never mind. We all make fools of ourselves
over matters of the flesh. Believe me, I know.'

The pained undercurrent in his words had Adrianna
lifting her soggy lashes and looking up at him. 'You've
been in love too, Alan?'

His eyes betrayed true pain before he turned to stride
across the room to the drinks cabinet. 'I'll get you a gin
and tonic,' he muttered. 'You look as if you could do
with one. I certainly could. Though I think I'll skip the
tonic.' He went about it with his usual efficiency, stalk-
ing out to the kitchen to get some ice, then returning to
hand over her glass and sink down in one of the roomy
armchairs, his face bleak.

'In love, you ask?' His sigh was weary. 'It's hard to
believe one falls truly in love with an eighteen-year-old
girl. It's more likely lust.'

Now it was Adrianna's turn to stare. 'You mean…'

'My ward. Yes—Ebony.' His face twisted into a grimace and he took a hefty swig of straight gin. 'I don't

understand it. For three years she's been flitting in and out of my life, a quiet little thing who hardly ever said boo to a grasshopper. Then last holidays Mother threw her an eighteenth birthday party and she came out all dressed up in this white lace dress, and immediately all I wanted to do was…' He shuddered.

'…make love to her?' Adrianna finished softly.

'What a delicate way of putting it!' was his black remark. 'Unfortunately I rarely feel delicate when I look at her these days.'

They both fell silent for a few seconds. Adrianna's mind was a merry-go-round of thoughts till one single realisation overrode all the others. 'Alan, is this the reason you asked me to marry you?'

His sigh was ragged. 'Yes. She finishes school in a month. She'll be in my home permanently from then on. I thought…'

'…that there'd be less danger for the girl if you had a wife by your side,' she finished gently.

'Yes,' he confessed.

An awkward silence fell between them till Alan spoke up again. 'I'm sorry, Adrianna, truly sorry. I didn't think of it as using you. You're my dearest friend. I guess I'm used to turning to you in my hours of need. Remember the night we first made love?'

'Yes,' she said warily.

'It was not long after Ebony's parents' funeral. I felt…distraught when I saw those two coffins being lowered into the ground. Distraught and…lonely. For years I'd done nothing but work, with few outside interests. My personal life had deteriorated into a night here and there with women I barely knew. Suddenly I wanted…no, *needed*…something more. Something decent and warm and special. You gave me that something, Adrianna, and for that I'll be eternally grateful. I'll never regret our relationship. I hope you won't either.'

She looked at him then and saw that he was very sincere in what he said. 'Oh, Alan, why couldn't I have fallen in love with you, instead of some crazy outback man?'

He gave a short, dry laugh. 'I might say the same, my love. Why couldn't I have fallen in love with you, instead of…' He broke off abruptly as he realised what he was saying. A dark frown bunched his brows together and he glared down into his drink. 'Must be the gin,' he muttered, and drained the rest.

Adrianna frowned as she sipped her drink. She knew Alan, and she knew the type of person he was. Much the same sort of man as she was a woman—serious, hardworking. Certainly not sex-mad. If he felt such strong physical feelings for the girl there was sure to be more to it than lust, just as in her case with Bryce.

'I think you're mistaken, Alan,' she argued quietly. 'I think you do love Ebony, but your desire for her is so strong that it overwhelms these deeper, finer feelings. I know what I'm talking about, because that was what I thought I was feeling for Bryce till I realised how much I liked and admired him as well. Love can be a very deceiving emotion. It plays tricks on us because sometimes we're frightened of love, frightened of the risks it entails.'

She hesitated then, her heart turning over with dismay at what she had just said. Who was she to talk about risk-taking? She wasn't prepared to take any, was she?

She claimed to like and admire Bryce. Claimed to actually *love* the man! But the basic truth was she didn't have the courage to put that love on the line...

She lifted the gin and tonic to her lips and gulped down a mouthful, only to find Alan staring at her when she lowered the glass.

'You've changed, Adrianna,' he said slowly. 'You've discovered passion. I almost envy Bryce McLean.'

The irony of his statement dragged at her heart. She stared down into her glass and swirled the remainder of the drink in circles. 'I wouldn't if I were you. I'm bad news for any man.'

'I don't agree. You have qualities a lot of men would kill for. Why don't you go after him?' Alan urged. 'Find some way to make it work. If anyone can, you can. You can be very determined, Adrianna, when you want to be.'

For a second his words sent a surge of hope into her heart. Did she dare do as he suggested? Was there some sort of compromise acceptable to both Bryce and herself? But then her heart sank. If there was she couldn't think of it. Bryce was a black and white man, a man who, once he had an idea fixed in his mind, could not be swayed from it. Just look at the way he still disliked Alan after all these years!

A thought popped into Adrianna's head and her eyes snapped up to Alan's. 'Would you mind if I asked you a highly irrelevant question?'

He raised a single eyebrow in mild surprise. 'Such as?'

'Why didn't you go to your father's funeral?'

He stared at her. 'That *is* an odd question!' But then

the penny dropped. 'Ah, I think I get the picture… McLean never did like me much. Neither did my secretary.' His smile was rueful. 'Believe me, I wanted to go to Dad's funeral, and if I could go back in time, I would do so. But at twenty-one, I didn't have the confidence to tell the bank to get stuffed.'

'The bank?' Adrianna repeated, puzzled.

'The bank who held the mortgages on the family home and business. They insisted on sending one of their auditors over that day to inspect the books and the business. They didn't believe I could pull it out of the mire of debt my father had run up in the years before he became ill. I couldn't see any way out of the appointment, so the funeral went ahead without me, though I held my own private service later that evening. I really wasn't the heartless bastard back in those days that I seemed to be. Just a young man under a lot of stress. Does that restore me in your eyes a little?'

'You never did need restoring in my eyes!' she assured him.

'Not even now,' he said slowly, 'that you know about Ebony?'

Adrianna's heart contracted slightly, but she kept a straight face. 'Not even now. As you said, Alan, we're friends. And friends understand and forgive each other.'

Alan smiled. 'OK, friend. Then might I make a suggestion?'

'Of course.'

'I gather going out to dinner is off, but why don't you go and put some clothes on and I'll have some food sent up. You look as if you could do with some sustenance.'

Adrianna stood up, then hesitated. 'Alan, you do real-

ise that there can never be any more…physical intimacy
between us, don't you?'

Again his smile was gentle. 'Naturally. You're in
love, and I know you'd never betray that love. I would
never ask you to.'

Adrianna turned then and walked into the bathroom,
a frown coming to her face. But aren't I betraying it
right now? she worried. Didn't I betray it the moment I
let Bryce walk out of here and out of my life so easily,
the moment I chose not to go after him?

You can still go after him, an inner voice intervened.
Of course, it will mean giving up everything you hold
dear, everything you've ever worked for…

Instinctively she recoiled at the thought. I can't, she
shuddered. I just can't!

CHAPTER ELEVEN

ADRIANNA circled the chartered Cessna over Dover Downs several times before setting the plane down on the private airstrip with only a few light bumps, then taxiing down to the hangars. She switched off the engine with a ragged sigh, only then admitting to herself that the flight—and the landing—had been almost as harrowing as the days leading up to it.

It hadn't occurred to her that she would be so nervous behind the controls of a plane—her previous accident had hardly been her fault, after all—but her heart had been in her mouth from the moment she had taken off from Darwin airport and she was very relieved to be safely on the ground.

Which brought her to another problem. The hangars looked deserted, no one coming out to see who had just arrived. She had thought someone would be there who could drive her up to the main house, but not a soul was in sight. She pushed open the door of the cockpit and the blistering heat hit her in the face.

'Just as well I wore light clothing,' she muttered, looking down at her ice lemon sundress and low-heeled white sandals. It would be a long, hot walk up to the house.

It was then that she spotted the approaching cloud of dust, preceded by a light blue Utility.

Would it be Bryce at the wheel? she wondered. The thought brought a surge of adrenalin and nerves.

She had never intended to come. After Bryce had left her she had finally and irrevocably decided that she would try to forget him, try to put him out of her heart and her mind.

She might as well have told herself not to breathe.

Still, it had taken her ten full days to give in, ten days of agonising and waffling and worrying, ten days of heartache and loneliness and frustration.

The arrival of her period a couple of days after Bryce left had made her oddly depressed, though it was only to be expected, and she had tried to get on with her life as usual, tried to find distraction in working.

But it had been useless. Most days she had merely stared at blank pages, her mind devoid of creative urges, though she should have been getting on with next year's winter designs.

How many times did she find herself reaching for the telephone to ring Bryce? Once she actually dialled his number, which she'd found out from Information, only to hang up before anyone had time to answer. Her hands had begun to shake uncontrollably, and what would she have said anyway? I love you, Bryce? I miss you, but I still can't live the sort of life you want me to? What would that have achieved?

So the calls had never been made.

Everyone in the office had commented how tired and strained she was looking and suggested she have some time off. They had all said they could cope without her for a while, which she didn't doubt at all. It seemed everything had swung along quite sweetly during her missing days in the desert, with her assistants making any necessary business decisions for her. Adrianna had always hired the very best. And the best were always waiting their chance to show what they could do.

In the end she had to admit that she couldn't go on as she was, going through the motions without energy or enthusiasm. Being away from Bryce and his loving had taken all the joy out of living. What did it matter if she had to give up her career? If she went on the way she was, soon she wouldn't have a career to give up!

Yet even then she hadn't been able to call him on the telephone. Perhaps she was half afraid he wouldn't talk to her, that he would still be angry. Whatever the reason, she felt it better if she just came and confronted him, told him she had changed her mind, that she did want to marry him, even though she still had her doubts about their long-term happiness. It wasn't the thought of children that frightened her so much now, but the sort of life Bryce would expect her to lead as his wife. And of course there was still that niggling little doubt that he might not be the most constant husband in the world. That was one thing Adrianna didn't think she could live with.

But perhaps she was wrong about that. Perhaps, like Alan, he had changed since those early days. Hadn't he claimed at Dover Downs that day that he could change, that she only had to show him the way? She hoped so. Anyway, all she could do was explain her doubts and fears to Bryce, and then it was up to him, wasn't it?

Yet now that the moment was at hand she was attacked by different doubts. He hadn't telephoned her, had he? He hadn't written either. He had, to all intents and purposes, wiped her from his life. Maybe she was wasting her time. Maybe he wouldn't want any more to do with her.

She climbed down from the cockpit, carrying the overnight bag she had packed when she'd been more optimistic, and walked with growing apprehension over to where the utility had pulled up at the edge of the tarmac. Because of its dusty windscreen she couldn't see who was at the wheel till she drew level with the passenger window.

A sigh of relief fluttered from her lips when she saw Mrs McLean sitting there in a pretty floral dress, beaming at her. 'Get in!' Bryce's mother called. 'I've kept the air-conditioning going for you.'

Adrianna quickly settled herself and her bag in the cool cabin. 'Thanks for coming down to meet me,' she said.

'No trouble. We always meet any plane that lands. Bryce is out in the far paddocks checking fences, I'm afraid. He won't be back for another hour or two.'

Adrianna gave the other woman a close look. How much did she know? she wondered. 'Has…has Bryce spoken to you about what happened between him and me?' she asked carefully.

'In what way?' The woman frowned.

'The day he flew me home to Sydney…we had a…a difference of opinion.'

'I see… That explains it, then.'

'Explains what?'

'Bryce's mood. He hasn't exactly been his bright breezy self this last week. I thought he was just missing you. He didn't say you'd argued or anything.'

Adrianna felt a surge of hope. So Bryce had been miserable too, had he? Clearly he hadn't been able to dismiss her from his life any more easily than she had been able to forget him. Though his moodiness could have been due to damaged ego. Or sexual frustration. 'Do you think he'll be pleased to see me?' she asked.

Mrs McLean's hesitation betrayed reservation at this. 'He doesn't usually like to be caught at a disadvantage,' she said by way of an answer. But then she smiled. 'Still, he's not likely to stay angry with the woman he loves for long.'

Adrianna's heart jumped. 'He *told* you he loved me?'

'He didn't have to. A mother knows when her son is in love. I knew it the moment he brought you home.'

'Oh!'

Her laugh was gentle as she put the Utility into gear. 'I always used to tease Bryce that he never brought a girl home for me to meet. He told me quite firmly that when and if he brought a girl home it would be the one he wanted to marry.'

Adrianna's heart turned over. So that was what Bryce and his mother had been smiling at that day!

Mrs McLean swung the Utility round and began heading along the rough road that led past the outbuildings back towards the main house.

Adrianna sighed.

It brought a sharp look. 'Don't you want to marry my son?'

She gave the other woman a pleading glance. 'I have to be honest with you. At first I didn't. I didn't think marriage was what I wanted at all.'

'But Bryce *has* asked you to marry him?'

'Well, yes…but…'

'You make it sound as if marrying Bryce is something to be wary of,' the other woman said indignantly. 'I'll have you know that he's a splendid man—simply splendid. And I'm not speaking through the blind eyes of a mother. Ask any of the cattlemen. Ask *anyone* around here! Oh, he went through some unsettled years when he thought he didn't want to even *see* another cow, let alone work with them. Went to Sydney to have a taste of the bright lights for a while. His father let him go, said it was good for him to see how the other half lived, give him a better basis to judge for himself what was right or wrong for him. When his father was killed, he came back like a shot to take his rightful position as head of the family. Not grudgingly either. He's told me many a time how much he's learned to value life on the land. Not that it's an easy life…'

She flashed Adrianna a narrow-eyed look. 'Is that what's been bothering you? The life you'd have to live if you married Bryce?'

'Partly,' she admitted.

'Humph! I wouldn't have taken you for a cowardly girl. OK, so it requires some sacrifices, but it's not as though you'd be poor. And since you can fly a plane, you could come and go to the city as often as you liked. There isn't anything Bryce wouldn't do for the woman he loved. You wouldn't even have to give up that business of yours. Though surely some of the creative work could be done from here, couldn't it?'

Adrianna just stared at Mrs McLean. Now why hadn't she thought of that? A burst of joy gushed through her. Even her earlier creative block disappeared, images from

her days in the outback jumping into her mind with in-
spired flashes. She would start a special range of outback
designs, using fabrics that reflected the strong colours
she had seen for herself—the red of the sand, the bronzes
and yellow ochres of the rocks, the bright blue of the
sky and the deep green of the gorge. And then there was
the black and orange of the cockatoos. The styles would
be light and cool, loosely fitting and comfortable. Oh,
her ideas were endless!

'Of course things might change when the kiddies
come along,' the woman was saying, snapping Adrianna
back from her flights of fancy to the reality of life. 'You
might have to stay at home a bit more then, but even in
that you wouldn't be alone. You have *me*, you know.
I'm as fit as a fiddle. I'd come and babysit my grand-
children as often as you'd like.'

Adrianna was startled by this generous offer at first,
but then she sighed and nodded. How silly she had been
to think that all mothering was like the one experience
she had been involved in! Most families were only too
happy to share the workload, making the inevitable
stresses and pressures of looking after children not only
bearable, but probably enjoyable.

'And then there's Helen,' Bryce's mother went on.
'She's a good one with children, as are all the Aboriginal
women who live at Dover Downs. Though I dare say
Helen will have a baby of her own soon, since she's
marrying Pete next month.'

'Helen's getting married?' Adrianna gasped.

'And none too soon, I'd say,' the other woman
sniffed. 'She's been impossible since she fell in love,
going round giggling and blushing all the time.'

'Then there's nothing between…' Adrianna's voice broke off before she could give voice to her jealous fears. A wry smile captured her mouth. Bryce had deliberately baited her with Helen. She could see it all so clearly now. His smiles had been no more than a ploy to make her jealous. And how well they had succeeded!

'Does that smile mean you've made up your mind?'

Adrianna glanced over at Bryce's mother, her smile widening. 'If he'll have me.'

Mrs McLean grinned back. 'If he doesn't I'll skin him alive!'

Adrianna settled back in the seat, feeling definitely happier, but not nearly as smug as Bryce's mother. It was all very well for the two women who loved Bryce to talk about him and settle his life for him. But would the man himself have the same ideas?

CHAPTER TWELVE

BRYCE swept into the house shortly after two-thirty and made straight for his bedroom, unaware that Adrianna was sitting in the kitchen, nervously awaiting his arrival. She had been keeping Helen company while Mrs McLean had an afternoon nap, and had found the girl quite delightful once she was past her shyness.

'That's Mr McLean now,' Helen said when she heard the front door bang. 'He always showers first, then goes into his study for the rest of the afternoon.'

'Do you take him coffee or tea or anything?' Adrianna asked, trying to think of some excuse to go to him quite naturally.

Helen shook her head. 'No, he usually has a beer. There's a small refrigerator in his study.'

'Oh…'

'Why don't you wait for him in there anyway? Unless you'd like to go along to his bedroom?' At this Helen giggled and blushed.

Adrianna smiled. 'No, his study will do. Show me the way, will you?'

It was another very masculine room with a polished parquet floor and wood-panelled walls, the furnishings in autumn tones. A large heavy desk sat on a rust-toned rug between the two long windows that faced the outside, a rich brown leather chair behind it, two armchairs in front—one a darker brown, the other a mustard gold.

A modern personal computer sat on one end of the desk, a fax machine on the other, both looking incongruous in the old-style décor.

Adrianna spent her time waiting for Bryce inspecting the various books in the sturdy Victorian bookcases. There were a lot on cattle and cattle management and several on modern computerised book-keeping. Clearly Bryce was not a man to fall behind the times.

She was standing at one of the windows, staring out at the hot, dry landscape, feeling sick with nerves, when the door opened abruptly. Bryce didn't see her till he went to close the door. His hand froze on the knob and he just stood there, staring at her.

Adrianna did a bit of staring herself, for Bryce wasn't wearing all that much. Just a pair of white shorts and a white, short-sleeved shirt open to the waist.

'Adrianna!' he breathed.

'Bryce…' Her taut face broke into an encouraging smile.

She saw his hand tighten where it still held the door-knob. His eyes hardened as they travelled slowly down her body, then back up again.

Oh, God, she thought. He doesn't want me any more.

She cleared her throat. 'Bryce, I…'

He clenched his jaw even harder and swung the door shut. 'What are you doing here, Adrianna?' he grated. 'Believe me when I say you will *not* be allowed to toy with my feelings again!' He strode over to the desk, where he snatched up a pile of mail and began sorting through the letters, not giving her another glance.

Despair was like a dagger in Adrianna's heart. She was too late.

No, she refused to think that! She loved Bryce and wanted him. She hadn't come all this way to give up now.

'I wouldn't do that, Bryce,' she tried to assure him, but her voice shook uncontrollably. 'I…I love you.'

The blue eyes were chilling as they lifted to hers. 'Is that so? And what, may I ask, does that mean? What does it entitle me to expect? An adoring little woman prepared to lay her life at my feet?'

Adrianna couldn't help her automatic cringe.

His mouth twisted cruelly at her reaction to his words. 'I didn't think so,' he scoffed. 'Playing the sweet submissive wife isn't in your line, is it? So where does that leave us? What, I ask myself, is behind this mission of *love*! Could it be…?' His gaze flicked over her body once more. 'Ah, yes… How silly of me not to realise that your visit might have an extremely basic aim.'

He put down the letters and began walking around the desk towards her, his face hard, his gaze mocking. 'I have to give you credit, my sweet—you've come well armed. I mean…have you got *any* underwear on at all? I can't see any bra or stockings. No petticoat either. The sunlight shining through the window is like an X-ray on that dress. That doesn't leave much, does it?'

He stopped in front of her and ran a contemptuous fingertip around the low square neckline of her dress, making her shiver. 'This is why you've come, isn't it?' he snarled, his hands sliding slowly down the sides of her dress, then moving back up, taking the skirt with them.

Adrianna couldn't seem to get her mind into gear,

shock and excitement warring a fierce battle inside her. Stop him! her pride screamed.

She staggered backwards against the curtains, her eyes wide, her throat swallowing convulsively. 'No,' she denied shakily, 'it's not why I've come.'

His laugh was scornful. 'You *don't* want me to make love to you?'

Her face showed total dismay at his derision. 'Of course I want you to make love to me. But not like this… Not with you sneering at me and thinking I'm some sort of…of…My God, Bryce, didn't you mean what you said before you left?' she cried. 'Don't you love me any more?'

'Oh, yes, I meant what I said before I left,' he jeered. 'And I still love you, more's the pity! But have *you* forgotten just how long it is since I did leave? I haven't. It's ten days. Two hundred and forty hours and God knows how many minutes, all of them spent loving you and wanting you and hoping against hope that you'd come after me or ring or write. Or any bloody damned thing!'

His hands shot out to grab her, his face suffused with anger and violent emotion. 'You don't know the meaning of love, woman. Love doesn't take a man's pride and grind him into the dust. Love doesn't leave a man for days without a single word of contact. Love doesn't make a man despair that he'll never have children because the only woman he wants as their mother refuses to have them!'

He threw her from him then, turning away to ram closed fists down on the desk before whirling back to glare at her. 'Get out of here,' he muttered. 'Get out before I do something I'll really regret.'

Adrianna glared right back at him, her heart pounding, her mind exploding with an answering fury. 'Don't you speak to me like that, Bryce McLean! And don't you dare speak to me of regret! I know more about regret at this moment than you do. I regret ever setting eyes on you. I certainly regret the moment I put my hand in yours back there at that gorge. And I infinitely regret coming here today. I came out of love for you, my crazy, hopeless love for you. And what have you done? You've just thrown that love right back in my face! Well, I'll keep it, thank you very much, and hopefully, next time, I might find a man who'll value it a bit more than you did!'

She turned then and stalked towards the door, head held high, her pride intact but her heart breaking into a million jagged pieces.

'Don't go!' Bryce called in a haunted, desperate voice that tore at her very soul.

She stopped for a second, then walked on.

The air in the room moved like a rushing wind as he raced to grab her, spinning her round and holding her captive against the door. 'I can't let you go,' he ground out, wild eyes roving madly over her startled face. 'I love you, Adrianna. I can't live without you. These last ten days have been hell. Hell, I tell you!' Suddenly his hands were in her hair and he was kissing her, hungrily, desperately. 'Tell me what you want,' he rasped. 'I'll give it to you. Tell me what I have to do…I'll do it!'

He groaned, and pressed hot lips to the madly beating pulse at the base of her throat.

Adrianna was breathless, both with shock and a quickly rising passion. Already her hands had stolen to his hair and she was pressing his mouth to her rapidly heating flesh, but when his hands began to fumble with the front buttons on the dress, she tried to push him away. 'No,' she gasped. 'No!' She couldn't let him waylay her with sex when there was so much still to be settled.

He stopped, but didn't let her go, his eyes determined and quite ruthless as he stared down at her. 'This is the last time you're going to say no to me, Adrianna,' he said, striking fear into her heart till a surprisingly gentle smile softened his face. He led her over to the large brown armchair, drawing her down into his lap as he sat down in it. 'Now,' he said, 'let's get all this sorted out. You love me?' he asked.

She nodded.

'And you'll marry me?'

Again she nodded.

'And you'll have my children?'

She smiled, thinking to herself that she hadn't forgotten what he had said a moment ago, all the concessions he was prepared to make. 'How many would you like?'

His sigh was deep and contented. 'Then what were we arguing about?'

'What indeed?' Her eyes were innocently wide.

His narrowed. 'What sneaky plan have you got up your sleeve, Adrianna Winslow?'

She took his hands and ran them up and down her bare arms. 'Not a thing, as you can see,' she said seductively.

He laughed. 'You can't fool me, city girl. I've got your measure.'

She only smiled at this, but made no further move to stop him when his hands returned to the buttons on her dress.

'It was nice of you to invite Alan to our wedding, Bryce,' Adrianna murmured.

'He's not such a bad bloke,' came the grudging reply. 'He's changed.'

'You're only saying that because you know now that I never loved him.'

'Mmm.'

'Did you see how his ward gazed adoringly at him when he wasn't looking? If she's not in love with him I'll eat my hat. And wasn't Alan awfully sweet to her when she spilled that drink on her dress?'

'What an incurable romantic you are, Adrianna!' her husband grinned.

'I just want Alan and Ebony to be as happy as we are.'

'Don't you worry about Alan Carstairs,' Bryce said, smothering a yawn. 'He's not the type of man to ever come out on the losing end.'

Adrianna lifted her head from Bryce's stomach to look at him. 'You're not going to sleep, are you?'

'Now why would I do that? It's only three in the morning, we've been going since dawn, what with the wedding at Dover Downs, then the reception, then the flight to Sydney, and we've only been making love continuously since we arrived at the honeymoon suite here around midnight.'

'Well, we want to be sure, don't we?' she pointed out reasonably. 'After all, today's one of my best days to conceive. I worked it out on my calendar.'

Bryce groaned. 'I said I wanted children, Adrianna. I didn't mean I want one nine months to the day after our wedding night!'

'The sooner we start trying, the better. It might take months before I fall pregnant!'

'I certainly hope so. I want you all to myself for a while. The only person I want waking you in the middle of the night is *me*!'

She kissed her way up his chest and hovered her mouth above his. 'And why would you want to wake me in the middle of the night, my darling sexy husband?'

'God only knows. With you I can imagine I'm going to need all the sleep I can get!'

'You're to blame,' she said, kissing him lightly on the mouth. 'You've turned me into a sex maniac.'

'*Now* she tells me!'

She kissed his mouth again, then his throat, then laid her head on his chest, sighing contentedly. 'It was a wonderful wedding, wasn't it?' she said softly.

'Mmm.'

'Mum likes you.'

'Mmm.'

'Even my rotten brothers like you. Though I can understand why. You shouldn't have bought them that cleaning business, you know—they don't deserve it.'

'Everyone deserves a chance, Adrianna. It's up to them to take it or not. Besides, it's only money.'

Adrianna could only admire Bryce's attitude to money. Enough was enough, was his motto. And they

both had more than enough, he said. Why not spread it
around a little?

'I love you, Bryce McLean,' she said simply. 'So
much that I'm prepared to forgive you for once being a
ladies' man.'

He laughed. 'What makes you so sure anything's
changed?'

Her hand slid down his body to enclose him in a rather
intimate hold. 'But it has, hasn't it, darling?' she threatened with smiling teeth.

He paled for a moment. 'You wouldn't dare.'

'Oh, wouldn't I?' Her hand began to tighten. 'How
about telling exactly what you did get up to all those
years ago when you were cavorting around like
Sydney's answer to Casanova?'

'If I confess will you have mercy on me?'

'I might.'

'OK—well, back in the old days I started with the
brunettes, then I moved on to the redheads, and finally
I polished off all the blondes. Present company excluded,
of course.'

'Bryce! I'm not amused.'

'Neither am I, my dear. Neither am I...' Suddenly he
tickled her, then whipped out from under her loosening
grasp to pin her laughing body to the mattress with his
huge body.

'Help!' she squawked. 'You're squashing me!'

'Good. Now that I have you at *my* mercy let me point
out that I don't fancy being given the third degree about
what's well and truly over. I'm not interested in knowing
your past conquests, Adrianna. I suggest you take a leaf
out of my book. The present is what I'm concerned

about. The present and the future. But, just to put that jealous little heart of yours at ease once and for all, let me assure you that I didn't bed all those ladies I dated. As a sweet and wholesome country lad I was quite content to give most of them a kiss and a cuddle. Admittedly, there were one or two that progressed further, but…'

'Only one or two?' she queried sceptically.

'OK, three or four. Who's counting?'

'*I* am!'

'Then make it five.'

'Five?' she echoed.

'You wouldn't have wanted me inexperienced, would you?'

'No.'

He heaved a sigh of mock relief. 'I'm glad that's all settled, then.'

'Hold your horses! What about since then? Who's been gracing those cool sheets of yours just lately?'

'Good grief, Adrianna! Do you also want to know what I've had for breakfast every day of my life as well?'

'No. Just every female you've had!'

He laughed. 'Then I'm afraid you'll have to learn to live with ignorance. I have no intention of giving you a blow-by-blow description of my past love-life. All I'm going to say is there was no female for nearly twelve months before you.'

'No one?'

'No one,' he pronounced firmly.

Adrianna was amazed. She was also pleased at the way Bryce always stood up to her. She had fallen in love with him when he was at his masterful worst, and underneath, she didn't really want him to change, for she admired his decisiveness, his strength, his slightly dominating maleness. But neither was she about to change either. 'Pull the other leg, Bryce McLean,' she countered drily.

'Scout's honour,' he insisted.

'Really?'

'Really. Even a suspicious woman like you has to concede that women aren't exactly thick on the ground around Dover Downs. And before you say it, no, I've never bedded Helen either. Not that she isn't an attractive girl, but I've known her all my life and I've always looked on her more as a kid sister than an available female. Mostly, since coming back to manage the station, I've restricted myself to the odd holiday affair, that's all. Funnily enough, as you get older, sex without love loses its appeal. But when I met you, my lovely siren… My God, I was climbing the walls in no time!'

He cradled her face and kissed her lightly. Then not so lightly. 'I will never want anyone else other than you, Adrianna,' he said huskily. 'Never. I love you to distraction. Forget about the past. The past is over, for both you and me. Today is the first day of the rest of our lives.'

Adrianna's heart turned over with happiness at the thought of living the rest of her life with this wonderful man. What would his children be like? she wondered, the thought still having the power to move her that if she had never met Bryce, never fallen in love with him, she wouldn't ever have even contemplated having a child. Now the idea was a driving force inside her, a goal that would give her more satisfaction than any career move ever could.

'And now,' Bryce murmured, 'where was I?'

Her movements beneath him were both direct and tantalising. 'You were just about to put those wonderful words of yours into action.'

His laughter was low and sexy. 'You've got a one-track mind, do you know that?'

'Yes.'

He gave a mock sigh. 'We husbands have it hard.'

'I hope so,' she smiled.

'Adrianna! You're wicked!'

'Not wicked, my darling. Just in love, in love with the most fantastic, sexiest man in the whole wide world!'

Jacqueline Baird began writing as a hobby when her family objected to the smell of her oil painting, and immediately became hooked on the romantic genre. She loves travelling and worked her way around the world from Europe to the Americas and Australia, returning to marry her teenage sweetheart. She lives in Ponteland, Northumbria, the county of her birth, and has two teenage sons. She enjoys playing badminton, and spends most weekends with husband Jim, sailing their Gp.14 around Derwent Reservoir.

Look out for
THE ITALIAN'S RUNAWAY BRIDE
by Jacqueline Baird
in Modern Romance™, December 2001.

THE RELUCTANT
FIANCÉE

by

Jacqueline Baird

CHAPTER ONE

BEA looked around the crowded room, her full lips twitching in a wry grimace. Music blared from two amplifiers, gyrating bodies were everywhere and the flashing lights were giving her a headache. She should be enjoying herself; after all she was in *her* living room! It was *her* twenty-first birthday party! *Her* friends!

She turned her back on the crowd and stared out of the tall Georgian window to the blackness beyond. Bea lifted a fluted champagne glass to her mouth and took a sip of the bubbly. It was as flat as she felt. It was futile to worry, she knew, but she did not seem to be able to help it.

Tomorrow she was travelling down to London, and on Monday she would start work as a junior partner in the firm of Stephen-Gregoris, an import and export firm started forty years ago by her late father, John Stephen, and his greek Cypriot friend, Nick Gregoris. But it wasn't the thought of work that bothered her, or the fact that the firm had diversified into other areas. No, her real worry was that she would have to meet Leon Gregoris again.

Leon Gregoris was the chairman and managing director, and a despot to boot, as she knew from past experience... Also, until today, he had been the trustee of her thirty per cent share of the business, left to her by her father.

As a child Bea had considered Leon a friend, even though he was fourteen years older than her. But that had ended when her father had died. For the last three

5

years any communication between them had been strictly business, conducted through lawyers and the occasional telephone call.

An orphan at seventeen, Bea had stayed on in the home she had shared with her father in Northumbria. Her mother had died when she was a baby and it was her honorary aunty Lil and her uncle Bob who had looked after her.

They still did. A fond smile curved Bea's full lips. She was going to miss the elderly couple when she was in London. She had never really had to take care of herself before. While attending the University of Newcastle upon Tyne she had simply travelled in every day. Now she was the proud recipient of a first-class degree in Maths and Accountancy, and on Monday she would take her place in her father's firm!

A frown creased her smooth brow. Leon Gregoris was the only fly in the ointment; she cringed at the thought of seeing him, not at all sure of her ability to face up to him.

For heaven's sake! Was she a woman? Or a wimp? She shook her head dismissively. She was bright, intelligent, and no longer the naive eighteen-year-old girl she had been when she had last seen Leon, in love with the idea of love.

'Humph!' she snorted, disgusted with the memory of her much younger, gullible self. 'You're a fool, Bea. You have nothing to worry about,' she told herself firmly, and, lifting her glass, she took another large swallow of champagne, unaware she had spoken out loud.

'If you say so, Phoebe, darling. Far be it from me to disagree with a lady.'

The deep melodious voice made the hair on the back of her neck stand on end. She would have known that voice anywhere. Her hand tightened, white-knuckled, on the stem of her glass. It couldn't be! She raised her eyes and stared at the couple reflected in the window pane.

Her own reflection showed a young woman of average height with straight silver-blonde hair and pale, bare shoulders. She wore a silver Spandex sheath dress that clung to the soft curves of firm breasts and on down to fit like a second skin over feminine hips, ending mid-thigh and exposing long, shapely legs.

All the colour left Bea's face. The picture she presented was almost ghostly, but there was nothing ghost-like about the tall, dark man hovering behind her. Warlock, more like! she thought grimly. Wide shoulders seemed to shadow her. The harsh, handsome features had not changed a jot, she realised, swallowing hard. Too long black wavy hair, and even blacker piercing eyes. Slowly turning around to face him, she silently added, And an even blacker heart…

'You, Leon,' she murmured, finally finding her voice and hating the way it quavered. She tilted her head back and looked up into his tanned, attractive face. He was watching her, laughter lighting his dark eyes. He knew damn well he had shocked her rigid. 'What are you doing here?' she demanded curtly. 'I didn't invite you.'

'An oversight on your part, Phoebe, but I forgive you,' he drawled mockingly. 'You know I wouldn't miss your twenty-first birthday for the world.'

He was the only person who ever called her Phoebe, and she hated it. She opened her mouth to tell him as much, but never got the chance. Two large hands settled on her naked shoulders and a firm male mouth descended on her parted lips.

Whatever she had been about to say vanished from her mind at the first touch of his mouth on hers. She closed her eyes.

Bea knew she should resist, and lifted her free hand

to press against the hard wall of his chest, but for some reason her fingers spread out instead, over the soft silk of his shirt.

It was Leon who broke the kiss, murmuring against her mouth, 'Happy birthday, darling.' Then, lifting his head and staring down into her flushed, beautiful face, he winked…

'The chemistry is still fizzing, Phoebe, which is more than can be said for the glass of champagne you're clutching with such tenacity.' And, taking the glass from her unresisting hand, he placed it on the windowsill. 'I'll get you another. Come on.' Capturing her hand, he added, 'Let's get out of here and into the study, where we can talk.'

Bea shook her head to clear her brain. He was doing it again, exactly as he had years ago. Mesmerising her, poor fool, with a kiss, and then ordering her about. That was Leon's *modus operandi* and she would do well to remember it.

'No, thank you, I've had quite enough to drink.' She snatched her hand free. 'And as for talking we can discuss all we need to at our meeting on Monday.' She was proud of her ability to speak firmly to Leon for once, and, bravely meeting his narrowed gaze, she added for good measure, 'But if you would like a drink please help yourself. The bar is in the dining room. You know the way.' Half turning, she would have walked past him, but Leon's hand closed around her upper arm, halting her in her stride.

'Not so fast, Phoebe.'

She fought down the tingling sensation the large hand curved around her flesh aroused, and looked up into his face. 'In case you hadn't noticed, I have guests. I must mingle.'

Black eyes raked her from head to toe in a blatant

sexual appraisal, lingering for a moment on the shadowy cleavage cupped in silver Spandex before returning to her face. 'Mingling with you was actually what I had in mind. How about it, Phoebe?' Leon asked with deliberate provocation, his long fingers caressing the bare skin of her arm. 'Interested?'

Bea looked at the man towering over her and recognised the sensual amusement glittering in his eyes. Leon hadn't changed in three years. He was still as devastatingly attractive as ever, and he knew it. It was there in his arrogant stance, an animal magnetism he exuded without even trying. Add wealth, power and sophistication, and he was a lethal cocktail to any member of the female species.

Tonight he was wearing a conservative business suit, dark navy, with a plain white silk shirt and a muted blue and red striped tie. His jacket was open and pleated trousers hung comfortably on his lean hips. For a second she wondered why he was dressed that way at almost midnight on a Saturday night, at a party he had not been invited to. But she refrained from asking. She simply wanted him out of her house.

'Will I do?' Leon asked, arching one dark eyebrow enquiringly, fully aware that she had been studying him. Bea could feel hot colour flood her cheeks, and was not sure if it was from anger or embarrassment.

'Does your silence mean you're considering my offer, Phoebe, darling?' he teased huskily.

His deep voice was awfully close to her ear, and, jerking her arm free from his hold, she shot back scathingly, 'Still the incorrigible flirt, Leon. I pity your poor wife and…family.' For some reason she could not bring herself to say 'child'. 'How they tolerate your many escapades I can't imagine,' she added, trying for a flippant note, horrified to realise that his touch, his closeness, still had the power to make her go weak at the knees. But there was no way she was going to let him see it. Never again…

He straightened to his full height and stepped back. 'My family, if you can call it a family, is fine. My step-mother and stepsister live in California, and I rarely see them unless they want something.' He stared down at her with eyes as black as jet, all trace of amusement gone. 'As for a wife, you should know the answer to that better than most,' he opined cynically.

'Sorry, I haven't kept up with your private affairs,' she said, drawling out the last word deliberately.

Bea's blue eyes, filled with contempt, flicked up over the hard planes of his face, his smooth, tanned skin, the faint shadow of his square jaw; she saw the sheer animal strength of him, and more. He was furiously angry, but hiding it well. Deciding discretion was called for, unless she wanted a fight in a room full of people, Bea added with a calm she was far from feeling, 'It takes me all my time to keep up to date on our business partnership. Your personal life is your own. Forget I mentioned it.'

'Forget?' Leon smiled, a cynical twist of his hard lips. 'How could I forget, when the nearest I ever got to fall-ing into the matrimonial trap was the abortive engage-ment you and I shared for a few idyllic months, my sweet Phoebe?'

Idyllic! My eye, she thought bitterly, and, looking anywhere but at Leon, she realised a good percentage of her guests were watching them with avid curiosity. Damn the man! 'I don't know what you want to discuss that can't wait until Monday, but you were right; the study would be better.'

'There now, Phoebe.' A large arm fell across her shoulders and urged her through the press of bodies towards the door. 'I knew you would see it my way in the end.'

Once in the relative peace of the elegant oak-panelled hall, Bea shrugged off Leon's guiding arm. 'I do know where the study is. This is my home.' She mocked him, walking towards the large door to the rear of the sweeping staircase with Leon a step behind her.

'True, but the bird is about to fly the nest at last.' He sighed, with a hint of irritation in his deep voice. 'Which is why we need to talk about your entrance into the wider world of London, and work.'

Bea glanced up at his handsome face; he looked older. A few lines crinkled at the corners of his black eyes, and more bracketed his sensuous mouth. And was that grey she spied in the thick black hair swept back behind his ear? Yet he could still have wowed the whole of the feminine population. Inexplicably she felt a sudden tenderness sweep through her for the man—after all, he had been a good friend once. Maybe they could be friends again.

Leon's long arm reached over her head and pushed open the panelled study door. He stood aside for her to enter. Bea walked in and breathed deeply. She loved this room, and even after all this time she still imagined the spirit of her father lingered in the air. It was a library-cum-study—a room where the man of the house could relax.

'I always loved this room,' Leon remarked, glancing about him appreciatively, and then, closing and locking the heavy door behind him, he gestured towards the sofa. 'Sit down.'

Bea seated herself stiffly on the edge of the sofa and tried not to look as nervous as she felt. 'So what is it that's so vital it can't wait until Monday?' she said in a rush. Suddenly being alone in a locked room with Leon seemed vaguely threatening. Bea watched as he strolled past her to lean one arm on the mantelpiece, tall, elegant and completely at ease, while her own nerves were stretched to breaking point.

'You are extraordinarily like your mother,' he remarked, ignoring her question, his glance flicking to fix intently upon her. His dark eyes slid over her with the sensual thoroughness of a professional womaniser. 'You have grown into an incredibly attractive woman, but then I always knew you would.'

'Really, Leon, if you've brought me in here to practise your chat-up lines, forget it… I'm immune to your brand of charm,' she lied, with a hint of mockery in her voice. 'Been there, done that, worn the tee-shirt.'

'Not strictly true, darling. I never actually did it with you,' he shot back, his sensuous mouth curved in a mocking smile. 'But who knows? I might oblige you some time, if you ask me nicely.'

Bea's colour deepened at the sexist comment, but she said nothing. Leon was the most extraordinary man she had ever known. He made no secret of what he wanted from a woman and yet he had them queuing up to share his bed. But she was determined not to be added to his long list of conquests. She'd had a lucky escape three years ago, and she needed to keep reminding herself of the fact.

'I'll take your silence as a compliment and live in hope,' Leon chuckled, and, after straightening up, in two lithe strides he was beside her. 'You're right, of course. I really do not have time for flirtation at the minute.' Dropping onto a sofa, he half turned to face her, suddenly all business. 'The company jet is waiting for me at Newcastle airport. I have to be in New York tomorrow, hence the detour to see you.'

Bea stared at him. 'You're incredible.' She shook her head in amazement.

'I know, Phoebe,' he drawled, with an element of seduction in his deep voice. He couldn't help himself, Bea thought wryly, fighting to suppress a grin.

'But enough about me. It is you we have to concentrate on. I will not be in the London office for at least the next two weeks, which presents me with something of a dilemma. I did want to be there for your first day with the company, but it is simply not possible. However, I have talked to Tom Jordan and everything is organised for your arrival. But first...' Slipping his hand into his inside jacket pocket, he withdrew a document and a pen. 'The reason for my whistlestop visit. Your official entry into the adult world.' Placing the parchment paper on her knee, he indicated where she was to sign. 'As of midnight tonight my trusteeship ends and you are the outright owner of thirty per cent of the company. Free and clear.'

'Oh! I see.' Taking the pen, she scribbled her signature where he indicated. So he had not called simply because it was her birthday, and now the conservative suit made sense. For a brief moment Bea felt a swift stab of something very like disappointment. She quickly dismissed the notion. Good heavens! It was a relief, surely, that she would not have to be around Leon. Hadn't she been dreading the thought of meeting him only half an hour ago? But as he continued speaking her relief was overtaken by a rising anger.

'I have arranged with Tom Jordan, the manager of the London office, for you to start work as an assistant to his PA, Margot. You'll like her, she's a great woman, and she knows almost as much as Tom about the workings of the office. Another plus—she also has an apartment in the same building where your father used to live when he was in town. I take it you will be using your father's apartment? So you will not be alone at all. You'll have a friend—'

'Wait just a minute,' Bea interrupted angrily. At another time she might have found the startled expression in his dark eyes amusing, but right now she was too furious. 'As of now I own a large slice of Stephen-Gregoris.' Shoving the document back at him to emphasise her point, she continued, 'And as such I have no intention of starting work as an assistant to somebody else's personal assistant. I have not spent the last three years of my life studying to end up as some office junior. I am no longer the little girl you knew. I am an intelligent woman who intends to take an active part in my late father's company. Junior partner, yes… Anything else, I don't want to know.'

Her blue eyes, glittering with anger, flicked over his impassive countenance, and then wildly around the room. 'Put that in your pipe and smoke it, Mr Leon Gregoris,' she quipped, probably because her glance had caught her father's pipestand, she realised. And instantly she wished she could take the childish words back. But she could not believe the cheek of the man… No discussion, no asking her opinion—typical Leon. Do this! Live there! Have this friend!

'So the kitten has developed claws,' Leon said softly, and, slipping the document into his pocket, he turned more fully to face her. But his eyes narrowed to slits of anger when he saw her furious blue gaze resting on him. 'Damn it, Phoebe, don't be so stupid. There is no way a girl of twenty-one, however brilliant, can walk into a company as a partner. I run the business, and I have made you a wealthy woman in the process. Content yourself with that. In fact you don't need to work at all. But, if you must, it has got to be the way I say.'

'No way,' she spat back.

His hands snaked out and tightened around her slender wrists, and she felt the pressure of his fingers biting into her flesh. Her pulse raced, but with anger, not passion, she told herself. She looked into his hard face and recognised the resolute expression there, but she refused to be intimidated by it.

'My way. Understand?' he said tersely.

'Oh, yes, I understand very well, Leon. Keep little Phoebe in her place or she's out of the business altogether. So you can remain the absolute dictator, the tyrant you have always been. My God! You were even prepared to marry me once, simply to keep your all-powerful position, until I wised up to what you were after.' As soon as the words left her mouth she knew she had gone too far.

His black eyes widened in astonishment, and then narrowed in anger as the import of what she had said registered in his astute brain. 'You little bitch!' he exclaimed. 'At last the truth is coming out. You broke our engagement not because I was too old—your desertion had nothing to do with my age,' Leon snarled, and, jerking at her hands, he dragged her across his lap. 'You actually thought I was trying to control your share of the company. You simply did not trust me.'

He'd got that right! Bea thought, and almost laughed at the incredulous expression in his dark eyes. But her own position was far from safe, so she bit down any response.

'My God, I should give you the good hiding you deserve. But, as you were at pains to point out, you're a woman now.' Twisting her around, he pushed her flat on her back on the sofa. 'A more adult punishment is called for.'

Confusion replaced her earlier anger and she could

hear the thunder of her own heartbeat. She saw his expression as he bent over her. 'No!' she cried, and then his face became a twisted blur as his hand tangled in her long hair and his hard mouth fastened on hers in a long, grinding kiss.

Bea fought against him with all the strength she possessed. Her small hands pushed at his mighty shoulders, and when that had no effect she dug her fingers into the nape of his neck. He retaliated by rearing back. With his free hand he grasped the front of her dress, and in a second it was down around her waist and his hand was clasping one firm breast.

She gasped, and, taking full advantage of her parted lips, his mouth covered hers again, his tongue plunging into its sweet, dark cavern. His full weight came down on top of her and long fingers nipped the perfect bud of her breast, teasing it into hard, pulsing life. Electric sensations shuddered through her even as she bucked beneath him, trying to throw him off. But she was no match for his superior size and strength, and, worse, when his kisses changed to a tempting fiery passion, she was helpless to resist.

His mouth never left hers but his hands were everywhere, stroking, teasing, tormenting. His muscled leg moved over her thigh and she felt the full pressure of his masculine arousal hard against her flesh… Her *flesh*!

Her passion-dulled mind came alive to what was happening. The lamé dress was now little more than a belt around her waist, and alarm returned to give her the motivation to fight. She lifted her hand and deliberately raked her long nails down the side of his face.

'What the hell—?' As he reared back she took her chance and slid from under him onto the floor. She didn't care what she looked like, and, struggling to her knees, she hauled up the front of her dress, then stood up and tugged down the skirt.

She backed away from where he sat rubbing his hand against his cheek. Her breasts heaving and her face flushed, she watched him warily. He looked down in amazement at the blood on his hand, and then back up to fix Bea with glittering black eyes.

'You little vixen. You drew blood!'

'Serves you right—you attacked me.' She had no idea how aroused or how young she looked to the seated man, or how beautiful. She was still reeling from the totally unexpected explosion of passion between them, and her own shameful reaction to Leon.

For a long moment they simply stared at each other, the sexual tension in the air almost tangible.

Leon finally broke the contact. He looked down at the floor and said quietly, 'Yes, I did, and I apologise.'

Bea's bewildered blue eyes searched his handsome face; Leon apologising was unheard of. 'You apologise?' she queried, as if she didn't believe what she was hearing.

'Yes, a hundred times over.' He glanced at her with a look in his eyes that she could not fathom. 'I am a lot older than you and I should have more control. But in all the years we have known each other it never once entered my head that you did not trust me.'

Bea, for some unknown reason, found it hard to look him in the eye. Yet he had made no attempt to deny her accusation. So why did she feel ashamed? It was Leon who should be ashamed, for having tried to trick a grieving teenager. But she doubted he knew the meaning of the word 'ashamed'. Leon moved through life supremely confident of his own abilities, a ruthless predator, cut-throat in business, overpowering the opposition with ar-

rogant ease. And, Bea realised, he was just as ruthless
in his private life.

He shrugged his broad shoulders, dismissing the question of trust, and ran his hands through his dishevelled
hair, sweeping it back from his brow. 'Also, Phoebe, I
should have explained in more detail your position in
the company.' He glanced at the slim gold Rolex on his
wrist and grimaced.

'I was in too much of a hurry. But please try and
understand, you will not be working as the office junior.
Tom and Margot have strict instructions to show you
every aspect of the London office and how the company
works. You will get to know all the staff we employ
there personally. Your job description as a PAA is modest enough, so they will not resent you. But if you insist
on walking in and declaring you're a part owner, and
also insist on starting as a junior partner, there is bound
to be resentment. Do you want that? The snide remarks
about nepotism at work? Perhaps even publicity in the
press?'

Bea had not thought about it from that angle, but she
realised Leon had a valid point. 'No, no, I don't,' she
said quietly.

'I didn't think you would. That is why I made the
arrangements I did. Only Tom and Margot know your
true status in the company, but it is up to you if you
want to tell everyone else. Personally, I only wanted to
give you some protection, at least for your first few
months in a working environment. I had hoped to be
able to stay in England for a few weeks, but it simply
is not possible.

'Branching out into the USA and the Far East in the
past few years has been a great success, but I seem to
spend most of my time jetting between New York, Hong
Kong and Athens—as you must know by the company

reports you receive.' He glanced at her, black eyes capturing blue. 'You do read them?' he asked with a smile, and her heart gave a curious lurch in her chest at the sight of it.

'Yes, of course.' She smiled back and took a step towards him. Leon was right. Since taking over the company he had expanded its business enormously. It had been successfully floated on the London Stock Exchange, but their two families still retained sixty per cent of the shares, thus ensuring that it remained a family concern. Leon's name was regularly featured in the financial newspapers all over the world, and the meteoric rise of Stephen-Gregoris as a leading international company was constantly remarked upon. As for the tabloid newspapers, they had nicknamed him the ''Swashbuckling Tycoon''—probably because when he'd first come to their notice, in his mid-twenties, he'd worn his hair in a ponytail.

'You're right,' she admitted. 'It was stupid of me to think I could walk into the firm as a partner. I realise that now. But I do want to learn everything, and perhaps eventually I can visit the overseas offices too, maybe even work in one.' The more she thought about it, the more she liked the idea. 'Maybe this time next year it will be me going to New York.'

'Why not?' Leon stood up and, crossing to where she stood, once more took her hands in his. 'Next week London, next year the world.'

Bea tilted her head back to look up into his face, her expression serious. 'Are you teasing, or do you really think I can do it?' she asked, in a voice that was surprisingly calm considering the way the pulses in her wrists were racing beneath his fingers.

He released her hands and dropped a swift kiss on the

top of her head. 'I think, Phoebe, you will do whatever you set your mind to, and the world had better look out.'

'You as well.' She grinned up at him, mischief dancing in her eyes. 'I might decide I want your job.'

Leon's mouth twitched, and then he chuckled. 'You're some woman, Phoebe.' He shook his dark head, still smiling. 'But I really must be going.' Withdrawing a small velvet box from his trouser pocket, he dropped it into her hand. 'Happy birthday, and good luck on Monday. I'll be in touch.' Turning, he started for the door.

'Wait. I'll see you out.' She hurried after him, but he stopped her with a hand on her shoulder.

'Not a good idea, Phoebe, unless you want your friends to get the wrong idea.'

'My friends?' He had lost her; she didn't know what he meant.

'Have a look in the mirror before mingling again, darling…' Leon drawled softly, and after unlocking the door he went, his laughter ringing in her ears.

Standing where Leon had left her, Bea slowly opened the box. Inside was a delicate pendant, a deep blue sapphire surrounded by diamonds, ringed in gold and suspended on a gold chain. After fastening the chain around her neck, she picked up the pendant and gazed at it in wonder. Leon was an incredibly generous but infuriating man.

CHAPTER TWO

STILL bemused by Leon's present, Bea wondered why he had not stopped to see her open it. What had he said? 'Look in the mirror!' Bea mumbled to herself, quietly slipping out of the study. She quickly dived into the cloakroom—luckily free.

One look in the mirror above the vanity basin, and the pendant was forgotten. Instead she wanted to die of shame. Her blonde hair was a tangled mess around her face—a very flushed face—and the remains of once red lipgloss were smeared over her skin, but none of it on her lips—lips that were unmistakably swollen. Worse, the dress she had hastily pulled up after escaping from Leon on the sofa clung decorously over one breast, then slanted down over the other, revealing the dark areola around her nipple to the world.

Bea groaned out loud. Never again would she wear the silver Spandex creation, she vowed. No wonder Leon had told her to look in the mirror. But the swine could have told her earlier about the dress, instead of feasting his eyes and having a good laugh at her expense. To think she had actually been considering they could be friends again!

Splashing her face with cold water, and tidying herself up as best she could, she felt a humourless laugh escape her. Would she never learn where Leon was concerned? He had arrived, got her to agree to what he wanted, and left... As for her birthday present, to a man of Leon's wealth, the pendant was a mere trinket.

She knew she was being irrational. She was a very

wealthy woman herself. But somehow she never thought of herself as such. Her parents, because they'd been from the north, had always lived there, though her father often stayed in London. As a child Bea had known they were comfortably off, but never thought much about it. And since Leon had taken over the running of the company, and then since the death of her father, she hadn't liked to think how much she was worth. It seemed indecent when she had done nothing for it. Which was another reason for her going to work in London. She felt it her duty...

Two o'clock in the morning, and she leant against the front doorframe, grateful for the breath of cool air and the support. She was dead beat. With a sigh of relief she closed the door, locked and bolted it. At last she was alone...

The caterers had cleaned up and left ten minutes earlier. Aunty Lil and Uncle Bob would have nothing to complain about when they arrived back in the morning from their night out in the city. She hoped they'd had a better time than she'd had...

Some party, she thought moodily, making her way up to the sanctuary of her bedroom, removing the sapphire pendant as she went. What should have been a great night in her life had turned out to be a horror, all because of Leon Gregoris. She supposed she should be thankful he had left early, and she was no longer going to have to face him in London on Monday. But somehow that thought gave her no consolation.

Walking into her bedroom and closing the door behind her, she slipped out of the silver dress and, clad in only the briefest of lace briefs, dropped the pendant on the dressing table. For a moment she looked at it, her eyes narrowing; it looked vaguely familiar. Yawning widely, she dismissed the thought and, picking up her cotton nightie from the end of the bed, headed for the *en suite* bathroom. Five minutes later, her toilet complete, she slid into bed. Pulling the pink duvet up to her chin, she closed her eyes and welcomed sleep.

But it was not to be. The dark face of Leon appeared in her mind's eye; she traced her swollen lips with one finger. She could still feel his kiss, the taste of him. Nothing she did would displace his image from her brain.

Turning restlessly, she lay flat on her back and opened her eyes. She didn't want to think about the past; there were too many painful memories, and Leon's reappearance tonight had reawakened a lot of them. The trace of a smile twitched her lips. She recalled the first time her father had sent her to this very room for being naughty. That had been Leon's fault...

It had been a Saturday, just like today—or last night, she amended. Bea had been eight years of age, and her father had had visitors for the weekend: Mr Gregoris and his son. Having spent all day with adults, she'd been bored.

But at about seven o'clock in the evening she had slipped out of the gate at the bottom of the garden, something she was strictly forbidden to do. She had met two older boys from the village, Jack and Ned, and they had allowed her to play with them. Cowboys and Indians, and—wouldn't you know!—as the girl she'd got to be the Indian, captured by the cowboys, and Jack had tied her to a tree.

It had been when Ned had withdrawn a knife from his trouser pocket, saying, 'Now try some of your own medicine and see how you like it,' and grabbed her long hair prior to scalping her, that she'd begun to scream. That was how Leon had found her.

At twenty-two he'd already been a man, dressed in shorts and singlet, obviously out for his evening run. He'd pulled the two boys apart, one in each hand, shaken them and sent them sprawling on their backsides. Then he'd untied Bea and lifted the terrified little girl into his arms.

She remembered clutching him around the neck, resting her head on his chest and between sobs and hiccups telling him he was wonderful for saving her. He'd been her hero, this big, dark man with a ponytail as long as hers. At least, she'd thought so for all of ten minutes, until he'd started lecturing her on how little girls should behave. But, worse, he'd actually told her father, and she'd been sent to her room without any supper.

Looking back, Bea could see that had been the start of the love-hate relationship she shared with Leon. She had not seen a lot of him after that; his father, her dad's business partner, had been a frequent visitor, but Leon had come maybe two or three times a year, some years not even as much as that. When she had seen him he was always nice to her, though he could be a bit bossy. But then she'd thought of him as an adult friend, and most adults were bossy...

Old Mr Gregoris had died when Bea was eleven. She could remember her father going to Cyprus for the funeral, but she hadn't gone. After that Leon had come on his own to visit her father, but as often as not they'd met in London.

Then, when she'd reached her teens and begun to read the more lurid tabloids that Aunty Lil was so fond of, she'd discovered Leon was quite notorious for his ladyfriends. His procession of women was well documented, and once, as a fifteen-year-old, she had teased him about it. Leon had told her not to believe everything she read

in the papers. He had for once lost his sense of humour
and had appeared quite upset.

Bea suddenly realised that this had been the last time
Leon had visited her home until the death of her own
father. Leon had appeared at his graveside on a bleak
January day and held her hand. He had been a tower of
strength to a very sad and frightened seventeen-year-old.
Having lost his own father earlier, he'd seemed to understand exactly how she felt.

Back at the house Leon had taken charge, explaining
her inheritance, insisting she complete her final year at
school, and making sure Lil and Bob would look after
her—though there had never been any doubt. Leon had
left after a week, due to pressure of business, but had
promised to return at the Easter vacation. True to his
word, he had. But it had been a different Leon...

Before Bea had seen him as a sort of jocular uncle—
a friend but an adult male. Then suddenly he'd begun to
treat her as a grown-up. When he had arrived she had
greeted him with the usual peck on the cheek, and to her
amazement he had grasped her around the waist.

'Surely at nearly eighteen you can do better than that,
Phoebe? I can see I'm going to have to educate you,'
he'd said, and covered her lips with his own.

From then on when he'd looked at her it had been
with a blatant male appreciation for a desirable female.
When he'd touched her his hands had lingered just a
fraction too long, and when he'd kissed her her legs had
turned to jelly.

Bea shivered and pulled the duvet tightly around her.
She had been such a naive young fool, and had lapped
it all up.

But Leon had played his part to perfection. He was a
man whose devastating charm and sophistication could
make the hardest-headed businesswoman feel gauche,

and he had turned the full force of his dynamic personality upon the young Bea. She'd been in awe of him.

The public success of the company since Leon had taken over was well documented. From a small import-export firm, Stephen-Gregoris had now developed into a force to be reckoned with in the world market. Leon had made them both millionaires, as he had casually pointed out on the last day of his visit...

It was a lovely spring day. A car was arriving at noon to take Leon to the airport; he would fly back to London and then on to Athens. Seated opposite him at the table in the breakfast room, Bea was feeling sad at the thought of Leon's departure; the past five days had been wonderful.

Last night he had taken her out to dinner at Twenty-One, an exclusive restaurant in Newcastle. On arriving home he had led her into the living room and pulled her down onto the couch beside him. She had snuggled up against his side with a sigh of pure contentment.

'Happy, sweetheart?' Leon had asked, and, not waiting for a reply, had turned her in his arms and kissed her. A long time later he'd raised his head and shifted slightly to look into her flushed, trusting face.

'There's something I want to ask you, Phoebe. I know...' And that had been when Lil had walked in.

'I heard you arrive so I've brought you coffee.'

Bea had not been pleased at the interruption. She'd had a sneaky suspicion that Lil was acting as a chaperone, and she'd been sure of it when the older woman had sat down and poured the coffee into three cups before asking about their evening out. An hour later Bea had gone to bed, still wondering...

Now, seated with Leon at the breakfast table, Bea sighed and drained her cup of coffee, her blue eyes resting wistfully on the top of his dark head. He was apparently oblivious to her presence, reading the morning paper. Whatever he had been going to ask her last night, he had obviously forgotten it this morning, she thought morosely. In a few hours he would be gone and it was back to studying for her, for her A level exams. A place at the University of Newcastle upon Tyne was waiting for her, providing she passed them.

'Don't look so sad. It might never happen.' Leon's deep voice cut into her morbid thoughts.

Glancing across at him, she almost said, It already has; you're leaving. But, young as she was, she had the sense to keep her true feelings to herself, and instead said, 'But it will... Exams start in six weeks' time; it's nose to the grindstone time for me. Whereas you will be flitting around the world, chatting up every beautiful woman you meet.' She tried for a teasing smile but it did not quite come off.

Her innate common sense told her Leon had simply been flirting with her the past few days. There was no way a man like him could really be interested in her on a personal level. He was kind to her because of their fathers' relationship, and because technically they were now business partners—though the reality was that Leon was her trustee, along with Mr Nicholson, her late father's lawyer, until she was twenty-one.

'Jealous, Phoebe?' he teased back, and, putting the newspaper down on the table, he stood up. 'There is no need.'

He was tall, well over six feet, and incredibly handsome; he had to be nearly thirty-two now. Far too old for her. But he looked so vitally male, so elegant in his immaculate, conservative three-piece suit, and yet subtly powerful and superbly healthy—which, given his lifestyle, was something of a miracle. If the papers were to be believed, he played as hard as he worked. Fascinated, Bea watched as he strolled around the table and reached out a hand to her.

'Come on, sweet Phoebe, a walk before I leave. And hopefully we will escape your guardian angel Lil for a while.'

Bea put her hand in his and was pulled to her feet. Five minutes later Leon, still holding her hand, opened the garden gate with his other hand, and then guided her onto the path.

They talked of her exams, her university course, her ambitions. It was only when they were out of sight of the house that Leon suddenly stopped a few feet away from a large willow tree.

'The infamous tree where you were held captive,' he declared, and grinned down at her.

Bea tilted her head back. She laughed up at him. 'Yes, and I haven't forgotten I got no supper. Because of you, I was confined to my room.'

His dark eyes narrowed for a moment on her young, girlish figure. She was wearing figure-hugging blue jeans and a blue sweatshirt. Her high, firm breasts, clearly defined against the soft fabric, made it obvious she wore no bra. Leon dropped her hand and curved an arm around her waist, pulling her against his lower torso. 'I wish I could confine you to my room.'

She looked at him, thrilled by his statement, but all her youthful uncertainty was reflected in her wide blue eyes. 'Why?' she asked.

'For heaven's sake! Don't look at me like that. You make me feel like… Never mind…' Leon hesitated, then walked on until they were at the tree. Leaning his back against the trunk, legs splayed, he turned her loosely in the circle of his arms, so she was standing between his hard-muscled thighs.

The light touch of his hands on her waist and the subtle male scent of him both conspired to make her heart leap in her chest. She wanted to move forward, just a fraction, enough to make contact with his hard body, to have that proud head bend and his firm mouth on hers. She didn't know herself. Bea had never felt like this with any man before. Only Leon had the power to turn her into a quivering heap of over-active nerves, passions, feelings…whatever! She only knew his virile masculine aura was such that it promised everything a female could desire, with the certainty that he could deliver…

'Did you ever see either of those two little monsters again?'

'What?' She jumped as his question cut into her overheated thoughts. 'Yes, as a matter of fact I did.'

Leon sent her a mocking glance. 'Not here, I hope. Surely you weren't stupid enough to be caught twice?'

If Leon had one fault, Bea thought mutinously, it was arrogance. He was so clever, of such towering intellect, he tended to think other people were dumb.

'No, actually. Jack, the older of the two—not the one who was about to scalp me—' she clarified, 'is a good friend. He's in his second year at Oxford, and doing well, already a rugby blue. We went to a couple of parties together when he was home for the Christmas break; we have the same friends. I got a card from him last week. He's spending the Easter break in Switzerland. He's also a keen skier—in fact an all-round sportsman.' As she spoke what she had wished for earlier happened.

Leon slipped one arm completely around her waist and hauled her hard against him. With his free hand he clasped her chin and tilted her face up to his.

'Is he now?' His lips were quirking as he cast her a curious glance. 'Well, I hope he breaks a leg.'

'Leon! That's rotten.'

'No, realistic,' he returned with a laugh. 'If anyone is going to tie you up ever again, it's going to be me.' And, swinging around, it was suddenly Bea who had her back against the tree.

'You wouldn't, and anyway you have no rope,' she shot back.

'Who needs one?' Leon murmured, and, fastening her to the tree with the pressure of his large body, his dark head bent and his lips brushed softly over hers. 'Will you let me tie you to me, Phoebe?' he asked huskily, his teeth nibbling her bottom lip while his hand clasped the nape of her neck and held her head firm. He scattered kisses over her brow, her eyes, her cheekbones, and back down to her softly parted lips.

She was helpless against his gentle persuasion as he trailed kisses down her throat, and then his hand cupped her breast through the thickness of her sweater, his thumb unerringly finding its rigid tip and squeezing ever so slowly. 'Will you be tied to me, metaphorically speaking, my own sweet Phoebe? Will you be my wife?'

Of course she said yes. She said yes to everything he suggested. Their engagement would be a secret until she had finished school, and on her eighteenth birthday, in August, he would take her to the family villa in Cyprus and declare it to the world. They would marry a few weeks later and, if she liked, she could still go to university.

Bea sailed through her last term at school. Her grief at losing her father at the beginning of the year still lingered, but her love for Leon and knowing he loved her somehow made everything better. She even applied herself to her exams with a new-found vigour.

Leon telephoned every other night, wherever in the world he happened to be, and with his support and encouragement she blossomed into a confident young woman. She did have one slight argument with him in June: school was to finish in July and she wanted to join him immediately afterwards, but Leon said no. But the 'no' was tempered the next day by the arrival of a huge bouquet of red roses, and the following day came a loving letter from America, explaining the difficulties of his schedule but promising to be in England the week before her birthday—mid-August.

One morning in August Bea stood in the hall, an envelope addressed to herself in her own handwriting in her hand. 'Lil, they're here!' she yelled. Her exam results.

'Well, open it, dear,' Lil commanded, joining her. 'They won't alter for the waiting, pet.'

With trembling fingers she slit open the envelope, took one glance and then she was whirling Lil around the hall in a wild polka. 'I've passed! I've passed! Four straight As.'

To make her happiness complete, after spending two hours on the telephone calling all her friends, Leon arrived. She was still on the telephone when a deep voice murmured in her free ear, 'Miss me, Phoebe?'

Bea squeaked, 'Got to go,' and dropped the receiver on the hall table. A strong arm encircled her waist and turned her around. 'Leon, you're back,' she murmured inanely, suddenly inexplicably nervous.

Leon's hand cupped her chin and tilted her head back as his dark eyes scrutinised her lovely face. 'Is that the best you can do in the way of a welcome, Phoebe, darling?' he drawled mockingly. 'Months apart and you say "you're back"?'

'One hundred and thirty-two days, actually.' Bea glanced at her watch, 'And twenty-two hours.' Wrapping her slender arms around his neck, with a wide, beautiful smile curving her full lips, she added, 'I have missed you during every one of them.'

A long, satisfying kiss later, Bea gazed dazedly into Leon's dark eyes. 'I wasn't expecting you until tomorrow.'

'Change of plan—I have to be in Athens tomorrow.' Leon spent the next ten minutes explaining why, but Bea barely took it in. She was too entranced to have him beside her, to hear his voice, to be able to feast her eyes on his large, all-male body.

Her happy, dazed state lasted until the aeroplane touched down at Athens airport, and beyond...

Sighing, Bea let the paperback book, number one on the *New York Times* bestseller list, fall to the ground beside the sun lounger on which she was reclining. She didn't seem able to get interested in anything today.

Leon's villa was set high on the hills above Paphos, in the Greek sector of the island of Cyprus. The view before her was magnificent: an enticingly cool-looking swimming pool and beyond it the garden, flowing down the hillside in a mass of flowers and shrubs, the whole enclosed by an undulating white wall. Beyond, in the far distance, the ancient port of Paphos and its magnificent fortress stood by the Mediterranean Sea.

Her only garment was a minuscule bikini, and yet the heat was still stifling. Glancing at her half-naked body, she hauled herself into a sitting position and idly picked up a bottle of sun lotion and began massaging it into her arms and legs, across her flat stomach. The trouble was, she thought wryly, it wasn't so much the heat outside that was making her so restless, but the heat within her.

Last night had been wonderful. Leon had held a huge party and they had become officially engaged. A tiny smile pursed her lips as she twisted the magnificent diamond and sapphire ring on the third finger of her left hand. Every time she looked at it she got a lump in her throat, not just for its beauty, but for what it represented.

Her engagement party had been perfect; she had danced the night away in the arms of the man she loved, the man she was going to marry, and she had met all of Leon's friends and his stepmother, Tany, who seemed a very nice lady. But Tany's daughter by her first marriage, Amy, Bea was not so sure about, and Amy's friend from America, Selina, Bea had certainly not taken to. The woman had given her the most peculiar look, and a positively evil smile. Still, all in all it had been a great party.

Bea sighed again, and lay back down. She only had one slight niggle—and she knew she was being stupid— but… After the guests had left, and the house guests had retired for the night, finally she and Leon had been alone. He had walked her to her bedroom door and taken her into his arms.

Her eyes fluttered closed—just for a moment—as she relived the sensations his kiss had aroused. Her lips had quivered beneath the light touch of his mouth, then he had lazily nibbled her bottom lip, his tongue exploring when her mouth opened to him. Her hands, of their own accord, had moved up his arms to cling to his broad shoulders, glorying in the strength of his taut muscles and the power of his broad frame. He'd deepened the kiss with an ease and sensuality that had made her whole body burn with a trembling need that reached the very core of her being.

She'd murmured his name: 'Leon.' At last they were engaged, and the bed was just behind the door. Her firm young body had arched into him, the power of his arousal against her pelvis making her ache with frustration.

'No, Phoebe,' he'd murmured against her lips. 'Ten days is not too long to wait.' He'd eased her away from him. 'I want you to have a perfect wedding, and a perfect wedding night. You deserve it. And that means keeping my desire under control until then.'

Sighing for the third time, Bea rolled over onto her stomach on the lounger. It had been a noble sentiment on Leon's part, but had done nothing for the frustration burning inside her… With her head resting on her folded arms, she dozed off…

She raised her head groggily and turned onto her back, not sure what had awakened her. The lounger, placed as it was near the house, was now in the shade. 'Thank goodness for that,' she muttered to herself, realising she could have been burned to a crisp. Then she heard it again. Her name being called from inside the villa.

Good, Leon was back. He had gone into Paphos to see someone on business earlier. She was just about to stand up and make her whereabouts known when another voice floated from the open window not three yards away.

'Looking for your proposed child bride, Leon, darling?' It was Selina, the American girl, who spoke. 'I don't think you'll be in such a hurry to find her after you hear what I have to say.'

'Selina, there is nothing you have to say that I want to hear.'

'Leon, don't be like this. This is me, Selina, you're talking to. Your lover for the last three years. You can't fool me.' A shuffling sound followed.

Bea gasped and, raising her hand to her mouth, she bit hard on her knuckle to stifle her cry of pain.

'Let go, Selina, you're wasting your time. I told you it was over months ago. You career women are all the same. You say you are equal to a man in every way, and you willingly enter into an open relationship, quite clearly defined, mutual pleasure only. Then, as soon as you are told it is over, instead of acting like a man and walking away, you revert to sniffling feminine tricks.'

'Please, Leon, you have to listen to me. I know you care for me—you can't possibly love that schoolgirl. Even your stepmother said your engagement was more about cementing the business partnership firmly under your complete control than about any love on your part.'

'My reasons are my own, Selina, and are not up for discussion. Now get out of my way and stay out of it.'

'That might be hard to do. Especially in seven months' time when our child is born.'

'Impossible, and anyway I always use protection—mainly to prevent just this type of blackmail. Do yourself a favour and leave, before I have you thrown out.'

Bea could not believe her ears. This was a Leon she had never heard before: hard and totally ruthless. But worse was to follow.

'Aren't you forgetting something, Leon? Two months ago, at the Mackenzies' house party in Newport? You flew in, partied half the night, and woke up in the morning in my bed. Protection was not something you bothered about. I know; I was there...'

For a long moment there was silence. Then, 'You bitch, Selina. You did it deliberately. Didn't you?'

Bea didn't hear the rest of the conversation. She had heard enough. Staggering to her feet, she silently crept around the outside of the house and entered by the kitchen. She took the servants' stairs to her room and once inside locked the door. She collapsed on the bed, but could not cry. She was too traumatised for tears. Instead she stared blankly at the white walls, asking herself over and over again, How could I have been such a fool?

CHAPTER THREE

BEA had been used, exploited by the first man she had ever let near her. Before Leon she had dated a few boys of her own age, and exchanged the odd fumbled kiss, but nothing like the passionate interludes Leon had introduced her to. She should have realised a sophisticated, sexually mature man like Leon couldn't possibly be interested in a naive young girl such as herself unless he had an ulterior motive. But she had blindly agreed with everything Leon had said. She'd even put up with him calling her Phoebe, when she much preferred Bea...

Nausea clawed at her stomach; the sense of betrayal ate into her very being. That she could be so wrong about a man she had known almost all her life, a man she would have trusted *with* her life, made her burn with shame at her own gullibility.

She thumped the bed with her clenched fists and shouted out loud, 'Fool, fool, fool!' Then the tears came. Bea cried until she had no tears left, and her throat was raw and dry. Finally she slowly sat up. She had no idea how long she had been in the bedroom, but it was already getting dark. Confirmation, if she needed any more, of how little Leon actually thought of her.

On his return to the villa, his eager calling of her name had roused her from sleep. But since his conversation with Selina he certainly hadn't bothered trying to find Bea again.

She heaved herself off the bed and walked into the bathroom. One look in the mirror, and if she could have cried again she would have. Red-rimmed, swollen eyes stared out of a face as white as a ghost's. She had no idea how she was going to face Leon ever again.

Stripping off her bikini, she stepped into the shower and turned on the cold water. She stood beneath the freezing spray, praying it would numb her body and brain, but it was no good. The image of Leon and Selina together tortured her mind. Three years… They had been lovers for three years, and they were having a baby together. She heard again Leon's furious outburst: 'You did it deliberately.' And that was what hurt most of all.

Leon hadn't tried to deny the child was his. He was simply furious at being caught by the oldest trick in the book. Bea stepped out of the shower, wrapped a towel around herself and walked back into the bedroom. She stopped by the dressing table, pulled the diamond ring off her finger and dropped it on the polished surface. Her engagement ring. What a joke! While she had considered herself engaged since Easter, when Leon had asked her to marry him and she had said yes, he had obviously felt no such commitment. He had continued sleeping with his long-time lover.

It was not so surprising, really, she thought as mechanically she set about getting dressed. She had always known Leon was the Lothario type, but in her youthful naivety she had let herself believe she was the one person who could change him. A hollow laugh escaped her. She remembered last night and their impassioned kisses, and then his denial of what she had quite obviously been offering, his high moral stance. He wanted her to have the perfect wedding, and wedding night. What a lie!

Sadly Bea realised he probably didn't even want her in a sexual way. No, what he wanted was control of her share of the company. With that thought her sorrow began to change, and by the time she was standing in front of the mirror once more, about to put on her make-up, she wasn't sad but mad... Mad with a cold fury. Then it came to her—a way to escape with her pride intact and without revealing what she knew.

In the end it was simple. Bea walked into the dining room, not a scrap of make-up on her pale face, her long hair tied up in a childish ponytail and wearing the simple blue and white candy-striped dress she had included in her luggage, thinking it would come in useful if she were messing around. She knew she looked ridiculously young, but that was the idea.

Tany, Leon's stepmother, Amy and Selina were elegantly gowned and already seated at the table. But Leon was standing near the door and crossed straight to Bea's side. He bent his head to kiss her. She saw it coming and deliberately moved so that his lips brushed her cheek and not her mouth.

'Something the matter, Phoebe?' he asked solicitously.

Bea almost snapped back, Yes, you, you snake! But, biting her tongue, she simply turned her face up to his, giving him the full benefit of her red, swollen eyes. 'Not exactly.'

'Please sit down, you two. We want to eat,' Tany commanded.

Leon cast Bea a worried glance, but held out a chair for her and then slid into the one next to her.

It was Tany who noticed first. 'Bea, where is your ring, child? You don't want to lose it. Knowing Leon, it will have cost a fortune. And what has happened to your eyes?'

Dramatically Bea pushed back her chair and jumped to her feet, acting for all she was worth. The last thing she felt like doing was sharing a dinner with this group.

'Please, you will have to excuse me. I'm not hungry.' Glancing down at Leon's upturned face, surprise and puzzlement evident in his expression, she added, 'I really am terribly sorry but it has all been a mistake. I realised this afternoon. It is beautiful here, but I—I am h-homesick.' She deliberately stuttered. 'I miss my friends and Lil, and the cool English summer, and I don't want to get married, not yet.'

A solitary tear rolled down her cheek, lending credit to her story, but in actual fact it was a tear of self-pity, an emotion she despised. Brushing her cheek with the back of her hand, she saw Leon's dark eyes narrow assessingly on her pale face. Then slowly he got to his feet, and tried to put an arm around her shoulders.

'Don't be silly, Phoebe. It's probably just bridal nerves.' He smiled. 'I promise everything will be fine.'

Patronising swine, she thought, and, twisting out from under his arm, she turned to face him.

'It will not be all right because I do not want to marry you. I want to go home and get on with my studies, my life. I'm sorry. I think it was because of my father dying so recently. I needed a father figure, and so I latched onto you. But that is no reason to get married.'

It took every ounce of nerve and self-control Bea possessed to hold Leon's now angry gaze and deliver her final comment. 'I realise now I'm not ready for marriage or commitment. I'm only just eighteen, far too young, and you…well, you're…' She trailed off, not so subtly implying that Leon was too old for her.

It had been the reference to age that had clinched it, Bea mused, safely ensconced on the aeroplane back to England the next day. In her mind's eye she could still see the look of frustrated fury on his darkly handsome face as Selina and Amy had had the temerity to laugh.

True, he had made another attempt to change her mind much later. He had walked into her bedroom and tried, with his sexual expertise, to kiss her into submission.

But knowing his lover Selina was downstairs had given Bea the strength to remain cold in his arms. How long she could have continued doing so was anybody's guess. Because she'd still wanted him, even as she'd hated herself for feeling that way. But the arrival of Tany to check that Bea was all right had stopped Leon cold. And, in Tany's presence, Bea had given him back his ring.

Yawning widely, Bea turned over and curled up into a foetal position. She yawned again. Tomorrow was the first day of the rest of her life. The past was past. Leon was no threat to her peace of mind any more, she told herself groggily. As for her reaction to his kiss earlier, it was simply because she had drunk too much champagne and he had caught her off guard. It would never happen again. Only a fool made the same mistake twice, and at twenty-one, with a degree in her pocket, Bea was nobody's fool…

The drive down to London was not as bad as Bea had expected. The Sunday traffic was light, and she arrived at the underground car park of the mansion block that housed her late father's apartment at five in the evening. It was a simple matter to transfer her two suitcases to the lift, and moments later she was plonking them on the bed in the only bedroom.

Her father had originally had his office in Newcastle, but after the death of Nick Gregoris, and Leon taking the place of his father, the firm had expanded rapidly. The English headquarters had been moved to London, at Leon's instigation. Bea had been twelve when her father had begun travelling to London on a Monday and staying two or three days, safe in the knowledge that Bea was at school all day and Lil was there to look after her.

Glancing around the familiar bedroom, Bea thought

fondly of the times in the school holidays when her dad had taken her to London with him occasionally. With a shake of her fair head, she told herself not to get sentimental, and set about unpacking her belongings.

Ten minutes later she stared in amazement at the kitchen table. Someone had anticipated her arrival. A huge vase full of red roses was at the centre, and propped against it was an envelope. Picking it up, she quickly slit it open and withdrew a sheet of notepaper. She recognised the bold, sloping writing immediately. It was from Leon—a rather childish poem.

> *Enjoy the roses while you may*
> *Tomorrow is a working day.*
> *The fridge is stocked, the larder too*
> *Behave yourself until I'm with you.*

A small smile twitched her full lips; she had forgotten. Almost every time she had seen Leon when she was a child he had made up a stupid rhyme for her. She racked her brain, trying to remember the first one.

> *The lovely lady fair*
> *Almost lost her hair*
> *By playing near a willow*
> *When she should have been asleep on her pillow*

Bea's grin broadened. Leon had been good fun as an uncle figure. Pity their relationship had not stayed that way. The smile faded from her face to be replaced with a frown.

What did he mean, *until I'm with you*? The note fell unnoticed from her hand and quickly she turned around. Bea opened the refrigerator door and was not surprised to see it stocked full, including a bottle of white wine.

The cupboard was the same. Uneasily she walked into the living room and glanced around. Had Leon been here? And, more importantly, how the hell had he got in? She had the only key. Anyway, he was supposed to be in America.

Suddenly the safety of her apartment seemed threatened, and she didn't like it, not one bit… Think, woman, think, she told herself. Of course! A sigh of relief escaped her and she sank down on the sofa. The caretaker had a master key. Leon must have sent the note and instructions to provide the goodies to the caretaker.

Relieved to have the mystery settled, she made full use of the food provided to make herself an omelette and salad, washed down with a glass of wine, then she went to bed.

'Ready to go yet, Bea?'

Bea glanced up and smiled at the tall red-headed girl asking the question. Actually, Margot was a woman in every sense of the word, about thirty-eight years old. As personal assistant to Tom Jordan, she knew everything about the business.

'I thought, if you have nothing special to do tonight, we could stop off for a pizza and a glass of wine or two on the way home.'

'Oh, sorry, Margot, I forgot to mention—I've arranged to meet a boyfriend for dinner and I'm going straight from here.'

'Ah, a heavy date with the male of the species—and you with only two weeks of living in the city. How do you do it?'

Bea grinned. 'His name is Jack, I've known him for years, and he comes from my home town.'

'Interesting, is he?' Margot queried, with a suggestive flicker of her eyebrows.

'Well, he did once tie me up.'

'Bondage… This I must hear. If you get back before eleven pop in and tell me all about him. It's about the only way I get a thrill nowadays. Vicariously.'

'Liar,' Bea chuckled. 'I've heard you on the telephone to a certain financial advisor in the office three floors above us.'

Margot winked. 'Enough said. Tom left half an hour ago, so I'm off. Enjoy yourself.' And, closing the door behind her as she left, Bea heard her shout, 'Don't forget to lock the outer door.'

A lingering smile played around Bea's lips. She could still hear a mumble coming from next door—probably Margot talking to herself. She was prone to speaking her thoughts out loud.

Though Bea hated to admit that Leon could be right about anything, he had been right about Margot becoming a friend. Over the past two weeks the two women had developed a good working relationship, and had also become firm pals.

The offices of Stephen-Gregoris occupied the first floor of a prestigious block in the heart of the city, and, arriving for work on her first day, Bea had naturally felt nervous. A rather superior blonde girl had shown her to what was to be her office, but in fact was a small partitioned section of Margot's much larger one, which in turn led straight to the manager's. Then Margot had walked out of Tom Jordan's office, apologised for not being there to greet her, and had immediately taken Bea under her wing.

Only Tom Jordan and Margot knew Bea owned part of the company, but Margot showed no resentment at the fact. She had taken Bea on a tour of the office, and introduced her to all the staff with the explanation that Bea was the new graduate trainee who was to work in each department for a few weeks to get the feel of the operation and would probably end up in the finance section.

The fact that Margot's apartment was in the same block as Bea's was an added bonus. They'd quickly decided to travel to work together, and had shared the occasional meal or a gossip over coffee.

Stretching, Bea glanced at her watch: it was after six. She was meeting Jack at Covent Garden, a short taxi ride away. Jack had done extremely well for himself; he'd gained a first at Oxford and for the past two years had held a high-profile job with a top merchant bank in London. It would be good fun to catch up on all his news.

With a contented sigh at the completion of the last spreadsheet, Bea switched off her computer terminal and stood up. It was very quiet, but then the building usually emptied early on a Friday.

Bea reckoned she had just enough time for a wash and brush-up, and, with a quick glance around the room, she picked up her bag from the desk, checked she had the office key, and left.

Crossing Margot's office, Bea hesitated. What was that sound she'd heard? She turned and looked around. That's funny, she thought, the door to Tom Jordan's office is half open. It's unlike Margot to forget to lock it.

She waited a moment longer, but everything was quiet, and so, with a shrug of her shoulders, she crossed to where she knew Margot kept a spare key in her desk drawer. And got another surprise. The key was not in the drawer, but lying on the desktop. The woman's mind was slipping; Bea would tease her about it tomorrow.

A couple of seconds later and Bea had closed and locked Tom's door, and the outer one behind her.

Singing softly to herself—she was looking forward to

tonight—Bea headed for the ladies' room. Stephen-Gregoris provided excellent facilities for the female staff. A pleasant restroom with a locker provided for everyone, two shower cubicles and the usual accompaniments. Opening her locker, she withdrew a towel and toilet bag and crossed to the row of vanity basins occupying one wall.

She was not going to change; the smart blue suit, with its double-breasted short-sleeved jacket and short straight skirt, which she had worn all day with a high-necked white blouse, would do for the evening—minus the blouse. Bea removed her jacket and the blouse and hung them on the back of a chair, and then quickly washed and redid her make-up. Slipping the jacket back on, she fastened the buttons and checked her image in the mirror.

She pursed her lips; the deep vee of the jacket lapels maybe revealed a little too much cleavage. She would have to remember not to bend forward and reveal the lace of her bra—or maybe she could remove the bra! What the hell? she told herself. You're in the city now... And she did. Then, rashly, she unpinned her hair from its rather severe chignon and let it fall loose about her shoulders.

Her jacket back in place, she stopped in the act of picking up her hairbrush. Was that someone hurrying down the corridor? Must be Security... Tipping her head forward, she brushed her hair until it crackled with life and then swung it back. The effect was rather good, even if she did say so herself. Having been pinned up all day, her usually straight silver-blonde hair had developed a rather nice bouncy curl around the ends.

A quick spray of her favourite perfume, and she was ready. Quickly she replaced her toiletries in the locker, with her discarded bra and blouse, and with a last look at her reflection she made for the door.

Bea stepped out into the hall. Just at that moment the office door she had so recently locked was flung open. She expected to see a security man, but what she actually saw stopped her in her tracks.

'You—you crazy little bitch. I might have guessed,' Leon Gregoris roared, and came barrelling towards her, a security man hard on his heels, apologising madly.

'Leave it—and us. I will deal with this,' Leon snarled at the poor man, and Bea watched in open-mouthed amazement as the security man disappeared at a run. She turned back just in time to have Leon grab her by the arm. 'I suppose you thought that was funny—a stupid, childish practical joke. My God! Are you never going to grow up?'

Bea shook her head. It was a dream—it had to be. One minute she was in an empty office building, preparing for a date, the next Leon had appeared out of nowhere, breathing fire and brimstone. She hadn't been far wrong when she'd thought he looked like a warlock. She glanced curiously up into his red, furious face; the devil himself might be nearer the mark.

'Well, woman, what have you to say for yourself?'

'I haven't the foggiest notion what you're talking about,' she offered, with another shake of her head. He was dressed in a dark blue suit and white silk shirt, with a maroon silk tie half undone around his neck. The white of his shirt only served to emphasise his darkly flushed features. 'Where did you come from?' she asked in obvious puzzlement.

Hell itself, if the flames leaping in his black eyes were anything to go by as they seared down into hers!

'Don't give me that wide-eyed innocent look. You deliberately locked me in that office. Didn't you?'

Suddenly she was aware of the fierce grip of his hand around her forearm; the heat of his large body seemed to reach out to engulf her. Swallowing hard, she tried to pull free. 'Locked you in the office?' she muttered inanely. 'I don't know what you're talking about. I didn't even know you were here,' she added, gathering her composure. 'I think you've had a brainstorm. Maybe you should see a doctor.'

'I sometimes wonder that myself. Why I put up with you I will never know,' Leon grated, scowling down at her. 'You drive me to distraction almost every time we meet. What is it with you? Is it your purpose in life to deliberately make me look a fool?'

'I don't have to; you do that very well yourself. That poor security man looked petrified. What on earth did you say to him?' She watched him warily; she saw him take a few deep breaths, his massive chest expand and contract beneath the soft fabric of his shirt. For a second he closed his eyes, and then he opened them again.

'Margot didn't tell you I had arrived, did she?'

'No, she left half an hour ago.'

'Oh, damn! And you, like the conscientious worker you are, locked all the doors before leaving?'

'Of course.' Bea wished he would just let go of her; now he had calmed down she recognised a much more disturbing glitter in his dark eyes.

'Sorry, sweetheart, it was my mistake.' And before she could say a word he hauled her into his arms and his mouth swooped down over hers.

She was too stunned to move. And after the first touch of his lips, so soft, so gentle, she found she didn't want to. He coaxed a response from her that she was helpless to deny.

A long moment later Leon lifted his head and stared

down into her flushed, bemused face. 'That is how I meant to greet you.'

An angry Leon she could deal with, but when he was being charming it was another matter altogether. Shoving her hand between their two bodies, she tried to ease away. 'I preferred you angry,' she breathed heavily, fighting down the urge to sink back against him. 'But I would like an explanation.'

A wry grin twisted his lips. 'I owe you that much, I suppose. I arrived at Heathrow almost three hours ago, and have been stuck in the Friday rush-hour traffic for most of the time since then. I intended going straight to my hotel and then calling you, but the office was nearer and, basically, I was desperate to use the bathroom. I dashed in as Margot was leaving. She opened Jordan's door for me and left the key on the desk for me to close it.'

Bea could feel the beginnings of a chuckle starting deep in her chest. It was ridiculous, she knew, but the idea of the great Leon Gregoris being caught short like any other human being was highly amusing. 'I thought I heard mumbling but presumed it was Margot talking to herself,' she offered quickly, in an effort to control her real desire to laugh.

'That would have been me,' Leon said quite seriously. 'I had no idea you were still here. So you can imagine my surprise when I tried to leave and found myself locked in. For a horrible moment I had a vision of spending the weekend in the office, until I remembered Security. I rang them and it did nothing for my temper when it took them over fifteen minutes to answer. Then, when I was finally free and saw you standing in the corridor, I jumped to the conclusion it was a practical joke on your part, and saw red.'

He had looked a bit like a charging bull, Bea thought

on reflection, and she could restrain herself no longer. 'The great Leon locked in the loo,' she spluttered, and burst out laughing.

'It wasn't funny.' His hands tightened on her arms. Glancing up at him, her blue eyes dancing with amusement, she saw his lips twitch, then break into a smile and finally into outright laughter.

The shared humour seemed to clear the air between them, and Bea, still smiling, glanced at the watch on her wrist as she pushed her hand against his chest again. 'It is good to see you, Leon, and I'm glad we can still share a joke, but would you mind letting me go? I have a date.' She felt the brief flicker of tension in him, and suddenly she was free.

He stepped back and really looked at her, his dark eyes skimming over the silver hair in tumbled disarray, the plunging neckline of her jacket and the short skirt, moving down her long legs and back to her face. 'He is a lucky man; you look ready for it,' he drawled mockingly.

So much for the brief moment of accord, Bea thought dryly. Leon just couldn't help himself. If it had been any other man who had said that to her, she would probably have slapped his face. But she had more sense than to try it with Leon. 'And you with your vast experience would know, of course,' she shot back, and, turning, walked away.

He caught up with her at the elevator. 'As I am the cause of your delay I insist on giving you a lift.'

'No, thank you.'

'Be reasonable, Phoebe; you'll never get a taxi in the rush hour, and in any case I feel it is my duty to check the man out.'

Bea's gasp of outrage was cut short by his hand at her

back urging her into the elevator. 'Now wait a minute, you pompous…'

'You don't have a minute; you're already late.' Leon grinned, and pushed the button for the foyer.

He was doing it again, taking control as though she were still a child. The trip to the ground floor was too quick for her to state her case. Before she knew it she was out on the pavement, with Leon's arm at her elbow leading her towards a low-slung black sports car. Parked on a double yellow line, and of course he hadn't got a ticket, Bea thought blackly, eyeing the traffic warden standing not two feet away. The swine had no doubt conned her as well.

'All right, Mr Gregoris, but don't make a habit of it,' the woman simpered, and was treated to one of Leon's megawatt smiles.

'Thank you, Officer. I won't, I promise.'

Like all his promises: easily given but with no substance, Bea thought with a sad shake of her head. Leon would never change…

CHAPTER FOUR

SEATED in the passenger seat of Leon's car, Bea cast her companion a baleful look. 'I wanted to get a taxi; this is totally unnecessary,' she said flatly.

She might as well have talked to a brick wall. Leon took not the blindest bit of notice, but simply stared straight ahead as he manoeuvred the powerful car through the busy city streets. He really was impossible, Bea thought for the thousandth time. Why she bothered trying to argue with him she did not know. For the rest of the short journey she ignored him.

'Where are we meeting this guy?'

'You are not meeting him, I am.' She instructed Leon to go to Covent Garden. Unfastening her seat belt on arriving, Bea opened the door and jumped out of the car. 'Thanks for the lift,' she cried jauntily, and, swinging on her heel, she set off down the road. Ten seconds later a large arm fell across her shoulders.

'No, Phoebe, my sweet. *We* are.'

Angrily she shrugged one shoulder, trying to shake Leon off. 'Will you let go of me? And don't call me Phoebe,' she flashed back.

'No to both, and a word of warning...'

'You—warn me? It should be the other way around. Women should be warned about you, you...you...over-sexed lech,' she spluttered in exasperation. The taste of him still lingered on her lips from that kiss in the office. If only he would take his arm from her shoulder, she would feel a lot safer. She shrugged again. Being held by Leon had a disastrous effect on her senses, sending

51

her pulse rate into overdrive however much she tried to control it.

'Please yourself. But if I were you I wouldn't shrug quite so energetically—unless you want the world to see you're not wearing a bra. Not that I mind; from my position the view is magnificent,' he opined, amusement lurking in his tone.

Colour flooded up her throat and over her face. A quick glance at her neckline and then up at Leon, and she realised that from his superior height he was staring straight down her cleavage. 'You're a pervert!' she spat. But if she thought that would dent his supreme confidence she was wrong!

'Sorry to disappoint, Phoebe, but I like my women beautiful and my sex straight.' He squeezed her shoulder. 'But for you I'll get kinky, if you want me to.' And he laughed out loud at her furious face.

She felt like stamping her feet with rage and embarrassment but, by a terrific effort of will, she controlled herself enough to stare boldly up into his amused eyes and say cuttingly, 'I don't want you, kinky or otherwise, and I wish you would go now.' For a second she saw a flash of something like hurt in his black eyes, but decided she had been imagining it two seconds later.

'Foolish Phoebe, you should never challenge a man like that.' Sweeping her up in his arms, he kissed her long and hard.

At first Bea could not believe it was happening again. But, standing in the middle of the pavement, locked against his hard body and with his mouth covering hers, she was too shocked to resist and then it was too late… Her traitorous body arched against him, and when his tongue plunged into her mouth she was lost.

A group of young men jostling them and shouting, 'Way to go!' finally broke them apart.

Bea, chest heaving, eyes blazing, glared up at Leon. He smiled—he actually smiled back at her. 'Are you mad? It's still daylight,' she cried rather inanely. As if it made any difference *when* he grabbed her, she silently fumed. He had to stop…

'No, just proving a point. Now come on, Phoebe.' Leon looked around over the top of her head. 'Where are we meeting this bloke?'

Her heart was still pounding from his kiss, and her legs were none too steady, so she gave up. It was a waste of time trying to defy Leon. When he made up his mind about something it was impossible to shake him off.

'Follow me,' she muttered, striding along the pavement. 'Here it is,' she said with an angry glance at Leon.

'It's certainly not the Ritz.' He grimaced and, opening the door, stepped back to allow her to enter.

The Muck and Money was obviously not a place Leon would choose to frequent. Served him right; he wasn't invited, Bea thought with a smug smile as she walked past him into the bar and looked around.

'Bea! Over here.' A tall, blond, strikingly handsome young man, smartly dressed in a grey Armani suit, pushed his way through the crowd.

Bea grinned up into his sparkling blue eyes, delighted to see him. 'Jack, trust you to find the liveliest place in town. What happened to the quiet drink?' she prompted, laughing. It was good to see him; he reminded her of home.

Planting a swift kiss on her lips, he replied, 'And it's great to see you too, Bea. Come and meet the gang.' He reached out his hand towards her.

Leon chose that moment to intervene. Stepping forward, he effectively blocked Jack from taking Bea's hand. His black eyes narrowed and shuttered, he studied the younger man. 'Introduce me to your friend, Phoebe,' he demanded hardily, not asking but ordering.

Bea looked from Jack to Leon. They were both tall, both incredibly handsome, but where Jack's face was open and laughing Leon's expression was one of bland social correctness. Her eyes clashed with his and she felt an inexplicable little shiver race through her. His tall, wide-shouldered presence exuded an aura of perfectly controlled powerful masculinity, and yet she sensed something in his stance, a threat of aggression barely held in check.

'Phoebe.' His lips tightened, as if her silence angered him, and quickly she burst into speech.

'Leon—my old friend Jack,' she said, and, turning to smile at the younger man, she added, 'Jack, dear, my boss, Leon.'

'How do you do, sir?' Jack held out his hand, the epitome of politeness.

'Pleased to meet you, but Leon will do,' Leon said curtly, looking anything but pleased.

'Why, thank you, sir...I mean Leon,' amended Jack, disconcerted by the obvious hostility emanating from the other man. 'Would you like to join us for a drink, sir...Leon?'

Bea, listening to the exchange, had to stifle a giggle. Leon did not like the 'sir' one jot. It put him firmly in a different generation. Suddenly she saw a chance to get her own back on the arrogant devil. She quickly intervened before Leon could answer.

'Leon kindly offered to give me a lift because I was running late, but this is not really his scene.' She raised cool blue eyes to clash with angry black. 'Thank you for the lift, Leon,' she drawled with thinly veiled sarcasm. 'But I know you're a very busy man. Please don't let us delay you any longer.' And, moving slightly, she slid her arm under Jack's, leaning in towards him.

For a moment she thought she had goaded Leon too far, when she saw his handsome features darken with fury, but, amazingly, he simply forced a smile to his hard mouth, and only Bea recognised that it did not reach his eyes.

'You're right of course, Phoebe. I am rather tied up at...' Then he quite deliberately hesitated. 'Tied up,' he repeated, and, turning the full force of his powerful gaze on the hapless Jack, he exclaimed loudly in mock surprise, 'I thought I'd met you before! You're the guy who likes tying up young girls.'

In the immediate vicinity there was a sudden hush, and as Bea watched poor Jack went red to the roots of his hair with puzzled embarrassment. 'Leon...' she said furiously, about to give him a piece of her mind, but Jack found his voice.

'Oh, that was you! I remember now. But we were just fooling around... It was a game...' Jack was making it worse with every word. 'It was a long time ago, sir.'

'Well, I trust you have grown out of the habit. Phoebe is a very close friend of mine and under my protection.' And, with a malicious grin at Bea's thunderous face, Leon added smoothly, 'Why, she was only remarking on the way here that she is not into kinky sex.'

The swine had done it again, Bea raged. Every time she tried to outwit Leon, he always got the last word. She felt like kicking him, and actually lifted her foot, she was so mad. He had quite deliberately embarrassed both Jack and herself. But, before she could give free rein to her anger, Leon stepped back, grinning, as if he knew what she had intended.

'Don't forget I'm picking you up for dinner at seven tomorrow night, Phoebe,' he said, and with a casual wave of his hand he added mockingly, 'Enjoy yourself, kids.' Then he was gone.

'Phew! Bea, are you sure you're just working for that man? I got the distinct impression he considers you his property,' said Jack, urging her through the press of bodies to a corner table where five people were already seated. 'And fancy him remembering that stupid childish game. He must have a memory like an elephant.'

'Right at this moment I wish a herd of elephants would trample the damn man into the ground,' Bea said feelingly. Where did Leon get off, telling her he was taking her out tomorrow night? 'In his dreams,' she muttered under her breath.

'Hey, lighten up, old girl. We're here to have fun.' And have fun they did... Much to Bea's surprise, after the disastrous start to the evening. A few more bottles of wine and a lot of laughter later, they all piled into two taxis and headed for some new restaurant Jack had heard of.

They fell from the cabs in a laughing bunch, a short walk from the entrance to the restaurant, but as they strolled towards the door all the amusement left Bea's flushed face.

On the point of leaving the premises, with the doormen in obeisance, was Leon Gregoris, elegantly dressed in a dinner suit, and not alone. Clinging to his arm was a model, as famous for her lovers as she was for her modelling career.

Bea slipped behind the group, hoping Leon would not see her. But she need not have worried; his whole attention was on the gorgeous woman as he ushered her into the passenger seat of a waiting car with a lingering kiss on her lips, before walking around and slipping into the driving seat.

Bea stared at the departing car, a sick feeling in the

pit of her stomach. It wasn't the wine she had drunk; she had been careful. hIt was the shock of actually seeing Leon kiss another woman. She watched until the car was out of sight, unaware of her surroundings.

Leon, her friend for most of her life. She had rationalised their brief engagement by looking upon him as the man who had done her a favour by introducing her to the sensual side of her nature as a teenager, without compromising her virginity. But the man who had kissed her in the street a few short hours ago really *was* a womaniser. Staring at the empty road, suddenly she felt icy cold although it was a warm night. It was one thing to think someone was a womaniser, but it was quite another to see it with one's own eyes, she thought sadly.

And in that moment she really grew up. She finally accepted that Leon was a good laugh, a good friend, but beyond redemption where women were concerned. A woman would have to be an absolute idiot to love the man. With a sigh and shake of her blonde head for something lost for ever, she swiftly joined her friends, who were discussing where to go next.

Obviously they were not going to get into the restaurant, she deduced from the conversation. But then none of them had the clout of Leon Gregoris, she thought wryly.

Leon! Odd, but in all the time she had known him she had never actually seen him with a woman. Oh, she had read the newspapers, knew his reputation. But she had never actually seen him in the flesh, so to speak, with another woman. Even in Cyprus, when she had discovered his betrayal, Bea had heard him with Selina but she had not seen him so much as touch the woman in her presence. Just imagining them together had been bad enough at the time.

Bea straightened her shoulders and looked around.

Seeing Leon with his model was the best thing that could
have happened to her, she realised honestly. She had
always known he was a rake, and any lingering romantic
illusions left over from her teenage years were finally
put to rest now. Leon had taught her a valuable lesson.
Love and sex were not the same thing. From now on
she was going to enjoy life and go for what she wanted,
with no regrets.

'Andy,' she called to a rather attractive young man of
Italian extraction who was one of their party. She had
apparently been paired off with him. 'Where are we going next? I feel like dancing.'

Bea groaned and rolled over on the bed. A thousand little
gnomes were playing a xylophone in her head.

No, it was not a xylophone; the gnomes were ringing
bells. Campanal—Campanol— What did one call bell-
ringers? It had gone—along with half her brain, she
thought groggily.

So, this was what one called a hangover! She tried to
think clearly. She remembered drinking and dancing half
the night away at a top nightclub. How had she got
home? That was right—it was coming back to her now:
that nice Andy had brought her home in a taxi.

'Oh, my Lord, my head—my stomach,' Bea groaned.
Never again—her first and last hangover, she vowed. But
why did the gnomes keep ringing? No, not gnomes! The
telephone!

Reaching out her hand, she felt around the bedside
table and knocked the receiver off; she groped a bit more
and finally her hand closed around it. Slowly she lifted
the receiver, and even more slowly forced her reluctant
eyes to open. She blinked in the harsh glare of sunlight
filling the room. But, thank goodness, the ringing had
stopped. Faintly she could hear a voice calling.

'Phoebe.'

Dragging herself half up the bed, she rested on one elbow. 'Yes,' was all she could get out.

'So you are there. I was beginning to wonder if you had stayed out all night.' Leon's deep voice vibrated in her ear.

She had not, but he probably had, she thought with sudden clarity, remembering the sultry seductress. 'What do you want, Leon?' she asked.

'That is a leading question, my sweet Phoebe,' Leon's mocking voice drawled suggestively. 'I never had you pegged as a woman who liked dirty talk on the telephone. But you know me, always one to oblige. So tell me, are you naked? I can see your long pale hair tumbled around your firm breasts—'

'Put a sock in it, Leon,' she cut in. 'I know you too well.' She was in no mood 'for his brand of teasing innuendo this morning. In fact, she realised, hauling herself into a sitting position, the sound of his voice, which usually brought her out in goosebumps, had absolutely no effect now.

'You mean you think you do,' he said, with an edge of cynicism. 'But down to business. I'll be a bit late tonight—something has come up.' Bea just bet it had, in the form of a luscious model, but she said nothing, simply listened. 'So I'll pick you up at seven-thirty.'

'Leon, I do not want to have dinner with you. We are partners in business, and anything you wish to discuss with me can be done in the office in working hours, nine to five, Monday to Friday.' She was quite proud of her response, given that her head was splitting. Maybe seeing him with one of his women and getting drunk had cured her of her stupid reaction to Leon. Amazingly she was no longer intimidated by the man. But equally she had no desire to go out with him.

'Nine to five? Nice if you can get it,' Leon drawled mockingly. 'Fortunately for the profitability of the company, *I* work seven days a week. Be ready and waiting. I don't want to have to come looking for you,' he concluded, an edge of steel in his tone.

Wincing, Bea pushed a hand through her tangled hair, her eyes half closed against the light. 'Okay, okay,' she reluctantly agreed. She hadn't the strength to argue, and actually she no longer cared much one way or the other. 'Bye,' she said, ending the conversation and dropping the receiver back on the rest.

Gingerly she moved her legs over the edge of the bed and sat for a moment, fighting down a wave of dizziness. Bad—but not too bad! Bea slowly got to her feet. Once in the shower with a refreshing stream of water massaging her flesh she was well on her way to recovery. By the time she was dressed in jeans and tee-shirt, with a cup of coffee in her hand, Bea was congratulating herself on having solved the problem of Leon.

Curled up on the sofa, sipping her coffee, she reached a conclusion: the events of last night had acted as a catharsis. Finally she could see Leon clearly for who and what he was, without the baggage of her teenager emotions and ideas to blur the picture. As for going out to dinner with him, no problem; they would discuss work and part friends...

She was still of the same opinion several hours later when the doorbell rang. She crossed to open the front door, pausing to glance at her reflection in the hall mirror. She was dressed in a simple halter-neck sheath dress, navy-trimmed, in cream—plain but sophisticated, she hoped. On her feet she wore three-inch-high stiletto-heeled strappy navy sandals.

She had taken care with her make-up, adding a grey eyeliner and a little extra eyeshadow to accentuate her wide blue eyes, a touch of brown-black mascara to her long lashes and a subtle dark pink lipgloss on her full lips. She was ready…

The bell rang again. 'Impatient pig,' she muttered, opening the door.

'I heard that, Phoebe!' Leon, looking dark, dangerous and incredibly attractive in a formal black dinner suit, stared down at her, a cynical smile twisting his firm lips. 'Gracious as ever, I see.'

Inexplicably Bea felt the colour rise in her face. 'Sorry,' she mumbled, and immediately wanted to take the apology back. It did not fit in with her new-found determination to deal with Leon on a mature level.

It was not a very auspicious start to the evening. But surprisingly, a couple of hours later, seated opposite Leon at a table set with the finest linen and crystal in a small, exclusive French restaurant, Bea felt totally relaxed.

Leon had been a model of decorum all evening. He had asked her how she was settling in at the London office, and asked her opinion on the staff, and how the place was run. More importantly he had listened to her views. They'd chatted about all aspects of the business, worldwide, and, Bea thought, for the first time ever Leon was actually treating her as an intelligent adult.

If now and then her eyes lingered too long on his sensuous mouth, or the soft fall of his black hair over his brow, or his long-fingered, expressive hands as he made a point, Bea had no trouble squashing her body's response to his potent masculinity. She simply conjured in her mind's eye the image of Leon last night.

Ironically, he had been leaving the same restaurant where they were seated tonight; maybe he had sat at the same table, and he had probably been wearing the same dinner suit. Bea recalled him kissing his glamorous model as he'd ushered her into his car...

She briefly looked around the dimly lit restaurant, noting the covert glances directed at Leon from almost every woman present. In a way, Bea didn't blame him. He was an exceptionally attractive, virile male, and wealthy with it. Why shouldn't he take advantage of what was obviously on offer? It wasn't up to her to pass judgement on his lifestyle.

Bea replaced her spoon on her plate and sighed. The meal had been perfect: smoked salmon pâté followed by Supreme de Volaille Alexandra—poached chicken breast with cheese sauce and asparagus, with slices of truffle added. And for their sweet there had been a delicious summer pudding.

'That was delicious. I'm absolutely stuffed full.'

'Stuffed, hmm?' Leon repeated smoothly, his expression remarkably bland. Bea glanced at him and caught the glint of wicked amusement in his dark eyes. His lips tilted at the corners in a brief, very masculine grin before he added, 'I could comment, but I won't.'

Mellow with fine food and fine wine, Bea grinned back. 'You're an impossible man, Leon,' she said, with a rueful shake of her head. How was it that Leon could make the simplest comment somehow sexual?

'Only to you,' she thought she heard him murmur, before he lifted a large bottle from the silver ice bucket. 'More champagne?' he offered urbanely, and refilled her glass. 'A toast to a beautiful woman and an impossible man.'

His black eyes met and held hers, a hint of challenge in their depths, and a wave of something very like fear washed over her. Until that moment she had succeeded in convincing herself that Leon was no longer a threat to her emotions. But, picking up her glass, then watching his long fingers curve around the stem of his own and lift it to his firmly chiselled mouth, she was not so sure.

'To partners,' Bea said firmly. She refused to be seduced by his brand of flirtation.

But her resolve was sorely tested when, after paying the bill, Leon waited until she was on her feet, and then slid a strong arm around her waist. The light of mockery dancing in his dark eyes, he bent his head and murmured, 'There, that wasn't so painful. Admit it, Phoebe,' and dropped a swift kiss on the top of her head.

Her immunity to Leon disappeared at the same speed as the masculine scent of him assailed her nostrils and the heat from his hard body seemed to engulf her. His fingers apparently idly kneaded her waist, but tightened perceptibly when she tried to move away.

'Lighten up, Phoebe. I am simply escorting you out of the restaurant. You look none too steady on those ridiculously high heels.'

Bea was not particularly tall, and she had worn the shoes in the faint hope that Leon would not tower over her quite so much, not to give him the excuse to hold her. 'They are not ridiculous, and I can walk by myself,' she snapped back.

'Temper fraying, sweet Phoebe?' Leon asked, a teasing light in his black eyes as he ushered her outside to where the car awaited them.

'No,' she denied, finally shrugging out of his hold. His soft chuckle did nothing for her temper. The trouble with Leon, Bea thought bitterly, was his complete and utter confidence in his masculine prowess. He knew exactly how he affected her, or any woman for that matter, and relished the knowledge.

'Not to worry, you'll soon be home now, and tucked up in your bed.' He opened the passenger door of the car, adding, 'Any chance of me doing the tucking, sweet Phoebe?'

She sent him one fulminating glance as she jumped into the passenger seat, and watched, appalled, as his dark head lowered. If he dared kiss her in a replay of the scene she had witnessed last night, she'd punch him on the nose. But he didn't. Instead he reached across her, carefully pulled out her seat belt and fastened it. Then he casually walked around the front of the car and slid into the driving seat.

'By your silence, Phoebe, I guess the answer is no,' Leon drawled with mock disappointment as she started the engine and drove off.

'Got it in one, buster, and why do you insist on calling me Phoebe?' Her exasperation and frustration finally spilled over. 'Everyone calls me Bea.'

'Bea does not suit you. When I think of a bee I think of an angry, buzzing yellow insect with a sting.' Taking his eyes from the road for a second, his glance slid over her flushed, angry face. His dark eyes gleamed briefly into hers. 'Then again, maybe it does. You certainly anger easily.' Turning his attention back to the road, he added, 'And I know you sting.'

'So call me Bea in future.' She did not like being compared to a stinging insect, but she preferred it to Phoebe.

'Never.'

'But why?' She cast him an exasperated glance. His clean-cut profile was illuminated by the glow from the streetlights, but shadows played over the rest of his face, masking any expression.

'The first time I ever saw you, as a young child, I was struck by how well your name suited you,' Leon responded quietly. 'I knew your name; your father, every time he came to our home in Cyprus, was always talking about his little girl. I can remember walking into your father's house in Northumbria, standing in the square hall and looking up at the large stained-glass window above the landing, halfway up the stairs. A single ray of sunlight was shining through it—a lot, given the state of English summers,' he opined with dry humour.

'Suddenly a tiny girl came whizzing backwards down the stairs, around the curve in the banister—a cloud of silver hair, a white dress and white legs. You shot to the bottom and fell. When you turned around the sun caught your face, and I saw you were truly a Phoebe. The name is from the Greek; it means shining, brilliant, and that is exactly what you were.'

'I don't remember that,' Bea said, oddly touched by his explanation.

'I'm not surprised. You landed on your behind and a second later you were bawling your eyes out. Aunt Lil swept you up against her ample bosom and carried you off.'

'Trust Lil,' Bea murmured fondly, letting her head fall back against the headrest. Heavens, she was tired.

'You're very loyal to those you trust, Phoebe. Which reminds me. I didn't have time to ask you on your birthday, but who or what gave you the idea I asked you to marry me simply to control your share of the company?'

Still dwelling on Leon's flattering explanation as to why he always called her by her proper name Bea wasn't paying much attention, and missed the underlying anger in his tone. 'It doesn't matter now. All water under the bridge, as they say.' She yawned widely, closing her eyes for a second, her previous late night catching up with her.

'Boring you, am I?'

The harshly spoken words made Bea sit up and take notice. They were parked outside her apartment block, the interior of the car illuminated by the overhead street-light. She glanced across at Leon. He was half turned towards her and his face was tight with anger; it glittered in his eyes.

'No, no, of course not,' she denied speedily. Although he no longer had the power to intimidate her, she saw no sense in provoking an argument. 'I have enjoyed our dinner date. But I had a very late night last night,' she offered by way of explanation.

'Your friend, Jack, keep you up all night, did he?' Leon asked crudely. 'Or should I say it?'

'Don't be so coarse,' Bea shot back. 'Just because you are incapable of having a platonic relationship with a member of the opposite sex, don't think everyone is the same. I have a lot of male friends, *friend* being the operative word. Not that it's any of your business.' Her mouth curled contemptuously. 'I certainly don't need advice on relationships from the Swashbuckling Tycoon.'

CHAPTER FIVE

HER words had found their mark. Leon, his eyes bleak and darkening with some emotion she could only guess at, said tersely, 'I apologise. The comment was uncalled for. But tell me, Phoebe, what did I ever do to you to give you such a terrible opinion of me? Surely you're intelligent enough to realise half of the stuff written about me is lies, or at the very least gross exaggeration?' A cynical smile twisted his hard lips. 'And, as I recall, three years ago it was *you* who dumped *me*. I was the innocent party, while you took your first step into love-them-and-leave-them mode.'

'Innocent?' Bea stared at him in amazement, wondering if the arrogant Leon Gregoris even knew the meaning of the word. He had probably lost his innocence not long after he'd left his mother's breast.

For a moment she was tempted to tell him the truth. That she knew all about Selina, the woman who had been his lover for years, the woman he had made pregnant *after* he had asked Bea to marry him and she had agreed. Agreed because Leon had played on her awakening sexuality like a virtuoso, exploiting her adolescent innocence until she was completely bemused by the sensual expertise of a sophisticated, experienced man and would have agreed to anything he asked of her.

Bea lowered her eyes from his enquiring gaze and bit her lip, remembering the most painful episode in her life to date. She wanted to blurt out her deep sense of betrayal, but the new, mature Bea had more sense. With hindsight she could almost feel sorry for Selina. Leon

67

almost certainly would have paid for the child, but he had not done the honourable thing and married his long-time lover! No—Bea would not tell Leon the truth.

Instead, marshalling her thoughts, she said calmly, 'Contrary to what you imagine, I do not have a poor opinion of you, Leon. In fact I think you're an extremely astute businessman. In the past two weeks I have learned a lot about the company and, to be honest, I feel guilty owning thirty per cent. I don't deserve it. My father, and probably yours as well, was quite content to run a small, successful firm and earn a comfortable living. The reason it's such a success worldwide now, according to all the pundits, and confirmed by Tom Jordan, is entirely down to you. And I believe it. You're a genius in the financial world.'

It was the truth and Bea freely admitted it. Leon deserved the accolade where work was concerned; as for the rest, it really did not concern her. She had been hurt once by this man and she had learnt her lesson well: business and pleasure did not mix. Her blue eyes were cold when she finally raised them to meet his.

'But as for your private life, it has nothing to do with me.' Tonight it had been her turn to be wined and dined, but she had not forgotten that last night a different woman had been in the exact same position. 'And by the same token mine has nothing to do with you,' she concluded bluntly.

He watched her for a moment, and Bea didn't like the predatory look in his eyes. So, feigning an ease she did not feel, with a dismissive shrug she turned her back on him to release her safety belt. She tensed as his hand fell on her shoulder.

'Subject closed—just like that—?'

'I'm tired,' she cut in, without looking at him. 'Thank you for a lovely meal.'

His long fingers tightened on her naked shoulder, sending a tingling sensation down her spine. He was too large, too vitally male, and far, far too close. She held her breath as she felt those astute black eyes observing her intently in the dark interior of the car.

She heard the chiming of a clock in the distance and added a breathless, 'It's late. Goodnight.' Amazingly, he agreed...

'Okay, sweetheart.' With surprising alacrity Leon was out of the car, around the front and opening the passenger door before Bea had steadied her breathing.

'You do look tired, so I'll help you to your door.' His hand was once more on her shoulder, and he was guiding her across the pavement to the entrance hall of the apartment block before she recovered enough to speak.

'There's no—' She had been going to say 'no need', but never got the chance.

'In fact, although I'm not the most domesticated of men, in this instance I will even make the coffee you so obviously need...'

'Now, wait a minute...' But it was like trying to stop the tide. In moments they were outside her door, and Leon was demanding her key. 'I never invited you in for coffee,' she muttered, rooting in her bag for the key. She opened the door and turned. Leon's hand reached out and she stepped back instinctively. She didn't want him touching her again.

Leon smiled a rakish grin as he switched on the hall light. It gleamed on his night-black hair and threw the too handsome features into stark relief. 'Lead me to the kitchen, Phoebe, sweetheart.'

'Don't keep calling me sweetheart.' Bea swung on her heel, muttering under her breath. The man was too damn confident for his own good.

She was angry with herself for allowing him to steamroller his way into her apartment. Then she reminded herself it was *her* apartment. 'I suppose there's not much point in telling you I don't want any coffee and asking you to leave,' she said as she walked into the galley-style kitchen.

'None whatsoever. Go and sit down, relax. I can manage.'

She obeyed, simply because the alternative—staying in the confined space of the kitchen with Leon—was not appealing. Or maybe it was *too* appealing, a tiny voice echoed in her head.

Kicking off her shoes, she sat down on the sofa, curling her legs up beneath her. Her eyelids drooped, and she stifled another yawn.

'This is a first. A woman falling asleep on me,' a mocking voice drawled softly.

Forcing her eyes open, Bea looked up. 'What?' She yawned.

'Nothing important, Phoebe,' Leon said dryly as he stared down at her from his imposing height. He had shed his dinner jacket and got rid of his bow tie, and the top three buttons of his shirt were undone. He was enough to make any woman catch her breath. Then Bea noticed the tray in his hands.

'Coffee—you made it…' Her blue eyes widened in amazement. He had actually laid out two china cups and saucers, with her best silver cream jug, sugar bowl and coffee pot—a twenty-first birthday present from Lil and Bob, supposedly for her bottom drawer! A trousseau was an old-fashioned custom Bea did not believe in, and she hadn't used the coffee service.

'I am not the complete chauvinist you seem to think, Phoebe, as you will discover if you give me the chance.' And, bending, he placed the tray on the occasional table and sat down beside her. 'Shall I be mother?' he drawled, and proceeded to fill two cups from the coffee pot.

So much for a quick cup of instant and then turfing him out, as she had hoped, Bea thought. Sitting up straight, she slid her legs to the floor. 'Thank you,' she muttered, taking the cup and saucer Leon offered her. 'But it really wasn't necessary.'

'Not for you, maybe, but it is for me. Something you said in the car disturbed me, and, looking around this pleasant if small apartment, it occurred to me it's time we set the record straight.'

A puzzled frown creased Bea's smooth brow as she looked around the familiar room. His jacket and tie, draped over the armchair opposite, were the only items out of place. 'What has the size of my apartment got to do with anything?' she asked, and, taking a sip of her coffee, glanced sideways at Leon.

He tilted back his dark head and drained his cup. Bea was reluctantly fascinated by the subtle movement in the smooth column of his throat. He bent forward and replaced the empty cup on the tray. The fine silk of his shirt strained across his broad back, outlining muscle and sinew, the slight indentation of his spine, and Bea had to fight down an incredible urge to run her finger down it. She clasped her hands together in her lap. He was a magnificent male animal whichever way one looked at him, she realised, and she was no more immune to his charms than a million other females.

'It is a symptom of your father's upbringing,' Leon responded as he sat back, spreading his long arms along the back of the sofa. One of his hands was perilously near her shoulder. He stretched his long legs out in front of him with negligent ease, his feet crossed at the ankles. He looked as though he was settling in for a long stay.

'How much did your father tell you about the origin

of the firm?' he asked quietly, his dark head turned towards Bea, his black eyes seeking and holding hers.

'Do we have to…?' Bea began.

'Humour me this once, hmm?' Leon demanded quietly.

She eyed him warily, but there was no mistaking the serious intent in his expression. Bea allowed herself a nonchalant shrug. 'Okay.' The quicker she answered him, the sooner he would leave. 'Dad told me he was in the army and posted to Cyprus, where he met and made friends with your father. When Dad left the army, he spent a holiday in Cyprus with Nick, and between them they decided to set up in business—*ergo* Stephen-Gregoris. It's no great secret.'

'It wasn't quite that simple. Your father saved my father's life. My father got into a bar-room brawl, and your father intervened and took the knife meant for my dad's heart in his forearm.'

Bea's eyes widened; she was intrigued. 'So that's where he got his scar!' she exclaimed. As a child it had fascinated her—the long, ragged slash down her father's arm. He had explained it as a battle scar—the result of ten years in the army.

'Yes, but there's more. The company flourished quite well for a number of years, until the Turks invaded the island in 1974. I was a boy at the time, and we lived in Northern Cyprus—the part that is now controlled by Turkey. My father lost almost everything, and once again your father came to the rescue. He supported both families for a while, until they could get the business going again. As a precaution they decided to set up the head office on the Greek mainland, in Athens; it seemed a safer bet and it looks like proving to be correct. Unfortunately there's trouble brewing again in Cyprus.'

Bea had seen the news and knew there had been a

skirmish recently, but it seemed to have quietened down again—though for how long was anybody's guess. But she was in no mood to discuss the political situation in Cyprus, or anywhere else. 'Why are you telling me all this?' she asked, because she really did not see the point.

'Because earlier you said you felt guilty at owning so many shares in what is now a very large concern.' His voice was almost terse. 'Don't ever think like that again, Phoebe. You are entitled to everything you have, and more. Our fathers were partners, and it was because of your father's trust and loyalty that the company continued to flourish. If it hadn't been for him I wouldn't be where I am today,' Leon opined hardily. 'The debt my family owes yours is unquantifiable.'

'I think you're rather overstating the case,' she said awkwardly. The passionate intensity in Leon's tone was so unlike his usual light-heartedness.

'No, it's how I feel. I am Greek and I promised my father on his deathbed that I would always honour the debt of gratitude and abiding friendship between our two families, that I would always look after you. So never again let me hear you say you do not deserve your wealth.'

He glanced at his watch, and Bea noticed again that it was an expensive gold one—but then everything about Leon was expensive. Hard on the heels of the thought, she frowned and looked around the simple room.

'Understand, Phoebe.' His harsh demand brought her eyes back to his face. 'Last night, if I appeared a little too concerned about you and your friend, now you know why. I have difficulty remembering you're a grown woman, but I am trying,' he said with a wry grimace. 'Though beware, Phoebe, I will never stop protecting you, if I consider you need it.'

'Now why does that worry me?' she jibed. The

thought of Leon looking after her was horrific, yet oddly comforting.

'Don't worry. I learnt my lesson when I tried to marry you to protect you.' She sensed the derision behind his words. 'First I thought you called it off because I was too old for you, but then I discovered it was because you didn't trust me. I hope after our little chat tonight you realise you can trust me, and why?'

He was astute, Bea acknowledged. She knew he had tried to marry her to consolidate his hold over the business, and he had failed. Now he was smoothly suggesting it had been friendship and his promise to a dying man to protect her that had prompted their brief engagement. The truth was probably somewhere in between, but Bea was not about to delve into that particular morass. Instead she simply said, 'Yes, of course, Leon.'

'Thank you,' he drawled mockingly. 'Such enthusiasm is quite overwhelming.'

The old Leon was back. His black eyes gleamed with devilment as he shifted his long legs and moved closer, allowing his arm to fall from the back of the sofa and encircle her slender waist. Bea was trapped between his arm and Leon's muscular thigh, hard against her own. Immediately she felt a burning sensation through the thin fabric of her dress. She felt his muscles tense and wondered for a second if it was because he felt the same sexual heat that afflicted her.

'Now we've got that settled, Phoebe, let me give you some advice.'

Obviously not the same affliction, Bea thought, maddened. Leon sounded as cool as a cucumber while she felt hot and flustered. He was back to being his arrogant self, dishing out advice whether she wanted it or not.

'Seriously, as your friend and partner, I am telling you

never to feel guilty about money. It is not a sin to be rich, or to enjoy oneself.'

She tried to inch away, but the grip of her waist tightened. 'You're suggesting I should stop worrying about money and start spending it?' The gleam in his eyes did not resemble the caring light of a true friend giving advice. More likely it was a very astute masculine awareness of exactly how he affected her.

'Well put.' Leon grinned, and, lifting one long finger, he slipped it under the halter neck of her dress. 'This is a lovely dress, and you look gorgeous in anything.' His eyes appraised her with deliberate slowness from head to foot. 'But you can afford to be clothed by the best designers in the world.'

'Maybe I don't want to…to be…' she stuttered, her nerves quivering in response to his nearness.

'Then look at this apartment. Your father was a cautious man, but it's a different situation now, Phoebe. Buy yourself a penthouse, if you want.'

'Like you, you mean,' she said coldly, but her flesh burnt where his finger idly stroked her breastbone. She could feel her nipples tighten into hard buds of arousal and prayed he would not drop his gaze and discover her embarrassment. Jerking forward, she placed the cup she was still grasping on the table, dislodging his marauding fingers at the same time.

'I don't actually own a penthouse,' Leon remarked, a hint of amusement in his tone. 'The company owns all the apartments in Athens, New York and Hong Kong. My one indulgence is cars. I keep a Maserati in Athens, a Ferrari in New York, a Mercedes in London and a Jaguar in Hong Kong. But the only house I own is the villa in Cyprus.'

Bea believed him. Leon always had to be in control. The thought of another person driving him anywhere was probably anathema to him. 'Where do you stay in London?' she queried, wondering how much longer it would take to get rid of him. The hand at her waist hadn't slackened its grip, and it was taking all her strength to remain perched on the edge of the sofa.

'I'm not very often in London, and when I am I stay with a good friend or at the Dorchester.'

The 'good friend' is a woman, no doubt, she thought, but did not say it. 'Nice for you,' she said, glancing back at him over her shoulder.

'Nice for you too, Phoebe. Technically the properties are yours as much as mine—feel free to use them any time.'

'Speaking of time, it is eleven and I'm bushed.'

'Your late night is catching up with you,' Leon drawled mockingly, letting go of her waist and getting to his feet. 'Okay, I don't want to outstay my welcome.'

What welcome? Bea thought, and immediately felt guilty. He wasn't a bad man. Her eyes followed him as, in a few lithe strides, he crossed the room and reached for his jacket. He was just an incorrigible flirt and so irresistible with it!

Turning towards her, he hesitated briefly, not quite his usual confident self. He glanced down at her.

'I'll call around about ten in the morning; we can spend the day together.'

'Sorry, I can't. I'm going out.' She saw him stiffen, but ploughed on—though she didn't owe him an explanation. 'It was arranged last night. My friend Nan is down for the weekend and Jack suggested we all go to Brighton for the day. It should be fun.' Bea saw no reason to tell Leon that Nan was Jack's girlfriend.

Leon dropped his jacket and took a step forward.

'There's an antiques fair on. I thought I might buy

something,' she babbled on, the atmosphere in the room suddenly fraught with tension.

Temper flashed briefly in his eyes, and was almost immediately overlaid by something much more sinister. He lowered his large body down onto the sofa beside her again, and lifted a hand to slide it once more around her waist. 'In that case I must make the most of tonight.'

'Thank you for tonight.' Bea battled on politely, wishing desperately that he would leave. She looked frantically round the room, anywhere but at Leon. His hand had crept up to the underside of her breast and her body was betraying her yet again. He was just so damn smooth! She could leap up like an outraged virgin, but she didn't want to give him the chance to laugh at her. Her gaze alighted on a flower vase. 'Oh, and I forgot to thank you for the roses and the groceries you bought for me when I first arrived here.'

'My pleasure. But the one thing I really want I find I cannot buy,' Leon said enigmatically, lying back against the soft cushions, looking for all the world as if he was settling in for the night.

Resolutely she resisted the subtle pressure of his hand on her side, tempting her to fall back against him. She could feel his breath on her bare back and she shivered, but not from the cold. Folding her arms over her chest to disguise her peaked nipples, she rabbited on, 'Yes, well, I'm sure you'll find a way. You always do. But, if you don't mind, I want to go to bed.'

His deep-throated chuckle did amazing things to her heartbeat. He bent his head, sliding his free hand into the thickness of her hair and brushing it to one side. Then she felt the warmth of his mouth on the nape of her neck and she shivered again. 'Sweet Phoebe. I want to go to bed as well.' The husky words brushed against the soft whorls of her ear.

Bea sucked in her breath and stiffened her back ramrod-straight. 'So go!' she snapped. She might have known he would make a pass. He couldn't help himself.

'Relax,' Leon drawled. 'I have to leave on Monday afternoon and so, as tomorrow is out, we must make the most of tonight. Remember what I told you earlier. You're a grown woman now. Let's enjoy ourselves together.'

Angrily she turned her head towards him. His lips curled into a smile as he caught her half-smothered denial with his mouth.

His lips against hers silenced her, and his hand held her head still beneath his. His other hand slid up her back, holding her closer to his broad chest. He deepened the kiss, letting her feel the possessive heat of his passion. Bea tried to remain immune to his assault on her senses but old memories, never far from the surface, welled up inside her, bringing with them the familiar rush of desire only Leon seemed able to arouse in her.

Her arms curved up and around his shoulders of their own volition. She felt her breasts crushed softly against the muscular wall of his chest, and suddenly she was responding helplessly to the promise of his lips. His tongue surged in her mouth as his fingers slipped the tie of her halter-necked dress. Her head fell back and she gasped as she felt his fingers trail down her throat and delve beneath the lacy edge of her strapless bra, grazing across her nipples.

Her slender body trembled in his hold and she only vaguely realised when her legs left the floor. She was held firmly in his lap by one strong arm while his free hand dealt with the front fastening of her bra.

Finally Leon lifted his head and stared down into her flushed, bemused face. There was a dark, demanding hunger in his eyes that stilled her frantically racing pulse.

'Leon, I don't think this a good...' Bea began.

'I want you...and I know you want me. Let me show you true pleasure,' he rasped throatily, his glittering eyes raking her beautiful face and then dropping to her firm, high breasts. His head swooped down, his tongue licking over each taut nipple in turn.

Bea bit her lip against the exquisite sensations flooding through her body. 'No,' she gasped in dismay, appalled by her own swift surrender.

'Yes,' he contradicted her, and bit lightly on her breast before raising his head and kissing her fleetingly. 'Don't think, feel. The chemistry between us has always been there, whatever else went wrong.' His large hand cupped the lush weight of her breast, his thumb grazing the aching tip. His dark, knowing gaze flicked from her face to her breast and back, to emphasise his point. 'You know it's true, Phoebe. Let's give ourselves a chance, see where it leads.'

Bea wanted to. She had never wanted anything so much in her life. But she knew where it would lead, she thought sadly: to disgust with herself and to another notch on Leon's belt.

As if sensing her uncertainty, suddenly Leon moved, turning her under him. She was trapped by his arms at either side of her and his large hands threaded through her long hair, framing her face, holding her head gently between his palms. His mouth closed over hers once more, hot and passionate, his tongue plunging its moist secret depths.

Bea was made achingly aware of the full weight of his rock-hard arousal, moving against her belly in rhythm with his mind-drugging kiss. She could barely breathe, but didn't care. Frantically her small hands slid beneath his open shirt and tangled in the soft hair of his broad chest, her fingers brushing a hard male nipple.

Leon groaned against her mouth and trailed a string of kisses down her throat and lower, until his dark head nestled between her breasts. Then he was suckling on their hardened tips, first one and then the other. A low moan escaped her, arrows of pleasure darting from her breasts to the apex of her thighs. She quivered helplessly as his mouth moved, tasting her skin. Her back arched, encouraging his ministrations even as some tiny corner of her rational mind reminded her he was an expert in the sexual stakes, and a confirmed womaniser.

But when he lifted his head and their glances collided Bea read the question in the fiery depths of his eyes. She saw the skin pulled taut across his cheekbones with desire, the dark flush on his tanned face. She also knew it didn't matter. She wanted him.

Bea reached a hand to his square chin, hypnotised by the undiluted hunger in his fiery gaze. Tonight he wanted her...only her... She traced his jawline and felt the beginnings of stubble. He always had been a hairy man. Her childhood hero. A soft smile curved her mouth, and Leon took it for assent.

'Phoebe.' His voice was a husky groan. 'You're so beautiful, so passionate, and God knows I've waited so long.' His hot mouth found hers once more, and they were swept up in a swirling tide of passion.

Leon's hands and mouth roamed over her body, stroking, kissing, and she needed no urging to return his caresses. Her fingers teased his chest hair, again discovered the hard male nipples, stroked his broad shoulders and tangled in the silky black hair of his head. She was delirious with excitement and pleasure.

'You're sure?' Leon demanded gutturally, easing her skirt up around her waist. He moulded her hips with his hands and slid between her thighs.

Blue eyes bravely holding black, slowly she lowered

her hands to the waistband of his trousers, her fingers finding the clasp. Bea felt his sharp intake of breath and the flex of his stomach muscles. The silence was laced with a sexual tension so acute, she could taste it. The musky scent of his powerful male body filled her nostrils. The clasp was undone... Bea hesitated, suddenly shy, then her fingers found the top of the zip, her knuckles brushing against hard, bulging male flesh. Leon groaned—a hoarse, aching sound...

Then the doorbell rang.

Bea's hand dropped from the zip. 'The door,' she murmured. 'Someone's at the door.'

'Ignore it,' Leon rasped, catching her hand in his and lowering it to his thigh as his mouth once more took hers.

The ringing continued. 'Leon, I must answer,' Bea murmured against his mouth, and, pushing against his chest with her small hands, she tried to wriggle free.

The bell rang again. 'Who the hell calls this late anyway?' Leon demanded, frustration lacing his voice, but he let her up.

Shocked by what she had almost allowed to happen, Bea staggered to her feet, her heart pounding and her legs like jelly.

'Wait!' Leon snapped, and she stood before him meek as a child as with swift expertise he fastened her bra and retied the halter of her dress. 'We don't want your late-night guest shocked out of their socks, do we?' he said.

Bea stared at him. The man mad with passion only minutes ago was now in complete control, and she felt like a quivering wreck. But then Leon was a past master at getting women in and out of their clothes—and why not? He had certainly had plenty of practice, she thought bitterly, and, swinging on her heel, she dived for the hall and the front door.

'Saved by the bell,' she muttered under her breath, and flung open the door.

'Hi, Bea. I saw your light on when I arrived and thought, Great! It's not yet midnight.' Margot walked past Bea into the small hall. 'I can't wait to find out how your heavy date went last night.'

Bea closed the door and, turning, stopped Margot from strolling into the living room with a hand on her arm. 'Still living vicariously, are we?' she teased—anything to delay her friend for a moment. It had suddenly hit Bea: she had left Leon standing with his shirt undone, his trousers half undone and with no jacket on. Silently she prayed he had had time to get dressed as she listened to Margot chatter on.

'Well, as it happens, I woke up at the crack of dawn and did catch a glimpse of you staggering out of a taxi with an incredibly attractive Latin-looking young man.' Margot walked on into the sitting room, heading for the kitchen with Bea reluctantly following her. 'I want to hear all the juicy details over a cup of cocoa, and—Mr Gregoris!' Margot exclaimed, stopping dead.

Bea hardly dared look at him, but when she did it wasn't too bad. Leon was standing by the fireplace. His shirt and trousers were fastened, and his jacket was draped casually over his arm. Only the bow tie was still missing.

'Hello, Margot. I'm glad to see you're taking such an interest in our young charge.' Leon looked across at Bea, a cynical light in his dark eyes. 'And I wouldn't mind hearing all the juicy details myself. An incredibly attractive Latin-looking young man, you say? How interesting,' he drawled silkily. 'I can see I shall have to keep a closer eye on my young partner.'

Bea bristled at the word 'young', and could guess what he was thinking. Leon had left her with Jack, a tall blond, and she had ended up with Andy, someone quite different. But Leon was as bad. No, worse, she thought scathingly. He had no right to take this moral tone with her. A picture of his model friend formed in her mind, and gave her the courage to reply carelessly, 'That was Andy, a really rather nice man. Something in the City, I think.'

But Margot seemed to have lost interest. Instead she was looking from one to the other of them, a thoughtful expression on her face. She turned to Bea. 'Sorry. I didn't mean to intrude. You should have told me you had a visitor.'

'Oh, please, Margot, stay. Mr Gregoris took me out to dinner, but it was strictly business. You're not intruding at all—in fact Leon was just leaving.' She glanced up at Leon defiantly. 'Weren't you?' she demanded, her blue eyes daring him to disagree.

'Yes, of course. I'll leave you two to your gossip.' Leon bent and casually picked his bow tie up from the arm of the chair, dangling it provocatively between his long fingers. Bea could have slapped him... But he wasn't looking at her. He was saying goodnight to Margot. Then, turning to Bea, with a wicked gleam in his dark eyes, he added, 'As it happens I have a rather pressing problem I had hoped to solve tonight. Show me to the door, Phoebe. Perhaps you can help me.'

Bea's face flamed. He was back with the innuendos. She only hoped Margot didn't realise it. Marching into the hall, she made for the door, her hand going out to open it.

'Wait a second,' Leon ordered hardily, trapping her hand with his. She glanced up at him in the dimly lit hallway. His face was in shadow, but there was no mistaking the determination in his eyes.

'Put your jacket on and go,' Bea said flatly.

'In a minute, but first you owe me, lady,' he hissed, pressing her hand beneath his folded jacket. 'Feel what you do to me.' Bea's face burned even more as he forced her hand flat against his still aroused male flesh. Now she understood why his jacket was draped strategically over his arm, and she quickly pulled her hand free.

'It's not my fault you're an over-sexed womaniser,' she hissed back, keeping her voice low. It was a very small apartment and sound carried. No way did she want Margot hearing the conversation.

'I gave up my womanising ways the day I realised it was possible to have an erection and be bored at the same time. I am much more discerning now, and I don't appreciate being led to the brink and left cold.'

Bea tried to choke back a totally unsuitable desire to laugh, and failed. 'Cold,' she chuckled, her blue eyes lit with laughter and clashing with Leon's. He was anything but cold! She could feel his heat reaching out to her.

His firm lips twitched and he couldn't suppress an answering grin. 'You think it funny, you little tease?' Ruefully he shook his head. 'One day, Phoebe, one day... Be warned, I am going to have you, and when I do you won't be laughing, but begging.' And, dropping a gentle kiss on the top of her head, he let himself out.

Dream on, buster, Bea thought, dismissing her earlier weakness as simply tiredness and proximity to a lethally attractive man. She was over Leon now, she reminded herself as she walked back into the living room.

Margot was standing in the doorway of the kitchen, a mug of cocoa in each hand. She burst into a hurried apology. 'Bea, I feel such a fool barging in like that; I'm so sorry. But it never entered my head that Leon Gregoris could be here, and I realise it should have done. After all, you are his business partner, even if you do seem just like one of the workers.'

'Can it, Margot,' Bea said bluntly, and collapsed onto the sofa. The last thing she wanted was for Margot to start seeing her as a boss figure, and with that in mind she gave her a carefully edited account of the evening. 'Leon was doing his usual heavy uncle act. Checking up on me to make sure I'm behaving myself and working hard. Nothing more.'

'Are you sure?' Margot asked, handing Bea a mug of steaming cocoa and sitting down in the armchair opposite. 'Do you mind if I speak frankly?' Margot went on, eyeing Bea's messed-up hair with a wry smile.

'Of course not.' Bea grinned at her friend. She had quickly realised Margot was outspoken to the point of bluntness. 'Why change the habit of a lifetime?' she quipped, and took a sip of the warm chocolate.

'I'm a lot older than you, Bea, and a lot more worldly, shall we say. Leon Gregoris is a very charismatic, powerful man, but if he has one fault it is women. Notice the plural, and beware. According to office gossip over the years, he only ever once got close to committing to a woman, and even that fizzled out. I'm warning you, Bea. From what I sensed tonight, when I walked in here, Leon Gregoris in no way sees himself as your uncle.'

'Well, that's how I see him,' Bea said flatly, gulping down the rest of her cocoa. Carefully she put the mug back on the table and glanced at Margot. 'Don't you start worrying about me as well, Margot. I can look after myself. Take last night, for instance.'

In a swift change of subject Bea gave Margot an exaggerated version of the previous evening. She described the hilarity of Leon being locked in the loo, and gave the impression they had parted at the office. Then she went on to describe her great night out with her friends. And if she accentuated Andy's charms while avoiding mentioning Leon's part in the evening, what did it matter? Finally, when she'd told Margot her plans for a day out in Brighton with Jack, Nan and Andy tomorrow, the older woman got up to leave, totally convinced Bea had her life well under control.

Bea went to bed telling herself the same thing, and the next morning, when she climbed into the back of Andy's Range Rover with the rest of her friends, she was convinced of it.

Brighton was a roaring success, and they finally returned to London just before midnight.

Bea jumped out of the Range Rover into Andy's open arms, and quite enjoyed his kiss. The ribald comments from her friends made her laugh, and she was still laughing as Andy showed her to her door.

She might not have been as happy if she had noticed the black car parked on the opposite side of the road. Or the thunderous expression on the face of its driver…

CHAPTER SIX

ON MONDAY morning Bea eyed the contents of her wardrobe with a frown. Leon was right; she should splash out a bit on clothes. Apart from a handful of dresses, she only had two outfits for work: the blue suit she had worn on Friday and a simple black suit in almost exactly the same style. She glanced out of the window. It was a beautiful sunny day, not a cloud in the sky, and suddenly she decided to hell with the suit, took one of her favourite dresses out of the closet and crossed to the dressing-table mirror.

She slipped the dress over her head and smoothed it down over her thighs. She eyed her reflection. Not quite…she mused. Then quickly she opened a drawer and took out a gold Chanel belt. She slung it around her hips and it immediately lifted the soft forest-green shift, with its tiny sleeves and slightly scooped neck, from simple to stylish—in the process shortening even further its already short straight skirt. She smiled at her reflection in the mirror, well satisfied with the result.

Bea breezed into the office half an hour later with Margot, not for a second admitting to herself that she had dressed with more care than usual because Leon might appear.

Appear he did. Bea had not even made it to her little office before he burst out of Tom Jordan's. 'What time do you call this, ladies?' His dark eyes swept over Bea from head to toe, narrowing slightly on the hemline of her skirt and her shapely legs.

Bea opened her mouth to speak, but Margot answered. 'Eight-twenty, Mr Gregoris. We're ten minutes early.'

With a hard look at Bea, Leon switched his attention to Margot. 'Never mind, get in here. We have work to do.'

'Good morning to you too,' Bea muttered, opening the door to her office. What or who had rattled his cage? she wondered as she switched on her computer and sat down at her desk.

Two minutes later her door was flung open. 'What is keeping you?' Leon growled.

Bea looked up. 'I—I didn't realise you meant me,' she stuttered, the fierceness of his expression temporarily unnerving her.

'You never do,' he grated inexplicably. Leaning against the door, he added, 'Move it,' and waited for her to walk past.

The morning was a revelation. Bea had always known Leon was clever, but watching him in action was an education. He created an electric atmosphere simply by his presence; power and dynamism radiated from him.

Seated at Tom's desk, Leon quickly went through the turnover of the London office. In rapid succession he spoke to the Athens and New York offices. Bea felt sorry for the poor person in America. It was a little after midday in London and, given the time difference, it had to be the crack of dawn there.

Tom and Margot hovered around, answering all Leon's questions and immediately implementing his suggestions. Bea's role turned out to be the coffee-maker, but she didn't mind; it was fascinating to see Leon at work.

Finally Leon stood up. 'A quick lunch before I have to leave. Tom, you'll join me?'

Bea hid a flicker of disappointment behind a bright

smile. 'Well, if you'll excuse me, I must get on with my own work.' She started for the door.

'Phoebe, the *four* of us are going to eat.' And then, turning his attention to Margot, he said, 'Get Reception to hold all calls until later, and let's get out of here.'

Over a light meal of pasta and salad Leon sought their views on the Far East. The discussion that ensued, on the advantages of trading with the Pacific Rim economies and how Leon intended to exploit them, left Bea speechless with admiration. An hour later they were heading back for the office.

Leon said goodbye to Tom and Margot but, grasping Bea's hand, he prevented her from following them inside. The kiss he bestowed on her parted lips left her speechless for quite another reason.

'Behave yourself. I'll be in touch,' he said, and was sliding into his car and gone before Bea could get her breath back.

She looked guiltily around, terrified that anyone she knew might have seen her, but the flow of people walking along the pavement was devoid of any familiar faces. She must stop Leon doing that! she told herself for the umpteenth time. But without much hope of success...

Sighing, she walked into the building and entered the lift. Sophie, the receptionist, was standing with her finger on the 'hold' button.

'Aiming a bit high, aren't you?' she said in her cool voice.

Bea blushed to the roots of her hair. Obviously Sophie had seen the kiss and had drawn her own conclusion. Bea couldn't say she liked the girl. She was the sort of woman who sparkled around the male sex but seemed to have little time for her own. But maybe Bea was being unkind; she didn't really know Sophie.

'I'm not aiming anywhere,' she finally said, forcing a smile as the lift moved. 'It was just a bit of fun.'

'So long as you remember that. Leon Gregoris is a great lover, but don't get any ideas. His sort will never marry a working girl. If he ever does marry, it will be to some filthy-rich society babe. Believe me, I know.' The trace of bitterness in her tone was undeniable.

'You're probably right,' Bea agreed, suddenly feeling inexplicably low. It was a relief to walk out of the elevator and reach the sanctuary of her own office. Sophie's comments shouldn't have got to her, but they had. Obviously the woman was another notch on Leon's belt.

Summer gave way to autumn—not that it was very noticeable in the heart of the city. In the weeks since Leon had left Bea had settled into an enjoyable routine.

Leon called her very occasionally at her apartment, from wherever he happened to be in the world, and always at the most ungodly hour, Bea thought with a wry smile as she sat down at her desk one day. More often she spoke to him at the office, when he rang to speak to Tom and she put his call through. She was quietly proud of her ability to manage these telephone conversations with a degree of efficiency and sophistication.

Another Monday, but she wasn't blue, and it had nothing to do with the fact that she had spoken to Leon last night. She glanced at her wristwatch. He should be in Hong Kong now, she mused, and on Saturday he would be back in England.

'Penny for them,' Margot said, walking up to her desk. 'You looked rapt. Dreaming about Andy, were you?'

Margot had met the young man and liked him, so Bea simply smiled, and said, 'Jealous?'

'Too young for me. Though when you're through with him I might fancy taking on a toy boy.'

'And what about your financial friend?' She tilted her head back. 'Up there.'

That was all it took to get Margot talking about her boyfriend and forgetting about Bea's love life.

By Thursday morning every little bit of information of the previous weekend's escapades was talked out, and relative calm reigned. But not for long…

'Bea.' It was a softly spoken word, and Bea's head jerked up from the program she was working on and she smiled. But quickly her smile turned to a worried frown.

Tom Jordan was standing in her doorway. Today he looked as if the weight of the world had fallen on his shoulders, and not a glimmer of humour lit his blue eyes.

'Come into my office, Bea,' he demanded quietly. 'We need to talk.'

The fact that he had come looking for her instead of simply ringing through was ominous enough, but the expression on his face was worse. Slowly Bea got to her feet and silently followed Tom through to his office. His curt command to Margot to hold all calls had Bea racking her brain for what disastrous mistake she must have made to be personally summoned in such a way.

'Sit down, Bea.'

She did. 'What have I done?' she blurted.

Tom, instead of sitting at his desk, pulled up a chair to face hers. 'Now, I don't want you to get upset, or worried…' he began earnestly.

Of course his words had completely the opposite effect on Bea. Her heart stopped. It had to be personal. 'Lil and Bob.' She said the names of the only two people she was close to. 'What's happened? An accident?' she asked, the colour draining from her face.

'No, no, nothing like that. Everything will be fine. But we have a bit of a problem.'

Bea breathed more easily. 'A problem?' she queried.

'I have just had a telephone call from head office in Athens. Apparently they were informed yesterday by the Hong Kong office that Leon has been kidnapped.'

'Kidnapped? Leon?' She couldn't help it; she started to chuckle—it had to be a joke. 'No one would have the nerve!' she exclaimed. She didn't believe it for a minute. She glanced at Tom, expecting him to share her amusement, but was shocked into silence by the grim expression on his face.

'Unfortunately, it's true. He's been kidnapped.'

'Kidnapped,' she repeated, like a parrot.

Reaching out, Tom took her small hands in his in a gesture of comfort. 'It seems he arrived in Hong Kong on Monday and drove out to stay with a friend in the New Territories for the night. He was supposed to be in the office on Tuesday, but never arrived. Instead a ransom note was delivered. The kidnappers want twenty million pounds. The demand was accompanied by a distinctive gold keyring, with the keys to his Jaguar attached, and, more ominously, a lock of wavy black human hair. The police were informed.'

'It could be anyone's keys or hair,' Bea said slowly, refusing to believe what she was hearing.

'The police have checked with the friend Leon spent the night with. It is Leon's keyring and it is European hair—not Asian; apparently there is a difference.'

'Oh, my God!' The full enormity of what Tom was telling her was beginning to sink in.

'The Hong Kong police are almost sure a Triad gang is responsible, and, while they will do everything in their power to find Leon, they suggest the money be prepared just in case. I don't know if you have ever been to Hong

Kong, but it's like a rabbit warren—trying to find one man must be extremely difficult. As the police said, the car would be more difficult to hide than the man.'

'So what are we going to do?' she demanded, panic edging her tone. 'I'll go there straight away. I'll get the next flight. No, the company jet.' Bea tried to rise, but Tom's hand forced her to remain seated.

'No, Bea, you must stay here. In fact a detective inspector from New Scotland Yard will be arriving at eleven to interview you.'

'Interview me?' She couldn't understand what was happening. 'Why me?'

'That's the part I'm coming to. You know your father and Leon's were great friends, and I know what your father would do now if he was alive. But I don't want to put pressure on you in any way. It has to be your decision.'

'For heaven's sake, Tom, what are you going on about?' If Tom had one fault, it was his inability to get to the point.

'Twenty million is a huge amount of money. Stephen-Gregoris is a highly successful company, but it does have to consider its shareholders. In most kidnap cases an appeal to the family would probably apply. But there's no point in asking Leon's stepmother, because her income is tied up to Leon's share of the company. So, for there to be any chance of assembling the money quickly, the head office in Athens need your consent. As the single biggest shareholder, next to Leon, basically it's your decision whether to pay up or not.'

'Yes, yes, of course—anything, Tom. What is money when a man's life is at stake?' Now she understood his remarks about her father. 'I'm surprised you need to ask.'

'I knew you would agree; you're a good kid, Bea.'

Standing up, he added, 'I'll get on the blower to Greece and set the wheels in motion.'

The rest of the day was a blur to Bea. She signed documents, banker's drafts—anything Tom put in front of her—and the inspector from New Scotland Yard arrived. He told her he was questioning her on behalf of the Hong Kong police and said that sometimes business partners knew more than most about each other. But Bea was no help. How could she be? She still didn't really believe it had happened. Leon in captivity was unthinkable.

But when the detective insisted on absolute secrecy, informing her that only three members of staff in Hong Kong were aware of the kidnap, in Greece only two people—the company lawyer and the director of head office—and in Britain only Tom Jordan and herself, and that it had to stay that way, it finally hit Bea just how perilous the situation was.

She jumped to her feet and paced agitatedly around Tom's office, her mind in a whirl. She suggested again flying out to Hong Kong, but neither Tom nor the police would hear of it.

'But when they find him he'll want to be met by a friend, at the very least,' Bea cried, the full horror of what had happened finally cutting through the fog in her brain. Then her imagination took over: Leon alone, in chains, in the dark, maybe already dead. It was a nightmare. 'I must do something. Go there.'

Tom put an arm around her shoulders. 'No, Bea. Your place is here. When Leon is free he won't be alone; you forget he was staying with long-time friends the night before he was taken. They'll be waiting for him just as anxiously as us.'

Tom was right, she realised sadly, and, knowing Leon, there was probably a lovely lady there somewhere too.

'All right,' she finally conceded, and, rubbing her bare arms, trying to instil some heat into her numb flesh, she sank back down on the chair.

Then the detective inspector told her that, as a precaution, she would be kept under surveillance for her own protection until the situation was resolved satisfactorily. The Triad organisation had long tentacles and was known to be active in London. She voiced no protest; she was frozen in shock.

Bea didn't want to leave the office that night, but Tom insisted she go home. Perhaps the worst part of all was that she couldn't talk about it to anyone; the information was strictly on a need-to-know basis, and even Margot hadn't been informed.

Ensconced in her small apartment, Bea paced the floor for hours on end. She telephoned Lil at home, but for Lil and Bob's sake she had to pretend everything was fine, when really she was crying inside. She couldn't eat, she couldn't sleep. Tom had promised to ring if there were any developments, and she lay in bed, her ears straining to hear the telephone.

On Friday lunchtime, Margot demanded, 'Come on, Bea, I'm not a fool. Something has happened to upset both you and Tom. You never said a word all the way to the office, and you've sat at that desk all morning watching the telephone and jumping out of your skin every time it rings. What's wrong?'

Bea looked at her friend with haunted eyes. 'Nothing—nothing at all—'

'Leave her alone, Margot,' Tom Jordan broke in sternly, walking into the office. 'It's a private matter and not to be discussed.' The tone of his voice was enough to warn Margot not to question further.

By Sunday Bea was quietly going out of her mind. She hadn't left her apartment all weekend. She was tormented by thoughts of what Leon must be going through.

Leon had always been such an active man, he'd used to run morning and night, and probably still did—when he was free. In the villa in Paphos the basement was his own personal gym. One only had to look at his physique to see it was honed to the peak of fitness. She had nightmares about his beautiful body, broken and bent.

She went to bed, but she didn't sleep through a whole night.

Leon might be a rake, a womaniser, but he was her friend. She forgot all her bitterness over their broken engagement, and remembered only the good times. How as a child she had adored him—his stupid rhymes and his wacky sense of humour. He had always been there for her; at her father's funeral his had been the comforting shoulder to cry on, and as her trustee he had taken care of everything for her. And then, on her twenty-first birthday, he had handed her inheritance to her with a smile and a present of a pendant, and she had never really thanked him for any of it.

Next morning Bea did something she hadn't done for years. She knelt by the side of the bed and, her slender hands clasped together, offered up a silent prayer for his safe return. Childishly she promised God anything, if only Leon was safe.

She did the same every day until finally, the next Thursday, her prayer was answered.

The call came through from Hong Kong just as Bea was about to leave the office after another futile day of waiting. It was the middle of the night in Hong Kong; the hand-over of the cash had been arranged, the police had been waiting and it had all gone smoothly. The kidnappers were caught, the money recovered and Leon had been discovered, gagged and chained to a wall, in a small compartment only two feet by four.

Ten days confined in such a way had taken their toll, but a doctor had seen him and declared there was no permanent damage. He was all right and recovering in a private clinic, and would be in touch after a debriefing by the police.

Tom declared a celebratory drink was in order, and, with Margot finally let in on the story, the three of them retired to the nearest wine bar and got very merry.

Bea's sense of euphoria lasted until the next morning. After a good night's sleep she skipped out of the apartment block with Margot, eager to get to work, sure that Leon would call to speak to Tom, if not her.

He did. 'Phoebe—Leon here.'

The sound of his voice over the phone was music to her ears. Her eyes filmed with moisture. 'Leon. Oh, thank God. It's so good to hear your voice. Are you all right? I won't believe it until I see you again. When will you be here? I was almost worried out of my mind.' She knew she was babbling, but it was such a relief.

'No need to worry, Phoebe, I'm fine—and so is your money. I believe I have you to thank for allowing the ransom to go ahead.'

'It was nothing. I'm just so glad you got away un-harmed.'

'Twenty million is quite something to most people,' Leon drawled cynically. 'Thank you again. Now, put me through to Tom; I don't have time to gossip.'

'Yes, yes, of course.' Bea did as he said. She should have been happy; Leon was fine, she had spoken to him. But something was wrong.

Bea sat staring blankly at her console, chewing on her bottom lip. It was Leon, but it wasn't. Gone was the humorous chat, the not so subtle innuendo; he had sounded curt almost to the point of rudeness. Reluctantly she turned her attention to the document on the screen. She was supposed to be working, not worrying about Leon, she told herself firmly. But somehow her earlier euphoria on learning of his safe return gave way to a feeling of anticlimax.

You're rotten, she remonstrated with herself. Leon was fine; he had spoken to her and thanked her. What more did she want? Bea didn't know the answer, or, if she did, she wasn't ready to face it… With grim determination she got on with her work, and heaved a sigh of relief when it was time to go home.

Bea walked into her apartment. A long hot soak in the tub was what she needed. Half an hour later, she made herself a light meal and then settled down on the sofa, a glass of white wine on the table beside her. Too upset about Leon, she had made no arrangements to meet anyone so she had the whole weekend to herself.

Picking up the remote control, she switched on the television. Picking up the glass of wine, she took a sip— and then nearly choked. The glass slipped from her hand and bounced on the carpet, spraying her with wine. The seven o'clock news was on Channel Four, and there, standing with his arms around the shoulders of a tall, fair-headed European man on one side and an exquisitely beautiful Oriental girl on the other, was Leon. The news of his kidnap and subsequent release had broken, and he was being interviewed live on television.

Bea hardly heard the words; her whole attention was focused on Leon. He looked tired, and pale, and his magnificent black hair was cut close to his head.

'How did it feel to be locked in a cupboard, Mr Gregoris?' the interviewer asked.

Bea watched as Leon gave him a withering glance. 'Try it and see.'

The fair-headed man spoke up. 'Mr Gregoris has answered enough questions. He has been through a great ordeal, he is tired, and on his doctor's instructions he intends taking a few weeks' R and R. End of interview.'

It was strange seeing another man speaking for Leon, and even stranger that Leon had allowed him to. But seeing Leon finally put Bea's mind at rest, even if it was just on the television. Leaning forward, she picked up the glass from the floor, got up and headed for the kitchen. A glimmer of a smile tipped the corners of her full mouth but did not quite reach her eyes. Trust Leon; captured and shorn, he could still pull the most gorgeous female the very next day.

The following day, her apartment was clean, her washing done, and it was barely noon. Bea strolled into her bedroom, the rest of the weekend stretching before her as a total blank. She straightened the coverlet on the bed, not that it needed it, and wandered around aimlessly. She opened the wardrobe door. Yes! she decided on impulse, and half an hour later was dressed in her blue suit, *sans* blouse, but with the sapphire and diamond pendant Leon had given her for her birthday around her neck.

She left her apartment and hailed a cab. Settling in the back seat, she said to the driver, 'Knightsbridge, please.' She was going to act on Leon's advice and go on a shopping spree! Harrods and Harvey Nichols, here I come...

Five hours later, a tired but happy Bea stepped out of a cab about fifty yards from her building. The driver couldn't get any nearer because of the parked vehicles. She paid the fare and, after gathering a multitude of packages in both hands, turned to walk the last few yards home. She frowned; there seemed to be a crowd of people around the entrance, some kind of accident, fire or...

Before she could complete the thought, a voice yelled, 'There she is!' and she was surrounded by dozens of people. A microphone was stuck inches from her face, cameras flashed and she reeled back under the press of human bodies.

'Miss Stephen, the heiress?'

'Yes—no. I suppose so.' She was caught wide-eyed and stunned.

'How did you feel when Leon Gregoris was kidnapped?' 'Is it true you sanctioned the payment of the ransom?'

The questions flew fast and furious, and Bea was completely out of her depth. 'Upset, obviously. Yes. No.' She didn't know what to say. She had never had any dealings with the press or television before, and she was horrified. Clinging onto her shopping bags, she stumbled through one of the most embarrassing half-hours of her life. Eventually she managed to battle her way to the foyer of the building, where mercifully the security guard let her in and firmly refused entry to the media.

By the time she reached her apartment, reaction had set in. She collapsed on the sofa, shaking in every limb, her parcels discarded unnoticed on the floor. My God, she thought. Now she knew how Leon must feel. How on earth did he deal with the press so easily? They had turned her into a nervous wreck in a few minutes.

After a cup of sweet tea, and the relative silence of her home, she began to feel a little better. Well enough to unpack her purchases and put them away, and to begin to wonder how the media had found out who she was and where she lived.

She was still mulling over the problem when her doorbell rang. Bea automatically got up to open it, then stopped with her hand on the doorknob. What if a reporter had got into the building?

'Who is it?' she called, and smiled with relief at the sound of Margot's voice.

But her relief turned to squirming embarrassment as Margot dashed past her and switched on the television. 'You're famous, Bea.'

Bea looked at the picture with horrified eyes. There she was, in her blue suit, diamonds at her throat, loaded down with parcels from the top shops in town, and the commentator was calling her the 'Reluctant Heiress'. Then followed a sketchy history of her life and her business partnership with Leon Gregoris.

She didn't think it could get worse, but the Sunday papers the next morning were even more detailed, going so far as to print her address in Northumbria and a picture of her family home.

Margot was a tower of strength. 'Hey, Bea, as Andy Warhol said, it was your fifteen minutes of fame. To-morrow someone else will be on the front page.'

And she was right. By Monday morning, when the two girls left for work, there was not a reporter in sight.

But as Bea walked into the office she began to realise the full extent of the damage caused by the press. Sophie, the receptionist, was the first.

'Good morning, Miss Stephen,' she said knowingly, and the rest of the staff followed suit.

Bea could see it in their eyes, the way they looked at her; a certain barrier was now in place. She was no longer Bea, the graduate trainee, but a person of power. By the end of the day she was forced to recognise that she was only comfortable around Tom Jordan and Margot.

Tuesday was even worse, but by Friday morning Bea was beginning to adjust to her new status. Leon was back in Cyprus, supposedly resting, but he rang Tom most days. Bea had spoken to him a few times and he seemed to be okay, if a bit abrupt. It was amazing how quickly things got back to normal, she mused.

Until Margot knocked on her apartment door and placed the daily paper in her hand.

'Sorry, Bea, some people just can't keep their mouths shut.'

'Why? What's happened?'

'Read the paper, take a look out of the window at the paparazzi, then decide if you want to go into the office.'

Bea rushed to the window. Margot was right; the reporters were back. Slowly she turned and crossed the room. She sank down onto the sofa and with growing horror read the newspaper article. It was full of sly innuendo that Leon and Bea were more than just business colleagues, that they were also lovers. An eye-witness account of Leon kissing Bea outside the office, which could only have been revealed by Sophie, the receptionist, seemed to confirm the fact. Also Andy, whom Bea had considered a friend, described her as 'a swinging girl who can't be pinned down'.

To cap it all, to Bea's utter amazement, some customer from the Muck and Money bar said he had seen Bea there with Leon and another man at the same time. Then he misquoted Leon's quip about bondage and kinky sex, making Bea out to be a cross between a sado-masochist and a *femme fatale*.

She did not go to work…

The next morning the ringing of the telephone woke her from a restless sleep. She groaned, and, reaching for the receiver, put it to her ear.

'Phoebe.'

It was Leon's voice, and she was struck by a sense of *déjà vu*. The last time he had awakened her with an early-morning call she had been suffering from a hang-

over. This time she simply felt tired and sadly disillu-
sioned.

'What do you want?' she asked.

With a return to his old teasing ways, he answered,
'You, Phoebe.'

'Leon.' She said his name softly. 'It's good to know
that after your ordeal you're still as incorrigible as ever.'
He might be the biggest rake in the western world—
what did she mean western world? He was as bad in the
eastern world as well, it would seem!—but he was an
old friend, and she felt as if she had very few left.

'No, I'm deadly serious. I've seen the newspaper reports and I know how much they must have upset you.
Apparently my stepmother was interviewed in California
and asked if she had put up the ransom. She gave them
your name, but, in fairness to her, any serious reporter
could easily have found out; it has never been a secret.
However, I also know the media; they'll hound you to
death until they get a statement. You can face them on
your own, if you want to. But I have arranged to take
care of it, if you're agreeable.'

'How?' she asked cautiously.

'I'll explain when I get there; expect me in twenty
minutes.'

'You're in London?'

'Yes, and don't answer the door to anyone but
me. Right?'

CHAPTER SEVEN

BEA slid out of bed and glanced from the telephone still
in her hand to the blue sky outside, and then carefully
replaced the receiver. She didn't have much choice.
'Damn the man,' she muttered.

Typical Leon; he had hung up on her before she'd had
a chance to respond. She grimaced at the sight of the
reporters already gathering on the pavement. Still, she
reasoned, if Leon had a plan that would get her out of
her apartment without having to run the gauntlet of the
press hounds, it had to be worth considering.

The telephone shattered the silence. 'Hello, Leon,' she
said, assuming it must be him calling back.

'Interesting! But no, Miss Stephen. This is Doug
Brown, from the *Sunday Herald*.

At the mention of that particular tabloid newspaper
Bea exploded. 'What? How did you get this number?
It's ex-directory.'

She had thought at least she was protected from reporters telephoning her. She didn't wait to hear the
man's answer but slammed the phone down, and, bending, unplugged it from the wall. Swiftly she dressed, then
paced around her apartment, anger boiling within her.
She felt like a caged animal, and suddenly she decided
that anything Leon could come up with was all right by
her. She had to get out or go mad...

By the time the doorbell rang Bea had calmed down
somewhat, but she still felt like a fugitive in her own
home. She whispered, 'Is that you, Leon?' When she
heard his voice she opened the door, grabbed him by the

arm and pulled him inside. 'Quick, someone might see you.'

'Don't be ridiculous, Phoebe; you sound like Inspector Clouseau on a bad day.' He walked along the short hall and into the living room, with Bea padding after him.

'Well, you never know,' she muttered defensively.

'With you, no,' Leon drawled sardonically, and, turning in the middle of the room, he flicked an unreadable glance over her. 'I did have to pass the press to get here, or did you imagine I was going to shin up a drainpipe, or lower myself in through a window off the roof?'

Leon could always be depended upon to make her feel like a fool. She reddened, because actually she *had* thought he would sneak in. 'Cut out the sarcasm and tell me this plan of yours. They have my telephone number now, though heaven knows how.'

She studied his darkly handsome face from beneath the veil of her lashes. The kidnap had taken its toll. His once long hair was now short, with the hint of a curl, and yet, if anything, it made him look even more attractive; he had a beautifully shaped head. But the lines had definitely deepened around his mouth and eyes. The ruthless strength and raw masculinity were evident as ever, but added to them was a coldly dispassionate cynicism, a world-weariness that the hero of her childhood, with his flowing ponytail and laughing eyes, would never have displayed.

She lowered her gaze down over his huge body. The elegant charcoal-grey suit hung not quite so perfectly on his tall frame. He had obviously lost weight, and suddenly her heart flooded with sympathy for him.

Acting on instinct, she crossed to where he stood in the middle of the room and wrapped her arms around him, her sole intention to give him a friendly hug. She tilted her head back to look up into his eyes.

'Sorry, Leon. Never mind my troubles. I should have asked. How are you coping?' Feeling the tension in his long body, and with a compassionate smile curling her mouth, she said softly, 'I really am sorry. I know it must have been terrible for you.'

Roughly he caught her upper arms and held her away from him, staring down at her with dark, almost angry eyes. 'Cut out the sympathy, Phoebe. I don't need your pity.'

So much for trying to comfort the man! she thought, feeling like a fool, and, shrugging off his hands, she stepped back. 'You're not going to get it,' she snapped. 'If it wasn't for you I wouldn't be in this mess.' Bea knew she was being unfair. Leon hadn't been able to help being kidnapped. But his curt dismissal of her offer of comfort had inexplicably hurt.

'I wondered how long it would take you to get around to blaming me,' Leon drawled cynically.

Bea took a deep breath, determined to hang onto her temper. After all, he had been through a harrowing ordeal. 'Look, Leon, let's not get into an argument.'

'You're right,' he said, and let his dark gaze sweep over her from head to toe, taking in her casual garb of old blue jeans and a red sweatshirt. 'First, get out of those clothes,' he added.

'What?' Her blue eyes widened in amazement. She hadn't let him into her flat to make a pass at her, but to rescue her.

'You can close your mouth, Phoebe. I promise I'm not going to seduce you. I simply want you dressed suitably. Put on that suit, the pendant and those shoes you were wearing in the newspaper photograph. The best form of defence is attack, so you and I will walk out of here together. I will make a short statement to the press that will satisfy them for the moment, but there's no reason to give them a different picture of you from the one they already have.'

She supposed it made sense. 'But then what?' she asked. It didn't seem much of a plan to her.

'Then you and I will take the company jet to Cyprus. I need a longer break, and a few days in the sun won't harm you, either. By the time you return to London, some other story will have hit the front page.'

'That's it? I go on holiday with you and hope the gossip blows over? I don't think so…' The thought of spending time alone with Leon on a Mediterranean island was all too seductive, and she doubted she would have the strength to resist him if he turned on his usual charm.

'Please yourself. If you want to face the press alone as the ''Reluctant Heiress'', as I believe they nicknamed you, or stay trapped in your apartment—fine. As a friend, I'm offering you a way out. But I'm leaving in ten minutes, with or without you. It makes no difference to me.'

'But—' She stopped. Her troubled gaze searched his face. He didn't seem concerned one way or the other, and the idea of a few days in Paphos was appealing. She hadn't been there long enough as a teenager to see anything, and he had said, 'as a friend'. But alone with Leon? Could she trust him? More importantly, could she trust herself?

'Before you ask, there are at least half a dozen staff at the villa. You won't be alone with me. And in any case I have work to catch up on. I promise you, flirtation is the last thing on my mind…'

She flushed slightly. How did he read her mind like that? 'I'll need time to pack,' she said, weakening.

'An overnight bag will do. I've told Tom Jordan you'll be away for a while, and I've arranged with Margot to pack your things and send them on. You'll have them by tomorrow night. So go and get changed and let's get out of here.'

Leon had thought of everything. And ten minutes later Bea learnt just what 'everything' entailed...

Leon slipped an arm around her waist as they exited the elevator on the ground floor. She tried to ease away—the warmth of his firm hand, even through the fabric of her jacket, had an unsettling effect on her already overstretched nerves—but Leon tightened his grip.

'Stick close to me, Phoebe, and let me do all the talking.' He slanted her a reassuring smile. 'Okay?'

She didn't have a lot of choice. They walked out of the front door and the flashing cameras blinded her. A dozen different voices yelled questions, so that Bea could hardly hear. She was glad of Leon's supporting arm, even if it did do funny things to her pulse rate. It was preferable to being pulled apart by what seemed like a pack of baying hounds.

When she did finally recover enough to make sense of what was being said, she got the shock of her life. She stared up at Leon in open-mouthed astonishment.

'Phoebe and I have been close for years. The pendant she is wearing was originally the betrothal ring I gave her when she was seventeen.' And with his free hand he lifted up the jewel while gazing like a besotted fool into Bea's upturned face.

'What?' she breathed stupidly. Surely no one could possibly believe such twaddle?

'I had it made into a necklace when we decided to wait until she had finished her studies before getting married. There's no longer any reason to delay. Phoebe and I are engaged and we are taking a short holiday in

South Africa, where Phoebe will choose her own uncut diamond and have it modelled exclusively for her as an engagement ring. I could do no less for my perfect bride.'

His captivity had clearly affected his brain. The man has gone mad, was Bea's first thought, and, tearing her gaze away from his, she looked down at the jewel he held between two long fingers. His knuckles brushed her throat, making her skin tingle, and she had difficulty concentrating. Originally she had only had the ring for less than twenty-four hours. Was it the same? she asked herself. And if so, why?

'Is that right, Miss Stephen? You and Mr Gregoris are to marry?' a reporter cried.

Then it hit her—why she had thought the pendant looked familiar when Leon had given it to her on her twenty-first. 'Yes, of course!' she exclaimed, finally recognising it. The gold ring was gone, and a slim gold base had been added, but it was the same. She shot a quizzical gaze up at Leon. What on earth did he think he was playing at?

'Wh—?' was as far as she got, before Leon's hard mouth descended over hers. His arms curved around her back, holding her firmly against his tall body while he kissed her with passionate possessiveness. She tried to resist. Eyes wide open, she caught the surprised but pleased faces of the crowd around them. Oh, no, she groaned inwardly, and then she was groaning aloud, for another reason, when Leon's tongue found entrance to the moist, sweet interior of her mouth.

Bea sagged when Leon finally broke the kiss, and only his arm around her waist stopped her from falling flat on her face. Before she could gather her scattered wits, Leon was pushing her into the back seat of a chauffeur-driven limousine and sliding in beside her.

The car was moving before Bea recovered her composure, and with it a rising tide of anger swelled in her breast. Face scarlet, her skirt halfway up her thighs, she turned her furious gaze upon Leon.

He was sitting beside her, one hand unfastening the tie at his throat and then the first couple of buttons of his shirt. He lounged back, his long legs stretched out in front of him, his jacket undone, apparently totally unconcerned by their recent hustle with the press.

He looked so damned satisfied, and in his rumpled state so infinitely attractive, that suddenly Bea saw red and exploded in a tirade of abuse.

'Are you stark staring mad, Leon? Has being kidnapped pickled your brain or something? Your plan was supposed to help me escape the press. Some plan! What on earth possessed you to tell that lot we were getting married? Tell the driver to turn the car around this minute, or I will. I'd rather be trapped in my apartment than trapped into an engagement to you.'

'And I have no desire to be trapped in an engagement to you.' Leon slanted her a cynical glance. 'But the strategy did work. The press are happy with their scoop, and we are free and clear.'

He made it sound so reasonable, yet Bea's feminine intuition was telling her there was something seriously wrong with Leon's scenario. He might have vastly more experience of the press than she did, but she was not a complete fool. 'I still think we should go back and tell the truth.'

The sardonic look he gave her made the colour surge in her cheeks. 'The truth?' he mocked. 'If you recall, my dear Phoebe, you were asked if my statement was true, and I, and the reporters present, distinctly heard you say, "Yes, of course!"'

She flung up her hands in a gesture of exasperation.

'But I meant I had recognised the pendant, not—not…' She stumbled to a halt as Leon grasped the waving hand nearest to him.

'Stop it—forget it. In a couple of weeks the gossip will have blown over and we can go our own ways.' Dropping her hand, Leon slouched back in his seat, effectively dismissing her objections.

'That's all very well for you,' she snapped. 'The press are used to your licentious ways. But I'll never live it down. They'll never leave me alone—or I'll be known as the dumped fiancée of the great Leon Gregoris. My God! I can't believe you.'

'You never did trust me,' Leon slashed back, brutally but quietly. 'So just shut up, Phoebe, and do as you're told.'

Leon had never spoken to her in such a ruthless manner before and it stopped her cold. She searched his harshly set features suspiciously. She didn't know this man at all; his dark eyes evaded her gaze and instead he looked out of the window.

She took a deep breath. 'The plan was a short holiday in Paphos; are we still going there, not to deepest Africa?' she demanded scathingly. She needed some clarification from Leon, some sign to allay her mounting disquiet at the situation.

'Yes, of course. The rest was a false trail for the benefit of the press.'

'Humph, some trail,' she snapped, still riled by his stupid engagement story. It was all right for him, he was a notorious womaniser, but when the truth came out she would look like another one of his pitiful cast-offs.

'Drop it,' Leon said harshly, but she noticed he still avoided looking at her.

The rest of the journey was conducted in almost complete silence. Bea, simmering with resentment at the

false position Leon had engineered, glanced around the
interior of the car. It was luxury personified. A glass
partition separated the chauffeur from the occupants—
all very private. As for her companion, he had the smug,
self-satisfied look of a man in total control. Her resentment bubbled over into sarcasm.

'The limousine is quite a change for you, Leon. I
never thought I would see the day when the great Leon
Gregoris would allow someone else to drive him.'

'I learn by my mistakes.' Leon swung around, and the
embittered black eyes that met hers sent an icy shiver
down her spine. 'In Hong Kong I stopped for petrol.
While I was paying for it the bastards hid on the back
seat. Never again.'

'Your one indulgence is your cars,' she said softly,
horrified by the brief glimpse she had seen of the kidnap
and how it had affected him.

'Not any more,' he said flatly, and returned his attention to the view from the window.

The flight to Cyprus was not much better, though Bea
had never been on a private jet before. She looked
around in awe at the thick-pile carpet, the soft cream
hide chairs and sofa and the heavy glass table bolted to
the floor, plus an extensively equipped bar in one corner.

'You certainly know how to live, Leon,' she quipped.

Black-lashed glittering eyes met hers in a challenging
glance. 'This is also yours, Phoebe. Do *you* know how
to live?' he demanded mockingly.

Bea retreated to the safety of a seat at the back of the
cabin without answering. Reluctantly she fastened her
seat belt, wondering if she was doing the right thing.
There was something different about Leon. She couldn't
put her finger on it.

She chewed her bottom lip nervously as the roar of
the plane engine signalled take-off. It was too late to

escape now, she thought, and then wondered why the word 'escape' had entered her mind. She was getting fanciful, she told herself firmly. This was a brief holiday in the sun, with a family friend, in a house full of staff. It would be a breeze, and then back to London and work.

She was still telling herself the same story when she stepped out of the aircraft at Paphos airport, the warmth of the late October sun lifting her spirits and her confidence. Another limousine was waiting, and it drove them through the countryside and up the twisting mountain road that led to the villa.

Her first shock was the twelve-foot-high iron gates, and the armed security guard on duty. 'Leon.' She swivelled round in her seat. He'd had his head stuck in papers from his briefcase virtually since leaving London. He looked up and out of the window.

'Good. We've arrived.'

'Yes, but I don't remember iron gates and a guard.' She looked around her, her eyes widening in puzzlement. The white perimeter wall was still there, but now it was topped with what looked suspiciously like six feet of electric fencing.

'Yes, well, more trouble surged up between the Turkish and Greek sectors not so long ago, and I decided on a little more security. As it turns out, it was lucky I did.'

She stared at him warily. 'Lucky? Surely the fighting wasn't that bad?' She had seen something on the news, but it had sounded more like an unfortunate skirmish than anything major.

'Forget it, Phoebe. Welcome to my home.'

The car slipped slowly between the massive gates after the security guard had carefully checked the driver and the occupants of the car.

'Fort Knox springs to mind,' she tried to joke, but Leon did not share her humour.

'It is necessary,' he replied bluntly.

The limousine came to a halt before white marble steps that led to massive double entrance doors forged in bronze.

The staff had emerged to greet them, and as Bea stepped out of the car she smiled in recognition at the old housekeeper and her husband, Anna and Spiros. She had met them on her last brief visit. The dark-eyed young maids were all strangers but Leon, taking her arm, duly introduced Bea to everyone as they walked up the steps.

The two burly men at the top guarding the door she could have done without knowing, Bea thought as Leon guided her into the shadowed coolness of the wide reception hall.

'I'll show you to your room.' He glanced at his wristwatch. 'You have exactly fifteen minutes to settle in. Anna insists on serving an English tea out on the patio at four.'

'That's sweet,' Bea said with a smile, and her smile broadened considerably when Leon ushered her into what was to be her room for the holiday.

At least he'd had the sensitivity not to put her in the same room as last time, and for that she was grateful. Plus, if memory served her right, this huge, elegant room had been his stepmother's room before, and it was at the opposite end of the villa to his room.

Why the distance should make her feel safe she did not query. Instead she turned smiling eyes to Leon. 'Thank you, it's a gorgeous room.'

One dark brow rose sardonically. 'Don't thank me, thank Anna; it was her idea. She's trying to impress you.

She never quite got over your hasty departure last time. Hence the tea and the master suite.'

'I will,' she murmured as he left.

A brief exploration of the room revealed a door leading to a dressing room lined with wardrobes and an ultra-modern functional dressing table. A further door opened into a luxurious bathroom.

She looked longingly at the spa bath, but, mindful of tea in fifteen minutes, she contented herself with washing her face and hands and running a comb through her long hair. Finding her way back downstairs, she consoled herself with the thought that she couldn't have got changed anyway; all she had in her holdall was a change of underwear, a nightshirt and her toiletries.

Anna had really gone to town for the tea. Bea smiled as she walked down the steps from the main living room onto the patio. A wrought-iron table was covered in a white damask cloth, and two places were set with delicately patterned bone-china cups and plates. A silver cakestand took centre-stage, loaded with a variety of delicious-looking, fat-making cakes. Three more plates stacked with finger sandwiches, and a plate of scones, completed the picture. Bea had barely sat down when Anna arrived, carrying a silver tea service on an elegant matching tray.

Leon reappeared as she drained her second cup of tea, having eaten two cakes too many. 'What kept you?' she demanded huskily. Poor Anna had apologised over and over again for his absence, but it was not that so much as the way he looked that affected her tone of voice.

Her wide blue eyes took in his appearance, from the sheen of dampness on his short black curling hair—obviously he had showered—down to his broad shoulders. The suit had been replaced by a plain black polo shirt that moulded his muscular chest and revealed his tanned forearms. Well-worn black jeans and a leather belt with an intricately designed brass buckle to support them hung low on his lean hips. He looked dark and dangerous, and a frisson of warning slid down her spine as he came towards her and stopped, towering over her.

'Well?' she prompted—anything to break the lengthening silence.

He studied her long blonde hair, which a slight breeze had tousled into tumbling disarray around her beautiful face, and the tight clasp of her fingers on the delicate handle of the bone-china cup. He took his time looking her over, a glitter of gold brightening his black eyes. A brilliant smile curved his sensuous mouth, making her aware of the virile sensuality he exuded without even trying. 'What kept me?' he echoed throatily. 'If I had known you missed me I would have been here like a shot.'

'I didn't miss you. I just...' She ground to a halt at his mocking laugh.

'Same old Phoebe. You certainly know how to make a man feel good,' he drawled, and, reaching down, caught hold of her hand. 'Come on, I'll show you around before the sun goes down. There have been quite a few changes since the last time you were here.'

She got to her feet and for the next half-hour she duly admired the new extension. By the time Leon led her out into the garden and insisted they watch the sunset she was almost relaxed in his company—until he put his arm around her shoulders.

Bea stiffened instinctively. They were alone on the terrace, their vantage point for watching the sunset. She tried to ease away from the disturbing warmth of his large frame, but he simply tightened his hold.

'The days are still hot in October, but at this time in

the evening the air cools rapidly, and you have no other protection but me. So be still, Phoebe, and watch.'

The sunset was magnificent, and she sighed with pleasure as together they watched the fiery red ball sink into the sea far away to the right.

'Worth the wait, but then the best things in life are,' Leon offered softly, turning her back towards the house.

She glanced up at him; it was hard to see his expression in the dim light, and for a second she thought she saw a gleam of triumph in his dark eyes. But once back inside she knew she was mistaken.

His arm falling from her shoulders, Leon smiled blandly down at her. 'Sorry, I have to leave you to your own devices until dinner at nine. I have work to do.' And again he walked away.

Once more in her bedroom, Bea kicked off her shoes and padded across to the bathroom. She turned on the taps of the spa bath, and, spying a collection of toiletries, chose a bottle of bath crystals and tipped half into the swirling water. Over the sound of the running water she heard someone knock on the bedroom door. Padding back through the bedroom, she went to open it and found Anna.

'Miss Phoebe, you like I press your clothes? The master say your luggage not yet arrived.'

'Thanks, that's a great idea. Come in.' In seconds Bea had stripped off her jacket and skirt and handed them to Anna. 'Just come in when you're finished. I'm going to wallow in the bath.'

Back in the bathroom she slid off her bra and briefs. As she bent to turn off the taps the gold chain around her throat fell forward. Her eye caught the pendant and she frowned. Turning off the water, she straightened up and removed the jewel, then she turned it over slowly in her small hand.

Walking back into the dressing room, she let the gold chain trickle through her fingers. Leon had told the truth: it was the original ill-fated ring. Strange that he should have bothered to have it altered. He could just as easily have passed it on to one of his many ladyfriends. No— he was far too cagey a bachelor for that, she realised. He would never give a mistress a ring. She might get the wrong idea!

Still, it was odd. Leon was a generous man; he could easily have bought her something new for her birthday. So why this? She picked up her bag from the dresser and slipped the pendant in the interior pocket. Whatever his reason, she was not going to wear it again; it made her uneasy somehow...

Half an hour later, feeling relaxed and refreshed, Bea stepped out of the bath and, wrapping a large towel around her wet body, swiftly washed her bra and pants in the vanity basin and hung them on the towel rail to dry. She was smiling to herself as she walked back into the dressing room; somehow, wet underwear hanging around looked oddly out of place in the luxurious bathroom.

She rummaged in her holdall for the spare set she had packed and, finding them, dried herself thoroughly and slipped on the matching white lace briefs and bra. Sitting at the dressing table, she quickly blow-dried her long hair, curving it under like a page boy's with the help of a hairbrush. Satisfied with the result, she applied the minimum of make-up: a moisturiser—her skin needed nothing more—a quick flick of the mascara wand to accentuate her long lashes, a touch of pink lipstick and she was almost ready.

Back in the bedroom, she looked around for her clothes just as Anna, after a brief knock, walked in.

'Thank you, Anna.' She took the garments with a smile and slipped on the skirt.

'It is my pleasure. For many years we have waited for your return. It is not good for the master to be alone.' Her eyes rested benignly on Bea's face. 'But now you are here to stay and everything is right again.'

'For a holiday,' Bea said awkwardly, not quite knowing what to say. The poor woman had obviously got the wrong end of the stick somehow. But it wasn't up to Bea to disillusion her; she would leave that to Leon, after she had left.

Slipping on her jacket, she strolled across to the French windows. Opening them, she stepped out onto the balcony. Taking a few deep breaths, she savoured the clear night air. It was a beautiful spot.

Best of all, there was not a reporter or photographer in sight... The pressure of the last few days and weeks fell away and she felt rejuvenated. Leon's plan wasn't all that bad, she conceded.

She looked around in pleasure at the beauty of the night, and then she stiffened. The serpent in Eden! she thought with a grim smile as her gaze caught the moonlight glinting on metal, and a man patrolling the wall with a gun.

Abruptly she turned. Finding her shoes, she slipped them on and left the room. After one or two false moves Bea found the dining room. It was an elegant room, overlooking the bay, and had an enormous table with seating for twelve. Standing by the window was Leon.

'Do we have to eat in here?' she blurted, disturbed by the sight of Leon in a white dinner jacket, a vivid reminder of the last time she had been in this room with him. 'And aren't you a tad overdressed?' she opined, suddenly no longer relaxed. Instead she could feel the tension simmering in the air between them. Was Leon remembering that last time, when she had broken their engagement? Had he dressed exactly the same again as a taunting reminder?

'I told you, Anna is insisting on doing everything correctly, and I wouldn't dare argue with her,' he responded, with an amused lift of his eyebrow, and, crossing to the table, he pulled out a chair to the right of the one at the head and indicated that she should sit down.

Studying his face, Bea was not convinced his reason was so simple. She had not forgotten his lie to the press that they were once again engaged. She couldn't put her finger on it, but she sensed something sinister lurking beneath his bland expression.

'That reminds me,' she said, sitting down and shaking out her napkin. She placed it on her lap before glancing up at Leon, who had taken his own seat at the head of the table. 'Anna seems to have some weird idea I'm staying here for a lot longer than a few days.'

'Have some wine and relax; you're imagining things.' He filled a crystal glass with sparkling wine and offered it to her.

She took it, and their fingers touched with a sudden tingle of awareness that made her pulse flutter. Hastily she took a gulp of the wine. She hadn't imagined his effect on her, and whispered under her breath, 'Oh, Lord, don't let him get to me.' But it was a futile prayer.

Anna served the meal—a mixed fish platter, which Bea found very appetizing, followed by roast lamb with an assortment of herbs, which gave it a tangy flavour. But halfway through Bea found her appetite dwindling.

Leon kept her glass topped up with wine and made pleasant, uncontroversial conversation. But she just couldn't relax. The silences between them grew longer. She found her eyes straying to his mobile mouth, found herself gulping as he unselfconsciously licked his lips. He sounded amiable enough, but she could not dismiss the feeling that underneath he was watching her with a brooding intensity that was not in the least amiable.

When he suggested they have their coffee in the main lounge, she jumped out of her seat before he could help her.

'If you don't mind, I'll give the coffee a miss. I think I'll just go to bed.'

'So soon?' Leon queried, and she flushed as she saw the sardonic gleam in his dark eyes.

'Well, with the press and everything, I haven't had much sleep the past few nights, and coffee keeps me awake,' she returned quickly, backing towards the door.

'Then of course you must go to bed. I'll see you to your room.'

'No, really.'

'I insist.'

Bea mounted the staircase with Leon a step behind her. She was sure she could feel his hot breath on the back of her neck, and she asked herself how she could have been so stupid as to get herself in this position. Turning at the door to her room to say goodnight and goodbye, she found her face only inches from his chest. Her head shot back and she put her hands on his chest to ward him off.

'Are you frightened of me, sweet Phoebe?' Leon drawled silkily, capturing her hands on his chest in one of his much larger ones.

'No, no, of course not.' But she lied. His black eyes burned down into hers and she recognised the glint of desire—and something else she couldn't name.

'Then why are you looking at me like a startled rabbit?' he demanded mockingly.

'I'm not,' she squeaked.

'Good.' With his free hand he opened the bedroom door and backed her inside.

'Goodnight, Leon.' She forced his name past her stiff lips, suddenly more afraid than she had ever been in her life, and hoping he would just go.

'One kiss, and then—'

'Please, you're being silly, Leon.' She cut him off, but stood frozen to the spot, caught between fear and fascination as he let go of her hands. In one deft movement he had undone her jacket and slid it from her shoulders to lie at her feet. His smouldering glance fell to the full curves of her breasts, cupped in a wisp of white lace.

'What do you think you're playing at?' she snapped belatedly, and felt the colour surge to her face even as she crossed her arms defensively over her chest. 'Don't be a fool, Leon. You promised.' She tried to reason with him, displaying a cool sophistication she was far from feeling. 'Friends, remember? No seduction.' Seemingly casually, she bent to retrieve her jacket.

His hand snaked out and fastened around her arm. 'No, once before I was a fool. I was stupid enough to leave you at the bedroom door. But never again.' Pulling her against him, and with his other hand lacing up into her trailing hair, he gently tugged her head back to expose her throat.

'No, no, you can't!' she cried, losing her cool. But his face became a blur as he lowered his head, and his lips trailed kisses of fire across the curve of her breast, up her throat, before his hard mouth captured hers.

CHAPTER EIGHT

IT ALL happened so quickly; one minute Bea was outside her room, the next she was inside, naked to the waist apart from a wisp of lace, and crushed against Leon's powerful body.

All thought of remaining sophisticated fled from her mind under the demanding pressure of his lips. Bea, hands flailing wildly, lashed out at any part of him she could reach in an effort to break free. But his mouth ravaged hers, and the all-consuming passion of his kiss evoked a response that insidiously drained her resistance.

'Tonight you're mine,' he growled against her lips, breaking the kiss to trail a string of kisses back down her throat. He stopped where the pulse beat madly in her neck and sucked on the tender flesh.

Her heart beating frantically, her breasts pressing painfully against the restrictive white lace of her bra, Bea groaned, 'No-o-o.'

He swallowed her denial with his mouth and swung her up in his arms. He carried her across the room and lowered her onto the bed. His mouth never left hers as he snapped on the bedside light, illuminating the room in an intimate golden glow.

When he finally released her, she found herself staring breathlessly up into the night-black darkness of Leon's eyes, and what she saw made her come alive to what was happening. Pure panic made her renew her efforts to escape. She struggled to sit up, but with one large hand he pressed her back down, and, with a dexterity born of vast experience, he shrugged out of his jacket and shirt.

'Stop it, Leon. You can't…' she cried, even as her mouth dried at the sight of his muscular bronzed chest, its dark covering of soft hair arrowing down to disappear beneath the waistband of his trousers. Trousers he was deftly unfastening, her mesmerised gaze discovered!

'I can,' he grated. 'I want you, and you can lie through your teeth denying it, but your body tells a different story.' His glittering gaze skimmed over the curves of her breasts as his trousers hit the floor, and he slid onto the bed, turning his powerful naked body towards her, partially blocking out the light and shadowing his handsome features.

His dark eyes bored into hers as she lay paralysed by a reluctant fascination. His strong arms at either side of her slender body caged her, and the weight of one long, muscular leg, thrown over hers, pinned her to the bed.

'You… Leon… You don't mean it. You'll hate yourself,' she babbled, hoping to deflect him from the avowed intent she read in his narrowed eyes. This was a Leon she didn't recognise: cold and determined. Gone was the easygoing, charming companion, and in his place was a man she instinctively knew would not take no for an answer.

'Leon, please…' She tried again as his long fingers deftly unclipped her bra and threw it to one side.

'Oh, I am going to please you, sweet Phoebe.' His hand stroked across her full breasts, his thumb casually grazing the rosy peaks. 'See how you respond?' His dark eyes lingered on her naked breasts, and a slow, sensuous smile curved his hard mouth as the rosy peaks hardened beneath his fingers.

A shaft of arrowing excitement shuddered through her as his hand moved expertly against her breast, cupping and stroking, rolling the sensitised peak between his fingers. She was helpless against his sexual onslaught, and a low moan escaped her.

'I tried to do the correct thing once. I let you tease me for years. But no more,' he grated, his hand stroking down to her waist.

Through a sensuous haze she heard his words. Had she teased him? Her confused mind tried to find the answer. But his clever, caressing hands robbed her of the power to think straight.

'I was a fool. I could have had you but I wanted more.'

Yes, that was the trouble. Her dulled mind suddenly cleared. The swine had wanted more. One woman was never enough for him; he wanted hundreds. The thought renewed her resolve to fight him off, and she lashed out with her fist. He caught her wrist and held it over her head, his glittering gaze raking her flushed face.

'Stop fighting me, Phoebe. I am nothing like the young boys you're used to. What did your friend tell the press?' he queried savagely. '"A swinging girl who can't be pinned down."'

'Andy did—'

'I don't want to hear what any other man did to you. I've ached for years, and tonight you are going to feel just some of what I have suffered, before finding pleasure you have never dreamed of with your young boys,' he drawled arrogantly.

Pinned beneath him, with the heat of his body enveloping her, it was hard to think straight, but she realised Leon actually thought she was experienced.

'No, Leon, you don't under—' She never finished.

Leon muttered something thickly in Greek and smothered her mouth with his, kissing her with devouring hunger. His hand stroked back up to cup her breast, then he grazed his lips down her throat until his mouth covered her hard nipple, and then with tongue and teeth he stroked and bit in an exquisite tormenting caress, while his fingers found her other breast and teased with subtle expertise.

The blood pounded through her veins, sheer pleasure lancing through her body, and she whimpered with delight. The rest of her clothes were removed without Bea even realising it until Leon knelt up on the bed, his arm curving around her back as he lifted her up towards him.

'You liked that, Phoebe,' he rasped, and kissed the tip of each breast before holding her a little away from him. 'Let me look at you, Phoebe.' His black eyes, lit with the flame of desire, studied her naked body. 'You are so beautiful. Your skin is as pale and as fine as a moth's wing. I can almost see your heart fluttering in your chest.'

Bea, her sensually drugged gaze slowly focusing, swallowed hard, and almost choked as she experienced a feeling more earthy. She had never seen a totally nude man in the flesh before, and Leon was magnificent. The light played across his broad shoulders and down over his flat belly to where the source of his manhood stood proud and erect. It was vaguely frightening. He was like a statue of a Greek god, perfect in feature and form, but very much alive, with the dark, domineering strength of a man who was supremely confident in his mastery of the female sex.

What was she doing here? Naked on a bed with Leon? Her worst nightmare! Or was it her ultimate fantasy? a tiny devil whispered in her brain. Panicking, she grabbed his shoulders and tried to push him away, but he simply slipped his hands around her waist and lowered his head to hers, and the force of his kiss drove her back down onto the mattress, his long body following.

The power of his kiss inflamed her senses, and the feel of his naked body moving smoothly against hers, flesh on flesh, was like being stroked by satin and steel. But still she made one last effort to deter him. She dug her fingernails into his shoulders. 'Don't do this, Leon.'

He looked down at her hectically flushed face, his black eyes glittering with gold. He moved against her again, then his hand stroked down over her stomach and slid between her legs, his palm cupping her feminine mound.

She gasped as his long fingers delved into the hot, wet warmth, and she shuddered uncontrollably.

'But you want me to…' Leon rasped throatily.

She was drowning in a sensuous world of physical pleasure. One finger pressed on the nub of her feminine joy. Her thighs parted slightly and she bit back a moan.

'Badly…' Leon growled. His eyes, brilliant with triumph, burned into hers, and deliberately he bent his head and licked the taut peak of one breast while his seeking fingers continued their devilish torment. This time she could not hold back the moan. Her hands snaked around the nape of his neck, and she was lost.

'Desperately,' he added roughly, capturing her swollen lips again in a passionate, teasing kiss.

Bea could not deny him. Her lips parted and welcomed the thrusting invasion of his tongue. Her small hands urgently roamed over the muscle and sinew of his broad back and she cried out when once again his mouth found her breast.

All the while his long, sensitive fingers explored her intimately, until she was a writhing mass of burning sensation. Muscles she'd never known she had were clenching and unclenching in aching, desperate need. Perspiration dampened her skin; her eyes lost their focus. She was aware of nothing but Leon, his strength and power, and the promise of pleasure unimaginable.

Only slowly did she realise he had stopped, that most of his weight had lifted from her.

'Open your eyes and say it,' Leon ground out between clenched teeth. 'Look at me.'

Slowly she opened her eyes and met his brilliant black gaze.

'Tell me what you want, Phoebe,' he demanded harshly.

She could not have denied him to save her life. 'You,' she breathed, and for a brief second wondered what else she had to tell him. But, reaching her small hands up to tangle in the soft hair of his chest and, more bravely, to stroke down to cup the core of his masculinity, she forgot everything.

His mighty frame shuddered. 'At last,' he groaned, and bestowed a kiss of infinite possession on her swollen lips.

Her legs parted wider to welcome him and his large hands cupped her buttocks, lifting her from the bed. He took her in a sudden mighty thrust.

Bea screamed, but her cry of pain was stifled moments later beneath Leon's lips as he stilled inside her.

'Hush, Phoebe. I did not know,' he murmured against her mouth.

'No... Please,' she begged, her body taut with the unexpected pain.

'Yes.' His lips brushed against her ear, sending a little shiver through her which intensified when he slowly withdrew, then eased gently back inside her. 'Trust me, Phoebe. Relax.' His deep, rough voice murmured comfort and encouragement. His hands moved to stroke the length of her legs. He continued to caress her, stroking.

her breasts, her stomach and the place where they were still joined.

Bea forgot the pain, forgot everything but the heady sensual emotions Leon was arousing in her. And, sensing her receptiveness, Leon thrust deeper. Bea's body arched convulsively, the pleasure so intense that she cried out again, but this time in ecstasy. She clung to him, her untutored body quickly adjusting to the rhythm he set. Wave after wave of indescribable sensation sent her shuddering to the edge, and she heard Leon's triumphant cry as his life force exploded inside her and she went careening over the edge, consumed by the fire of fulfillment into a moment of complete oblivion.

From a long way off she heard Leon's voice and opened her eyes. She was conscious of nothing except the thudding of her heart—or was it his?—and Leon's long body stretched out beside her. So that was what it was all about, she thought in awe. A rapturous feeling of complete union between two people, at one in body and soul.

'Phoebe?' Leon raised himself up on one elbow and frowned down at her. 'Are you all right?'

'Mmm,' she murmured, lazily studying him. His black hair was flat to his head with sweat, and beads of moisture glistened on his curling chest hair. She reached up a finger to trace around the sensuous line of his mouth. He had a wonderful mouth. But he caught her hand and pushed it away.

'Why didn't you tell me you were still a virgin?'

'Does it matter?' she sighed, wallowing in the glorious afterglow of loving.

'Not to me. Not now.' And, lowering his lips briefly to her breast, where her nipple instantly responded to his touch, he grinned in satisfaction and drawled mockingly, 'In fact I can almost feel sorry for Andy and the rest.'

Collapsing back on the bed, his hands behind his head, he added, 'Obviously you were a touch-but-don't-take tease. A type I always avoided in the past. But not any more; you were quite a revelation, Phoebe.'

His reference to her sexuality and supposed past boy-friends brought her down to earth with a thud. No tender words of love or reassurance... The greatest moment in her life, and for Leon she was nothing but another lay. What had she done? Her emotions raw, tears welled up in her eyes, but she blinked them back. She would not give him the satisfaction of knowing he had hurt her.

Sitting up, she found the sheet and drew it up to hide her nakedness. He had even left the light on, and some-how that only seemed to add to her shame and humila-tion. How could she have given everything to this man? The one man she had vowed not to get involved with.

She turned her head and glanced down at Leon. He was lying there, a perfect picture of the satiated male, with about as much sensitivity as a brick wall...

She had not the strength to be angry; instead a blessed numbness enveloped her and, with what little self-esteem she had left, she forced herself to speak.

'Yes, well, if you say so. Who am I to argue with a man of your vast experience? But would you please leave? I want to sleep.' Her decision was made in an instant. She was leaving tomorrow—getting off this is-land and out of his life. She would rather face the world press than end up as another one of Leon's playthings.

Bea brushed the hair back from her forehead with a shaky hand, wondering how she could have been so foolish as to imagine they had shared an almost mystical experience. Two people joined in body and soul! Leon had long since lost count of the women who had shared his bed. As for his soul, she doubted he had one...

Slowly, Leon sat up. Naked and unashamed, he turned

his dark gaze on her pale face. 'What the hell are you talking about?' he said, with a softness that was more threatening than shouting. 'You belong to me, and we share a bed.'

'No,' Bea said firmly. 'It was an interesting experience, and you can mark another notch on your belt. You got what you wanted. Now go.'

His dark eyes flared with anger. 'No way,' he snapped. The light went out at the touch of his hand, and the room was plunged into darkness.

Bea could make out his large shape and felt his hand tug the sheet from her grasp. 'What are you doing?'

'Expanding your education, Phoebe. Obviously you know very little about men if you imagine once is enough,' Leon's deep voice drawled silkily. He ran a taunting hand down over her breasts. 'That was for starters, if you like. The main course is the fun.'

His lips touched hers, and to her never-ending shame she was too weak to resist. Or maybe a tiny part of her brain said, Why not? She was leaving tomorrow. Who could begrudge her one night of passion? It might be the only passion she would ever know.

That thought scared her more than anything. It was tantamount to admitting Leon was the only man for her... She closed her eyes tight and gave herself up to the pleasure of his kiss, and within moments she was drowning in a sea of sensuous delight...

Bea opened her eyes. Dazzling sunlight made her blink sleepily, and the delicious smell of fresh coffee teased her nostrils. She tried to sit up and it was then she realised that a very masculine tanned arm, lightly dusted with black hair, was clamped firmly around her waist. Please let me be dreaming, she prayed, but she turned her head slightly and her gaze fell upon the sleeping face of Leon. 'Oh, God!' she groaned.

'Good morning.'

It got worse… Anna appeared at the side of the bed with a tray loaded with two cups and saucers, coffee jug, cream and sugar.

'Anna,' Bea murmured weakly, and, carefully lifting Leon's arm from her waist, she sat up. 'I…you…' Her face turning scarlet with embarrassment, she battled on, 'It's not what…'

'Shh, I understand,' Anna said in a whisper, a broad smile lighting her plump face, and, placing the tray on the bedside table, she added, 'We no wake the master. It is long time since he sleep.'

With the events of last night giving an instant replay in her mind, Bea's blush deepened even further. Trust the pig to sleep on, she thought bitterly. Again and again in the night he had turned to her, and she had been putty in his hands. Now she had to face Anna, stricken with guilt and embarrassment, while he snored. He had no conscience. But then she had always known that.

'Thank you, Anna.' Casting a glance around the room, she spied her scattered clothes. 'Would you mind pressing my suit again?' she asked. It was all she had to wear, and she wanted to get out of here as quickly as possible.

'No need, Anna.' Leon sat up, very much awake. Curving an arm around Bea's waist, he nuzzled her neck, the morning stubble on his jaw grazing her skin. 'Phoebe, darling, we can stay here till your luggage arrives, or there are some clothes my stepmother left in the wardrobe. Take your pick. But I know which I prefer,' he drawled throatily.

Anna, beaming benignly on what she perceived as the happy couple, scooted out of the room. Bea, with a hard fist to Leon's chest that sent him sprawling back on the pillows, scooted out of bed. Grabbing the sheet and wrapping it around her naked body, she let her gaze skim the tray. Two cups. *Two* cups! And then it clicked.

She spun around, the full fury of her blue eyes blasting the man reclining stark naked on the bed. 'Two cups... You planned all this. You even told Anna,' she spluttered in her rage. 'It's one thing to be seduced on the spur of the moment, but, but...' Words failed her.

'Seduced? You? You couldn't get enough,' Leon responded with a shout of laughter. Bea dashed to the dressing room and into the bathroom, his mocking laughter ringing in her ears.

She locked the door behind her and, dropping the sheet, entered the shower and turned on the water, before giving way to tears of hurt, anger and bitter humiliation.

He was right. She had acted like a woman possessed. She had gloried in his lovemaking, had willingly followed him down the paths of erotic delight that he, with his vast experience, had revealed to her. The unfamiliar aches and a light bruise on her naked body bore testimony to the fact, she sadly admitted to herself as she scrubbed and rubbed her naked flesh in an attempt to wash away his touch.

But never again, she silently vowed. After removing the lingerie she had left to dry on the towel rail the night before and slipping it on, she unlocked the bathroom door and entered the dressing room. Fearful that at any moment Leon might burst in, she hastily searched the wardrobes. Finding a pair of plain black chinos, she pulled them on; they were a bit tight, but would do. A skimpy white knit cropped top completed the ensemble. With her long hair still damp, and stuck behind her ears, she straightened her spine and, picking up her bag from the dresser, marched back into the bedroom, expecting to face her Nemesis.

The room was empty, the bed made afresh—no sign of her night of debauchery, or of Leon. Bea breathed a sigh of relief and, spying her blue high-heeled pumps, slipped them on her feet. Hardly haute couture, if the press were waiting when she arrived back in London, she thought grimly. But what the hell? So long as she got away from Leon.

The kitchen was empty, much to Bea's relief, and, crossing to where the telephone was fixed to the wall, she picked it up. Ten minutes later, she slammed it back down in exasperation. It had been easy enough to get through to the British Airways office—most Greek Cypriots spoke some English, probably because the British armed forces had been a presence on the island for decades—but, unfortunately, the earliest she could get a seat on a flight back to London was tomorrow.

Worrying her bottom lip with her teeth, Bea moved around the kitchen, making her breakfast. Anna was probably at the vegetable market. Finally, she sat down at the kitchen table and pondered her dilemma.

By the time she had finished eating, a kernel of an idea had taken root in her mind, and, draining the last of her coffee, she stood up with a determined expression on her face. Leaving the kitchen, she headed for the study.

Taking a deep breath, she opened the door and walked in. Leon was sitting behind a large leather-topped desk, his dark head bent over some papers. He looked up at her arrival, the beginnings of a smile curving his sexy mouth.

'Good. You have recovered from your sulks, Phoebe?' Rising to his feet, he strolled towards her. 'It is not un-usual after a girl's first time for her to feel upset—angry, even. But—'

'But nothing,' she cut in, astounded by his arrogant

complacency. Her eyes took in his large form, casually dressed in blue jeans and a blue denim shirt; he looked disgustingly, vibrantly male. His hand reached out to her shoulder, but, hanging onto her anger, she shrugged it off, moving around him. 'I want to contact the company jet.' She swung on her heel to face him again. 'I am leaving. Today.'

'Are you, now?' Leon drawled softly, closing the door and leaning back against it.

'Yes,' she said curtly. 'As you have reminded me more than once, I am a partner, and the company assets are at my disposal just as much as yours. And that includes the company aircraft.'

'True, but unfortunately the jet is out of commission.'

'I don't believe you,' she said through clenched teeth. 'It was perfectly fine yesterday, when you set out to— to seduce me!'

His gaze rested on her rigidly held body, then sank to her clenched fists, and an expression of derision tautened his hard bone structure. 'Do you honestly think I would have had to fly you across a continent, at great expense to the company, to seduce you, when I could have had you in your apartment, your home, any time I chose?' he mocked as he stepped away from the door, lessening the distance between them until he towered over her like the devil she thought him to be.

Bea flushed scarlet, but she refused to be intimidated. 'That's where you're wrong, Leon. And, anyway, I don't care what you think. I want that aircraft today,' she ended furiously, only to find her shoulders gripped with fingers of steel.

'And, as I told you last night, I want you, Phoebe.' His voice was low and dangerous. 'But you obviously did not understand me correctly.'

'You can't force me to stay here; you have no right,'

she protested hotly. 'In any case I have a seat booked tomorrow with British—'

'That will be cancelled,' he interrupted, his hands biting deeper into the soft flesh of her upper arms. His nearness was an aching reminder of the night they had shared and it severely drained her confidence. 'You are not leaving here.' Thickly lashed black eyes rested inscrutably on her hot cheeks. 'I brought you here to protect you, and that is what I am going to do.'

'Protect me?' she protested heatedly. 'Is that what you call it? Invading a girl's bedroom—'

'Be careful what you say, Phoebe,' he cut in ruthlessly, 'or I will be forced to remind you just how willing a bed partner you were.' His hand touched her cheek and stroked back to tangle in her hair. 'And you will be again.'

'No,' she denied.

'Yes. We want each other, and in two weeks' time it will be legal. We will be married.'

For a second, shock held her silent, but then, as the import of his words sank in, a brittle laugh escaped her. 'What is this, Leon? An action replay of years ago, but without the supporting cast?' The memory of Selina was a constant reminder of his perfidy, even if her traitorous heart had leapt at his words. 'You must be crazy!'

'I almost was, Phoebe. Locked in darkness for days on end,' he said savagely, with seething bitterness. 'Chained by the feet like a dog. I had a lot of time to think between struggling to break free, my blood lubricating the chains, and wondering if I would die... But not any more—I learnt a valuable lesson.'

Caught in the turmoil of her own emotions, Bea had forgotten Leon's recent ordeal. Her compassionate heart touched, she studied his handsome face. His dark eyes blazed with fire but he didn't seem to see her. He was lost in the hell of his kidnap. 'What was—?'

Ruthlessly he cut across her. 'A man must protect his own against the world. I was a fool. I promised my father to look after the business and his partner, and I thought I had succeeded. Before your father died, I made him a very wealthy man, more than he ever dreamed. But what happened? Yet again, for the third time, a Stephen had to bail out a Gregoris.'

Bea listened in amazement, and with a growing sense of unease as he continued, 'You, Phoebe…' His hand felt like a steel band around her arm, and his black eyes clashed with hers, no longer unfocused, but deadly in their intensity. 'You, whom I had vowed to protect.' His other hand tightened in her hair, tilting her head back further, 'you, sweet Phoebe, ended up paying the ransom.' He dragged her up against him. 'You! Whom I should have married years ago. But instead I let you wander around at will.'

The hard contact of his body against her own attacked her senses. Bea felt the colour leave her cheeks and beneath her top a trickle of perspiration ran down between her breasts, but it was more from fear than arousal. Leon was not joking. It had bruised his male ego, being kidnapped, and it was a woman that had had to bail him out. She knew him well enough to understand how he must feel.

It did not matter to Leon that the money had been recovered. He was a very proud man, and to discover he was not invincible must have been devastating, the injury to his pride incalculable. But the fanaticism in his gaze terrified her. She lifted her free hand to his chest, hoping to pacify him in some way. Licking her dry lips nervously, she murmured, 'It wasn't your fault.'

'Oh, yes, it was. I was arrogant and headstrong. I believed the world waited on me. Now I know better, and I never want you to have to learn the same lesson. Which is why you and I are getting married, and why you are staying here. Here I can vouch for your safety.'

He meant it, Bea realised, with a sickening lurch in her stomach. The electric fence, the guards—they all made sense. But wait a minute. She told herself not to panic. He had only been free a little over a week—he couldn't have arranged everything so quickly!

'I was already in the process of improving the security here because of trouble at the partition line between Greek and Turk; it was a simple matter to hire the armed guards.'

Unfortunately, he had accurately read her mind, and his answer made sense. Dazedly she surveyed him. 'But I can't stay here.'

'Rubbish. After last night what else can you do?' And, planting a swift, hard kiss on her trembling lips, he slanted her a ruthless smile as he set her free. 'Here you will be totally secure. The guards have strict instructions—you only leave with me.' The matter settled to his satisfaction, he brushed past her and resumed his seat behind the oak desk.

'You…are…mad…' Bea said, enunciating each word slowly and clearly, as if talking to a child. 'I'm getting out of here, and you can't stop me. I'll get Anna to help me…'

Leon lounged back in the leather chair, one black brow arched sardonically, a glimmer of a grin twisting his hard mouth. 'Really, Phoebe! Anna, who brought us coffee in bed this morning? I think not. She is a very old-fashioned Greek lady. She already considers you my wife.'

'Or Lil and Bob. You can't guard the phone.' She was casting around for a way out.

'I have already spoken to them both. They agree with me. As a very public heiress, your security is vital. Northumbria is not known for kidnapping since the Border reiver days. But even so I have set in motion plans to have the house at Mitford secured just in case. Don't worry, darling; in a few months we will be able to go for a visit.'

'We…we… I'm not going anywhere with you. Can't you get that into your stupid head?' Bea exploded.

'I know you're staying here,' Leon whipped back in silky derision. 'Call Lil, if you like, but remember our engagement is front-page news all over Britain today, and I have already told them we're getting married. I felt it was the correct thing to do, as they have acted *in loco parentis* for so long.'

At the mention of the newspapers, Bea's mouth fell open in shocked horror. She listened to the rest and was left standing in the middle of the room, gazing at Leon with her mouth working like a goldfish. She was lost for words, and only slowly beginning to comprehend what was happening. Dear heaven, the swine had thought of everything!

The suit, the pendant he had so casually told her to wear. 'Your plan wasn't to help me escape the press, it was to help yourself,' she said, almost to herself. 'How long…?' How long had he been planning to marry her? She couldn't put her thoughts into words. Since the kidnap? Or sooner? Since her birthday…?

'I always intended marrying you one day, Phoebe, but I hadn't decided when to give up my freedom. But being kidnapped concentrates the mind marvellously, along with a few other not so nice emotions. Hence your presence here now… As for my plan, I didn't really have one—until I saw your photograph in the newspaper, in which you were wearing the pendant. I bought the ring for you originally, and I had it altered on a whim for your birthday. You gave me a golden opportunity to announce to the world we were engaged, and I took it...'

'But why?' If it was her share of the company that he wanted, he could have it. 'Leon, if this is about the business you can have it,' she said urgently, crossing to the desk where he sat lounging back in a black hide chair, looking remarkably unconcerned, while a very real fear was building in Bea's mind. 'I'll sell you my share. I don't care. You can do what you like. Just let me leave.'

Dark colour stained his bronzed skin, and a flash of naked anger lit his eyes. 'Care does not come into it, or business.' He shoved back his chair and stalked around the desk. A hard hand spun her round, his fingers exerting pressure on her narrow shoulder. 'Can't you get it into your head, Phoebe? I am going to protect you. From the minute the world knew you were wealthy, you, Phoebe, became a possible kidnap victim. The only way I can be sure you are safe is to keep you with me all the time. And the obvious way to do that is for us to get married.'

Bea backed against the edge of the desk, nervously licking her dry lips. 'What on earth are you talking about? Don't you think you should see a doctor?' He was totally serious. The days in captivity really had affected his brain. In a weird way she could understand his motivation—he was paranoid about her safety—but he didn't seem to realise the irony of the situation. By making her a prisoner in his home, he was no better than the kidnappers.

Leon cast her a hard, triumphant smile. 'No, Phoebe, but in a few weeks' time *you* may need one. Have you thought you could already be carrying my child? I don't recall that we used any protection, and I seriously doubt you are on the pill, given your virginal state.'

White as a sheet, she stared up at him. 'You ruthless bastard,' she burst out unsteadily. The thought of pregnancy had never entered her head.

His fingers tightened on her shoulder and he jerked her up against his hard, masculine body. 'Maybe, but our child won't be.' He swore roughly before his dark head bent and he brought his mouth down fiercely upon hers, forcing her soft lips to part at the possessive thrust of his tongue.

A swift, unexpected surge of need lanced through her body as his hand settled low on her back, pressing her against his hard-muscled thighs. Only when she lay supine in his arms, defeated by her own instinctive arousal to his touch, did he desert her lips to lift his dark head.

'We have been friends for years, Phoebe. Don't spoil it by fighting with me now. Everything you want or need I can provide. A beautiful home, clothes, jewels, servants, even a family. And you know we're compatible. What more do you want?' Lowering his head, he let his lips feather across hers. 'You're young, but trust me on this, Phoebe. I know... We're great in bed together; the chemistry is there. Everything will be fine.'

Bea fell back from him, shaking like a leaf. 'Fine?' He was so bloody confident, and she had never hated herself as much as she did at that moment for surrendering to his sensuous persuasion. With self-loathing came anger, and with the fear of pregnancy fresh in her mind she lashed out at him in the worst way she could think of.

'Fine?' she repeated scathingly. 'And did your mistress Selina think it was *fine* when you left her holding the baby? Is one bastard child in the family enough for you, Leon? And don't give me the ''old friends'' routine, or your high moral view on marriage. I don't believe you.'

He stepped back as if she had struck him, his face draining of all colour. 'Who—?'

'Who told me?' She cut across him. 'Why, Leon, I heard you,' she drawled, warming to the subject. For years it had festered in her mind, the fact that she knew of his duplicity and had never revealed it. 'I was outside on the patio when your mistress of three years told you she was pregnant. I can even quote your response: "You bitch, Selina. You did it deliberately"—or words to that effect.'

'You heard?' Releasing his breath slowly, Leon stared across the room at her. 'You knew.' He bit out a harsh laugh, his hands clenching at his sides as if he would prefer them around her throat.

'I was young, but I wasn't totally stupid,' Bea lashed back. 'I could count, Leon. Engaged nearly five months, and with a mistress two months pregnant, does not add up in any woman's book,' she said sarcastically.

Something raw and primeval flashed in his black eyes as they clashed with hers. She shivered, and a sliver of fear trickled down her spine. This was more than anger.

'You devious little bitch. You had me believing I was too old for you, and then years later you let slip that it was business; you didn't trust me. None of it was true. Your excuses were all lies,' Leon hissed. 'It was just typical female pique. You overheard a conversation and condemned me.'

'Come on, Leon,' Bea prompted cynically. The man's arrogance was incredible! Trying to make *her* out to be the guilty one! 'With good cause. A party in Newport, wasn't it?' she queried, with an arch of one delicate brow.

Leon took a step towards her and she shrank back, fear churning her stomach. But to her amazement he stopped. His face was an impenetrable mask as he stood looking down at her—a mask carved out of granite. His temper was firmly under control, Bea thought as she warily raised her eyes to his.

'If you say so, Phoebe. Who am I to argue?' His dark eyes were cold and remote. 'But it changes nothing. You will stay here. It is for your own good.'

'My own good?' she parroted. The audacity of the man was incredible!

'Yes, and we will share a bed.'

He left her standing there, speechless, and walked out of the room.

CHAPTER NINE

STUNNED by the utter finality of his last statement, Bea stood looking at the door for a long moment, hoping against hope that Leon would return, grin, and tell her it was all a joke. He'd used to like teasing her, she thought pathetically, and then cringed at her own mawkishness. That was the Leon of her childhood; the Leon who had issued his ultimatum this morning was a totally different man. Cynical and coldly dispassionate, he had told her she was staying, and that was that...

Well, he wasn't getting away with it, Bea vowed. Galvanised into action, she shot out of the study and made straight for the front door. An hour later, after walking around the perimeter wall, she was about ready to give up. When she had tried to leave, the guard on the gate had simply grinned and pretended he didn't speak English, but Bea would have bet her last penny that he did.

The midday sun was fierce, and Bea wiped her sweat-soaked brow with the back of her hand. She was just about back to where she started and had found no way out. Then she espied Anna's husband, Spiros. He was walking along, head bent, pushing a wheelbarrow full of what looked like geranium plants.

With any luck Anna might not have had a chance to tell Spiros yet about finding Bea in bed with the master. The old man could be her chance to escape. The guards would not stop him. All she had to do was persuade him to take her to the town, the market—anything, so long as she got outside.

His happy smile of greeting lifted her spirits. His English was good so she had no trouble conversing with him. She spent some time enthusing over his beautifully kept garden, but then was flattened when he congratulated her on her engagement. But, her mind working quickly, she saw a way to use his knowledge to her advantage. She accepted his congratulations with a smile, and then, confiding in him, asked if he would mind walking down to the town with her. She wanted to buy a surprise betrothal gift for Leon.

Spiros was delighted to oblige.

Tucking her bag firmly under her arm, Bea approached the entrance gates. It was going to work, she thought exultantly. Spiros spoke to the guard, explaining the situation. Like most Greek Cypriots, he was a romantic, and with a beaming smile for Bea he opened the electronically controlled gates.

She was free. Now all she had to worry about was how to give Spiros the slip, but she couldn't see it being a problem; the man was sixty if he was a day, and as a last resort she could out-run him, she thought, grinning all over her face as each step took her further away from the villa.

A car screamed around in front of them, the wheels skidding as it stopped dead, throwing up a cloud of dust. When it cleared, Bea just had time to recognise a furious Leon before he grasped her around the waist and hauled her hard against him. Her back slammed into his chest, forcing the air from her lungs, leaving her winded and choking.

But Leon ignored her and turned his attention on the hapless old man who had accompanied her, letting go in a tirade of Greek which, by the time he had finished, had Spiros looking balefully at Bea, then hanging his head and walking slowly to the car.

She felt guilty for using Spiros, but she was also mad as hell. Grabbing Leon's forearm, she tried to prise it from her waist. 'Let go of me!' she cried. 'I'm not going back with you, Leon. I don't care what you say.'

He spun her around to face him. 'Oh, but you are, Phoebe.' His deadly drawling voice sent a shiver down her spine. 'Tricking an old man.' He raised one eyebrow, his expression icy. 'A bit low, even for you.'

'How did you find out I'd left?' she demanded, staring up at him in angry frustration.

He smiled and her blood ran cold. 'The guard reports every person entering or exiting directly to me.'

Her shoulders sagged. 'I want to go home, and you can't stop me.' But her words had lost their bite. She might have guessed Leon would have back-up. He was noted for being thorough in everything he did. She suddenly felt sick. But then, looking up at him through a mist of anger and humiliation, she caught a gleam of something that looked remarkably like tenderness in his black eyes.

Their gazes met and fused. Bea was suddenly conscious of the warmth of his arm against her bare midriff. She felt herself start to tremble, her heart thudding heavily in her breast, and she swallowed hard. 'Let go of me. You have to let me go, Leon,' she whispered, desperation edging her tone.

Held in his arms, she had little or no resistance to him, and deep down she knew that if she did not escape from his disturbing influence soon, very soon, she would never leave him…

Leon's gaze burnt on her upturned face for a long moment. 'You don't mean that,' he said in a chilling, quiet voice, and, urging her forward and opening the car door, he propelled her inside. He walked to the other side and slipped in beside her. 'Never try that again,' he said flatly as he started the engine.

Too dejected to reply, Bea turned her head and looked out of the window. In a matter of minutes they were back in the villa and Anna, with a reproachful look at Bea and a scathing comment for poor Spiros, declared lunch was served.

Lunch was a silent affair, with Bea seated at Leon's side in the formal dining room, morosely pushing what she suspected was a very tasty moussaka around her plate, quite unable to eat it. The events of last night and the morning had left her feeling like a washed-out dish-rag, and it was all Leon's fault. She shot him a frustrated glance. They obviously hadn't affected him at all; he was eating as if he had not touched food for weeks. 'Pig,' she muttered to herself, but he heard.

'Sorry, Phoebe? What did you say?' he enquired silkily, lifting his head and fixing her with his unsmiling gaze.

'I said you look hungry,' she compromised, not wanting to start an argument. She was too weary.

'I am a big man; I have a big appetite—as you know,' he replied, and his sensual mouth curved in a wicked smile at the sudden surge of colour in her face.

'You're a pig,' she retaliated, all thought of appeasing him vanishing at his sexual teasing.

'Ten days without food take a lot of making up,' he offered, and returned to eating, leaving Bea stricken with guilt at her callousness in forgetting his imprisonment, even as she burnt with resentment at his ability always to get the last word.

After strolling around the grounds once again, in the futile hope that she might have missed a way out the first time, Bea returned hot and exhausted to her bedroom. The sight of her suitcases, all her possessions from her London apartment, stacked in the middle of the room, did nothing for her temper. She was damned if she was going to unpack them, she swore. But was thwarted by Anna, who insisted on doing it for her...

Bea's furious resentment was still simmering when Leon joined her at the dinner table that night. She listened as he talked quietly but impersonally about the island, but she made no effort to prolong the conversation. Instead, as soon as Anna had served the dessert, she excused herself with, 'Not for me. I might get fat,' and bolted from the room.

She went to bed, taking care to lock the door behind her. The stress and strain of the past forty-eight hours had finally caught up with her. She knew that she should be making plans to escape to England. But how to face the press, her friends, her workmates, Lil and Bob, and try to explain without looking a complete and utter fool, was beyond her. Groaning, she buried her head in the pillow, and surprisingly quickly she fell asleep.

Bea awoke some time later from a beautiful, sensuous dream, in which her perfect mate was declaring his undying love, to find that a large male hand was cupping and caressing her breast. Another was tracing the line of her thigh, and a warm male mouth was nuzzling her ear.

'Leon.' She swallowed. 'How did you get in?' she asked in a voice that trembled.

'I climbed up onto the balcony, but does it matter?' he demanded, and then her lips were covered with a hard mouth and he was kissing her with a devilish sensuality that made her mind spin.

He was right again; it didn't matter... She tried to resist, but in the lingering aftermath of her dream-filled sleep her languorous body was all too eager to respond to his touch. Leon's lips left hers to seek the rosy peak of her breast, then moved lower down, touching her body with tantalising, teasing strokes and kisses. At this point she gave up the fight. She clasped her hands around his neck and offered up her body in willing surrender.

'You want me. You can't help yourself,' Leon declared with silky triumph. 'You have the face of an angel and the body of a wanton.'

She could not deny him.

Much later she lay, wide-eyed, beside him, her body boneless but her mind in turmoil. The most beautiful act between two people in the world, and all she felt was a burning shame at her helpless surrender. She eased herself up the bed and looked down at Leon. His large body was slanted across the mattress, naked and totally relaxed, his muscular chest moving gently in the even rhythm of sleep.

Her eyes lingered on his face. With his eyes closed, his firm mouth relaxed in a soft smile, he looked so much younger, and she was reminded of the first time they had kissed.

At seventeen he had swept her off her feet, and then betrayed her girlish dreams. But with the idealism of youth and enthusiasm for life she had quickly recovered, neatly slotting Leon into the Don Juan category: okay as a friend, but to be avoided as a lover. The man didn't know the meaning of the word 'commitment'.

But with the first light of dawn illuminating the night sky Bea finally admitted to herself what, deep down, she had known all along. She loved Leon. She always had and always would. But the knowledge gave her no joy.

She could do as he said. Marry him, let him protect her in his own misguided way, and glory in his lovemaking and constant companionship. Live on this paradise island. But she would be living in a fool's paradise…

Common sense told her Leon had not been his usual self since the kidnap. But eventually he would get over the trauma. Security would lose its interest for him, his burning desire to keep her safe would fade with time, and she would be left with a husband who didn't love her and not a cat in hell's chance of him staying faithful to her.

Sighing softly, Bea eased herself off the bed. She glanced at Leon as she crossed stealthily past the foot of the bed. His brow furrowed into a frown as she watched. His sleeping thoughts were no more uplifting than her waking ones, she thought sadly, strolling across to the window and staring sightlessly out.

It was no good ranting and raving at Leon, she realised. Because basically he was ill, suffering from a terrible fear of captivity and obviously feeling some kind of macho guilt that a woman had had to bail him out. Maybe there was even a scientific name for his disorder. Bea didn't know. But if she wanted to be free she had to reason with him, appeal to his better nature. Eventually he would recover his equilibrium and be the same old womanising rake he always had been. Sadly, of that she was certain...

'No, no, no!' The shout rent the air and Bea nearly jumped out of her skin.

'Leon!' She dashed back to the bed. He was groaning, muttering unintelligible sounds and words. His handsome face was contorted in agony, his long legs thrashing around the bed. 'Leon, please.'

His naked body was bathed in sweat. He was having a nightmare, that much was obvious, but Bea had no idea what to do. Tentatively she reached out her hand and stroked his fevered brow... Like a steel manacle Leon's hand closed around her wrist.

'Now I've got you, you scum,' he growled. His eyes

opened, wild and unfocused, and Bea felt herself being dragged across his mighty torso.

'Leon—Leon, please. It—'

'Phoebe?' His dark gaze settled uncertainly on the tumbled mass of her silver-blonde hair. 'Phoebe, you're not a dream?'

Putting her free hand on his chest, she pushed herself up slightly. 'You were having a nightmare, no dream.'

His big arms curled around her and he hugged her to him. 'God, I'm sorry. I didn't frighten you, did I?'

'No.' She tried to wriggle out of his embrace, but he held her firm.

'Shh, Phoebe. I've got you. You're safe now. Go back to sleep.'

'No, Leon. I don't want to be safe. I want to go home.' She felt his body tense beneath her. 'I want to see my friends, go back to work. You must understand. You can't make me a captive to your obsession. I realise the kidnap has left you with a fanatical desire for security,' she said quietly, 'but your nightmares will soon pass and you won't want to be stuck with me.'

She'd thought she was reassuring him, but she was wrong…

'I understand all right,' he snarled. 'Get to me softly, when I need your comfort, and maybe you'll win. More feminine wiles, Phoebe?'

Bea alternately begged, pleaded and yelled, trying to get Leon to see sense, but it was no good. When Anna arrived with the coffee Leon was up and dressed, and Bea was glowering at him in sick frustration.

For the next two days Leon went out of his way to try to entertain her. At breakfast the first day he suggested a trip to Limassol, and the next day a trip to the Troodos Mountains. But she rejected all his overtures, determined to ignore him.

But at night it was not so easy. The key to her bedroom door had mysteriously disappeared. Leon simply walked in and within minutes overcame her pathetic attempts at resistance. But she was fighting herself as much as him. She wanted him; she loved him. And, even though she never said the words, he was experienced enough to know she was with him all the way.

On the fifth morning, after another night as a helpless slave to his sexual expertise, Bea was drinking the coffee Anna had provided with the sheet tucked firmly around her breasts. It was stupid, she knew. Leon had seen her naked, knew every inch of her body, but she couldn't feel comfortable with him. It was not that sort of relationship. They came together in the night, like two passion-starved lovers, but in the light of day she could barely look at him.

Her coffee finished, she put the cup down on the tray by the bed and raised her head. Leon was leaning against the railings of the balcony, looking out across the bay, a coffee cup in one hand. His only covering was a white towel, slung low around his hips. Why didn't he just get dressed and leave? she thought bitterly, her blue eyes fixed on the back of his head.

He turned and their eyes met, hers burning with resentment, his distinctly mocking. 'Clutching that sheet does not hide your charms, Phoebe. I don't know why you bother.'

'Not everyone is an exhibitionist like you,' she shot back, giving his bronzed chest and muscular legs a derisory glance that did not quite come off. She gulped at the obvious bulge beneath the white towel and looked away.

'Give yourself a break, Phoebe. It's a beautiful day.' He crossed to where she sat huddled on the bed and lowered his lips to the satin softness of her shoulder.

Then he straightened up, adding, 'You must be bored, hanging around the garden all day. When I brought you here I didn't mean to stay in the villa every minute of the day.'

She glanced up at him, her blue eyes wide with surprise. The gall of the man. 'Excuse me,' she drawled, 'but that is not the impression I got when I was hauled back here the other day after barely getting a hundred yards with Spiros.'

'That was unfortunate, I admit. But Spiros, much as I admire him, is not the man to protect you.'

Bea's eyes met Leon's, and for once there was no trace of his usual mockery. And when he smiled her heart missed a beat. It was so much like the old Leon's grin. There was nothing remote about him.

'Let me take you out. We can go down into Paphos for lunch and then on to Petra tou Romiou. Legend has it that the goddess Aphrodite was born from the sea-foam. A large rock, the Rock of Aphrodite, marks the spot. It comes into sight about sixteen miles east of Paphos—not far. Bring your bathing suit; it really is a gorgeous day and you might like a swim.'

Whether it was the touch of his lips still lingering on her shoulder, whether it was simple boredom or something else...Bea heard herself agree.

They spent the rest of the morning walking around Paphos. To Bea's fascination, not more than five hundred yards from the harbour were the ruins of the Villa of Theseus.

She turned to Leon, blue eyes shining. 'I had no idea Paphos was so old, or had so many ancient ruins.'

'Like me, you mean,' Leon joked, with an indulgent smile at her vibrant face.

'Fool.' She punched him on the arm.

Later, sitting at a table outside one of the restaurants on the harbour, Bea said, 'I can't believe how lovely it all is.' Her glance went to the mighty fortress at the end of the harbour. 'Is that Roman as well?' She gestured with her hand, and turned a beaming face to Leon.

'No, Turkish, and mind your hand!' he exclaimed with a chuckle.

She followed to where his eyes were focused, and laughed out loud. A big pink pelican was attempting to snap at her waving fingers. 'What the…?'

'He's a fixture around here. The restaurant is named after him,' Leon informed her with a grin.

It was like a day out of time, Bea thought happily as she sat next to Leon in the passenger seat while he manoeuvred the car along the highway.

'How come you still drive yourself here in Cyprus, when you won't anywhere else?' Bea asked idly, recalling his outburst in the limousine in London.

Leon cast her a sidelong glance and smiled. 'Because here, as I have been trying to impress upon you, it is virtually safe. Everyone knows me, and we Cypriots look out for our own. Any crime committed around here, and the people will give the police every bit of information. A criminal rarely escapes for much more than an hour or two. It helps, of course, being a small island—nothing goes unnoticed.'

It made sense, Bea realised, but even so she couldn't see Leon being happy to remain here for ever. He was too much a man of the world. She turned her head to say so, but Leon lifted a hand and pointed ahead.

'Look.' And there in the sea was a rock.

'It's not that big,' Bea remarked, vaguely disappointed.

But once the car was parked, and the two of them had scrambled down onto the pebbly beach, Bea was oddly impressed, and somehow saddened. The birthplace of the goddess of love, she mused, glancing at Leon.

He was standing looking out to sea. That air of masculine virility which always surrounded him usually blinded her to the man inside, but with the sun glinting on his short curly hair, highlighting the grey strands, she was struck by how tired and lonely he looked. Physically he was perfect, but the horror of his imprisonment must haunt him, and, however much she might resent his treatment of her, it did not alter the fact that she loved him.

Here this place, if legend was to be believed, was where love was born, and Bea had an overwhelming urge to go to him and put her arms around him. Did it matter that he didn't love her? He was prepared to marry her, and maybe with time he might grow to love her. She had to take the chance.

She took a step towards him, prepared to tell him how she felt.

Leon looked around unexpectedly and caught her in the act of staring at him. For a long moment they simply looked into each other's eyes. Then Leon moved and his arms were around her. 'Enjoying yourself, Phoebe?' he asked tentatively.

She reached up on her tiptoes and gently put her lips to his. 'Yes,' she murmured, the kiss freely given with all the love in her heart.

'I will make you happy. I promise, Phoebe,' Leon vowed, his dark eyes gleaming golden into hers, and in that moment something intensely personal, a recognition of their need for each other, flowed between them.

'I know you will,' Bea confessed, and Leon found her lips again with his own. The ground seemed to shake beneath her feet as Leon deepened the kiss, his strong arms holding her firmly against his hard body. It was a kiss of infinite tenderness, a promise of commitment.

So it was all the more surprising when Leon yelled, 'My God!' Staring over her shoulder, he tightened his grip on her. 'Quick! Off this beach, away from the rocks. It's an earthquake!'

Bea looked down in horror; the pebbles on the beach were really moving, and as Leon dragged her along she realised he was right. The grass was moving, and the trees, and yet there was no wind. The car was shaking; two more had crashed into each other on the open road. The telephone poles shook—everything was moving.

It was like walking on jelly—impossible to know if your feet would support you. Leon found a bit of open ground and simply held her. Terrified, she buried her head in his chest and clung to him for dear life. She had no idea how long it lasted, but it seemed like hours. Then Leon took her back to the car, which was, amazingly, undamaged, and turned on the radio.

An earthquake measuring 6.3 on the Richter scale, with its epicentre in Paphos, Cyprus, had also been felt in Israel, Lebanon, Syria and Turkey. People were warned to stay as far away from buildings as possible, and to expect the aftershock.

It was a tribute to Leon's nerve and skill that they managed to get back to the villa. The house was undamaged, but part of the perimeter wall had collapsed and, worse, Spiros had been caught by the falling masonry and taken away in an ambulance to hospital.

By nightfall the first aftershock had hit, and with it came the news from the hospital that Spiros was dead.

That night would live in Bea's memory to her dying day. She sat trying to console Anna, in between drinking the coffee and brandy Leon kept plying her with. No one considered going to bed—the shock of the day's events was too severe. Only Leon was a tower of strength, doing what had to be done.

The next day the radio reported that two people were dead. A woman in Egypt, whose house had collapsed on her, and a man in Cyprus, where a wall had collapsed on him and he had suffered a fatal heart attack. Spiros. But altogether the damage was not too bad; Cyprus had been lucky. The epicentre had been twenty miles out to sea, off Paphos; if it had been under the island, the country would have been split into pieces.

Bea walked along the hall, having finally got Anna to lie down and sleep on the sofa at about eight in the morning. She didn't feel lucky; she felt like crying. She needed to see Leon. She found him in the study, leaning against the desk and talking on the telephone. As soon as she entered he put down the phone and crossed to her.

'Is Anna all right?' he asked immediately.

'She's sleeping. But all right?' Bea queried sadly. 'How can she be? Her husband is dead.' She wanted nothing more than to have Leon take her in his arms and comfort her. But instead he stepped back.

'You're right, Bea. It was a stupid comment.'

Bea. He had finally called her Bea! she thought, a smile curving her full lips. She tilted back her head and looked up at him. He had found time to change and was wearing a beautifully tailored navy suit and white shirt. No one could have guessed from his expression that he had been up all night, or that his friend had died, Bea noted. Only the black tie at his throat and the slight pallor of his skin revealed the horror of the last few hours. But there was not a flicker of emotion in his dark, shuttered gaze. No reciprocal grin…

'And, you, Bea, dare I ask?'

'Oh, I'll survive. I'm tougher than I look,' she said

chirpily, hoping to elicit a smile, but a curious sense of foreboding clutched at her heart.

'Good, good. In that case I will leave you to look after Anna while I make the arrangements for the funeral and contact a few people.' He went to walk past her.

'Don't you want breakfast, and—?'

'No. No…' Leon cut her off, avoiding her gaze and heading for the door…

She raised her hand and then dropped it again. It was as if he couldn't get away from her fast enough.

The feeling persisted all day, and that evening, when she finally saw him again and asked him what he would like for dinner, he coolly informed her he was dining out…

Bea made an omelette for herself and Anna, but the older woman could not eat. So, after seeing Anna safely to her room, Bea went to her own bedroom, and for the first time since arriving on Paphos she occupied the large bed on her own. Of Leon there was no sign.

She lay awake for hours, listening to every little sound, hoping Leon would arrive. She went over and over again in her mind the last kiss they had shared on the beach, when the earthquake had hit. She would have staked her life that Leon cared for her, but as the hours passed and his side of the bed remained empty she began to doubt.

A howling wind woke Bea from a restless sleep. She glanced towards the window; rain was lashing at the glass, threatening to break it. She picked up her wristwatch from the bedside table, and had to look twice. Nine o'clock in the morning, and yet the sky was a deep, dark grey.

Rolling out of bed, she quickly washed and dressed in jeans and a sweatshirt. Poor Anna was in no fit state to wait on anyone, and possibly Leon would want something to eat. That was if she could find him, she thought, casting a glance at the wide bed, the undisturbed pillow on his side, before dashing down to the kitchen. She need not have worried; one of the maids she had met on her arrival was obviously in control, but of Leon there was still no sign.

Bea drank some tea and ate some toast, gathering from the smattering of English the other girl possessed that Leon had taken Anna to stay with relatives and that they were now in the middle of a terrific storm.

She walked along to the lounge and gazed in awe at the view from the large windows. Water ran down from the mountains, forming mini-rivers, and the wind was uprooting plants. As she watched a huge palm tree bowed and broke. The aftermath of the earthquake, Bea presumed, and, finding a book, she curled up on the sofa and tried to read. But she couldn't concentrate. Fear for Leon consumed her.

Bea tried telling herself it was a natural fear for anyone out in such a ferocious storm. But in her heart of hearts she knew it was more. She had missed him in her bed last night, the one night more than any other when she had needed the comfort of his arms around her.

His sudden use of Bea, instead of Phoebe, should have filled her with triumph; at last he was using the name she preferred. But instead it simply added to her growing conviction that perhaps he was already tired of her...

CHAPTER TEN

THE conviction became a certainty when, at one o'clock, the maid informed her that lunch was served, and that she was off duty until six in the evening.

Bea ate a solitary meal, then wandered around the huge villa, the echo of her own footsteps the only sound to be heard. She had run the whole gamut of emotions in the past few hours, from fear for Leon's safety to anger, and finally to a fatalistic acceptance of the truth.

If Leon cared anything for her at all, he would at least have phoned to say where he was, Bea thought bitterly, wandering back into the lounge. She glanced out of the window and realised the storm had passed. A watery sun was fighting its way through the last remaining clouds. But there was no sun in Bea's heart, just a dull foreboding.

She loved Leon, and she had thought the kiss they'd shared on the beach of Aphrodite was somehow special, full of promise and a clear indication that Leon truly cared for her in the same way. But twenty-four hours later he had gone out to dinner and left her to sleep alone. And again today…

Were all women in love such fools? she wondered sadly. She shook her head in negation. The relationship was hopeless; she simply wasn't the type to be walked over by any man, and certainly not twice by the same man…Leon! She threw herself down on the sofa and, retrieving her book from the floor, she opened it, determined to read this time. But countless glances at her wristwatch played havoc with her concentration. Hope didn't die so easily...

It was three o'clock before Leon returned home.

'Good, I was hoping to find you here.' He strolled into the room. He looked as powerfully masculine as ever in an immaculate dark suit, but he also looked as if he had been up all night. The events of the past two days were reflected in the dark shadows beneath his eyes and the lines of strain etched around his firm mouth. He closed his eyes briefly, pinching the bridge of his nose.

'Where else would I be?' Bea remarked cynically, refusing to be influenced by his obvious exhaustion. 'You forbade me to leave, remember?' A tense silence followed her coldly spoken reminder, and he stared down at her with barely concealed anger in the taut line of his jaw.

'I remember. That is what I want to talk to you about,' he replied hardily, and sank down onto the armchair opposite, his long legs slightly splayed. He sat with his forearms resting on his knees, twisting his strong hands together between his thighs. His usual aura of dynamic self-assurance was no longer quite so evident.

Bea stared at his glossy bent head and waited, but the lengthening silence, the rising tension stretched her already fraught nerves, until finally she could stand it no longer. 'You missed lunch,' she blurted inanely. 'And the maid has gone home.' What she really wanted to say was, Where the hell were you last night? But she did not dare.

He bit out a harsh laugh. 'Missing lunch is the least of my troubles. I suppose I should have phoned you, but I didn't have time. Arranging a funeral for an old friend is quite a traumatic experience.'

'I understand,' she said stiffly, wanting to be convinced that this was his only reason for neglecting her.

'Do you?' He sighed. 'I think not.' And, lifting his head, he glanced across at her, black eyes clashing with wary blue. But Bea could not read a single emotion in his cold-eyed gaze.

'I had no right to bring you here, and I had no right to keep you here and force myself upon you. And if I thought an apology would do any good you'd have it… But at the very least I owe you an explanation.'

He spoke so flatly, so impersonally, Bea felt an icy hand grip her heart. 'There's no need,' she interposed. She didn't want to hear his explanation, because instinctively she knew it meant the end of their relationship.

'Yes, there is. Being kidnapped left me paranoid about safety—not just for myself but my friends too. In my conceit I presumed I knew what was best for everyone, especially you. And with the expenditure of enough money I was convinced I had succeeded. I hired chauffeurs, guards, every kind of protection I could think of. I turned this house into a fortress, and congratulated myself on doing so. But I was wrong.'

Bea's fingers curled into fists, her knuckles white. She felt sick with the dread of what was to come. She loved Leon, but it was becoming more and more obvious that he didn't care for her in anything but the most basic way. He had come to his senses, as she had known and feared he would, and was about to give her the brush-off…whichever way he worded it.

'You told me so, over and over again, and I refused to see it,' he went on wryly. 'But you were right all along. I hate to admit it, but ten days in captivity affected me more than I thought, and I panicked. I realise that now. But my deepest regret is that it took an earthquake and the death of Spiros—a death I was responsible for—to bring me to my senses—'

'It was an accident, Leon—' Bea cut in.

He rose abruptly to his feet and silenced her with a wave of his hand. 'No. You deserve to hear it all. I visited the pathologist this morning. The wall did not kill Spiros. The electric charge in the fencing, which I insisted on having installed, though not enough to kill a man, was probably enough to bring on the heart attack that did kill him.'

'You can't know that,' she protested weakly. No man should have to carry such guilt. Not even a cold-hearted devil like Leon.

'But I do. I tried to play God, to protect everyone around me, and instead nature had its revenge. The earthquake showed me quite graphically there is no such thing as absolute safety. Man might rule the world but nature rules man. I can do nothing for Spiros; it is too late. I have to accept that and get on with my life. But you I can and will set free.'

'Free?' Bea stared at him bitterly, the pain like a knife in her heart. She would never be free of Leon. She had known him all her life, and loved him for most of it. She almost told him...

But a searing memory of the last time she was here and the reason for her hasty departure—Selina, his pregnant girlfriend—froze the words in her throat. 'Thank you.' If he heard the sarcasm in her voice he did not show it.

'Yes, you're free to go. No marriage. Nothing...' His mouth twisted into a cynical smile that only confirmed her fears. 'I must have been unhinged to want to marry you—or anyone else for that matter. You're going back to London, back to your life.'

She looked at him, and through the pain common sense told her that, though she might love the man, in one aspect Leon was right. Nature ruled man. Even if by some miracle he had declared undying love for her, she knew Leon's nature far too well to ever trust him. The word 'fidelity' was not in his vocabulary.

'But I have one last request.' Leon's voice broke into her tortured thoughts. 'Would you mind waiting until tomorrow to leave? My stepmother is arriving in a couple of hours. She lived in this house for twelve years and considered Spiros a friend. She's going to attend the funeral in the morning, and then I have arranged for the company jet to take you and Tany to London tomorrow afternoon.'

Bea stared at him as if she had never seen him before. His darkly handsome face and long, lithe body, his air of casual elegance—all were there. Along with his total disregard for the feelings of others. He was insulting in his complacency. He had arranged her departure with the same ruthless efficiency that had got her here in the first place. She suddenly recognised with blinding clarity that the outcome had been inevitable from the start. It had taken an earthquake to bring Leon to his senses, but now the old Leon was back, and he didn't need her. Any last shred of hope she might have entertained was swallowed up by a burning rage at the man.

'Unless you want to stay longer? I did promise you a holiday,' Leon drawled casually.

It was Bea's turn to leap to her feet. 'My God, Leon, you have some nerve,' she yelled, staring him straight in the eye. 'I can't get away from you and off this benighted island fast enough.' Brushing past him, she ran from the room. Before he could see the tears in her eyes.

Sitting at the dinner table, with Leon at the head, Tany, his stepmother, on one side and Bea on the other, Bea had a horrible thought. She actually found herself feeling grateful to be going to a funeral in the morning. It explained her hollow-eyed, ashen-faced appearance, and excused her from having to look happy as she listened to Tany's reminiscences.

Bea couldn't help but like the woman. Tany had to be nearly sixty, but looked about forty. She was the type of woman who thought 'work' was a dirty word and expected the men in her life to look after her. Definitely lightweight, but quite witty in her own way.

She kept the dinner conversation flowing with stories of when she'd shared the villa with Leon's father and a much younger Spiros and Anna. The maid served the food, and the only sticky moment came as dessert was served and Tany turned to Bea.

'Tomorrow will be a sad day for all of us. But at least you and Leon have sorted out your differences at last. I was so glad to hear you were engaged again, even if I did have to read it in the newspaper.'

Bea was saved from answering as Tany, with a playful tap on Leon's arm, added, 'That was naughty of you, Leon. You could at least have told me first. After all, I am the only family you have. It was bad enough when the police informed me you'd been kidnapped. It seems to have done you no harm—thank God! But it was most embarrassing to find out from the media that my stepson was getting married.'

Get out of that! Bea thought with a scathing glance at his bland face. Because she had no intention of trying to explain. But with his usual charm, and lying through his teeth, in moments he had Tany believing there was no engagement, that it had all been a ruse to escape the press. The same trick he had pulled on Bea, for the opposite reason, she thought bitterly.

'Bea and I are just good friends and business colleagues. And whereas I'm used to the press hounds, poor Bea isn't. She needed to get away for a while, to let the scurrilous rumours die down. But now, what with the earthquake and the tragedy of Spiros's death, she has decided to go back to London after the funeral with you. Isn't that so?' he demanded, turning his attention to Bea, his dark eyes catching hers, willing her to agree.

Poor Bea, indeed! She was so furious that for a moment she was sorely tempted to tell Tany the truth. But what was the truth? How could she tell Tany that her stepson, the man she depended on for her income, the almighty Leon, had suffered from some kind of temporary trauma? Seducing Bea and insisting on marrying her one day, and the next, when he had recovered his senses, telling her to get lost. No, she couldn't do it…

With a last blistering look at Leon, leaving him in no doubt as to how she felt, Bea concentrated on Tany. 'Yes. Leon's right. I am going home tomorrow. Perhaps you and I can hit the shops together one day while you're in London?'

Tany enthusiastically agreed, and shortly after Bea excused herself, ostensibly to complete her packing.

Midnight, and a quiet like the grave had settled over the villa. Bea, her packing completed, left the suitcases in the dressing room and, after a quick shower, wrapped a towel sarong-style around her body and walked into the bedroom. Dropping the towel to the floor, naked, but wearing her anger like a shield, she got into bed, not expecting to sleep, but vowing she would not shed another tear over Leon.

She leaned over to turn off the light, and unexpectedly there was a light tap on the door. The door opened and Leon walked in. Bea sat up. He had changed, she noticed distractedly, into a thigh-length burgundy towelling robe, loosely tied around his waist, and revealing a vast amount of muscular hair-covered chest—he wore nothing else…

What was he trying to do? Drive her mad? She swallowed, recalling all too clearly how it felt to have that marvellous body possessing hers. She felt his eyes on her and belatedly remembered she was naked. Dragging the sheet up to her chin, she watched him with cold eyes as he approached the foot of the bed, but inside she was simmering with anger and more...

'What do you want?' she demanded curtly.

A glimmer of a smile flashed in his black eyes, and she could have kicked herself for leaving herself open to one of his sexy innuendos. But surprisingly the smile vanished as quickly as it had appeared.

'I probably won't have time to talk to you tomorrow. And I don't want you to leave without me telling you.' He hesitated, his usual poise deserting him.

'Telling me?' Bea prompted.

'Assuring you that if there are any unfortunate repercussions from our recent intimacy, then of course I will support you—marriage, money, any way you wish.'

'Unfortunate repercussions'. For a second Bea was puzzled, and then it hit her. He was talking about a child. Wide-eyed, she stared at his impassive countenance, pain searing through her and leaving in its wake a rage such as she had never known. In that moment she hated him enough to kill him. How dared he remind her? Now she knew how Selina must have felt when the devil had dismissed her pregnancy, and it gave Bea the strength to respond.

'That's very generous of you, Leon, but not necessary. I am not pregnant.' Lying like a professional, she added, 'Maybe it was the shock of the earthquake, but I can assure you, I am fine.'

'Oh.' For a fleeting moment Bea imagined she saw a flicker of disappointment in his hard-eyed gaze, but it was an illusion. 'That's all right, then,' Leon said abruptly, and, turning on his heel, he left.

Bea sank back down on the bed, pulling the sheet over her, and wished she could bury her feelings for Leon as easily as she could bury her head beneath the covers. But it was not to be.

She tossed and turned all night, going over in her mind every moment they had spent together in the past week, every kiss and caress. Every word, every argument.

Finally her own innate honesty forced her to admit that it was not all Leon's fault. Bea had to take some of the blame. She had known Leon all her life; she knew what he was like, warts and all. Immediately after the kidnap she had recognised he was not his usual self. But barely a week later, when he had offered to save her from the press by taking her on holiday to Cyprus, she had taken very little persuading. Realistically she had known, being a strong-minded woman, that once over the shock she could have easily learnt to deal with the press on her own.

To heal her wounded pride Bea could tell herself that Leon had seduced her. But in her heart of hearts she knew her own ardent response to his lovemaking had, in a way, fuelled his obsession. In fact she had begun to believe in it herself.

In the darkest hour before dawn, tears she had vowed not to shed rolled softly, silently down her cheeks as she realised that this was the saddest part of all. She had deluded herself into thinking he might love her...

The church was full to overflowing; the whole of Paphos seemed to have turned out for the funeral. Bea stood beside Tany and was glad of her company. The sound of sobbing was a constant background to the priest's sombre voice. Leon supported a distraught Anna all through the service and at the graveside.

Later, at the villa, there was nothing for Bea to do, and in the end she was relieved when, shortly after a heartbroken Anna had said goodbye and left, the limousine arrived to take herself and Tany to the airport.

Tany slid into the back seat and Bea got in beside her. The chauffeur was about to close the door as Bea glanced back at the villa for the last time, when Leon came sprinting down the steps. What now? she wondered. They had already said goodbye in front of the remaining guests, with a handshake... The handshake still rankled.

'Phoebe,' Leon said, staying the chauffeur's hand on the door. His dark eyes flashed golden. 'Phoebe, I can't let you go...'

Bea stared up at him. He was calling her Phoebe again, and for some reason the name she had always hated suddenly sounded wonderful.

'Phoebe.' He repeated her name, their eyes met and clung, and the expression in Leon's made her heart leap with hope.

'Yes?' she prompted hesitantly.

'I can't let you go...' He paused, and Bea could almost see his brain ticking over. She knew the exact moment he changed his mind. He slowly stepped back. 'Without saying...' His deep voice was wry as he went on, 'Thank you for everything, and good luck.'

'My pleasure,' she managed to respond stiffly. 'Goodbye.'

'What was all that about?' Tany asked a few minutes later as the car sped down the hillside towards Paphos.

'Nothing.' Bea dismissed Leon with a word, and prayed she could dismiss him from her heart and mind as easily. But she had not counted on the tenacity of Tany.

'I don't believe you. Leon has never run after a woman in his life except you. I know my stepson.'

Bea tried to ignore Tany, but it was hard. Half an hour into the flight to London, Tany renewed her attack in a more subtle form as they relaxed.

'The funeral today was like saying goodbye to an era,' Tany remarked quietly. 'Leon's father, Nick, and Spiros were great friends, although employer and employee, and now they're both gone. I loved Nick, you know, Bea.'

'You married him. Of course you did,' Bea said idly.

'He didn't love me. Not in the same way. Oh, he cared about me, but the love of his life was Leon's mother, Pandora. I met him three years after she had died, and he had been completely faithful to her memory.'

Her interest aroused, Bea said, 'Tell me more.' Her blue eyes rested on the still lovely face of Tany.

'I was an American on holiday with my daughter when I met Nick. It was love at first sight on my part, and I chased him unmercifully—until finally he laid his cards on the table. He said he would never love anyone again, but he was lonely. He wanted a companion, someone to host a dinner party, to socialise with, and three years without sex was becoming difficult for a virile man like Nick.' Tany grinned. 'I soon cured his problem, and six months later we were married. I got the man I loved and a secure future for myself and my daughter, and I like to think I made Nick happy.'

'I'm sure you did.' Bea grinned back.

'Yes, but my point is, Leon is very like his father. I couldn't really be a mother to Leon, because he was already thirteen when I married Nick. Even at that age Leon was very much a young man. But I do know him extremely well. Like his father, Leon is a one-woman man.'

Bea's blue eyes sparkled humorously. 'You're joking! I hate to tell you this, Tany, but Leon has had more women than hot dinners.' And if there was an edge of cynicism in her tone, who could blame her?

'Maybe, but he has only ever loved one,' Tany responded seriously. 'And that is you, Bea.'

The coffee Bea was drinking went down the wrong way and Bea almost choked. Coughing and spluttering, she raised startled eyes to Tany's. 'What on earth gave you that idea? You couldn't be more wrong!' Bea exclaimed, red-faced.

'I'm right. Leon loves you,' Tany assured her. 'And I think you love him.' Then, diverting the conversation slightly, she continued, 'I remember, when Nick died, all the flowers, the messages of condolence, and one in a childish hand from an eleven-year-old girl. Leon asked if he could keep it, and he put it in his wallet. Odd behaviour for a grown man.'

Bea felt a flush rise in her cheeks, and with it a tiny seed of hope took root in her heart. 'Leon is odd,' she said disparagingly, but lacking her usual force.

'Maybe, but he was always fascinated by you. When he was a student in England, and spent the half-term holidays at your home, you were only four. But all his letters were full of "little Phoebe's" achievements—the first time you rode a pony, the first time you took a jump. Over the years I heard about all your exploits. I can remember once—oh, Leon must have been nearly thirty at the time—he came back from visiting you and your father in a foul mood. Apparently you had been reading about his women in the newspaper, and asked him about them. The poor man was mortified. He always wanted to be your knight in shining armour, and you had discovered he was as human as the next man.'

'We were good friends,' Bea said softly. And he had

been her childhood hero. Looking back, she saw the truth in Tany's comment. Leon had been angry when, as a fifteen-year-old, Bea had teased him about his women.

'And now you're lovers,' Tany declared outrageously, leaving Bea speechless. 'Don't bother to deny it. I never fell for his explanation of a pretend engagement for the benefit of the press. I'm not a fool. He wanted to marry you when you were eighteen and he still does.'

The longer Tany spoke, the more convincing she sounded to Bea.

'In a way I blame myself for your break-up three years ago. I was married for the first time at eighteen, and it was a disaster. When Leon brought you to Paphos and put a ring on your finger I thought you were too young, and I was proved correct. But you have no excuse now.'

Tany's green-eyed gaze was unwavering when it met Bea's. 'My dear, don't give up your chance of happiness for a silly argument. I watched you and Leon at dinner yesterday, and the air literally shimmered with sexual tension. Then I saw Leon going into your room last night, and I heard him leave minutes later. Whatever he's done, forget it, and grab him with both hands. Or you'll regret it for the rest of your life.'

There was no point in denying it, Bea realised. Tany was a much more astute person than Bea had given her credit for. 'Supposing I *did* care for Leon that way,' she began tentatively, 'unfortunately I'm not the sort of woman to put up with his philandering ways. And whatever you say, he *is* a womaniser. I know,' she argued, not prepared to believe that Leon was capable of being faithful. There was too much evidence to the contrary.

'Look, my dear,' Tany said with some exasperation as she leaned towards Bea and placed a hand on her arm, 'Leon is a man of thirty-five. Of course he has sowed a few wild oats in the past. But I know for a fact he was devastated when you gave him his ring back the last time, and he has barely looked at a woman since. Whatever the press say…' She leaned back and a reminiscent smile illuminated her green eyes as she continued.

'I remember the day after you left. Selina made a great play for Leon. They'd had a bit of a fling before, and she was hoping to catch him on the rebound. Leon sent her packing. But you would not believe the lengths she went to.' Leaning forward again, Tany added, 'Confidentially, the woman made a complete fool of herself. She actually tried to con him into thinking she was having his baby. How on earth she thought she would get away with it I cannot imagine. But she stuck to her story for months.'

Bea, who had been listening but not really believing until then, suddenly gave Tany all her attention.

'She finally gave up when Leon arrived in America and insisted on a DNA test. She married the father of her child—a lawyer she worked with—and by all accounts they're quite happy.'

Slumped back in her chair, Bea tried to take it all in. She had been wrong about Selina! How much more had she got wrong? For years she had tried to deny her love for Leon, convinced he was simply a man on the make. Now she was not so sure. Maybe she had been looking at Leon and seeing only what she wanted to see, ignoring his myriad kindnesses over the years. He had always been there for her when she needed him. On the death of her father. During her first foray into the workplace. In her first disastrous brush with the press. And, most important of all, he was her first lover.

'Leon is a very wealthy, personable man. There will always be women chasing him, but he is also very wily, and makes sure he is never caught—except where you are concerned. Take my advice, Bea, and when we arrive in London turn around and go straight back to him.'

'Go back to Cyprus?' Bea murmured, and amazingly the idea did not seem half bad.

'Why not? You have nothing to lose and everything to gain. I had twelve glorious years with Nick, and Leon is his father's son. You will never find another lover like a Gregoris. I know. Why do you think I've stayed a widow all these years?' She grinned. 'Once you have had the best sex, you won't be content with less.'

'You're incorrigible, Tany. Sex isn't everything,' Bea quipped.

'You can say that because you haven't had to do without it for the last ten years!'

There was no answer to that, and Bea didn't even try to give one.

Tany paused, her green eyes studying Bea's flushed face. 'Joking apart,' she said, on a serious note, 'you and Leon were meant for each other. Go back. Give him another chance and I'm willing to bet you'll never regret it. There, now I've said my last word on the subject. The rest is up to you. Think about it.'

CHAPTER ELEVEN

BEA did, for the rest of the flight. She saw Leon again, in her mind's eye, running down the steps to speak to her one last time. 'Phoebe, I can't let you go,' he had said, and for a second she had believed him. But then he had changed his mind.

She relived the nights she had spent in his arms. Could a man really make love so exquisitely without caring at all about his partner? What was it Leon had said once? 'I gave up my womanising ways the day I realised it was possible to have an erection and be bored at the same time.' Sex was new to Bea, but she knew enough to realise that Leon had been anything but bored with her.

Tany thought Leon loved Bea, but if that was so, why had he told her to leave? Guilt, maybe? He thought he had forced himself on her, when in actual fact Bea had been quite desperate in wanting him. But did he know that? No—she had never told him. Leon was a proud man. He had always looked after Bea, always been there for her. And she? What had she done? At various times she had told him he was a womaniser, a devil, not to be trusted, too old, and, to cap it all, the father of a bastard child, which she now knew to be totally untrue. Was it any wonder he was reluctant to express his true feelings? And she was no better…

Bea liked to think she was a mature adult, and as the plane touched down at Heathrow she decided to act like one. She would put her pride on the line and go back to Leon.

The decision made, she said goodbye to Tany in the airport terminal, and, in her position as a partner in Stephen-Gregoris, instructed the captain of the aircraft to refuel and return to Cyprus.

By the time she walked down the gangway at Paphos airport, in the middle of the night, she was having second thoughts. No waiting limousine this time; she wasn't expected. So she simply took a taxi.

The first shock was that the gates of the villa stood wide open, with not a guard in sight. The second was that the doors of the house were also wide open, but there was no sign of anyone. Bea paid off the taxi and walked up the steps and into the hall. She wandered through all the ground-floor rooms; the caterers had cleaned up every trace of the funeral party, and were long gone. More disturbing, there was no sign of Leon. She called his name a few times, but silence was the only response. What did she expect? It was three o'clock in the morning…

Despondently she made herself a cup of coffee in the kitchen, and pondered on what to do next. He had probably gone off with one of the funeral guests for the night—and why not? He wasn't expecting any visitors, she thought, with a tired sigh.

It was too late to return to the airport—she had dismissed the taxi anyway—and so, concluding there was nothing to be done until morning, she decided to go to bed.

After opening the door of her old room and switching on the light, she stopped. There was no longer any need to wonder where Leon was. He was stretched out, face down on the bed, cuddling the pillow Bea usually used like a teddy bear. Gently snoring, he looked heartbreakingly attractive and oddly vulnerable.

Bea walked quietly across to the side of the bed, and

stared down at Leon's sprawled body. He had shed his black suit and shirt, retaining his underpants and socks. Apart from a few incoherent ramblings, he appeared to be out for the count. With a tiny smile curving her mouth, she bent down and ran her finger over the back of his head and down the indentations of his spine. She couldn't resist the temptation.

'Leon.' She said his name softly.

'Phoebe. Phoebe, my love,' he groaned, and rolled over on the bed. His eyes fluttered open and then closed again. 'No, she's gone, left me…' he muttered, his eyes opening again.

Bea sat on the edge of the bed. He had said 'Phoebe, my love'. Perhaps there was hope for them yet.

'I haven't left you, Leon. I'm here,' she said huskily. 'I came back.' She stared down at him tenderly. Was that a trace of dried tears she saw on his cheeks? His black eyes looked up into hers, clouded with sleep, but intent.

'Is it really you, Phoebe?' he asked uncertainly. 'You're not a dream?' Dragging himself up, he lunged at her. His strong arms folded around her, pulling her across the bed, and he clasped her to his chest as though his life depended on it. 'It's true. You're here,' he murmured into her hair.

With her face pressed hard against his chest and his arms like bands of steel around her, Bea could hardly breathe. 'Please, Leon, you're suffocating me,' she managed to get out, trying to sit up.

'Oh, God! I'm sorry.' Immediately he let her go, but not completely. Pulling her up hard against his side, he kept one arm around her shoulders, and with his other hand he tilted her chin so he could look into her lovely face. 'I wouldn't hurt you for the world, Phoebe. I love you. I couldn't harm a hair of your head. Please believe me.'

Her pulse leapt violently. His breath smelt slightly of whisky, but not unpleasantly, and as her gaze met his for a few seconds she saw his heart in his eyes. The sophisticated mask he presented to the world was stripped away, his true feelings laid bare, and his dark gaze burnt with love and a touching vulnerability that warmed her to her soul.

'I believe you wouldn't deliberately hurt me,' she said in an unsteady voice. 'But…' She hesitated, about to ask the most important question of her life. 'Did you mean it when you said you loved me?' She waited, holding her breath, her blue eyes fixed on his handsome face.

'God, Phoebe! How can you doubt it? I love you, I worship and adore you. I always have, and I always will.' His deep voice shook with emotion. 'What are you trying to do to me? Do you want me to beg? Plead?'

The anguish in his tone touched her heart. 'No, Leon,' she murmured, raising her hand to cover his where it clasped her chin. Tany was right, she thought with wonder—he *did* love her. 'I simply want you to love me, as I love you.'

Caught up in his own emotions, for a moment he didn't seem to hear her. 'Because I will beg. Twice I have let you walk away, but…' And then he stopped. An incredulous expression lit his dark features. 'You said you loved me…'

Tears of joy sparkling on her long lashes, she smiled. 'Yes, Leon. I love you.'

For a moment they simply stared at each other. Then, with a low groan, Leon wrapped his arms around her and eased her down onto the bed. His dark head descended and Bea's lips parted for his kiss. But then he stopped again.

'You love me, Phoebe,' he said deeply, his fingers brushing the hair from her brow while his black eyes devoured her. 'And you will stay with me?' he asked, his deep voice hesitant, as though he was afraid to believe her completely.

'Yes,' she whispered, lifting her slender arms around his neck. She wanted to feel the warmth of his mouth. What was he waiting for?

'I hope to God you mean it, Phoebe,' he said, and with a return to his usual arrogance added, 'Because there is no way on this earth I will let you leave me a third time.' Then he covered her eager, tremulous mouth with his own.

He kissed her with an achingly tender passion which stirred her more deeply than anything had ever done before. Her arms tightened around his neck as he held her hard against him, threatening to crack her ribs, but she didn't care; she was lost in the wonder of the moment. Leon loved her... Her heart sang, and soon her whole body was singing to Leon's tune.

Clothes were discarded in wild haste. It had only been three nights apart but it felt like an eternity.

'Phoebe, I want you so badly I can't help myself,' Leon groaned as, naked, he held her beneath him. His mouth burned against her skin as he scattered kisses over her face and throat. He found the rigid peaks of her breasts and eased the ache within her with his mouth and tongue. His hands slid down over her body, his knee nudging her legs apart. 'God help me, I can't wait.'

Bea didn't want him to. She was trembling so badly she couldn't stop, and as she pressed feverish kisses to his chest, her small hands skimming over his broad frame, she remembered and relished the feel, the taste of him. 'I love you, Leon,' she cried out as he entered her. At last she was free to express herself as never before.

He moved inside her and she murmured wild avowals of love until his mouth found hers, his kiss mimicking the hunger of his great body. Locked together, fierce primeval pleasure engulfing them, they cried out their love as they reached the pinnacle together.

Bea, languorous and loved, cradled Leon's dark head on her breast, softly stroking his short hair and listening to his laboured breathing. How she loved this man... And by some miracle he loved her...

A long time later Leon raised his head. Rolling off her, he pulled the cover up over them before turning towards her, and, balancing on one elbow, he stared down into her beautiful flushed face.

'More feeling than finesse,' he said, with a rueful grin. 'But I needed you so badly. If only you knew.' With a finger he traced the delicate arch of her brow, down her small nose and around the swollen fullness of her mouth.

'Knew?' she murmured as his finger moved along the line of her jaw and up over her cheekbone, as though, like a blind man, he was learning her features by touch.

Leon sighed deeply. 'The ten days I was a captive, tied up like an animal in a cage, the only thing that kept me sane was the picture of you I held in my mind. You are the most extraordinarily lovely woman.' His hand slid lower, over the soft peaks of her breasts beneath the sheet, cupping her gently. Bea had never felt such utter contentment as she cuddled closer and listened to his deep, melodious voice.

'If I fell asleep it was your lovely face I saw, your voice I heard, your laughter. Not that I slept much,' he said bitterly. 'When I was first released, and taken to the hospital, the doctor wanted me to stay in for a week, but

I refused. Then he insisted that at the very least I should seek counselling. But I ignored all his advice.

'My one thought was to get out of Hong Kong and back to Cyprus, the one place I could legitimately call home. I was convinced I was mentally strong, and a few days in captivity was not going to affect me. I was wrong.' His hand stroked up her shoulder to the soft curve of her cheek in a tender gesture. 'You witnessed my nightmares; you knew.'

'Yes,' Bea murmured softly, encouragingly, realising he needed to talk about his experience.

'Deep down inside, I think I felt afraid. But I couldn't face the thought. Instead, I behaved like a man possessed, more arrogant than ever. I insisted on every type of security, convinced I was in control—'

'Shh, Leon, you don't need to tell me,' Bea cut in.

'Yes, yes, I do, Phoebe. I love you and I want you to understand why I behaved the way I did.' A wry smile twisted his firm mouth. 'Actually, you're the only person I can talk to about it. Locked in that hellhole for days on end, with death a very real possibility, I went over my past life and realised perhaps I could have been more generous, more kindly to a few people. I began to think it wouldn't matter if I died the next day. Except for one overwhelming regret. And that was you.'

'Me?' Bea murmured, not really sure what he was trying to say.

'Yes, Phoebe, you,' he said, and, curving his arm over her slender frame beneath the cover, he cuddled her closer to his side. 'I vowed if I got out alive I was going to have you. When I was released, and saw the photograph of you in the newspaper wearing the pendant, I suddenly saw how I could do it.'

'Just like that,' she tried to joke, but Leon was not amused.

His dark eyes burnt intensely into hers. 'No, not just like that,' he derided softly. 'My first reaction was fury that the press had discovered who you were, and named you the ''Reluctant Heiress''. My second reaction was that you had to be protected at all costs. The thought of you being kidnapped was too horrible to contemplate. I have no excuse for tricking you into coming to Cyprus, or for forcing you into my bed—'

'You didn't force me, Leon. I was more than willing,' Bea cut in.

'My darling Phoebe.' Leon smiled and then they were kissing each other again, until Leon raised his head. 'You're far too generous, Phoebe. I know what I did. You were right when you told me I was making you a captive to my obsession, but I wouldn't listen to you. I couldn't let you go. It took an earthquake and the death of Spiros to make me realise I was as guilty as the scum who kidnapped me. I had taken away your freedom, and I had to give it back to you…'

'I didn't want to be free of you, Leon. I used to hate it when you called me Phoebe, but on the day you called me Bea I hated that more. Because I knew it meant you didn't care about me one way or the other,' Bea told him, her eyes clouding with remembered pain.

He stared at her in shocked silence, his eyes probing hers with a burning intensity. 'Phoebe, Phoebe,' he muttered thickly. 'Not care…' He shook his dark head in amazement. 'How could you believe that for a second?'

'I did.'

Leon tightened his arm around her. 'But you must know I've loved you for years!' he exclaimed. 'I thought you were delightful as a child—my brilliant and glittering little Phoebe. But there was nothing more then, nothing sexual. But you were still hopelessly young when I realised I was falling in love with you. Fifteen, to be exact. I remember sitting in the kitchen of your home in Mitford, and you challenged me about my womanising ways, as revealed in Lil's tabloid newspaper. I was almost thirty years old and I blushed like a boy as you stood there, all long legs and totally beautiful, your flashing blue eyes laughing at me.

'I was furious. I stayed away. I told myself I couldn't possibly love a schoolgirl, and for the next couple of years I avoided you. But when I heard of your father's death I dashed to your side. As soon as I saw you I knew I'd been fooling myself...

'It was then that I made my plan. Three months to get over the worst of your grief, and then I was going to return at Easter and begin my campaign of courtship. There was no hurry, you were still far too young, but I planned to lead you gently along for a couple of years.'

Bea reached up to his face and stroked his jaw with a gentle hand, stunned but flattered by his revelations. 'Typical Leon—make a plan and go for it,' she teased.

He grinned back. 'Except it backfired. In my conceit I thought you were well protected in the wilds of Northumbria, with Bob and Lil to watch over you. A few kisses was all I planned, and then I was going to ask you to spend the summer holiday in Cyprus with me. Well chaperoned, of course, by my stepmother and sister.'

'But you asked me to marry you?' Bea interjected.

'Yes. We walked along the riverbank and I casually mentioned the young tearaways of your childhood. When you told me you were friends with one, had even dated him, I was sick with jealousy, and all my good intentions went out of the window. I decided to marry you as quickly as possible.'

'And I said yes and floated off to Cyprus with you in the summer. And then I heard Selina,' Bea said sadly.

If only she had been more mature, not so in awe of her sophisticated fiancé, she might have been able to talk to Leon at the time, instead of believing all the lies and running away.

'It was never serious between Selina and me. I'm not proud of how I behaved, though she was a willing woman when I happened to be in America, but I swear, Phoebe, it was over between Selina and me the Christmas before your father died. Whatever you may have thought you heard—'

'It's all right, I know,' Bea cut in. 'She didn't have your child.' Leon looked down at her quizzically. 'Tany told me all about Selina. But you could have told me yourself,' she scolded lightly.

'Pride stopped me, Phoebe. You had told me I was too old for you, and then, years later, it turned out that you didn't trust me. And then finally you flung Selina at me. I didn't feel like explaining myself. I wanted you to love me unconditionally.'

'I do.' Bea quickly reassured him with a quick kiss.

'Thank you, Phoebe. But as we're being honest I have to admit to a certain amount of guilt. I *did* wake up in bed with Selina at Newport. But, believe me, I don't know how. I had business to discuss with Mackenzie, and no knowledge of any party. I arrived at his home late, having flown across the Pacific from Hong Kong that morning. I was jet-lagged, the house was full of people, I had one drink and crashed out. In the morning, when I saw Selina sprawled out beside me, I leapt out of bed. I swear I never touched her.'

Bea believed him, because she wanted to. 'It doesn't matter,' she said with a smile. 'I was probably too young to get married anyway.'

'I was devastated when you gave me the ring back. I didn't make a fuss because deep down I knew you were too young. But I didn't give up hope. Instead I decided to give you time, and renew my campaign when you were twenty-one.'

Snuggling into his warm body, she pressed another kiss to his bare chest. 'Let's forget about everything,' she said huskily, running her hand along the curve of his waist. They had talked long enough.

Leon captured her hand as it slid along his thigh. 'No, Phoebe. Let me finish. As soon as I kissed you on the night of your birthday, I knew the sexual chemistry was still as hot as ever between us. I was furious when I met you in London and discovered you had a date. But I felt much more confident when I took you out to dinner, and then afterwards, in your apartment, you went up in flames in my arms. Until Margot put her oar in.'

Leon shook his head ruefully. 'I thought Margot would take care of you, but the only person she chaperoned you with was me... I watched you come home the next night from Brighton with your friends, and I saw the steaming kiss you gave that Andy boy. No sign of Margot then...'

Bea chuckled delightedly. 'You really were jealous!'

'Too right I was. The next day I kissed you in the middle of the street when we parted, determined to settle things between us once and for all the next time I was in London.'

'I remember, and Sophie, the receptionist, saw us.' Then Bea remembered something else that made her heart sink. 'Was Sophie one of your ladyfriends?' she asked bluntly.

'Sophie? What are you talking about?' Leon demanded hardily. 'I barely know the woman. She sits at the front desk, I say hello to her, end of story.'

Bea wanted to believe him, but another doubt surfaced, bringing a frown to her face.

Leon grimaced and tightened his arm around her. 'I know you don't trust me, Phoebe, but I swear to you I have never made love to any woman but you in the three years since I first asked you to be my wife.'

Leon, celibate for three years! Bea couldn't believe it! She wanted to trust him, but…

'The night I went out with Jack, I saw you leaving a restaurant with a model—the same restaurant you took me to the next night.' She couldn't keep the tremor out of her voice. She loved Leon, and she was convinced Leon loved her, but was he capable of staying faithful?

'A model?' He looked at her as if she was crazy. 'You're jealous, Phoebe,' he said with a grin. 'You have no idea how good that makes me feel.' And, swooping down, he kissed her senseless.

'You still haven't explained,' she murmured breathlessly as his muscular thighs hardened against hers.

Cupping her head in the palms of his hands, his long body spreadeagled on top of her, Leon rubbed his nose against hers in a gesture of affection. 'Remember I told you I usually stay with a friend when I'm in London. His name's Jason Wells; we went to university together. Unfortunately, on my last visit he had a ladyfriend staying with him and I had to stay at a hotel.'

Relieved to hear his friend was male, and with the warmth of his breath brushing her face, Bea wished he would just shut up and kiss her. But no such luck.

'He's a doctor at Great Ormond Street, and that night he'd been paged in the middle of his meal. His girlfriend refused to leave until she was ready. Jason is a conscientious man, so he called me and asked me to pick her up, before leaving for the hospital. By the time I arrived she had downed another bottle of champagne and was definitely the worse for wear. I had to virtually carry her out of the place, and then she tried to make a pass at me.

'Personally I think Jason could do a whole lot better. Any man with money will do for that particular lady. But it's not up to me to give him advice on his love life. God knows, mine has been a disaster until now,' he said with feeling.

'But not any more,' Bea husked throatily, and, running her hands up his back, she beamed up at him with all the love in her heart. She didn't want to discuss his past loves, so long as from now on she was his only love.

'Thank heaven!' He grinned, and brushed her lips with his own, again and again…

Bea opened one eye. 'Leon?' she asked drowsily. 'Is that you?' She could feel the warmth of a large, masculine body enfolding her.

'It'd better be!' a rough voice growled in her ear. 'Now and for ever, girl, and don't you forget it.'

She turned in his arms and stared up into his face, a soft smile curving her lips. 'Just checking,' she said with a little laugh, and twined her arms around his neck.

'Tease,' he chuckled, and rubbed his rough morning chin against her cheek. 'The quicker we're married the better. I want you to be in no doubt whatsoever that I am the only man you will ever find in your bed.'

'You haven't asked me yet.' Bea pretended to pout.

'Well, I am now.'

'Not very romantic, Leon. After all, if I'm only going to be married once, I want a *proper* proposal. Down on your knees at least.'

Leon brushed a strand of hair from her brow, his smile indulgent. 'You have had me on my knees for years. Once more won't matter.' He rolled off the bed and knelt by the side, grabbing Bea's hand in his.

'My darling Phoebe, light of my life, keeper of my heart.' Leon dramatically placed his hand over his chest, hamming it up for all he was worth. 'Will you marry me, and make me an honest man?'

Struggling to sit up, Bea burst out laughing. 'Yes! Get up, you fool, you're stark naked!' He stood up, grinning down at her.

They didn't see the door open, but the almighty crash as a tray loaded with coffee hit the marble floor had them both turning towards the door. Unfortunately Leon was still naked.

The young girl from the village screamed, put her hand to her mouth, and shot out.

Leon turned to Bea. 'Was that a yes I heard?' he asked, and fell on top of her, roaring with laughter.

'Yes, but what I want to know is, who's going to get the coffee?' Bea managed to ask, between giggles.

A long time later they made the coffee together.

Born and raised in Berkshire, **Liz Fielding** started writing at the age of twelve when she won a hymn-writing competition at her convent school. After a gap of more years than she is prepared to admit to, during which she worked as a secretary in Africa and the Middle East, got married and had two children, she was finally able to realise her ambition and turn to full-time writing in 1992.

She now lives with her husband, John, in West Wales, surrounded by mystical countryside and romantic, crumbling castles, content to leave the travelling to her grown-up children and keeping in touch with the rest of the world via the Internet.

You can visit Liz Fielding at her web-site
 www.lizfielding.com

PRISONER OF THE HEART

by

Liz Fielding

CHAPTER ONE

'GOT you, Chay Buchanan!' Sophie Nash's triumphant exclamation was a tightly contained whisper. Perched on a rocky ledge fifty feet above a rock-strewn bay, she had waited too long—all an apparently endless afternoon, while the sun had crept around the headland, stealing her shade, beating into the exposed crevice with barely enough room to ease her aching back or flex her legs—to risk giving herself away now.

And she had almost given up. The sun was sinking fast, taking with it the precious light. Another ten minutes, she had promised herself, and she would end the torture and climb the fifteen or so feet back up to the top of the cliff. She had pressed herself a little closer to the comfort of the rock-face. The ledge had seemed larger viewed from the safety of the cliff-top and she had been so certain that she would be able to see the wide expanse of terrace between the tower and the sea. But she had been wrong. Only the tantalising glimpse of the pool had kept her riveted to her eyrie, praying that the sudden rise in temperature would tempt her quarry out for a swim. And finally it had.

The man fixed in her sights was staring out to sea, his hand raised against the westering sun. She released the shutter and the motor-wind drove the film forward as the wind whipped up a dark lock of hair and feathered it across his forehead. He was relaxed now, at ease in the safety of his keep. All that would change if he discovered that he was being observed. She shivered involuntarily, despite the heat. He had made

himself more than clear. Warned her to stay away.
Warned her that if she was ever unfortunate enough to
be found anywhere near the old watch-tower that was
his home with a camera in her possession she would
discover that the dungeon was still a working feature.

Sophie shrugged away the disquieting thought of
being locked inside the dark recesses of his tower. He
had been simply melodramatic, trying to scare her off.
Well, he would find out that she didn't scare off that
easily. His dungeon was undoubtedly nothing more
threatening than a wine cellar these days. Besides, she
wasn't trespassing. There wasn't a thing he could do to
her. Oh, no? The thought was in her head before she
could stop it. No! His property began on the other side
of the great overhanging rock that so effectively protected his privacy. All but the pool at the sea's edge.
And he would never know she had been there until the
photographs appeared alongside Nigel's feature in
Celebrity.

She twisted the zoom lens, closing in on the tanned
profile and a pair of well-made shoulders, naked but
for the towel thrown about them. The skin of his back
gleamed like bronze silk in the early evening sun,
smooth, packed with muscle, like an ancient statue of
an athlete she had seen once in a museum. Her mouth
dried as she panned the lense downwards, but the
briefest black swimsuit clung to his hips, and the
smallest gasp of something that might have been relief
escaped her lips.

She quickly swung the long lens back up to his face,
almost jumping as she adjusted the focus and he
suddenly appeared close enough to touch. That first
sense of triumph evaporated as she acknowledged that
her response to such compelling masculinity, even at
this distance, was as immediate and disturbing as on
their first encounter. She felt a hot, remembering flush

of shame at the way his knowing eyes had declined the imagined invitation.

He wasn't even handsome, Sophie thought furiously. Chay Buchanan possessed no feature that might lay claim to such an adjective. His face was rugged, lived-in. No, slept-in. She shifted, uncomfortable with the memory of the naïve way she had knocked at the door of his fortress to ask if he would let her take a photograph of him. She should have known that it couldn't possibly be that simple or Nigel would never have asked her. . . Her foot disturbed a small shower of stones and in a sudden panic, sure that the whole world must hear, she flattened herself against the cliff and held her breath as they rattled down to the sea.

But there was no shout of rage and finally she braved a peek over the ledge. He hadn't moved, his fierce profile fixed upon a distant yacht, sails straining against the wind as it cut through the brilliant blue of the Mediterranean.

Turn, she willed the man. Look this way. If he would just turn towards her, every painful, cramping moment on the ledge would be worthwhile. And turn he did, as if her mind had somehow reached out and touched his.

She took a deep, steadying breath as the lens was filled with that unforgettable face. Dark brows jutted fiercely over the sea-green eyes that this morning had seemed to bore into her to search out her secrets, and she had to remind herself very firmly that he had no idea that she had found a chink in his armour and was at this very moment intruding on his seclusion. If he had, he certainly wouldn't be standing relaxed and at ease at the edge of his pool.

Chay Buchanan had made it only too plain that trespassers were not welcome, and she wondered briefly if his nose had been broken defending that privacy. The most recent library photographs of the man had been more than six years old. He had been standing grim-faced at his brother's graveside, and in that shot his nose had been arrow-straight.

It had been set without much thought as to the aesthetics of the matter, and with his sun-darkened skin it gave him the hawkish look of a corsair. Just the kind of man to keep his enemies in a dungeon, Sophie thought uncomfortably. His mouth was wide and might be pleasing when he smiled. She wouldn't know. When she had seen it last it had been little more than a thin angry slash over an uncompromising chin. She released the shutter and claimed the image for her own.

He pulled the towel from around his neck, and dropped it on the rocks at his feet. Her finger hovered over the shutter release, capturing the moment of sheer power and grace as his body unwound and he dived into the water of a pool carved out of the rocks, fed and cleaned by a narrow channel from the sea.

With a series of workmanlike pictures of the reclusive writer safely on film, Sophie leaned back against the rock to catch her breath. A slight frown creased her brow as she watched the man carving his way through the water.

Chay Buchanan had once strutted the literary stage like a young lion, the darling of the media. But it was years since he had appeared on every prestigious arts programme as the literary find of the century. Years since his last book had done the almost impossible feat of flying to the top of the bestseller lists in London and New York before capturing one of the greatest literary prizes on offer.

Since then, nothing. No more books to win prestigious prizes and fly to the top of the bestseller lists. No more photographs of him accompanied by beautiful women to fill the gossip pages. He had simply disappeared.

According to Nigel, he had turned his back on the world, sold his London home and retreated to this island fastness. With an up-to-date photograph it would make a good feature. Long on speculation, short on facts. He was an ideal target for the kind of magazine that lived off scandal and well-known faces.

Sophie's fingers tightened around the cassette of film as she anticipated what would be done with her photographs. After this morning she had no reason to feel anything but antipathy for the man yet, slightly sickened by what she had done, she had to resist a sudden urge to fling the thing into the sea. She hated magazines like *Celebrity*. Sophie eased her shoulders, pushed back a wayward strand of fair hair that had escaped her plait to cling clammily to her forehead and watched her quarry, now slicing relentlessly through the water.

She stared down at the cassette, then, before she could do anything so utterly stupid, she dropped it into the button-down pocket of her shirt. She had no choice, she reminded herself. If Chay Buchanan had nothing to hide then Nigel couldn't hurt him. And she very firmly shut out the insistent voice that told her she was fooling herself.

Automatically she reloaded the camera with film, her eyes straying once more to the powerful figure of Chay Buchanan. But he had stopped the apparently effortless crawl and was lying on his back in the water, looking back towards the tower. Sophie watched, almost mesmerised by the beauty of his body glistening through the sheen of water as it rose and fell against the restless sea surging through the narrow gap in the rock. A tiny crease furrowed her forehead as she frowned, wondering what he was doing. Then, with a jolt, she knew, almost froze, as a buzz of excitement rippled her skin to gooseflesh. He was watching someone. There was someone else on the terrace.

She flattened herself as close to the edge of her rocky perch as she dared and strained to see. Who was it? A woman? Please, please, she begged the kindly Fates, let it be a woman. Someone famous. A well-known actress. A model. Something sensational enough to make up for not getting inside the tower, something that would please Nigel enough to hand over that precious envelope. . . And if it was somebody else's wife? Her conscience jabbed at her. She pushed the thought to one side. This was not the moment to dwell on moral dilemmas. She would worry about that later. Right now, if she didn't keep her head, there would be no photographs.

She hung over the edge a little, blotting out the dizzying drop to the sea in her effort to gain a few extra inches of terrace, but the great overhang of rock that protected the tower from prying eyes was still obstructing her view. Chay Buchanan raised his arms in encouragement to his unseen companion and a flash of white teeth confirmed that he was laughing. And she had been right about his mouth. Long seconds passed before she remembered her task and captured the moment on film.

A sudden movement galvanised her into action, but the body that leapt into those inviting arms was no famous beauty. It was a child. A dark-haired, straight-limbed boy, five or maybe six years old, and as at home in the water as his father. For a moment surprise held her transfixed. There could be no mistake in the relationship, the likeness was too marked. But Nigel had said nothing about a child. Or a wife. And Chay Buchanan certainly hadn't had the look of a married man.

She shook away the thought and the film ripped through the spool as she kept her finger on the release. With almost trembling fingers she dropped the used film into her bag and fed in another. There was barely enough light now for long-range photography. The sun was dipping relentlessly towards the sea, but still she carried on, her eye glued to the camera and the two figures framed in the viewfinder. Then she saw the boy pointing towards the cliff. Towards her.

Chay Buchanan's eyes creased as he scoured the cliff, and the mouth once again became that angry slash as the lowering sun gleamed against the hooded lens, betraying her. For a particle of a second their eyes clashed as the distance that separated them shrank to nothing.

There was no hurry, she told her trembling fingers as she flipped the film from the camera. By the time he was dry and dressed and halfway to the cliff-top, where her car was hidden from casual view, she would be gone. There was plenty of time. She repeated the words over and over in her head like a mantra. Just a short, easy climb and she was away. But her hands trembled a little as she hurriedly pushed her camera into the soft cocoon in her carrying bag. She slung it over her shoulder, glanced up at the route she had to take and reached for the first handhold.

It was unexpectedly difficult. Hours of being cramped, unable to stretch properly, had left her stupidly weak, and her legs began to tremble as she forced them to push her upwards, and her hands slipped sweatily on the suddenly elusive handholds as she thought of Chay Buchanan hurrying to intercept her. She was forced to stop, draw deep breaths into her lungs, remind herself that it was easy. She hadn't been about to kill herself over a few photographs. If it had been dangerous she would never have risked it.

Not even for Jennie? The thought of her sister lent her fresh strength. She had seen the way clearly down to the ledge. Now it was simply a matter of keeping her head, forgetting the drop below her and climbing back up to the cliff path before Chay Buchanan got there. The thought of meeting him again urged her on.

She clenched her teeth as the pain burned in her forearms. And with every agonising inch up the cliff-face she cursed Chay Buchanan. All she wanted was one photograph, a simple portrait to illustrate Nigel's article. And she had asked politely. If he hadn't been so damned rude she might have taken his refusal. It wasn't her way to sneak around corners, taking pictures of people who would rather be left alone. But a stab of guilt seared her cheeks as she recalled the extraordinary thrill of triumph when she had had the man in her sights.

Her fingertips reached upwards; she was desperate now for the ledge. Surely she was nearly there? But fifteen feet suddenly seemed more like fifty as there was just more rock to tear at her nails and scrape the skin from her fingers. Going down, it had all seemed so simple. Plenty of footholds. No more daunting than the bank in the local park where she and Jennie had played as children. The difference being that when she had slipped in the park there hadn't been a vertiginous drop down a sea-lashed cliff. Stop it! she warned her imagination. If she fell she would crash back on to the ledge. Nasty, painful—that was all. *All*? And if she hit her head? Rolled off?

Panic made her glance up, and her shift in weight almost undid her. She threw herself back at the rock-face, closing her eyes to shut out the dizzy spinning, and for the first time felt real fear cold-feather her spine. She clung on, wondering just how long she could stay there before the pain in her arms and the trembling weakness in her legs became too much and she simply fell.

'Can I offer you a hand, Sophie Nash?'

Her whole body lurched with shock at the harsh invitation. Taking great care not to overbalance, she glanced up once more, to find herself being regarded by a pair of fathomless eyes. He had flattened himself against the ground and stretched a hand down towards her. So close? She had been that close? She felt like weeping with frustration. But pride kept the tears at bay. Instead she glared at the strong, square hand and quite deliberately ignored the proferred lifeline. 'I can manage,' she ground out, and, as if to demonstrate this, grabbed the nearest rocky protrusion to ease herself up another few inches.

'I really think you should take my hand,' he advised coldly. 'I won't drop you, despite the undoubted provocation.'

But this small triumph had given her new heart. Adrenalin surging through her veins, she made another foot of height before she was forced once more to stop. She pressed her cheek against the rapidly cooling rock and tried to ease the strain on her limbs and drag air into her lungs through her parched throat. She hadn't known it was possible to hurt so much.

'Don't be stubborn, Sophie.' His voice was urgent now. 'You're not going to make it without help.'

His hawkish face was nearer, the lines carved deep into his cheeks, and he reached for her. 'Leave me alone,' she gasped, but the words were little more than a croak.

'Fine words. Remember them,' he ordered, 'if you live long enough.'

'I can manage!' she repeated, the words turning into a scream when her foot slipped and her forehead collided sharply against the rock as she scrabbled with her toe for a hold to halt the sickening slip. She was jerked to an agonised halt as Chay Buchanan's hands grasped her wrist and he hauled her over the edge, grabbing her in a vice-like grip as he rolled away from the yawning chasm.

'You've dislocated my arm!' she complained bitterly, as the pain of torn muscles brought tears swimming to her eyes.

'You would rather have fallen?' She didn't answer, couldn't answer through pain and tears. 'And I haven't dislocated anything.' He moved her arm, none too gently, and she groaned involuntarily and let her head fall forward on to his naked chest. 'See? Still in working order. No thanks to you.'

No wonder he had been so quick to reach her, she thought. He hadn't bothered to dry himself or put on more than a pair of shorts. But she was too weak with pain and exhaustion to move. Instead she lay very still, her cheek pressed against the dark hair that stippled his chest, listening to the steady thud of his heartbeat, while she tried to recover her strength. But he wasn't finished with her yet.

'You have dangerous hobbies, Sophie Nash.' He grasped her plait and yanked up her head, forcing her to confront him. 'But then, it isn't a hobby, is it?' She yelped and fresh tears started to her eyes, but he didn't care. His grasp only tightened, so that it was impossible to move without pain. 'Nevertheless, climbing alone, without a safety line, is just about the most stupid, reckless. . .' He stopped, clearly too angry to continue. Really angry. Those pirate's eyes were fierce enough to kill. 'Does anyone know where you are? If you'd fallen would anyone ever have known what had happened to you?'

How could he be so utterly heartless? Surely he must see that she was in agony? 'Someone would have found my car,' she gasped out.

'Someone would have found your car?' he repeated, in utter disbelief. '"Here lie some bits and pieces of

Sophie Nash. We know it was her because we found her car." Some epitaph.' Then the fact that silent tears were by now pouring down her face and on to his chest apparently penetrated, because he loosened his grasp of her hair and she almost whimpered with relief. But he hadn't finished. 'Let me tell you, girl, that you don't have much of a career as a paparazzo ahead of you if you ignore the simplest safety precautions.'

'I'm not a paparazzo,' she protested.

'You're giving a very good impression of one. For God's sake, is a photograph of me so valuable that it's worth risking your life? Whoever commissioned you must have promised to pay you a very great deal of money.' He frowned, then rolled over, pinning her against the rock-hard ground, crushing her breasts against his naked chest until she could hardly breathe. 'Who was it, Sophie?'

Pay? He thought she would do this for *money*? Days trailing around holiday resorts at the crack of dawn when they were deserted, making the best of hotels so that they should look exotic and desirable holiday destinations, that was what she was paid for.

Her attempt to get a photograph of the great Chay Buchanan while she was on the island had not been for the vast sums paid to professional paparazzi. It had been for something infinitely more precious. For a moment she was tempted to tell him. Ask him. . . She met his eyes and hope died. Chay Buchanan hadn't just turned her down when she had wanted to take his photograph. He had been. . .contemptuous. Anger, determination, sheer bloody-mindedness, had blinded her to the folly, the very real risk, of what she was doing.

She lay, too weak to move, her head thudding with pain from his maltreatment of her scalp. More likely the bang on your forehead, that know-it-all inner voice

immediately contradicted her. She would have liked to
touch the tender spot, check it out to assess the
damage, but his weight fixed her to the spot and she
lay quite helpless. She opened her lids to meet the
angry onslaught of his eyes.

'Well?' he demanded.

She had been stupid. She knew it, was prepared to
admit it. To herself. But she certainly wasn't going to
give him the satisfaction of telling him so. And she
wasn't going to tell him about Nigel. She had the
feeling that Nigel wouldn't like that at all.

'I wanted a photograph of you to hang on my
bedroom wall,' she managed to snap out. 'I'm a fan.'

For a moment he seemed taken aback. Then his lips
curved in a parody of a smile. 'I don't think so, Miss
Nash. I believe it would take a great deal more than
that to send you down that cliff.'

'You're too modest, Mr Buchanan. Besides, it was
easy enough,' she gasped, but the pain in her shoulder,
her head, and torn and bleeding hands made a liar of
her. Easy enough getting down.

'Easy?' he sneered. 'If it had been easy you wouldn't
be lying here, you would be racing to Luqa airport now
with your ill-gotten gains.'

She lay back against the hard rock. He was right, of
course, and now he would take the films and she would
have to tell Nigel she had failed, appeal to his sense of
honour. A hollow little voice suggested that Nigel was
not overburdened with the stuff. But Chay Buchanan
mustn't know how much it mattered.

'I wasn't in a hurry,' she said, as if strolling up a
rockface was an everyday occurrence. 'I was. . .admir-
ing the view,' she added, with a slightly wobbly attempt
at airiness.

'You won't admit it, will you?' he replied, clearly
infuriated by this unrepentant display of bravado. Then

he eased himself away from her, letting his eyes trail insolently from a pair of clear grey eyes, by way of a very ordinary nose and a full, over-large mouth, to linger on a bosom that rose and fell far too rapidly. 'But you're right about one thing. There's absolutely nothing wrong with the view.'

Sophie felt the colour flood to her face as she realised just how vulnerable she was. Pinned to the ground by his body, she had made not the slightest effort to free herself. 'How. . .how dare you?' she blustered, attempting to fling herself away from him, but he had her effortlessly pinioned between a pair of powerful thighs.

'Don't go all shy on me, Sophie. This morning you were quite prepared to offer me anything I wanted for that photograph.'

'That's not true! Let me go!' she demanded. Then, breathlessly, as his fingers brushed against her breast and the tip involuntarily tightened to his touch, she squeaked, 'What are you doing?' her grey eyes widening in alarm. 'Stop it!'

'You don't really mean that, Sophie Nash,' he said, knowing eyes dwelling momentarily on the tell-tale peaks thrusting against the thin white cotton of her shirt. 'There's no need to be embarrassed. Sex is the obvious response to a brush with death. It's simply nature's prompting to ensure the perpetuation of the species. But I'm afraid that right now I have something else on my mind.'

He flipped open the button of her breast-pocket and removed the film she had stowed there for safety. Then, without haste, not deliberately touching her but making no effort to avoid the inevitable intimacy, he thoroughly searched the rest of her pockets, while she squirmed with embarrassment. 'Just one roll?' he said at last.

She swallowed, then, very slowly, she nodded. For a moment he stared at her and she held her breath, certain that he would challenge her, would see the blatant lie. But her cheeks were already flaming from the intimacy of his touch and apparently satisfied he stood up, pulling her to her feet and half supporting her as her legs refused to work properly. He propelled her back towards the edge of the cliff.

'No!' She tried to step back but he held her fast, and she was too frightened of falling to attempt to jerk free. 'What. . .are you going to do?' He didn't answer, but took one gashed and bleeding hand, placed the spool of film into it and wrapped her stiff, rapidly swelling fingers around it. She glanced up at him uncertainly.

'Throw it into the sea, Sophie Nash,' he commanded, his words eerily echoing her own thoughts as she had perched on the ledge. But that had been before his hands had ransacked her pockets without a thought for her feelings. And his feelings? her over-active conscience prompted. But she was in no mood to listen to such stuff. He had no feelings. He was just a great big bully.

'No!' She defied him.

His hand gripped her arm more tightly. 'Do as I say.'

'No, damn you. I worked hard for those pictures. Do your own dirty work.'

'That's rich, coming from someone who spies on other people for a living. Throw it!' For a long moment she outfaced him, chin high, eyes blazing. 'Throw it!' he demanded.

Slowly, almost against her will, she turned to stare down at the white sea boiling around the rocks. It was oddly hypnotic, almost mesmerising. She began to sway towards it, only to be snapped back by Chay with a fierce oath. With a faint moan she turned and buried her face in his chest, and for a moment he held her and she knew he had been right. She could so easily have fallen.

And he was right about something else. Held against the warmth of his chest, almost drowning in the scent of his skin, the sharp tang of sweat and sea-water so strong that she could almost taste the salt, she wanted him to pull her down to the ground and take her, right there in the open air, with the sound of the sea pounding in her ears. The knowledge was as brutal as a slap in the face.

Horrified by desire so raw she could practically taste it, she tore herself away from him on legs weak from more than the terror of falling. It was far more frightening than that. She had to get away from this man. As quickly as possible, and not just because of her appalling reaction to him. He had found one film but she· might still get away with the others. Might still snatch her moment of triumph.

She bent to pick up her bag, wincing as its weight bit into her fingers, staggering a little as the ground dipped and swayed. The feeling was beginning to come back to her hands with a vengeance, the cuts and grazes stinging viciously and making her feel nauseous.

'Nice try, Sophie. But I'll have the film.' He caught her wrist, turning her roughly, and for a moment she thought he had guessed. But he forced open her fingers, still curled tightly around the little cassette, and she cried out involuntarily. For a moment he stared at her hand, then with a sharp impatient movement he said, 'You'd better come inside and clean these.'

'I'm all right,' she protested hoarsely. He hadn't suspected. 'I'll go back to my hotel,' she said quickly. Except that she'd already checked out. Her bags were in the car. She would be driving straight to the airport where she could clean up and change back into the pristine two-piece she had been wearing when she had called on him earlier. And, once she was inside the departure lounge, she would be beyond his reach.

'You think you can drive in that state?' he uttered in disbelief.

'It's nothing,' she said desperately. All she wanted was to get to the car and sit down for a moment, until this sickening weakness passed. She paused. 'I suppose I should thank you for saving me,' she added, a little grudgingly.

'Yes, you should,' he ground out. 'But we're so far beyond the niceties of good manners that I'd prefer it if you didn't bother.'

Hackles rose at his sharp, contemptuous tone. 'I won't! In fact, Mr Buchanan, you can rest assured that I won't bother you ever again.'

'I wish I could believe that, Sophie Nash. Why don't I?' His eyes fastened on the bag biting painfully into her shoulder, and before she could prevent him he had slipped it away from her and was hefting it thoughtfully. 'Perhaps I'd better keep this to be on the safe side.'

Her grey eyes widened in horror and she flung herself at him, making a grab for the bag. 'No!' she cried as he effortlessly whisked it out of her reach. Everything spun horribly from the sudden movement.

'No?' he enquired.

'It's just my camera. I can't work without it.'

'That is supposed to appeal to my better nature? Frankly, I can't think of anything that would please me more.'

'I doubt you have a better nature!' she flung at him.

'Then you are beginning to show some sense at last.' He glanced at the bag. 'This is just your camera? You went to a lot of trouble for just one roll of film. How long were you down on the ledge?'

'Hours,' she admitted. 'But you were only there for a few minutes.'

'True. But how long does it take with a motor-drive?'

'Not long,' she admitted. Then she took a gamble. 'In fact there are about sixty exposed films in my bag. I've been working all week for a tour company, taking pictures for next year's brochures.'

'You expect me to believe that?' he asked.

Her hands were beginning to throb horribly and she lifted them in a helpless little gesture. 'Why not? It's the truth.' She swallowed as saliva began to flood her mouth. Another moment and she knew she would be sick. If only he would let her go so that she could just sit down for a minute. But he was relentless.

'Come on, Sophie Nash. You can't expect me to believe that you would risk all that work?' he said incredulously.

'Risk?' Nothing was making much sense. She was the one who had been at risk.

'You might have dropped your bag while you were climbing down.'

'I. . .' She blinked as he began to recede. 'I was very careful.' She took a step, but the ground seemed to be made of foam rubber. Surprised, she reached out a hand to steady herself and he caught it.

'What is it?'

'I'm sorry.' Her voice seemed to come from a long way off. 'I'm afraid I'm going to be. . .' She lifted her hand to her head and saw the blood running down her fingers. Then, mercifully, everything went black.

CHAPTER TWO

SOPHIE woke with a throbbing head and dry mouth, every part of her aching. The room was dim, what light there was slanting through two pairs of louvred shutters closed on tall windows. She raised her wrist to see what time it was and heard a groan. It was a moment or two before she realised the sound had come from her own lips.

She stared at bruised, swollen fingers, that looked as if they might have been through a wringer, and winced. Her fingers. And memory began to rush back, a little confused, but with the basic facts intact. The slow motion nightmare as she had tried to make it to the cliff-top. And she had nearly made it. Would have made it. Only Chay Buchanan had been waiting for her.

She looked around her at the strange room and then with a rush of horror she knew. She was in the lion's den. Worse. She groaned, and this time the response was quite deliberate. She was in the lion's bed.

The thought was enough to drag her protesting body from the smooth linen sheet, but as she propped herself against the great carved bedhead and the sheet slipped from her body something else became startlingly obvious. She was naked. She gingerly grasped the sheet between her fingers and lifted it. Utterly naked. Someone had undressed her.

Who? It seemed vitally important that she remember. Then, rather hurriedly, she blotted out the thought before she did. She didn't want to contemplate the possibility of her unconscious body being undressed by

22

Chay Buchanan. Instead she focused her attention on her surroundings.

She was in a long, wide room, the stone walls painted matt white, with two large panels, glowing blue-green abstractions of the sea, the only decoration. The floor was of some dark polished wood. On it were laid rich Bukhara rugs, barred with faint stripes of light that filtered through louvred shutters closed over floor-to-ceiling windows. Apart from the bed, flanked by night-tables and a pair of tall Chinese lamps, the only furniture was an enormous chest of drawers with heavy brass handles and an equally impressive wardrobe. A man's room. Completely devoid of any woman's touch.

She rose unsteadily, dragged the sheet from the bed, clumsily wrapped it about her with fingers that refused to bend properly and staggered to the bathroom at the far end of the room. Halfway there she questioned her knowledge that it was a bathroom, but with the question came the all too shocking answer. She remembered. And blushed hot and painfully at the memory.

He had brought her here. She had been dimly aware of being carried up a wide staircase. Then he had propped her up and the sudden rush of water had brought her gasping back to life as he had stood with her in the enormous shower-stall, stripping her while the cascade of warm water had washed away dust and sweat and blood.

She tried to swallow, but her tongue seemed to cleave to the roof of her mouth as she remembered how, too weak to stand unaided, she had simply leaned against him, her head against his shoulder, her breasts startlingly white against the dark tan of his chest. She had been incapable of protest as he had held her around the waist and briskly soaped her with a huge sponge, rinsed her, dried her and wrapped her in a soft white bathrobe and bathed her hands with antiseptic,

his fingers gentle, even if the straight, hard lines of his
mouth and his angry eyes had made his feelings more
than plain.

The mirror alongside the bath reflected bright spots
of colour that rouged her cheeks like patches on a rag
doll's face against the whiteness of her skin, the pale
gold shock of hair. And he had threatened her with a
dungeon. She had the unnerving feeling that his dungeon would be far safer than his bathroom.

But one question was answered. There was no Mrs
Buchanan. No wife, however tolerant, would have put
up with such goings on. She glanced around, and the
lack of feminine accoutrements confirmed the fact that
whoever usually shared Chay Buchanan's king-sized
bed she certainly wasn't a permanent fixture. She
forced herself to her feet and opened the bathroom
cabinet. Not even constant enough to have left a
toothbrush. She quickly closed the door. It was none
of her business, she told herself firmly.

But it was too late to blot out the image of his
personal toiletries, his exquisite taste in cologne, the
fact that he used an open razor.

'Have you seen enough? Or do you want the guided
tour?'

She spun round, then wished she hadn't as the room
lurched sickeningly. She leaned momentarily against
the cool richness of Catalan tiles that decorated the
wall. Then, as she followed the direction of his eyes,
tugged desperately at the sheet, which had shifted
alarmingly as she turned, a sudden coolness warned
her that it had left her rear exposed. She edged
sideways as she caught her reflection in the mirror
alongside the bath. How on earth had she got that
bruise on her shoulder? She lifted it slightly and the
pain brought instant recall of the tearing jerk as he had
hauled her over the edge of the cliff to safety.

'I was looking for some painkillers,' she said, with a brave attempt at dignified suffering.

His lip curled derisively. 'Of course you were.' He took her arm and led her firmly back to the bed. 'Lie down and I'll bring you something.'

'I'm not an invalid.'

'No, just a pain in the backside. But you'd better lie down before you fall down.' She sat down abruptly on the bed, but only because her legs were so wobbly. It was nothing to do with his telling her to and she stubbornly refused the cool enticement of a down pillow.

'If you'll bring my clothes, I'll stop being a pain in the——' she started angrily, then stopped, gathered herself a little. She couldn't afford to aggravate the man any further. 'If you'll bring my clothes, I'll be happy to leave,' she said, with exaggerated politeness.

'Please?' he suggested.

For a moment her large grey eyes snapped dangerously. 'Do I have to beg for my own clothes?' she demanded. He didn't reply, merely waited. And waited. Apparently she did. 'Please,' she ground out through clenched teeth.

'That's better. But I'm afraid your clothes are being washed. Perhaps you can have them tomorrow.'

'Tomorrow! But I have a plane to catch——'

'*Had* a plane to catch. I contacted the airport and cancelled your booking.'

'You did what?' she exclaimed, ignoring the sharp reminder that scythed through her head that anything much above a whisper was inadvisable. 'You had no right to do that!' No right to go through her handbag. Look at her personal things.

'Since you were in no position to use it, and since it's an open ticket, I thought you might be grateful to have the opportunity to re-book. I suppose I should have known better.'

'I'm fine!' she declared, with a careless disregard for the truth. 'You can keep your washing. I'm leaving.' She rose a little shakily, hitching the sheet up and taking a step in the direction of the door only to find him barring her way. 'Right now,' she said.

He immediately stood back and offered her the door. 'As you please. I moved your car into the garage.'

Along with her suitcase with all her clothes. She would have liked to march out, chin high, but the wretched sheet made that impossible. She was all too aware of a mocking little smile twisting his mouth as she edged sideways and backed towards the door. He made no move to stop her but watched her attempt at a dignified departure with scarcely veiled amusement, and suddenly she knew it couldn't be that easy. She halted uncertainly.

'But?' she demanded.

'But,' he agreed, his green pirate eyes glinting wickedly. 'Alas, the keys are not with it. But maybe you're a dab hand with a hot wire? In your job I imagine it would come in useful.'

'Of course not!'

'No? What a pity. Perhaps you should learn. Then again, you would still have the problem of clothes. Because I removed your bag, too. For safe-keeping. Or maybe you don't mind arriving at a hotel wearing nothing but that rather ineffectual attempt at a sarong.'

She clutched the sheet a little tighter, unwilling to risk dropping it from stiff fingers if she tried to wrap it around her more thoroughly.

'And since time seems to have passed rather more rapidly than you imagine, I have to inform you that the plane you are so eager to catch left several hours ago.'

Sophie stared at him, then turned to the windows

and the light filtering through the shutters. 'How long have I been here?' she demanded. 'What time is it?' She dropped a glance to her wrist. 'Is my watch in the laundry too?' Not waiting for his answer, no longer caring about modesty—after all, he'd already seen a great deal more than her backside—she swept across the room and threw open one of the shutters to admit a whisper of light and stared out. The sea was flat calm, a pale milky blue under a thin veil of mist that curtained the sun. An early-morning sun.

'I've been here all night?' But it wasn't really a question. The slightly unnerving answer was confronting her.

'All night, Sophie Nash,' he affirmed. 'Wouldn't that have made an exciting caption for your photographs? "My night with Chay Buchanan,"' he offered, with just enough conviction to bring the colour flooding to her pale complexion.

'Don't be ridiculous. I didn't spend the night with you,' she said, but her mouth was dry and she steadfastly refused to give in to the temptation to turn and check the other pillow for evidence that the bed had been occupied by two.

'You did, but it's all a matter of intepretation, isn't it? And the doctor insisted that someone must keep an eye on you.'

Her eyes flew wide open and this time she could not help herself. But the swift involuntary glance at the huge bed told her nothing. 'An eye on me?' she asked huskily.

'In case of concussion.' His long fingers combed back the tangle of sun-bleached curls from her forehead and he lightly touched the dark shadow of a bruise. 'You took quite a knock, Sophie Nash.'

She winced, raised her own hand to the spot and felt the slight swelling. She drew a long shuddering breath, whether from the pain or the cool touch of his fingers she could not have told—perhaps didn't want to know. But she did know that it wasn't possible for her to stay a moment longer in Chay Buchanan's tower. She drew herself up to her full height, and five feet and six inches in her bare feet had never felt quite so insubstantial. 'Then I really mustn't put you to any more trouble, Mr Buchanan,' she said with all the dignitiy she could muster, wrapped inadequately as she was in nothing but a sheet. 'I should like to go now.'

'That isn't possible. Even if I were prepared to let you go, you're in no fit state to travel. But if you do as you're told and get back into bed I'll go and fetch some of the painkillers the doctor left.'

Doctor? It was the second time he had mentioned a doctor, but she didn't remember one. She must have taken a much harder crack on the head than she had thought. But right now that didn't matter. There was something far more important to get straight. 'What do you mean?' She dug her toes into the rug as he took her arm, resisting his firm urging towards the bed. 'If you were prepared to let me go. . .? You can't keep me here against my will. That's. . .' Her mouth dried. 'That's kidnapping.'

'Is it?' Heavy lids drooped slightly, concealing the expression in his eyes. 'Would you like me to ask the local constabulary to despatch an officer to listen to your complaint?' he offered, with every evidence of civility. But there was a muscle working dangerously at the corner of his mouth.

'Yes!' she flung defiantly, daring him to do just that.

He nodded. 'If you'll excuse me.' He gestured vaguely and walked to the door.

'But. . .' She took an uncertain step after him. 'You're really going to do it?'

'Of course. Kidnapping is a very serious charge,' he

said crisply. 'You should press it home with all the force at your command.'

'I will,' she declared. Then her challenge faltered under his unwavering gaze. 'Why do I feel another "but" coming on?'

'Could it be that common sense has suggested that you were about to make a fool of yourself?'

'Why should it do that?' she demanded.

'Just think about it for a moment,' he instructed her. 'Think about the fact that I rescued you from a very dangerous situation. That I——'

'I could have managed!'

He didn't even bother to comment on the absurdity of that remark, but continued as if she hadn't spoken. 'That I brought you to my home, bathed your wounds——'

'And a great deal else.' She flushed as his mouth curved in a provoking little smile. Stupid. Stupid to have mentioned that. Why couldn't she have forgotten that?

'I bathed your wounds,' he repeated, 'before I put you into my own bed and sent for a doctor, who advised several days of rest.' He paused. 'It doesn't sound much like kidnapping to me. But——' and he shrugged '—if you think the police will be interested I'll get them right now.' He waited for her response—imperious, tyrannical, scornful and infuriatingly right.

She didn't need to have it spelled out for her in words of one syllable. He would make himself sound like a hero with her playing the role of an ungrateful idiot. If he threw in the fact that she had been trespassing—she didn't think he would worry too much about the finer details of truth—he would probably be beatified. Given his own feast-day. With fireworks. Damn! 'Forget the police,' she muttered. 'But I don't want to rest. I just want to leave.'

'If you think that having you as a house-guest is an undiluted pleasure, Miss Nash, I have to tell you that you're mistaken. I value my privacy and you'll go the minute it's possible. We'll discuss terms after breakfast.' He turned abruptly to leave. 'I recommend a lightly boiled egg.'

'A boiled egg? I thought bread and water was the traditional prisoner's fare,' she threw after him.

His eyes darkened. Sea-green? Maybe. But what sea? The Arctic Ocean in mid-winter, perhaps? 'If that's what you want. . .' He snapped the door shut behind him.

'Wait!' But she was already talking to herself. Then in a sudden quiver of panic she ran across the room, and ignoring her painful hands almost tore at the door. But it wasn't locked. For a moment she stood there, in the open doorway, wondering whether to make a run for it down the thickly carpeted stairway. She glanced down at herself. He wasn't that careless. He didn't need a lock to keep her confined. How far would she get in a sheet, without any shoes? Without any money. She retreated into the bedroom and closed the door.

Think, Sophie, she urged herself. You need a plan. Forget the plan, she answered herself a little caustically. What you need first are some clothes. Her glance fell on the chest of drawers and, for the first time since she woke, her mouth curved in the semblance of a smile.

She gripped the brass handle of one of the drawers and pulled, biting back a cry as pain shot through her shoulder where Chay Buchanan had hauled her over the edge of the cliff. She gave up all attempts to cling on to the sheet as she eased it, recalling with a tiny spurt of anger the huge bruise that decorated her back. Monster! He hadn't needed to drag her up like that. She could have managed. Oh, really? Yes, really, she told the irritating little voice inside her head. Of course she could. But the recollection of that sickening lurch as she had missed her foothold and started to slip made her flesh rise in goose-bumps, and she shivered despite the warmth stealing in through the window as the early morning mist was burned off the sea. She had to get out of here.

She regarded the chest with loathing, but to escape she needed something to wear. This time she grasped both handles and the drawer slid open to reveal piles of beautifully ironed shirts. And this time she really smiled, with an almost irresistible curve of her lips.

She helped herself to a pale blue cotton shirt, easing her painful shoulder up to slide into the sleeve. The shirt was too big, hanging almost to her knees, but that was good. At a pinch, with a belt, she could wear it as a dress. She tried to fasten the buttons, but her fingers were stiff and painful, slowing her down, and she gave up after a couple.

She rifled through the remainder of the drawers, ignoring the ties but helping herself to a pair of thick white socks that would cushion her feet against stone. Pants? She regarded Chay Buchanan's taste for plain white American boxer shorts with dismay. They would never stay up. What she really needed was a pair of jeans and a belt. Her fingers grasped the handles of the bottom drawer as she heard his voice speaking to someone on the stairs.

She flew across the room to the bed, and as the door opened she was demure beneath the sheet. He backed in with a tray and there was just the slightest hesitation, as he regarded the shirt that now covered her anatomy, before he placed it on the table beside the bed.

'Feeling a little better?' he asked.

'Well enough to leave,' she replied brightly, ignoring

heavy, painful limbs and the overwhelming sense of weariness that her exertions had produced.

'I think that is a decision for the doctor to make.'

'Doctor?'

'He'll call in to see you later.' He regarded her thoughtfully as hope betrayed itself in her eyes. 'He's a friend, Sophie, so don't bother to bat those long eyelashes at him. He won't be impressed.'

'I've never batted an eyelash in my life!'

'No?' He sat on the edge of the bed and regarded her impassively. 'I must have mistaken the signals. I had the distinct impression that you were batting like mad yesterday morning when you asked me to sit for you.'

'That's not true!' she protested. She just hadn't been prepared for the instant response of her body to the perilous masculinity of the man, the unexpected pull of dangerous undercurrents tugging her towards something new and exciting and wonderful. She swallowed. He had seen it. Was that why his rejection had hurt so much? Because he had quite wrongly assumed that she was offering herself as a reward for his co-operation and had still said no?

He sat beside her on the bed and handed her a cup of tea, holding her clumsy fingers around it with his own. And it was still there. The urgent fire surging through her veins as he touched her. She felt the sudden start of tears to her eyes. It wasn't fair.

'Come on, Sophie, drink this,' he said. 'It'll make you feel better.'

'I doubt it,' she sniffed. It wasn't a cup of tea she needed. Her face, her whole body grew hot as she privately acknowledged that what she needed was Chay Buchanan. To be held in his arms, to. . . Oh, lord! She had always imagined herself feeling this kind of bewildering desire for a man she had fallen deeply, wonderfully in love with.

She buried her face in the cup. She hardly knew this man. And what she knew of him she didn't like. It was lust, far from pure, and shockingly simple. What she should be doing was standing under a cold shower, not lying in his bed with his warm thigh pressed against hers, separated only by the single thickness of a sheet, his hands wrapped close around hers. Why couldn't the wretched man wear a pair of trousers instead of those tailored shorts that blatantly offered his well-muscled thighs and beautifully shaped calves to her hungry eyes?

She gulped down the tea and he took the cup from her. 'Can you eat something?'

'Bread?' she asked, making an effort to keep the exchange hostile, but suddenly too weak to care much.

'The bread and water will keep,' he replied a little sharply. 'Try some toast.' She shook her head. Then wished she hadn't. 'All right. Just take these and lie down.'

She stared suspiciously at the white tablets. 'What are they?'

'Paul left them.'

'Your friendly doctor?' She withdrew slightly.

'For heaven's sake! Do you think I'm trying to drug you? He's a respected consultant with a wife and considerable quantity of children. These are just something for your headache.' He glared at her. 'You have got a headache, I hope?'

Of course she had a headache. She took the pills, swallowed them with the aid of a glass of water that he held for her as if she was an invalid. Then, as the door closed behind him, she gave up the struggle to maintain the façade of defiance, and slid down between the sheets and tried to work out just what kind of a mess Nigel's 'little favour' had got her into.

She hadn't much relished the task and had left it until the last day. . .perhaps hoping that he wouldn't be there. Nigel could hardly blame her for that.

But finally she had driven out along the coast road until she had seen the tower, just as Nigel had described it, four-square and massive, one of the many that had been built on the island to keep watch against pirates. A few in the more built-up areas had been turned into restaurants for the tourist trade. Most were abandoned. This one was surrounded by a garden.

Flowers tumbled from beds raised from the rocky ground and clambered over the walls, making the tower look more like some lost fairy-tale keep. With the impressive golden cliffs at its flanks, and the sea beyond, it had quite taken her breath away.

Close up, the tower had seemed rather more forbidding, despite the softening effect of the flowers, its entrance barricaded by a pair of heavy studded doors. But she had pinned a smile to her lips and lifted the traditional dolphin-shaped knocker.

For a long time nothing had happened. She had been trying to pluck up the courage to knock again when the door had swung open, and the figure that had filled the doorway took Sophie's breath away for the second time in less than five minutes as every cell in her body had swivelled in his direction and jumped to attention.

She had seen photographs of the man, seen him on the television, but nothing had prepared her for his overwhelming physical presence, a compelling masculinity that drew her to him like iron filings to a magnet.

'Yes?' His curt manner released her, her quick step back observed by a pair of knowing eyes that after the most cursory inspection seemed to know more about her than she did herself.

It took every shred of self-possession to keep the smile fixed to her mouth and offer her hand. 'Mr

Buchanan? Mr Chay Buchanan?' He ignored her hand,
and a little self-consciously she pushed back a strand of
hair that had fallen over her cheek before letting her
own hand fall. 'My name is Sophie Nash.'

'Sophie Nash?' He tested the name, as if trying to
recall it.

'Yes, I——'

'Maybe my memory is failing me, Miss Nash,' he
interrupted without apology, 'but I don't recall an
appointment with anyone of that name.' His tone
invited her to prove him wrong, but with the absolute
confidence of someone who knew it to be impossible.

'Well, no, I don't have an appointment,' she admitted, somewhat taken aback by this unexpected
challenge.

'In that case. . .' He shrugged, stepped back and
began to shut the door.

'But. . .Mr Buchanan. . . I'm. . .' Almost instinctively she reached out and held his arm. His skin was
warm, very brown beneath the whiteness of her fingers,
coated with silky dark hair. She snatched back her
hand as if she had received an electric shock, and when
she looked up again his eyes taunted her. But he didn't
shut the door. 'I'm here because——'

'I know why you are here, Miss Nash,' he said,
confounding her. 'Or were you deluding yourself that
you were the first eager. . .fan. . .to find me? I have to
admit that you are more appealing than some.' And his
eyes took a slow tour of her body. 'From the top of
your glossy blonde head to your pink-painted toenails,'
he conceded. 'Although most have the tact to carry a
copy of one of my books for me to sign. . .?' He raised
a querying brow and glanced towards her bag. But she
had no book to offer and silently cursed such a stupid
oversight. 'That's about all I can do for you.'

She was afraid that her cheeks had gone as pink as

the despised toenails. They were certainly very hot and she would have liked to cover them with her hands, but that would be stupid. Would only draw attention to them, and to the fact that she had painted her fingernails as well. Because she had taken a great deal of trouble with her appearance.

'Wear something pretty,' Nigel had advised. 'And plenty of make-up. He can't resist a pretty face. All you'll have to do is use that winning smile of yours and you'll be in.' Well, Nigel had been wrong. It was true that she wasn't wearing much make-up. It was too warm. But the charcoal smudges on her lids emphasised the size of her large grey eyes; the mascara thickened and glossed the lashes. And she had taken infinite care to outline her lips and colour them.

She had no experience of photographing major celebrities and she had been determined to appear cool and professional. Clearly the white sleeveless jacket with its deep revers and the flirty navy and white spotted skirt had been a misjudgement in some way that totally eluded her. But it was too late to worry about that now.

'I didn't come here for your autograph, Mr Buchanan. I'm a photographer. I'm sorry if this is an awkward time. I would have telephoned to make an appointment,' she rushed on, 'but you aren't listed——'

'That,' he informed her, 'is because I don't have a telephone. It's supposed to be a strong hint that I have no wish to be disturbed by. . .casual callers.'

She was missing something. What on earth did he think she wanted? Then, with a shock, she knew. He thought she was some kind of literary groupie! It was awful. Off-the-scale embarrassment. She wanted to turn tail and run but she couldn't. Now she had found him, she had to give it everything she had got. Remem-

bering Nigel's advice, she tried the smile. 'Mr
Buchanan,' she surged on, before he could stop her or
finally close the door on her. 'You've made a
mistake——'

'It's you who's made the mistake, Miss Nash,' he
said harshly.

'No,' she protested hotly, determined to disabuse
him of his mistaken notion. 'Please listen. I simply
want to take a photograph of you.' He said nothing.
He didn't move. Not one muscle. It was utterly unnerving. She ran her tongue nervously over her lips as she
fumbled in her bag for a card, any excuse to look away
from those disturbing eyes. Her trembling fingers
finally found what they were seeking and she held it
out and eventually he took it, without taking his eyes
from her face. 'You see?' she said, encouraging him to
look at it. 'I'm a *professional* photographer.'

If she had thought that this would clear up the
misunderstanding, make everything better, she had
been wrong. He didn't even bother to look at her card,
simply tore it in two and handed it back. 'Goodbye,
Miss Nash.'

A pin-prick of anger stirred the delicate hairs on the
nape of her neck, darkened her fine grey eyes, but she
wasn't about to give up.

'A friend of mine is writing an article about you. . .
about your work,' she rushed on quickly, before he
could ask what kind of article. 'I hoped to persuade
you to let me take a simple portrait. It wouldn't take
long. Ten minutes. Less,' she promised. 'There's no
need to change. You look fine.' Much more than fine.
He presented a picture begging to be taken. His green
T-shirt might be old, faded, but it was a perfect foil for
his dark colouring, and the sleeves had been ripped
from it, exposing strong, well-muscled arms and for-
midable shoulders; white tailored shorts displayed an

equally powerful pair of tanned legs. He looked more like an athlete than a writer.

Still he didn't move, apparently waiting for something more. She swallowed. 'I would, of course, be prepared to pay. . .' His eyes darkened slightly. 'Whatever fee you. . .think fit.'

'Anything?' he asked, finally breaking the ominous silence.

'Anything,' she agreed recklessly, as he appeared to weaken. She wasn't about to lose him for a few pounds. Then, realising how naïve she must have sounded, she added, 'Within reason, of course.'

'And if I was. . .unreasonable?' Suddenly, without the necessity for words, she knew that this was not, had never been, a discussion about money. He had seen her reaction to him, misunderstood, thought she was actually prepared to go to bed with him to get what she wanted. Then, with a jolt, she realised that it was far worse than that. He believed that she *wanted* to go to bed with him.

Mesmerised by the idea, she remained rooted to the spot, quite unable simply to turn and walk away. Not because so much depended on getting him to sit for her. But because her legs had apparently turned to rubber. His mouth curled in a cruel parody of amusement as he made a move towards her, forcing her to look up or retreat. Sophie had no choice, and as she looked up he lifted his hand, touched the delicate hollow of her neck with the tip of one long finger, his brows lifting just a fraction as she felt the shock start through her body.

'Well, well,' he murmured. 'Such flattering eagerness.' Then, as his eyes held her fixed like a rabbit mesmerised by the headlights of an oncoming car, his finger traced the line of her breastbone with agonising slowness, until it came to rest against the white linen where it crossed between her breasts. Her lips parted on a sharp, anguished breath as her nipples tightened against the cloth.

'Nice try, Miss Nash. But your friend should have warned you that I don't talk to reporters or photographers. No matter how appealing the inducement.'

With a superhuman effort she raised her hand to slap away the fingers that lingered against the soft swell of her breast. 'How dare you?' she croaked.

'Dare?' He had ignored the slap, but now he withdrew his hand and she could breathe again. Just. 'For my privacy I would dare a very great deal. I give you fair warning, Miss Sophie Nash, that if I find you anywhere near my home with a camera in your possession, you'll discover that the dungeon is still a working feature. And that's where you'll remain until I decide otherwise.'

Now, lying in his bed, Sophie almost jumped again as she recalled the slam of the great front door. She knew she had to escape. Get away from this insufferable man as quickly as possible. A yawn caught her by surprise and her lids, suddenly unbearably heavy, drifted shut. It was important. But she would just have a little sleep first.

CHAPTER THREE

SOPHIE woke, stretched, regarded her unconventional sleeping wear with a slight frown and pulled herself upright, wincing as the aches immediately re-established themselves, to confront a pair of dark, inquisitive eyes regarding her with open curiosity. The same dark eyes that had spotted the flash of her lens against the sun. They belonged to a boy of about five or six years of age who was sitting cross-legged at the end of the bed.

'Hello,' she said.

He leaned forward a little, excitement barely contained. 'What was it like?' he asked.

'I'm sorry?'

'On the cliff.' He flung an arm in that general direction.

'Oh.' She wondered what he expected. Breathless excitement and danger? The truth would probably be best. 'It was hot and dusty,' she offered, and hid a smile at his open scorn. 'And very. . .frightening.'

'I wouldn't be frightened,' he said, clearly dismissing her fears as something to be expected of a woman. 'I'm going to climb it. . .one day. All the way.'

The thought made her feel suddenly queasy. 'Well, make sure you take a rope,' she advised.

'You didn't,' he pointed out.

'I was stupid. Your father had to rescue me.'

He regarded her with something like pity. 'But you're a girl.'

She could offer no argument to that. Male chauvin-

40

ism lives, she thought, passed down from father to son. 'What's your name?'

'Tom! What are you doing in here?' The boy scrambled off the bed guiltily. 'I told you to leave Miss Nash alone.'

'I didn't wake her up, Papa. She did it all by herself. Didn't you?' He appealed to Sophie.

'All by myself,' she agreed. 'He didn't disturb me. Really.'

Chay Buchanan was not to be so easily placated. 'Go and have your tea. Theresa is waiting for you.'

Tom gave her an uncertain little smile, bravado extinguished. 'Sorry,' he muttered.

'Don't be, Tom. Enjoy your tea.' She watched the door close beind him with regret as she was forced instead to confront his stony-faced father, who leaned towards her and grasped her arm.

'What were you asking him?' There was no mistaking the raw anger in his voice, his face, the way his fingers bit into the soft flesh.

'I didn't ask him anything. Despite your low opinion of me, I am not in the habit of interrogating children.'

'You're suggesting that such a thing would be beneath you?' he demanded, disbelief stamped in every line of his face.

She glared at him. 'I'm not suggesting it,' she retorted coldly. 'I'm telling it like it is.' For a moment their eyes clashed.

'So what were you talking about?' The fingers bit deeper and she tried not to wince visibly.

'He. . .he asked me about the cliff.'

'The cliff?' He paled visibly. 'What did he ask you?' There was an urgency about him that intrigued her, despite her attempt to hold herself apart. He gave her a little shake. 'What did you tell him?'

'He just asked what it was like. I told him it was frightening and that I had been stupid. . .'

'And?'

'He took the view that I was feeble because I was a girl.' She paused, then added, because she thought he should know, 'He said he was going to climb it himself one day.'

'Damn you,' he said, through tight lips.

'Frankly, Mr Buchanan, I don't think it had anything to do with me. But perhaps some simple lessons in rock-climbing would be a wise precaution,' she advised, with feeling. 'Let him have a taste of the pain as well as the excitement.'

He swept his hand through a dark lock of hair that had fallen over his forehead. 'No.' A muscle was working furiously at his mouth. 'He's not going anywhere near that damned cliff.' He glared down at her. 'I don't have to ask how you are,' he snapped. 'Obviously a great deal better.'

'Yes,' she replied. And some small devil prompted her to add a gentle, 'Thank you for asking.' It brought her a sharp look. 'Quite well enough to leave.'

'You'll leave when it suits me, Miss Nash. In the meantime you'll stay where you are until Paul has checked you over. Don't say anything stupid to him,' he warned.

Stupid? Like what? Help me, I'm being held prisoner? She managed a sweetly insincere smile. 'What could I say? You're a hero. A positive saint——'

'Stop it!' She shrugged and subsided against the bed. He leaned over her and grasped her chin, forcing her to look into his eyes. 'Behave yourself, Sophie Nash. Or I'm warning you, you'll never see your precious films again. Is that quite clear?'

Oh, wouldn't it be utter bliss to tell him to take her films and go to hell with them? The temptation was almost overwhelming. But she would have to do the work again, at her own expense. And he didn't only have her films. He had her camera. And there was Jennie. She hadn't quite given up on the chance that she might yet snatch her films and run. 'Quite clear,' she said demurely.

For a moment he scrutinised her face, as if not quite believing in such a quick capitulation, and she forced herself to meet his disquieting gaze head-on and ignore the sudden quickening of her pulse, the intoxicating sense of her own fragility as she was confronted by the man's almost barbaric magnetism.

Finally, he released her, but the imprint of his fingers remained burned into her face. She was breathless, her pulse jumping, not quite in control. Unlike her gaoler, who was regarding her without any trace of emotion to disturb his arrogant features. 'You must be hungry,' he said prosaically, as if to confirm her opinion. 'When Paul's finished with you, come downstairs for supper. Theresa's made you some soup.'

She plucked at the shirt she was wearing. 'Could I have some clothes?'

'Not for the moment. Not until I've decided what to do with you.' He regarded her steadily. 'You seem to be pretty resourceful. I'm sure you'll manage.'

A tap on the door interrupted the flash of annoyance that sparked her eyes, threatening to erupt and undo all her hard-won attempts to be civil to the man. Chay rose from the bed and admitted the slight figure of the doctor.

'Don't take her blood pressure, Paul,' he warned as he turned to leave. 'I have the feeling that it will blow your machine.'

But the doctor did not take the warning seriously. He checked her eyes, listened to her chest, took the dangerous blood pressure and declared it to be fine, delicately probed her shoulder and finally examined her hands.

'Take it easy for a few days, Miss Nash,' he finally advised her. 'Get plenty of sleep and you will be fine.' He rose. 'I'll look in again tomorrow, but I hope to find you outside, sitting in the shade.' He paused. 'And stay away from cliffs in future. Particularly that one.'

'Why?'

Dr Paul Manduca regarded his patient thoughtfully. 'Some questions, Miss Nash, are better not asked.' He picked up his bag. 'I'll see you again tomorrow. Good evening.'

Evening? This time she didn't even bother to query the time. Chay Buchanan had invited her downstairs for supper. If she was hungry. By her somewhat unreliable reckoning it must be at least thirty hours since she had eaten an apple, something to do to break the boredom of the endless wait as she had hoped that Chay Buchanan would take a swim. She had eaten it with the thoughtlessness of someone who knew her next meal would only be an hour or two away. If she was hungry? She swung her legs from the bed. She was ravenous. But before she left this room she had to make herself decent.

She washed, used his comb to disentangle her hair painfully, then quite shamelessly helped herself to a fresh white shirt. Her fingers were hurting less and she made herself fasten all but the top two buttons. Then she tackled the bottom drawer. But there were no jeans. Just sweaters and shorts.

She held a pair of navy shorts against herself. Not bad. She pulled them on, but the minute she let go they fell about her ankles. She glared at them. She wasn't about to be beaten by a pair of shorts. All she needed was something to hold them up with. A tie. She found the drawer with the socks and ties and quickly threaded one tie through the loops and knotted it firmly in place around her waist. Then she took another, rather beautiful silk tie in deep red and tied it over the shirt, grinning appreciatively at her reflection in the bathroom mirror. She decided against the socks. She had the feeling they would rather spoil the effect.

She opened the bedroom door and jumped, confronted with the tower's disturbing inhabitant. But she didn't miss the glitter of a pair of vivid eyes as he absorbed her attempt at sartorial elegance, or the deepening of the lines etched into his cheeks.

'You took so long, I thought that something must be wrong.'

'Wrong? Whatever could be wrong, Mr Buchanan?' she enquired smoothly. 'I was simply taking my time deciding what to wear.'

'It's an interesting combination.' He walked around her, inspecting the result of her raid on his wardrobe. 'In fact, it's oddly sexy.' His eyes met her furious glance. 'But I imagine it was your sex appeal, rather than your skill with a camera, that won you this particular assignment.'

Sex appeal? The idea was so alien that she was for once left without a reply. She had certainly taken Nigel's advice and tried to look. . .tempting. . .when she had set out to persuade Chay Buchanan to let her take his photograph. That she might have succeeded was disturbing, especially as she was now quite at the mercy of her intended victim.

Sophie sat back and sighed with contentment after eating her fill of a thick vegetable soup in the style of minestrone, but with beans and pork added to it. 'That was wonderful, Theresa,' she said, and added two of the few Maltese words she had learned. '*Grazzi, hafna*.' The middle-aged woman who kept house for

Chay Buchanan beamed briefly, before turning on him to launch into a rapid speech in her native tongue. Then she flounced back into the kitchen with the dishes. Sophie watched her go and then turned to Chay. 'What was all that about?' she asked.

'Theresa is rather old-fashioned. She does not think it quite "proper" for a young lady to be wearing clothes that belong to a man. Especially a man she doesn't know.'

Sophie, hunger assuaged by Theresa's excellent cooking, was feeling considerably mellower. 'I agree with her,' she said, quite seriously, 'but since the alternative was the sheet. . .' She left the sentence unfinished, tucking away the knowledge that she might have an ally of sorts in Chay's housekeeper.

For a moment his eyes lingered on the opening of his shirt at her throat and it took all her self-possession to restrain herself from clutching it together. After what seemed an eternity he raised his eyes to hers. 'There was nothing wrong with the sheet,' he said.

'You weren't wearing it,' she replied crisply. 'And I think Theresa has been scandalised more than enough for one day.' She thought his lips twitched slightly as he contemplated that fierce lady's likely reaction to the sight of Sophie wrapped in a sheet that refused to stay put. Indignant that he should find amusement in her predicament she snapped, 'You might as well let me have my own clothes, Mr Buchanan, since, as you took such gratification in pointing out, I'm not going anywhere without my films or my camera.' She paused. 'Assuming, of course, that you haven't already done what you threatened and flung them into the sea.' And she held her breath, half expecting him to say that he had.

But he didn't. He didn't mention them at all. 'Theresa has made up the guest-room for you. You'll

find your clothes have been unpacked and put away.'
He stood up. 'We'll have coffee in the living-room,' he
said, taking her arm to help her to her feet.

'What a pity she's gone to so much trouble,' she
said, in an effort to provoke him, to ignore the warm
touch of his fingers at her elbow, 'I'll only have to
repack them all.' He refused to rise. Common sense
told her to leave it. But where Chay Buchanan was
concerned she seemed to have no sense at all, common
or otherwise. 'And my camera bag?' she demanded. 'Is
that all laid out and ready for me as well?' Then she
held her breath, waiting for him to explode. But he
merely glanced down at her.

'No, Sophie. It isn't. But I haven't flung your camera
into the sea. It's quite safe for the time being.' He
opened one of a pair of doors and ushered her into a
room similar in size and shape to his bedroom. Perhaps
it was slightly larger, thirty or forty feet long, but the
evening had closed in and the soft illumination from
the lamp on a table didn't reach that far. 'Sit down.'
He waved her to a chair. 'You'd better make yourself
at home.'

Home! Of all the nerve. . . And she'd sit when she
was good and ready; she had far more important things
on her mind than sitting down. 'What about my films?'
she demanded. He hadn't mentioned them and she
feared the worst.

'Black or white?' he responded aggravatingly, as he
lifted the heavy silver coffee-pot.

'Neither—they were colour transparencies,' she
snapped.

'So they were.' He relented a little as he saw dismay
cloud her eyes. 'They still are. For the moment. Sit
down, Sophie.'

She remained where she was. 'What are you going
to do with them?' she insisted.

He put down the coffee-pot and moved towards her with an air of purpose. Before she realised what he was about to do, could utter a protest, he had scooped her up into his arms and carried her towards a large squashy leather chair and dumped her in it. The moment was brief, over almost before she could register the pleasurable warmth of his bare arm against the back of her knees, the thud of his heartbeat as, for a second or two, her cheek had been pressed against the broad expanse of his chest.

Instinctively she drew her knees to her chin and curled up in a self-protective attitude. She wasn't used to a man being able to light her up with nothing more than a touch, a look. She didn't like the power it gave him. It frightened her. But she said nothing. She'd got the message loud and clear. Do as she was told. Sophie hid her pique under lowered lids as he returned to the coffee-pot.

'Black or white?' He repeated the question as if nothing unusual had happened. Her hands curled into tight, painful fists. Nothing *had* happened. Only in her head.

'White, please,' she murmured, her voice meekly obedient, and received a sharp look for her trouble as he passed her a cup.

Sophie sipped her coffee, trying to disregard the sense of the absurd, the complete unreality of her situation, as she faced him from across the wide expanse of a stone hearth. She was a grown woman, with a career and a growing respect in her profession, behaving just like a good little girl, waiting to be told what he had decided to do with her property. Worse. She was being held a virtual prisoner by the kind of man mothers warned their daughters about. Not that she had needed warning. She had recognised the danger signals the moment those knowing eyes had regarded her from his threshold.

Oh? that inner voice queried, with irritating percipience. So why didn't you run away when you had the chance? So, why *hadn't* she? Heaven knew that he had warned her in no uncertain terms to stay away from him.

He was sitting opposite her, relaxed, totally at ease, his long legs stretched out before him on a worn Persian carpet, balancing a coffee-cup in one hand, watching her from beneath heavy-lidded eyes. She blinked. It had been worth the risk. It was still worth any risk.

'Well?' she demanded, her voice thick with tension. 'Don't keep me in suspense any longer, Mr Buchanan. What are you going to do with the films?'

'That's rather up to you, Miss Sophie Nash,' he said softly.

She regarded him with utter disbelief, but he was apparently waiting for some response. She made a good attempt at a casual shrug. 'Well, that's easy,' she said. 'Just hand them over and I'll be on my way.'

'I'm sure even you can't believe it would be quite that easy.' He regarded her steadily for a moment. 'You have only two choices. And I'm being generous.'

'I'm glad you think so.'

'The first,' he continued, as if she had not spoken, 'is simply to destroy the lot. I don't think anyone would blame me.'

'*I* would blame you. In fact, Mr Buchanan, I should be very unhappy,' she pointed out.

'Your happiness is neither here nor there. Right now the only thing I care about is my privacy.'

'Why?' she demanded.

'Why not?' he returned with infuriating urbanity. 'Or maybe you would enjoy having a long-lens camera pointed at you from some hidden vantage point?

Perhaps when you were in the bath? Or sunbathing topless in the garden? And the results published in the newspaper?'

'I've never sunbathed topless in my life,' she protested, then blushed as one dark brow rose askance at her vehemence. 'Besides, no one would print it,' she continued defiantly. 'I'm not——' She stopped, suddenly realising where this was leading.

'You are not famous?' he suggested. 'Should that matter?'

'Maybe not,' she said, unable to stop herself squirming a little, letting her eyes drop from his penetrating gaze. 'But it does.'

'Yes, it does,' he agreed. 'So I made a conscious decision to stop being famous. I intend to keep it that way.' The question, Why? sprang to her lips once more, but this time she didn't let it beyond them. 'And for goodness' sake call me Chay,' he said. 'Mr Buchanan makes me feel about ninety.'

She recalled the sight of his sleekly muscled body as it had curved into the water. There was nothing remotely old about Chay Buchanan. He was a man at the peak of his power, the peak of his life. So what was he doing here, living alone with a small boy? Had his wife deserted him? Broken his heart? Was that the story Nigel was going to write? She found that she wanted to know, but a direct question was unlikely to produce an answer. 'You might as well be,' she said casually, although her heart was thumping furiously. 'After all, you've retired. Given up on life. . .just for the sake of a little privacy.'

'Who says I've retired?' The cool voice rippled with the warning that she was treading thin ice. She chose to ignore it.

'You haven't written anything in years, you've hidden yourself away in this place. You've simply

stepped off the end of the world and stopped living.'
She challenged him to deny it.

'And you're anxious to remind me of what I'm
missing?' he retaliated smoothly, his eyes glittering.
For a moment she took on the anger, met him head-on
while her pulse-rate accelerated alarmingly. Then she
found herself staring at her battered hands, her breathing too rapid for comfort. This was a man, she discovered, that you challenged at your peril. 'No? Then
shall we stick to the matter in hand?'

She swallowed hard. 'I believe I had two choices?
What was the second?'

He didn't answer, but stood up and fetched her
camera bag from the dim recesses at the far end of the
room. When he dropped it carelessly on the table in
front of her she reached out, wanting to grab it close,
protect it from him. But his strong fingers fastened
about her wrist and stayed the anxious movement.

Then he folded the long length of his body until his
eyes were on a level with hers and, poised on his toes
beside her chair, he held her, dominated her with the
careless arrogance of a man who knew he was invincible. 'As I said, we destroy the films now, Sophie. All
of them.' He ignored her sharp protest and with his
free hand flipped the bag open and took one out. 'It's
quite simple.' The pad of his thumb whitened against
the cassette and Sophie physically jumped as the film
burst free of its confinement and spewed into her lap.
Utterly ruined. She let out a low groan. All that work
for nothing. Unmoved by her dismay, he picked up
another cassette. 'That was the one I took from your
pocket,' he reassured her. 'This one might be anything.' His hand tightened over the spool of film.

'No!' Her hand flew to rescue her precious film, but
his fist tightened about it.

'Sure?' he demanded.

She swallowed. 'You've destroyed the film I took of you. There's no need to ruin the rest.'

He regarded her with something like pity. 'I have destroyed *one* of the films you took of me.'

'I only took one,' she said, but perhaps just a little too quickly.

'Sophie, Sophie,' he said, remonstrating softly. 'I can understand your eagerness to impress me with your probity. Doubtless a considerable amount of money rides on your being able to get away with your pictures. But I'm afraid that your record-keeping is too thorough.' He tossed the film back in the bag and, releasing her wrist, he produced a small hard-bound notebook from its interior. 'There are fifty-seven films listed in this little red book of yours. You've had a busy week.' He turned the pages, scanning her entries. 'Hotels, villas, a holiday village,' he said, looking up. 'I'm glad you've found time for a little culture too. Ancient sites, museums, Mosta Dom,' he listed as he flicked through the pages. 'Then there was the obligatory trip to Gozo to see the lace-makers and Calypso's cave. And we mustn't forget the perennial favourites. The Blue Grotto, a variety of picturesque harbours, the *dghajsa*-man and the pleasures of the *karrozzin* ride. Everything, in fact, that the tourist would want to see in Malta. All annotated with precision.'

'Of course,' she agreed. 'I always make notes as I take photographs. So?'

'So?' he echoed mockingly. 'There are *fifty-nine* films in your bag, Sophie. Plus the one I took from your shirt-pocket. There appear to be not one, but two cuckoos in the nest.'

'Oh!' The sound rushed from her in a little sigh.

Satisfied that he had her full attention, he continued. 'Of course, it may be that you simply forgot to record them?' He waited for her to confirm that this was the case. But she didn't bother. She knew he wouldn't believe her.

'No. I didn't forget.'

'No. You simply didn't have time to record the last three films, did you, Sophie?' He flung the notebook on the table and stood up. 'You were too busy trying to kill yourself in your hurry to get away with your ill-gotten gains.'

She ignored this, unwilling to think about what had happened. 'Your first offer of choice was destruction. What is the second?'

He stared down at the bag of films. 'We could have them processed.'

'Processed?' she repeated with astonishment. But a little spark of hope kindled in her breast. 'And you would keep the photographs I took of you? That's very generous of you, Mr. . .Chay.' And she managed what she hoped was a truly grateful smile.

'Yes,' he agreed, his own smile mocking her. 'In the circumstances, I think it is.'

'Of course,' she said slowly, 'you may not realise that they will have to go to Kodak in Paris. It will take a few days.'

'To Paris?' he asked with a slight frown. 'Why?'

Because Kodak would despatch the processed transparencies to their London office to await her collection, as they always did, no matter where in the world they were sent from. She would still have two rolls of film. It took iron control to hide her triumph. Any sense of guilt about her long-distance photography had rapidly dissipated in the heat of his aggression. 'Because it's professional film. For professional reproduction,' she said seriously. 'I'm afraid the quality control at some backstreet chemist shop in Sliema won't quite do.'

He smiled back. At least, his mouth smiled. His eyes

were not joining in. 'You, of course, will stay here until they return.'

Her eyes widened. She hadn't expected that. But then she shrugged, as if it didn't matter. Once they were out of his hands she would surely find some means of escape, but it wouldn't do to concede too quickly. 'Surely. . .there's no need. I'll give you my address,' she offered, diplomatically choosing to overlook the fact that, since he had all her belongings, he certainly already knew her address. 'You can just send on anything that doesn't include you.'

His eyes narrowed. 'You're very trusting.'

'Shouldn't I be? You wouldn't keep them, would you?' she asked.

'You'll never know, Sophie, because you are going to stay here, under close supervision, until they return.'

'As your prisoner?' she demanded.

His eyes darkened. 'I could still be tempted simply to trash the lot right now.' His hand hovered over the bag.

'No.' She leapt to her feet, reaching out a protective hand to grasp his wrist before he could carry out his threat. 'You. . . You'd better show me to your dungeon.'

His mouth straightened in a smile. Not a very big smile. Just horribly self-satisfied. 'Forget about the dungeon, Sophie. I have something far more entertaining in mind.'

She snatched her hand away from his wrist as if burned, eyes wide as her thoughts immediately flew to his huge bed on the floor above. Surely he didn't mean. . .? 'Can't sing, can't dance. . .' she almost croaked.

'No?' he asked, as if he didn't quite believe her. 'But then I'm not looking for a cabaret act. How are you in the kitchen, Sophie?'

'The kitchen?' she repeated, as if the word was strange to her. Not the bedroom?

'Yes,' he confirmed, 'the kitchen. Theresa has asked for a few days' holiday. I think it would be a happy solution all round if you were to take her place for a week. A small repayment for all the bother you have caused.'

'You mean, stay here alone with you?' she asked, horrified at the prospect.

He seemed to find her response amusing. 'Not quite alone. There's Tom.'

'Tom? I don't think he would make a very satisfactory chaperon.'

'You want a chaperon? A modern young woman who would risk her life to get a scoop? Come along, Miss Nash, surely you're not afraid?' His eyes offered her a dare. 'I've stepped off the world, remember? Retired from life. What kind of a threat can I possibly pose?'

She didn't want to consider the threat he represented, but was prepared to concede for the first time in her life that mothers knew a thing or two. 'Just how old are you?' she asked. 'As a matter of interest.'

'As a matter of interest?' He regarded her thoughtfully. 'Thirty. . .something.'

Four? Five? No more. 'That old?' she asked, her heart beating ridiculously fast. She made a play of looking around, then quite deliberately raised a pair of grave grey eyes to meet the ocean depths of his. 'So? Where do you keep your walking-frame?'

'You, Sophie Nash,' he said, grasping her shoulders with a fierceness which warned her that resistance was pointless, 'are a very foolish, very impertinent young woman. And quite definitely in need of a lesson in respect when speaking to your elders. I ought to put you over my knee and spank you, right now!'

'Do you think you could manage it?' she persisted in defiance.

'You choose to live dangerously, Miss Nash,' he ground out. 'But you've got enough bruises for one day.' He jerked her towards him. 'Consider this a down payment.'

CHAPTER FOUR

SOPHIE'S instinctive protest played straight into his hands, but by the time she realised that it was too late to clamp her mouth shut. He was quite unmoved by her attempts to free herself, carelessly releasing one shoulder before capturing her waist to pull her close against the warmth of his body, force her to acknowledge his dominance.

She immediately stopped struggling. It didn't need the urgent flicker of response from her own body to warn her that, clamped against his hard thighs, struggling would be foolhardy in the extreme. Instead she remained perfectly still. Determinedly unresponsive. Then an exquisite shiver ran through her body as it refused to co-operate with her brain. No one could remain unresponsive to such a man.

His mouth was a revelation. She had known it would be. Anger had not disguised the well-cut sensuality of a full lower lip that, without haste, was now demolishing the few shreds of self-possession she had managed to cling to.

He had said she should be taught a lesson and she had expected a hard, bruising kiss. Easy to resist. He knew that as well as she did. Chay Buchanan was too subtle for such caveman tactics. Instead the delicate, teasing caresses of his mouth, the heady pressure of his body against hers, were the kindling that lit a fire in her veins; his lips and tongue were the fan to her desire, until it was she who was kissing him, tempting him, demanding more. And it was Chay Buchanan who broke away, his eyes unreadable in the lamplight.

'Now, Miss Nash,' he demanded, 'would you care to repeat that remark about a walking-frame?'

She gasped, pulled away from him. While she had been lost to the world, cloud-waltzing on desire, he had been intent upon simply making a point, humiliating her. Some lesson! One that she would be slow to forget. She would hang on to her temper, stow her pride in the attic and remember the old adage—don't get mad, get even. Somehow, some way, she would make him pay for that.

And, with that silent promise of retribution, she lifted her chin, pinned a smile to her mouth and turned to face him, only the little black flecks that darkened her irises a betrayal of her true state of mind for those lucky enough to interpret the signals and run for cover.

'I withdraw it unreservedly, Mr Buchanan. Despite being thirty——' and she shrugged slightly '—something, you are clearly still a little way short of your dotage. Now, shall we pack up the film? Then perhaps you would be kind enough to point me in the direction of the servants' quarters?' He regarded her steadily, almost, she thought, with a touch of grudging appreciation for her acting ability. What had he expected? Hysterics? It was as well he couldn't see behind her cool façade to the seething mass of emotions that were churning around her brain and sending confused signals sparking through her body. Hysterics were nothing to what she felt like throwing.

'I'll see to the films in the morning,' he assured her. 'I think perhaps you've had enough for your first time out of bed.'

More than enough. More than enough of Chay Buchanan to last a lifetime. 'I've been in bed all day,' she reminded him. 'I'm not tired.' There was something important that she had to do. Casually, she took a roll of tiny sticky labels from her bag and began to fasten one to each of the films with fingers that trembled just a little.

'What are you doing?'

She looked up with what she hoped was nonchalance. 'Just indentifying the films with my account number.' She forced her lips to offer a smile. A very little smile. 'I can hardly expect you to pay for the processing.'

His eyes narrowed slightly as he stared at the bag. 'Leave it now. If you're not tired you might as well come out on to the terrace and have some fresh air.'

She hesitated for just a second before dropping the film back in the bag. If she protested, he would become suspicious. 'That would be. . .lovely.'

He opened the tall French windows and warm, moist air, laden with the scent of the sea, rushed to meet them. She took a deep breath and devoured the panorama spread before her. The little island of Comino was almost close enough to touch, and beyond that the light-strewn shape of Gozo, where the enchantress Calypso imprisoned Odysseus for seven long years, glittered in the dark sweep of the sea. 'Lord, but this is a beautiful spot,' she murmured.

'I thought you disapproved.'

'Disapproved? Why should I do that?' She glanced at him. 'This is a retreat. A place to go when you want to get away from everything.' She turned back to the sea. 'Not a place to live, though, unless you're a lotus-eater.'

'And is that what you think I am?'

No, she didn't think that. She didn't think that Chay Buchanan was idle, or even particularly happy in his island paradise. But she didn't say so. 'I can see the temptation,' she said, with apparent sympathy. 'The danger is that, like poor old Odysseus, you won't be able to escape. It's too easy just to stay put.' She turned to him. 'Why did you stop writing, Chay? What are you hiding from?'

His eyes flashed a warning. 'Surely your commissioning editor gave you the smallest hint?'

Commissioning editor? She wanted to laugh at the idea. Or cry. Nigel was nothing more than a hack freelance journalist. But she wasn't about to tell Chay that. 'Why don't you give me your side of the story?' she suggested.

'Nice try, Sophie, but, despite the fact that for the moment I choose not to be published, I write every day of my life, and if I were hiding I promise you would never have found me. So you'll just have to make it up as you go along. That's the usual method, so it shouldn't be difficult.'

'I wouldn't know; I don't make up anything. I just take the pictures.' Damn! That had come out all wrong. As if she spent her life hiding in corners and taking photographs of reluctant celebrities. 'I just take pictures,' she corrected herself.

His cynical smile suggested that he was not convinced. 'Would you like a drink? A small brandy, perhaps?'

'Thank you,' she said quickly, glad of any change of subject.

'Sit over there and I'll fetch it.'

He pointed her in the direction of the kind of swinging garden seat that had featured heavily in American romantic comedy movies in the late fifties and early sixties. The sort where a tremulous virgin, trying to prove how sophisticated she was, came perilously close to being seduced by a wicked older man, usually with the assistance of a large glass of brandy, only to be rescued by the hero in the nick of time.

Chay bent over her and offered a beautiful crystal goblet in which a small amount of amber liquid reposed. She stared at it for a moment, then glanced up at him, trying to read his expression in the dim light. Who would rescue her, she wondered, if Chay Buchanan decided to take advantage of the weakness she had already betrayed?

She took the glass, jumping nervously as her fingers brushed his, and he stretched himself alongside her, his arm along her shoulders, and began to rock the chair, very slowly. 'Who are you working for, Sophie?'

'What?' His question had been so far from her own disturbing train of thought that she jumped.

'It was a perfectly simple question.'

'Yes, of course it was.' She took a ragged breath. 'Island Holidays. I did the Canaries for them during the winter. Apparently they were pleased enough with the result to give me Sicily and Malta this year.'

'That's very interesting. Now perhaps you would be kind enough to answer my question.'

'But——'

'Sophie!' he warned.

'I'm not employed by anyone,' she said, abruptly conceding defeat.

'You were simply doing a little freelancing on your own account?'

What could she say? She glanced at him. Could he possibly understand why she had been driven to such desperate measures.? She shivered a little. Of course not. What could a man like him know of such things? But if she lied, said she was doing it for herself, for what she could get, it would confirm his view that she was someone who robbed people of their privacy for money. She discovered that she didn't want him to think that badly of her.

'A friend asked me to try and get a picture of you while I was in Malta. I told you, he's writing an article about you. It was simply a. . .favour. I won't be paid.'

'And how far would you have gone,' he drawled, 'for a favour?'

'How far?'

His fingers trailed beneath the collar of her shirt and began to stroke the nape of her neck. She tensed and tried to move, to escape, but he was too quick, capturing her throat with his free hand, cupping it in his palm, tilting her head back until she was staring up into his eyes. 'All the way?' His thumb brushed lightly across her lips.

'No!' She pushed him away.

He laughed softly but made no attempt to hold her. 'Do you really expect me to believe that?'

Something snapped. 'I don't care whether you believe it or not.' She put the glass on a small table and tried to stand up, but the treacherous swing of the chair caught her off-balance and she was thrown back against him. He caught her round the waist, pulling her down on to his lap, his eyes dark as he searched her face.

'He must be a very special friend, if you're prepared to risk so much—even your life—to please him.'

'I didn't. . .' she protested, then, catching his tormenting eye, she lifted her shoulders in a tiny shrug. 'I didn't mean to.' He raised a disconcerting brow and she blushed furiously as she realised that her denial fitted both scenarios. But maybe she should emphasise her friendship with Nigel. Although heaven knew that nothing could have been further from the truth, it might be wise to suggest that there was someone out there to worry about her. 'Yes, if you must know. Nigel is very special. Now, will you let me go?' She tried to pull free.

'Your lover?' he persisted.

'How dare you?'

His grip at her waist tightened warningly. 'The

prisoner must expect a certain amount of interrogation. Tell me about him,' he insisted.

But she didn't want to talk about Nigel. She thrust her hands towards him. 'Here. If you want my secrets, you'll have to use thumb-screws. I'm sure you must have a pair tucked away in your dungeon.'

If she had hoped to make him angry, she failed. He took one of her hands in his, turned it over. 'I think not. Your hands have suffered quite enough.' He lifted it to his lips and kissed the pad of her thumb. The warmth of his mouth sent a dangerous charge of longing surging crazily through her body, and she snatched her hand away as if stung. He grinned, quite suddenly, taking her quite by surprise. 'And I don't really think I'd need to employ torture if I wanted to learn your secrets, Sophie. Do you?'

'I don't know what you mean,' she protested, making a further unsuccessful effort to pull free of his grasp, the infuriating swing of the chair simply rocking her back against his chest.

'Of course you do, Sophie,' he murmured. 'Or you wouldn't be quite so anxious to escape.'

'Can't you stop this thing?' she demanded.

'Whenever I want. But I'm perfectly happy for the moment.' He shifted slightly, so that her head some-how became cradled in the hollow of his shoulder and there was nothing to struggle against. Instead she held herself as rigid as she could.

But the gentle rocking of the seat, the warmth of the brandy inside her, the steady thud of his heartbeat beneath her cheek was a bewitching combination. She could well understand any *ingénue* succumbing without a struggle to such an assault on her senses. The wonder of it was that she should be grateful to be rescued by some priggish young man.

She started. What on earth was she thinking? What was she doing, lying back in the arms of the enemy?

She cleared her throat. 'I seem to be falling asleep. Perhaps I'd better go to bed after all.' She tried to move, but his arm pinioned her against his chest.

'Just one thing before you go, Sophie.'

'Yes?' she queried, suspicious of the velvet-smooth drawl to his voice.

'Tell me what happened to the films you took in Sicily.'

She opened her eyes wide and stared at him. 'Sicily?' she repeated as her mind clicked into overdrive, playing for time in which to think.

'You were commissioned to take photographs in Sicily for Island Holidays. Didn't you say so?'

'Did I?' she asked. Would he believe her if she said she was on her way there next? A small ray of hope offered the possibility of escape. If she could convince him that she was expected there tomorrow. . .that if she didn't arrive people would worry and raise the alarm, search for her. . . Then she met a pair of hard eyes, gleaming in the darkness, and hope died. Of course not. He had her airline ticket. He knew perfectly well that she had already been there.

'Well?'

'I sent them to Paris before I left Palermo.'

'I see. And what happens to them after that?' She had the uncomfortable feeling that he knew very well what happened to them. That all the time he had been playing with her.

'They're sent back, of course.'

'Of course,' he agreed. 'But not to Sicily.'

She gave a small laugh. 'Well, no.'

'Well, no,' he repeated, and offered a nasty little parody of her laugh. But he wasn't amused. And when he spoke again his voice had lost its velvet caress. It struck at her like flint against steel. 'They get returned in accordance with your standing instructions, don't they? Straight back to base.' He stood up abruptly and dumped her on her feet. 'Your little labels have been bothering me, Sophie. But now I see the point. Very clever. Too clever by half. I think I'd better take you up to your room right now, before I change my mind about the dungeon.'

'Frankly, Mr Buchanan,' she declared furiously, 'I'd prefer the dungeon. At least then we could forget this pretence of civilised behaviour!'

'You don't know what the word means,' he growled. 'In the circumstances I've behaved with wholly admirable restraint!'

'Admirable restraint?' she gasped. 'Words fail me.'

'Now that would make a pleasant change,' he said. 'But I don't think I'll hold my breath.'

'You are truly the rudest, most infuriating and downright obnoxious man it has ever been my misfortune to meet,' she declared fervently, close to tears but determined that he shouldn't see.

'Am I? Well, it's a misfortune you brought entirely upon yourself. And I think you've pushed your luck quite far enough for one day.'

'Oh? Have I, indeed? And what about you? Aren't you just a little bit afraid that I'll tell everyone exactly what you've done, when you do eventually let me go?' She brushed aside his attempt to interrupt. 'And I don't mean the police,' she rushed on, 'I'm talking about the newspapers.'

'You don't come out of the encounter exactly covered with roses,' he retaliated harshly.

'No?' She scowled at him. 'Well, if I were the sort of person you seem to think I am, Chay Buchanan, would I actually *care*?' She made a gesture with her hands, indicating a banner. '"Bestselling author held me cap-

tive".' She paused briefly, then repeated the gesture.
'"I was Chay Buchanan's slave". Or, what about——'
She raised her hands once more, but this time he
caught her wrists in a vice-like grip.

'Enough!'

'You'd be famous enough then,' she advised him
recklessly. 'Your precious privacy wouldn't stand a
chance. . .'

Her voice trailed away as angry eyes compelled her
to silence. 'That was a mistake, Sophie,' he said, his
voice like chips of ice in her veins. 'A very big mistake.
I'm afraid you're going to have to stay here for rather
longer than I had anticipated.'

'What do you mean longer. . .? You can't——'

'Can't I? Who's to stop me?' She swallowed nervously as his ransacking glance pinned her helpless to
the spot and, releasing her wrists, he grasped a handful
of her long fair hair to twist about his fist. 'I could keep
you prisoner at the top of my tower for so long that,
like Rapunzel, you'd have to let down your long hair
and hope that some passing sailor would be tempted to
climb it and set you free.'

Her mouth dried. 'You're crazy!'

'Am I?' He tightened his grip and began to lead her,
using her hair as a halter, towards the tower, and she
had little choice other than to follow him like an
obedient spaniel as he tugged sharply at her scalp.

'What are you going to do with me?' she demanded,
still defiant despite the quiver of anxiety which told her
that she had, indeed, gone too far. Much too far.

His glance raked her. 'We made a deal, Sophie
Nash, but you never intended to keep your end of the
bargain.' He shook her. 'Did you?' She bit her lip
rather than cry out as pain shot through her scalp,
filling her eyes with tears, but something must have
shown on her face because he released her hair,

transferring his grip to her arm before she even registered the possibility of escape. 'Did you?' he demanded.

She glared at him, her eyes huge, overbright, as she angrily refused to let the tears fall. 'Why should I? You've no right to keep me here. You've no right to destroy my work. You would have done the same in my shoes!'

'Oh, no, I wouldn't. I would never have taken the damn things in the first place,' he said savagely.

That was too much. She wrenched herself free of his grasp, flinging her fists against her hips as she launched her own attack. 'Oh, lordy!' she declared. 'You are *far* too shy, Mr Buchanan. The world must learn that hidden away in this remote corner of Malta lives one of the last of that endangered species, the *noble* male.' She raised her eyes skyward in ironic appeal. 'Heaven help me if I fall for that one.'

'Perhaps you should improve the quality of the men you. . .associate with.'

'Associate with?' she repeated in disbelief. 'Well, there's a fine, high-sounding euphemism for what you really mean.' And finally she was unable to prevent eyes brim-full of tears from overflowing, but she was too angry to care any more. She dashed her sleeve against her cheek. 'Just who do you think you are, Chay Buchanan? You lounge around here, having made enough money to retire at the advanced age of thirty——' she almost exploded '—something——'

'If you believe that, Sophie Nash, you must be mad,' he retaliated.

She was too far gone in rage to register this outburst, her pulse racketing like an express train, huge eyes sparkling darkly. 'What would you know about having to earn a living?' she charged on. 'The day-after-day grind of it? It's not all spent taking pictures in holiday islands, you know! My next booking is in Liverpool for a mail-order catalogue. Vacuum cleaners and computer games and knickers——'

She never had a chance to finish. His mouth cut off the words as it swooped to obliterate them with a kiss that owed nothing to finesse. This was no gentle caress to disarm or please her. It was the fierce stamp of authority that demanded she obey. Submit to his will. Useless to struggle, useless to fight, she knew, even as her fists pummelled at his shoulders.

Too late she sensed the subtle change, the easing of the hard grip of his hands at her waist until his long fingers were gently cradling her ribcage, the heel of his hand nudging the soft swell of her breast. By the time she realised that his mouth was no longer punishing her, was caressing her with a fierce passion that was sending her heart spiralling to the stars, it no longer mattered. Her fists had ceased their battery, had become long, slender fingers that slid up to his shoulders and clasped firmly about his neck, and her lips had parted in welcome. It was a long time before he finally raised his head to stare down at her.

'Why did you do that?' she finally whispered.

For a moment he didn't say anything. He just continued to stare at her. Then, abruptly, he turned away, ran his fingers through his dark hair, pushing it back from his forehead. 'You were getting hysterical,' he said sharply. 'I had to shut you up somehow. It was a choice between slapping you or kissing you.'

'Oh!' She took an instinctive step back, her hand flying to her mouth, as if to wipe away the taste of him. He might as well have slapped her. His words had had much the same effect. An abrupt reminder that she was in danger of making an utter fool of herself. 'Then I suppose I should be grateful.'

'Grateful?'

She lifted her shoulders slightly. 'That you chose the slightly less violent alternative. I already have enough aches and pains. Although. . .' She touched her finger to her bruised and swollen lip.

His eyes followed the gesture. 'Did I hurt you?'

'I'll recover,' she said woodenly. 'It was no worse than a slap.'

'I doubt you'd have enjoyed a slap quite so thoroughly,' he retaliated sharply.

She bit back the angry retort that flew to her tongue. He spoke no more than the truth, after all. It was time to put an end to this charade. Before she said, or did, something so unbelievably rash that she might never recover from the consequences.

The almost electric effect that Chay Buchanan had triggered from the moment she had first set eyes upon him was making her say and do things light-years away from the cool self-possession she so prided herself on. Things so wildly out of character that people she had known all her life would scarcely recognise her. Chay had seen it, had thought she was brazenly flirting to get what she wanted from him. He couldn't know that she didn't know how to flirt, that this reaction was as unwelcome to her as it was to him. But she was certain now that she had to get away before one of them exploded, because, whichever one of them it was, she was the one who would be hurt by the resulting fall-out.

If he insisted on destroying her films she could do nothing to stop him. She would find a cheap hotel, work at top speed; she knew the shots she wanted now, and that would save a considerable amount of time. There would be precious little left from her fee, but at least she would retain her reputation as a reliable photographer. And her self-control.

There were worse things in life than losing a week's

work. Far worse. She pulled herself up to the full
extent of her five feet six inches. 'Do what you want
with my films, Mr Buchanan,' she said. 'I want to leave
here right now. I. . .I have a lot of work to catch up
on.'

A small muscle was working angrily at the corner of
his mouth. 'You're not going anywhere, Miss Nash. I
thought I had made that quite plain.'

She made a move towards him. 'Don't you understand? You can do what you like with the wretched
films. I just want to leave. Now!' she added, with some
force.

'I warned you what would happen if I caught you
trespassing,' he reminded her, his face hard as the cliff-
face.

And the fact that he was in deadly earnest finally
penetrated. 'But. . .why?'

'The reason is none of your business. But we have
gone far beyond the minor problem of a few photographs. Until certain. . .negotiations have been final-
ised, I'm afraid I can't risk your nasty little headlines.'

'But I wouldn't——'

'You were very convincing, Sophie.'

'But. . .I didn't meant it. Truly.' She had been
angry, that was all. 'I have to get home. It's——'

'What?' His lips twisted into a savage little smile. 'A
matter of life and death?' His voice had an unpleasant
little sneer to it that made her hackles rise, but she
fought back the desire to slap him. It was too important
that she convince him. 'Well?' he demanded. 'Is that
what you were going to say?'

She gave an awkward little shrug. 'Perhaps I was,'
she admitted, her eyes pleading with him. 'But it is. . .
very important.'

'You should have thought of that before you started
your sordid little job.'

She took a deep breath. 'Please let me go, Chay.' She whispered the plea, her eyes huge.

'Don't do that!' He was staring at her blankly, and for a moment she thought she was getting through to him. Then he lifted his hand to her heated cheek, to graze it with the hard edge of his thumb. 'Or I'll have to kiss you again.' His heavy-lidded eyes regarded her dispassionately. 'Until you beg me to let you stay.'

She stumbled back, but his hand was there, at her waist, to steady, hold her. 'You've got a great notion of your physical attraction,' she declared roundly, refusing to acknowledge the heat licking through her veins at the merest touch of his hand. Did that husky voice really belong to her?

'Have I?' Her eyes followed his apparent fascination with the front of her shirt, and she blushed deeply as she realised that the tips of her betraying breasts were thrusting hard against the fine cloth. His fingers traced a circle around the dark areola faintly visible against the whiteness, his thumb brushing the sensitive tip, and, apparently satisfied with her shuddering response, he raised his eyes to meet hers. 'Are you confident enough of your willpower to put it to the test?'

No! Her head screamed the word. Her mouth seemed to find it a great deal more difficult. Just as her body refused her bidding to pull away from the hand tucked against the small of her back.

What on earth was happening to her? Wild sensations were lashing at her body. Undreamed of desires that made her breasts feel tight and swollen, that heated her skin and pulsed in an almost unbearable ache deep in her loins. None of the sensations was precisely new. She was twenty-three, too old never to have felt the throb of arousal, even if she had always rejected it, afraid that because she and Jennie were twins—mirror-images of one another—it was inevitable that she must make the same mistakes.

It had been like waiting for the other shoe to drop, her mother had once told her, in a moment of weakness, on one of the few occasions she had managed to talk about it.

But she instinctively knew that what she was feeling now was different, more intense, as if the world had been nothing but a monochrome blur and had suddenly been transformed into brilliant, rainbow-bright focus.

'I. . .er. . .' She cleared her throat. 'I think I. . . perhaps. . .I. . .' There was no point in lying. He already knew.

'I think you'd better go to bed right now.'

She almost slumped against him, weak with relief that he hadn't actually put her to the test. Then, panicking that he would misread the signals her body was flashing out like a firebug in heat, she tried to yank free of his drugging touch. 'No! That is. . . I didn't mean. . .'

'Didn't you, Sophie?' He shrugged slightly. 'Shame your body wasn't co-operating.' But before she could protest he had stepped back. 'I'll show you to your room.' He paused briefly as they passed the table, and gathered up her camera bag. 'And, in case you're wondering, this will be locked away with the rest of your belongings, where you can't get at it. So don't get any bright ideas about running off in the middle of the night.'

A yawn caught her unawares, as if to demonstrate that she wasn't capable of running anywhere. She was suddenly quite exhausted, and it took all her strength simply not to lean against him. 'I couldn't run on the spot,' she murmured.

'You'll forgive my natural scepticism. It's stood me in good stead so far.'

His words were like a douche of cold water, driving all thought of sleep from her head. 'You are unbearable!' she exclaimed.

'You'll find that "unbearable" is one of my more endearing characteristics.' His fierce glance choked off the rejoinder that sprang to her lips. 'Upstairs, Sophie. Now.'

The sun woke her, dragging her reluctantly from sleep. But the brightness was not to be resisted, and Sophie opened gritty lids to acknowledge the day. The light was streaming in clear and bright through the open window and she stretched, tentatively trying out her aching limbs. She was stiff, it was true, but only her shoulder still gave her any real pain, and that was something she could live with. It was certainly no more unbearable than Chay Buchanan.

She sat up, eased her feet to the cool polished boards and went across to the window. Her room was on the opposite side of the tower from Chay's bedroom and the terrace, overlooking a flat stretch of open ground before the land began to rise beyond the road in the rocky terraces of small farms.

The week before she had cursed the squall of spring rain that had delayed her work. But now tiny irises, no bigger than her thumb, bee orchids and other small flowers were spreading a thick carpet of bloom across the baked earth, and a hedge of mimosa was decked out in fluffy yellow blooms.

Reluctantly she turned from the window. No time for that. The sooner she was ready, the sooner she could leave, and get on with the business of explaining to puzzled hoteliers why she had to repeat her work.

She went into the bathroom that adjoined her bedroom and stood for a few moments until the needle-sharp spray of the shower had her gasping. Then she washed her hair, threatening herself for the hundredth time that she would have the tiresome mop cut as she combed it out and dried it with the battery-operated drier that went everywhere with her. Her hair kinked at the slightest hint of humidity, despite every atttempt to tame it. It was only the fear that if she had it cut it would make her look like a poodle that had so far kept the scissors at bay. At least long she could clamp it down with hairpins, if all else failed.

Theresa had unpacked her clothes and laid out her cosmetics on the dressing-table, as if Sophie were a lady. But she had no time to waste on make-up. She quickly tugged on a fresh chambray shirt and long tailored navy shorts that echoed the pair she had 'borrowed' from Chay the night before.

She pushed her feet into a pair of sandals and buckled on the watch that had appeared beside her bed since she fell into an almost immediate and dreamless sleep the night before. Had he put it there while she slept? She shrugged away the thought. It hardly mattered. But, as she pulled the strap tight, her fingers shook a little at the thought of him standing over her defenceless sleeping body.

Stop it, she warned herself. He might have kissed her, but it wasn't because he desired her. He'd made that more than plain. She glanced in the mirror and after a moment fastened one more button of her shirt, leaving only the top button open. She didn't want a repetition of his accusation that she was batting eyelashes or anything else at him. It was too important that she convince him to let her go. He *had* to let her go. She opened the wardrobe door, took an armful of clothes and flung them on to the bed ready to pack. But there was no suitcase.

She took a deep breath, opened the bedroom door and marched downstairs, determined to thrash it out with him. But Chay wasn't there, only Theresa, greeting her as an old friend, drawing her excitedly into the kitchen and sitting her down at the table. It was difficult to follow what the woman was saying—she switched from Maltese to English and back again without apparently noticing. But, as she produced coffee, melting scrambled eggs and bacon, it gradually became clear that she was expressing her delight that Miss Sophie was going to look after Tom while she was away.

Sophie opened her mouth to protest that this was just not possible. But Theresa, beaming, removed her apron and donned an impressive black hat. '*Grazzi*, Miss Sophie, *grazzi, hafna*,' she repeated, taking her hand in both of hers and shaking it vigorously, departing once more into her own language.

'Theresa,' she interrupted urgently.

'*Iva*?'

'Where is Mr Buchanan?'

'He's out. At his marina.' Marina? At a time like this, he had decided to go boating? Sophie was stunned by the sheer nerve of the man, but it didn't matter where he was. She had a chance to escape. But Theresa hadn't finished. 'Tom. . .he is in the garden.'

She pulled Sophie to the door. Tom looked up from the small enclosed garden below the terrace, that was sheltered from the cool April breeze blowing in from the Mediterranean. He was playing with a large yellow toy crane, shifting a pile of sand to an equally handsome dumper-truck. The child was an unlikely gaoler, Sophie thought. But just as effective as chains.

'Hello, Tom.'

'Hello,' he said, suddenly shy.

'I go now,' Theresa declared, and turned to leave.

'No, wait!' The woman paused, eyebrows slightly raised at the touch of panic in her voice. 'When will Mr Buchanan be back?' Sophie continued, more carefully.

Theresa shrugged. 'Later.'

Later. That was just great. But she might usefully take advantage of his absence to regain control of her possessions so that she could make a run for it when he did get back. 'Do you know what he has done with my camera? My car keys?'

'No worry.' The woman patted Sophie's hand. 'Safe.' She indicated the rapidly cooling breakfast. 'Eat!'

'And my suitcase?' she persisted. At least she could pack in readiness for his return.

'Upstairs.' Theresa pointed at the ceiling.

Sophie sank into the chair. It wasn't much help, but it was a start. 'Thank you, Theresa,' she said, temporarily resigned to her fate. At least until the return of Mr Chay Buchanan. 'Have a good holiday.'

CHAPTER FIVE

SOPHIE stared at her breakfast, furious and yet oddly touched that Chay had trusted her sufficiently to leave Tom in her care. She glanced at the dark-haired boy visible through the open door. How could he have been so sure she wouldn't just walk out and leave him? After all, if she was everything he believed. . .

Idiot! Who did she think she was kidding? Of course she was going to stay. He had her camera locked away as assurance for her good behaviour. And her passport. Even her suitcase. Sophie Nash wasn't going anywhere until Chay Buchanan was good and ready.

She glared at her breakfast. She would go on hunger strike. He would have to let her go then. She stood up and seized the plate, determined to smash it and its contents against the nearest wall. One thing stopped her. The absolute certainty that he would derive great pleasure from making her clear up the mess. She sank back into her chair. Besides, she was hungry.

She washed her dish and placed it on the rack and glanced around. If she was going to cook the child lunch, she'd better know what was available.

She swung open the huge fridge door, checking over the contents. Then she stopped. What on earth was she doing? She would be getting out the vacuum cleaner next, to run over the living-room carpet. Coming to heel like a well-trained dog. She slammed the fridge door shut and turned to find herself being regarded solemnly by a pair of almost black eyes. Not that mysterious ocean-green like his father's.

77

'Is it time for lunch, Miss Nash?' Tom asked tentatively.

'Lunch?' She glanced at her watch. Half-past ten. Ten! Could she really have slept that late? She looked at her watch again. Apparently she could. Tom was watching her anxiously and she smiled reassuringly, saving her anger for his father, and crouched down so that she was on his level. 'Not yet, Tom. Perhaps elevenses. What would you like?' she asked.

'Honey?' he suggested hopefully.

'Bread and honey?' He nodded. 'Milk?'

'Yes, please,' he said, and wriggled on to a kitchen chair. 'Miss Nash?'

'Why don't you call me Sophie?' she suggested, reaching for a crusty loaf of homemade bread. Homemade? If Mr Chay Buchanan expected her to pound dough on his behalf he had another think coming. She had never made bread in her life.

Tom looked doubtful. 'Papa said I was to call you Miss Nash.'

'Did he? What else did he say?'

'I must be polite and. . .and not make you cross, or you won't stay and look after me while Theresa's away.'

Well, clever old Papa. What a pity he didn't take his own advice. 'I'd like you to call me Sophie, Tom. Then we can be friends.'

He immediately brightened. 'OK. Sophie. Will you swim with me this afternoon?'

She looked at the boy's hopeful face, but wouldn't make a promise she might not be able to keep. 'I might not be here,' she said.

'Papa said you were staying until Theresa comes back.'

'Did he?' Well, Papa could think again. 'You're a very good swimmer,' she said.

'How do you know that?'

She handed the boy a thick slice of bread spread with honey. 'I saw you yesterday——' And then she stopped. She didn't want to think about the cliff. 'What would you like for lunch, Tom?' she asked quickly, to divert his thoughts. To divert her own thoughts.

'Honey?' he sugested.

'I don't think so.' They settled on pizza, then Tom took her outside to show her the garden.

Dr Manduca found them there, sitting in the fragrant shade of a carob tree thick with pink blossom. 'You look better today, Miss Nash. No, please don't get up.'

'I feel fine,' she replied.

'Good. I saw Chay in Valletta this morning. He said you were brighter. He's left you babysitting, I understand?'

'I'm not a baby,' Tom said. 'I'm nearly six.'

The doctor laughed. '*Very* nearly six,' he agreed. 'On Sunday, in fact.'

'How do you know?'

'Because I was there when you were born. Are you having a party?' The boy shrugged and the doctor's eyes softened. 'I'll have to remind your Papa. My children will be very disappointed if you don't.'

Tom turned to Sophie. 'Would you come to my party, Sophie?'

'I. . .don't know if I'll be here, Tom.'

'But Theresa's going to be away for a whole week,' he replied with a small frown.

'Run along and play with your truck, Tom,' the doctor said, unexpectedly coming to her rescue. 'I just want to look at Miss Nash.'

'I'm fine, really,' Sophie protested.

'Shall I be the judge of that?' But when he had checked her over he agreed. 'Just as well, since you're looking after Tom.' He smiled as he closed his bag.

'It's good of you to offer to cover for Theresa. She rarely gets a break. Not that she complains. Bring him over to play with my brood one day,' he suggested. 'I'll get Gian to arrange something.' He stood up. 'Have a good holiday. And no more climbing, eh?'

She offered what sounded horribly like a hollow echo to his cheerful laughter. 'No,' she promised. 'I plan to steer well clear of the cliff from now on.' She walked with him to the door, shook his hand and watched as his car pulled away. She must be mad, she thought. If she had just told the doctor the whole story, he would almost certainly have talked some sense into Chay. She closed the door and leaned against it. All supposing Dr Manduca would believe her. The men were friends and men stuck together. No. She had got herself into this stupid situation and she would have to get herself out of it.

After lunch Tom went upstairs for a nap. He seemed a little old for this, but Sophie had noticed that children stayed up much later here than at home. They all seemed to sleep in the afternoon. And it suited her very well. With Chay out and Tom asleep, it was as good a chance as she was likely to get to search for her things.

She began upstairs. Theresa had said the suitcase was up there and that was a start. But a quick tour of Chay's room proved fruitless. The only hiding place large enough was the wardrobe, but that revealed nothing beyond a well-tended selection of clothes. She had begun to close the door when she noticed a small card on the floor. A business card. It must have dropped out of a pocket. She bent and picked it up. The logo, a dark green tower, belonged to Castile Developments. She had seen it all over the islands on construction sites and at the new marina, even at a hotel she had photographed that had had the developer's board still in place. It was one of the biggest companies on the island. But what on earth. . .? A stirring from Tom's room sent a warning prickle across her scalp.

She slipped the card into her pocket and hurried on to the landing, but when she peeked into the child's room he had simply rolled over and was still fast asleep. But it was a warning that she didn't have time to waste on speculation.

There was a flight of stairs leading to the next floor and she took it, expecting to find a similar layout to the first floor. But the stairs ended in a small landing, with further progress blocked by a heavy door. She seized the handle and pushed. Nothing happened, and she didn't need much convincing that throwing herself at it would damage her far more than the door.

On a hunch, she stretched on her toes and felt along the small ledge above the frame. Nothing. Disappointed, she gave the door a sharp kick to relieve her feelings. She glanced at her watch. Tom wouldn't sleep for much longer, and the knowledge that Chay might return at any moment lent further urgency to her search.

The study was the most likely hiding place for her camera bag and she could always throw her clothes in the back of the car. If she could find the keys.

Impatiently she tugged at the desk drawer, expecting it, too, to be locked. It slid smoothly open to reveal a stack of lined writing-blocks close-covered with a bold masculine script. A tiny flicker of excitement raised her pulse-rate and just a few lines confirmed her suspicion that she had stumbled across the first Chay Buchanan novel for six years. Was this his big secret? For a moment her fingers hovered over the smooth paper. . .

Then she snatched her hand back and closed the drawer quickly. No time for that.

The long centre drawer contained nothing more exciting than pens and pencils and other small writing accessories.

The last drawer contained notepaper and envelopes. On an impulse she wrote a brief note to the neighbour who looked after her flat while she was away, warning her that it might be for a few more days. She would ask Chay to post it for her. He could only say no. On reflection, he would almost certainly say no. But maybe she would get the chance to post it herself. She returned to the centre drawer, pulling it wider in her search for stamps. No stamps, but something else. A key. To the upstairs room? Her fingers began to close on it, then she saw something else.

A small photograph in a frame. It was a girl. A girl whose eyes glowed with happiness. She was dark and beautiful. In the corner she had written, 'Forever, Maria'. Sophie had thought that Tom looked like his father. But he had his mother's beautiful dark eyes.

The click of the door-latch was like a bullet, shattering her reverie. With a guilty start she hurriedly pushed the photograph back where she had found it and closed the drawer, leaping to her feet, her heart hammering, an excuse forming on her lips. But when she turned round it was not the accusing eyes of Chay Buchanan that confronted her.

'Well, sweetheart, this is cosy.' And Nigel Phillips sauntered into the study.

'Nigel? Where on earth have you sprung from?' Confusion, relief, made her shrill.

'That's not a very warm welcome for a friend who's come all the way from London to look you up,' he said.

Sophie knew she should be glad to see him. He

represented an immediate source of rescue. But she was far more concerned with Chay's reaction should he return and find them together in his study. 'H-how did you get in?'

'The front door wasn't locked,' he said, moving over to the desk and eyeing the computer. 'Country folk are so trusting.'

He reached for the switch and she grabbed his hand. 'Don't touch!' His pale blue eyes regarded her strangely. 'He'll know if you turn it on,' she said. 'The timer. . .'

'And he'll know you've been snooping.' He grinned. 'What a bright girl you are, Sophie. We'll make a good team. What have you found out so far?'

She jerked her hand back, sickened at the implication. 'You must go. . .he'll be back in a minute.'

'Don't panic. I've no intention of interrupting your little idyll, my sweet. It's just that when you didn't turn up with your photographs, I thought you might be planning to renege on our little deal.'

'No——'

'You weren't at your flat,' he continued, turning his attention to the drawers, 'and when I phoned your hotel they told me you'd booked out two days ago. So I thought I'd better find out what was happening.'

'I'll tell you what's happening,' she said. 'He caught me taking photographs with a long lens and he's keeping me here. . . He won't let me go, Nigel.'

'Really? I can't see any chains,' Nigel replied, with a knowing little smile. 'But then, men like him don't need them.'

'What is that supposed to mean?' she demanded, but a searing blush betrayed her.

'Come on, sweetheart, there's no need to be bashful. I'm really pleased with you.' He lightly flicked her cheek. 'Really pleased. I didn't think you had it in you.'

She stepped back sharply, hating him to touch her. 'What. . .? What do you mean?'

He grinned. 'You'll be able to give me a whole lot more than a photograph now, won't you?'

'I. . .I don't understand.' But there could be no mistaking his meaning, and he drove the message home without mercy.

'If you want to find your sister,' he said, with a leer that turned her blood cold.

'For pity's sake, Nigel. . .'

'I'll give you a few days.'

'But. . . You expect me to stay here?'

'You'll stay,' he said confidently. 'Not for me. For Jennie.' He stroked his hand down her cheek in a gesture that made her skin crawl, and she jerked away. 'Relax, sweetheart. Anyone would think. . .' He shrugged. 'There's no need to feel guilty about enjoying yourself. It's for your sister, right? I'll park up the road after dark. . .when? Sunday? Will that give you enough time? I'll flash my headlights at about ten o'clock. Just make sure you have all the juicy details. There'll be a nice little bonus in it for you.'

'I don't want a bonus. Or your filthy money.'

'That's up to you.' He shrugged. 'But your sister might be glad of it. The last time I saw her——' He shook his head. 'Some of those bed and breakfast places. . .'

Pain stabbed at her. She had been kidding herself for long enough. 'All right! I get the picture.' All pretence of a 'little favour' was at an end. This was blackmail. His hand reached for the drawer with the photograph. Sophie swallowed. How far back had she pushed it? 'You'd better go before Chay gets back,' she said urgently, but Nigel had already straightened and was staring at the doorway. Sophie's head swam as the blood drained from her face, and she held her breath, waiting for the explosion.

'Hello, there. What's your name?'

'I'm Tom.' As she heard the childish voice she almost sobbed with relief. 'Who are you?'

'I'm Nigel. I'm a friend of Sophie's.'

'Nigel's just leaving, Tom. Why don't you go and get into your swimming costume?' Tom needed no second bidding, and, giving Nigel a little smile, he disappeared.

'Who's the kid?'

'The housekeeper's boy.' He stared at her, taking in the bright colour that stained the pallor of her cheeks. She had always been incapable of telling a lie. 'She's away for a couple of days.' She walked quickly to the front door. 'You'd better go, Nigel,' she said.

'What's the hurry? I'd like a look around while you're on your own.' He moved towards the living-room door.

'I'm expecting Chay back any minute.' He hesitated, suspicious of her anxiety to be rid of him. 'He's late already,' she said, straightening, her voice a little firmer. 'Unless, of course, you would like to stay and meet him?' she invited. 'I have a feeling he would enjoy the opportunity of a word with you.'

'I take your point.'

She was shaking when she closed the door, locking it after him and leaning weakly back against it. She hadn't realised until this morning just how truly despicable the man was. He knew where her sister was, but his price for the information had been a photograph of Chay Buchanan in his hideaway. In her desperation it had seemed small enough. But it wasn't small, she discovered. She felt as if she had been touched by something very nasty, and she shuddered.

'I'm ready now, Sophie.' Tom's voice seemed to come from miles away. 'Sophie?' He tugged at her hand.

She glanced towards the study, the key, the possibility of freedom. It would have to wait.

A few minutes later, Sophie stood on the edge of the pool. She had no illusions about the water. It was too early in the year for it to be warm. But she welcomed that. It would be cold and clean and would wash away the touch of Nigel Phillips. Tom dived in without hesitation. She would have liked to follow his example, but her shoulder was in no condition for such a jolt and she lowered herself in, catching her breath as the water reached her stomach.

It was not water to hang around in, and she began to swim up and down the pool at a brisk pace. She was beginning to flag when a splash startled her. She had been so determined to keep a close watch on Tom that she had not seen Chay until his head surfaced beside her.

'Enjoying yourself?' he asked, with the kind of smile that suggested he knew exactly what she was suffering and was enjoying every moment of it.

'It's very. . .bracing.'

He laughed, disconcertingly, displaying a set of even white teeth. 'You should try it in winter.'

'No, thanks. In fact, since you're here now, I think I'll get out before I succumb to hypothermia.'

'Nonsense. It's not cold.' A pair of strong hands caught her around the waist and pulled her down. She came up, spluttering and gasping for air.

'You——' She didn't get a chance to call him the name that sprang to her lips because he ducked her again. The second time she erupted, gasping, from the water, she didn't bother with insults. She needed all her breath for retaliation.

The immediacy of her response, the shock of her hands crashing into his shoulders as she launched herself at him, took Chay by surprise. But he recovered instantly, and as he was knocked backwards by her furious onslaught his arms snaked around her waist, and he pulled her down with him, twisting over in the water so that he was above her and in control. And he was right. As his legs tangled against hers, and his arm pinioned her against his broad chest and hard flat stomach, she was no longer cold.

As he surfaced with her he grinned broadly. 'Better?' he asked.

Immeasurably better. Stupidly, dangerously better. Her hands were clinging to his shoulders, his skin was smooth beneath her fingers and the water pinned her against him. How much better could it get?

At that moment Tom leapt on them and Chay released her, turning with a roar to dunk the boy, chasing him up the pool in mock rage. Then they both turned on Sophie. With a little scream she struck out for the side of the pool. Chay's hand caught her ankle just as she reached the safety of the edge of the pool and he hauled her back. She twisted in the water, determined to fend him off, but he caught her round the waist, holding her up, so that despite her furious kicks she was quite helpless. For a moment something sparked in the depths of his eyes as they roved her body, and she caught her breath. But when he tightened his grasp around her waist it was simply to lift her up and sit her on the side of the pool.

'You are free to go, ma'am,' he said, with measured irony, and then quite deliberately removed his hands. 'For now.' It was oddly disturbing. As if he had been reinforcing his ability to hold her for as long as he wished.

Sophie scrambled to her feet and stepped back out

of his reach. Turning away to pick up a towel that she had dropped on a nearby rock, she began drying her hair with furious concentration. But she could not resist Tom's yells of delight as his father threw him up in the air, Chay's shouts of feigned rage as the boy's splashes found their mark.

She sank on to the rock, watching the two of them. The graceful little minnow swimming beside the shark. Tom a small promise of the man beside him. Chay, his body rippling with contained power, holding back as he swam alongside his son. Sophie scarcely realised that she was smiling. Then Chay rolled on to his back, and as their eyes met he smiled too. The smile of one adult to another in their conspiracy to amuse a child.

She immediately became absorbed in the meticulous drying of the ends of her hair, and when she looked again he had turned away to scoop up Tom and dump him on the side of the pool before hauling himself out.

She wrapped Tom in a towel and began to rub him dry. 'I'll see to Tom,' Chay said, taking over from her. She almost jumped as his shoulder brushed her arm, feeling suddenly very naked as his eyes flickered over her modest fuchsia one-piece bathing suit. He glanced up. 'You'd better go and make some tea,' he said, dismissing her. 'Plenty of milk for Tom.'

Her eyes snapped. 'Is that what Theresa would do?'

'She wouldn't have to be told.'

She opened her mouth, firmly resolved to tell him to go and make his own tea. But confronted with his broad tanned body, clad only in a scrap of black material that accentuated rather than concealed his blatant masculinity, and the spread of dark hair that curled across his chest, down his flat belly to his loins, she simply swallowed. 'Right,' she said, backing away, then she turned and fled.

Her hand shook as she filled the kettle. 'This is

ridiculous,' she said out loud to herself. 'Get a grip of
yourself, girl. He's just a man.' An arrogant bully of a
man, who had made his feelings on the subject of Miss
Sophie Nash very clear. And, while the kettle was
boiling, Miss Sophie Nash would be well advised to go
and cover herself up. She had made the hallway when
the front doorbell rang.

Sophie physically jumped. Had Nigel changed his
mind? Come back for her? The peremptory ring was
repeated rather more vigorously, and she moved
quickly to open it before Chay heard and came to
investigate.

It was difficult to say who was more startled—the
elegant woman on the doorstep, who looked as if she
had stepped out of the pages of a glossy magazine,
possibly in her late thirties, although it would take a
practised eye to tell for certain, dressed by Jean Muir
in a pastel suit that was neither blue nor grey but the
most sophisticated merging of the two, and with sleek
dark hair fresh from the stylist, or Sophie, in her
damply clinging swimsuit and with salt-stiffened hair
drying out into what her mother unkindly described as
something resembling tow.

The other woman regained her voice first. 'Poppy
Curzon,' she said coolly. 'Please tell Chay that I'm
here.' And she stepped over the threshold without
invitation.

Sophie stiffened at the woman's tone. She had
spoken to her as if she was a servant. And if she was
going to be treated like one, she was quite capable of
acting the part. 'Is he expecting you, Miss Curzon?'
she asked, in her best starched imitation of a maid.

But the question was academic. She brushed past
Sophie, her face wreathed in smiles, her arms extended
theatrically. 'Chay, darling.'

'Chay, darling' had taken the trouble to pull on a

polo shirt and a pair of shorts over his swimsuit and suddenly Sophie felt very underdressed.

'Poppy.' Chay took the newcomer in his arms and kissed her warmly on the cheek. 'Why didn't you let me know you were coming? I would have come to the airport.'

'Join the twentieth century and install a telephone and I will, darling.'

'Not a hope,' he laughed, obviously delighted to see the woman. 'Come on through to the garden. We're just having tea. Bring an extra cup, Sophie.'

At this reference to Sophie, Poppy turned, and gave her the kind of speculative glance that despite its fleeting nature would have earned a man a slap. 'Have you finally replaced Theresa with a younger model, darling?' she asked, with a small suggestive laugh. 'I do hope she can cook as well.'

For a moment Sophie's grey eyes flashed thunder and lightning, but Chay intervened before she could say anything outrageous.

'Poppy, meet Miss Sophie Nash,' he said, introducing her with grave formality. 'She's Tom's nanny.' His look was a sharp warning.

'Isn't he a little old for a nanny?'

'It's a temporary arrangement.'

Sophie drew in a sharp breath at this brazen lie.

But this time Poppy forestalled the threatened explosion. 'Very temporary, I should imagine, by the look of those goose-pimples. If she doesn't get dressed soon she's going to catch her death of cold.'

'Darling, if you wanted a nanny you should have let me know. I would have found someone for you. Someone properly trained.'

Sophie arrived just in time to hear Poppy's remark, to witness the long white fingers with immaculately polished nails curved possessively around Chay's arm. She placed the tray of tea very carefully on the garden table, catching sight of her own battered nails and hands and wincing at the comparison.

'She is trained, Poppy,' Chay said evenly, insolent eyes meeting Sophie's without the slightest shame. She had taken a quick shower and dressed, but with her hair still damp she was conscious of looking rather less like an old English nanny in the Norland tradition than an old English sheepdog. No competition for the well-groomed elegance of Poppy Curzon.

Poppy evidently agreed. Having turned a searching eye upon her, she finally asked, 'In what?'

'I promise you,' Chay said, with a very thin smile, 'she's utterly dedicated to her job. You've only brought two cups, Sophie. Go and fetch another.'

'I have to organise Tom's tea,' she said quickly. She had no wish to be a part of his cosy tête-à-tête with Poppy Curzon. And it was more than plain from the fixed smile on the other woman's face that she harboured no lingering desire for Sophie's company either.

But Chay had other ideas. 'Tom's gone down to the stables with Twany,' he said. 'He won't be back for at least an hour and, as you can see, Poppy can't wait to grill you on your qualifications.'

Twany? Who was Twany? But Sophie met his glance. If she was to be cast in the role of nanny, the least she could do was make some pretence of doing her job. She pursed her lips, in a manner perfected by her grandmother. 'I do hope,' she said primly, 'that you dried Tom thoroughly before he went.'

'Have you forgotten so soon?' he asked, his voice a silken ambush. 'How very thorough I can be?' The colour flooded to her cheeks at this reference to the way he had showered her. And dried her. Her stupid mouth should be fitted with a zip-fastener.

'I'll fetch that cup.' Anything to get away from his sardonic eyes and the flicker of amusement that crossed the lips of Poppy Curzon. Amusement that clearly suggested she was wasting her time if she thought Chay Buchanan would ever take more than a passing interest in the likes of her.

I don't want him to take an interest in me, she swore silently, as she clung to the edge of the kitchen table and tried to ignore the soft ripple of laughter that floated through the kitchen door, tried to fight down an almost irresistible urge to throw something. I just want to get away from here. Away from Chay Buchanan.

She was still simmering as she passed around Theresa's excellent cake. 'Are you here on holiday, Miss Curzon?' she asked, with excessive politeness.

'Holiday?' The idea clearly took the woman by surprise. 'No, I'm here on business.' She shrugged. 'I am Chay's literary agent.'

'Was, darling,' he corrected her. 'Since I no longer write, I don't need an agent.'

'Of course you do. It may be a while since your last novel, but I'm still handling overseas sales, reprints, translations. There's a repeat of the mini-series of your first book scheduled for this autumn.' Chay did not look paticularly pleased with this news. 'There's an enormous amount of interest still, darling. You could name your own price.'

'I don't understand,' Sophie said, and they both turned to her.

'What don't you understand?' Poppy snapped, clearly wishing that the 'nanny' would remember her place.

Sophie kept her eyes fixed upon the tall, glowering figure of her nemesis. 'I don't understand why Chay said he doesn't write any more.' Poppy's eyes narrowed, but Sophie was transfixed by the momentary flash of disbelief that crossed Chay's face. 'He writes every day of his life. He told me so himself.' Take that, Mr Buchanan, her eyes clearly told him. You might be able to keep me your prisoner and amuse your sophisticated women-friends at my expense, but you can't gag me. Then, as his eyes turned to steel, she suddenly wasn't so sure.

But before the explosion happened, before he could say or do anything, Poppy exclaimed, 'A new book? Tell me? What are you working on, Chay?'

From across the table his eyes finally relinquished their hold on Sophie, but she was left in no doubt that retaliation had only been delayed. And when he turned slowly to Poppy, he was wearing a small, disparaging smile. It was a daunting display of self-control. 'I'm afraid that Sophie is mistaken.'

Poppy glanced at Sophie. 'But she said——'

'That I write every day?' He shrugged. 'I keep a diary. Doesn't everyone?'

For a moment she was speechless. 'But Chay, that would be——'

'It's not for publication,' he said sharply. Then, as he saw from Poppy's intent expression that he had only aroused her interest further, he leaned back in his chair. 'I hardly think two hundred and fifty pages of "Got up. *Lounged* around——"' he looked pointedly at Sophie as he repeated the word she had used in her withering description of his lifestyle '"—went to bed" is likely to hit the bestseller list, Poppy.'

Poppy stared at him, then at Sophie, picking up the dangerous undercurrent that tugged between them. 'That would depend on who you went to bed with, darling,' she murmured, and a secret little smile curved her lips as she met Sophie's eyes.

'Kiss and tell was never my style, Poppy,' he said. 'In fact, I'm far too busy these days to——'

'I know. I've seen Castile Developments everywhere, sweetheart, and I'm very impressed, but that's not you. . .'

'It is now.'

Sophie's brows flew up in surprise. 'Castile Developments?' Her fingers touched the card in her pocket. 'Is that you?'

'Didn't you know?' Poppy asked, apparently amused.

But Sophie, staring at Chay, didn't bother to answer. It was hardly surprising he had taken umbrage at her assertion that he had 'retired'. The only surprise was that he had time to put pen to paper at all. But there *was* a book. But since he clearly had no intention of publishing it, there was something else driving him to keep her prisoner.

But Poppy hadn't given up. 'You could leave the management of the development company to someone else, Chay. Anybody could do that. But you have a gift.' His gesture was dismissive. 'Well, think of Tom,' she pressed him. 'You have his future to consider. For a three-book contract we would be talking telephone numbers.'

'Perhaps. But this way I don't have to stand up and bare my soul every time I complete a deal. Writing was something I did a long time ago. I don't do it any more because the books are not enough. They want more and more—chat-shows, interviews, lecture-tours—and when they have all that, and they can't think of anything pleasant to say, it gets more personal. . .' His glance at Sophie was quelling. 'They never give up.'

'Chay, I promise——'

He stopped her with a look. 'Don't promise what you can't deliver, Poppy. Somewhere in that contract,

in words so obscure, so small that it'll need a magnify-
ing glass to find them there will be a water-tight clause
about the author co-operating with publicity. There
always is,' he said bitterly, 'as I know to my cost.'

'The absolute minimum, I promise.'

Sophie almost winced as he turned hard, provoking
eyes upon her. 'You see, Sophie, that I was able to
sharpen my natural scepticism on an expert.' But she
rose to the challenge.

'You never seemed to object to co-operating with
publicity in the past,' she retaliated. 'You always
appeared to be extremely happy in the photographs
that were printed in the newspapers.'

'And the camera never lies?' His eyes were
expressionless. He replaced his cup on the table. 'I'm
sorry you've had a pointless journey, Poppy.'

'Not pointless,' Poppy said, and once more her hand
strayed to his arm. 'Come and have dinner with me
tonight, Chay.' Her voice was husky. 'It'll be like old
times.'

'Excuse me.' Sophie stood up abruptly, and swept
the tray back to the kitchen.

When Chay had seen Poppy to her taxi he leaned
against the kitchen table, watching while Sophie concentrated very hard on washing the dishes. She made it
last a long time, knowing full well that he was waiting
for her to turn and face the music. Finally, however, it
was done, and the moment could be put off no longer.
She stripped off the over-large rubber gloves she had
found in the cupboard beneath the sink and took a
deep breath to calm the butterflies dancing in her
stomach.

'So, you won't be in for dinner tonight?' she asked
brightly as she turned to face him.

'No, unfortunately, because you must be quite a

cook. If that demonstration of stirring is anything to go by.'

'If you think that's all there is to cooking, you have clearly never tried it yourself.'

'Never,' he confirmed, folding his arms. There was something about the way he said it that made her doubt the truth of that statement.

'Who is Twany?' she asked, abruptly changing the subject.

'He's Theresa's brother. He looks after the horses and does the gardening.'

'Then I'm surprised you haven't given him the week off as well. However did you resist the temptation to set me weeding and mucking out the stables?'

He took a step towards her, and she almost flinched as she saw the warning glint in his eyes, edging back until the sink brought her to a halt. 'It was tough, Sophie Nash, I promise.' He caught hold of her hands, held up as if to ward him off, and turned them over to look at her palms. 'But unfortunately these are in no state to wield a shovel.'

She ignored with difficulty the ripple of excitement at his touch as he cradled her hands. The memory of Poppy Curzon's throaty voice helped. 'What a great disappointment that must be for you!'

He stared at her fingers, still bearing the marks of her desperate scramble up the cliff. When he looked up all trace of gentleness had disappeared. 'Perhaps they'll be sufficiently healed for you to put in a day or two before you leave.'

'Why don't you go the whole way and put me to work on one of your construction sites?'

'Don't tempt me!'

'Forget it, Chay,' she said. 'I'm leaving today. Right now, in fact!'

His grip tightened painfully on her fingers. 'No,

Sophie. You'll stay for as long as I choose to keep you here.'

'You can't!' He didn't answer. He didn't need to. 'How long?' she asked, a little shakily.

'A week. Maybe a little more. So take a few days' holiday and forget why you came here. I do mean that.'

'This is your idea of a holiday?' she demanded.

'Tom's not hard work.'

'I've no objection to Tom's company,' she retorted pointedly.

'Then looking after him for a few days will be precious little penance for all the trouble you've put me to.' Sophie took a breath, but he hadn't finished. 'I sent away your films this morning.'

'Oh!' The exclamation escaped in a little rush of air. Despite her attempt to deceive him he had still kept to his part of the bargain. 'Where?' she asked anxiously. 'Which laboratory did you send them to?'

'You don't really expect me to tell you that?' he demanded, and she gave a little gasp. Always, she forgot. The minute he touched her she forgot everything. She snatched her hands away and he smiled slightly. 'You needn't worry. I took advice. They'll be of professional quality,' he promised.

'Thank you,' she said stiffly.

His eyebrows rose dramatically. 'Can this be gratitude?' he enquired.

She ignored the sarcasm. 'How long will they be?'

'Why? Do you have something more important to do? Some other unsuspecting soul to point your long lens at?'

'No, I don't!' Once had been enough. More than enough.

'Then, what's your hurry?' He shrugged. 'Theresa

wanted to go and see her latest grandchild. She should be back in about a week.'

'But you're not keeping me here to give Theresa a holiday, are you, Chay?' she demanded. 'You just want her out of the way, because if she knew you were keeping me here against my will she wouldn't stand for it. Would she? So what's the real reason?'

CHAPTER SIX

CHAY glared at her. 'That is none of your damn business, Sophie Nash. All you have to do is behave yourself for a few days, then you can go.'

'How many days?' she demanded.

'As many as it takes!' For a moment the air crackled as the two of them squared up to each other. Then he swept a hand through the lock of hair that had fallen across his brow. 'Believe me when I tell you that I don't want you hanging around any longer than necessary. I spent today trying to move. . .certain matters forward.'

What 'certain matters'? She made a determined effort to dampen her natural curiosity. She didn't want to know. She didn't want to know anything. But she regarded him with disapproval. 'You took a heck of a chance leaving Tom alone with me. Suppose I had just walked out and left him?' A worse thought struck her. 'Suppose something had happened to him? There's no telephone, no car——'

'I gave up leaving anything to chance years ago,' he said abruptly. 'Twany was near by, keeping an eye on things.'

'And to stop me leaving?' she demanded.

'Leaving? And where would you have gone, pray? On foot, without any money or a passport? I don't think so. But the true reason for your stay remains our secret.'

'Your secret,' she amended. 'One of them.'

'The only one you'll be privy to.'

'How many do you have?' She squared up to him

again. 'For instance, is it common knowledge that you own Castile Developments?'

His hand shot out and grasped her arm. 'It's what I do here.' Not all he did, she thought. But she had already said far too much. She didn't want him to know she had been prying through his desk. He released her. 'I'm a businessman. A very good one. There's no scandal in that.'

'None,' she agreed quickly.

'So. We'll keep the reason for your stay between the two of us. Clearly you prefer it that way, or you would have spilled the beans to Poppy.'

'You saw to it that I didn't have much opportunity for that. Was that why you insisted I stay for the tea ceremony? To keep me from writing a cry for help and slipping it into her car?'

'How bright you are, Sophie,' he said quietly. 'What a pity to waste all that beauty and intelligence on such a sordid occupation.' He regarded her thoughtfully. 'You're right, of course. And if you could have alerted Poppy you would have had an ally.'

'Would I?' She gave an awkward little shrug. 'It didn't feel much like it.'

'Didn't it?' He laughed softly. 'Then you were wrong. If Poppy had known your true purpose in being here she would have fallen upon you like a long-lost sister.'

'A long lost——?' She stopped. Took a deep breath. It was just a figure of speech. He knew nothing about the real reason why it had been so important to get a photograph of him.

But he was frowning. 'What is it? What did I say?'

'Nothing. It was nothing.' Change the subject. Something. Anything. 'I. . .I think it's a pity you don't publish what you write,' she said quickly. To her relief she saw that Chay was amused.

'That came perilously close to a compliment.'

'You don't need me to tell you how good you are. Were,' she corrected herself carefully. 'I. . .I have some sympathy with Poppy. It must be infuriating to have represented one of the hottest literary properties in the world, only to have him. . .drop out.'

'She has other authors,' he replied, the smile switched off as quickly as it had appeared.

That was better. It was easier when he was angry. 'Perhaps, but you must have seemed like the equivalent of the golden goose. And, let's face it, you've gone off-lay.'

He stared at her. 'You know nothing about it.'

'No? Then why don't you tell me? Is the great Chay Buchanan suffering from a terminal case of writer's block?' she demanded. She already knew the answer. He couldn't stop writing, but he would rather not publish than face the publicity. There must be some good reason. . . What exactly did Nigel know? Or suspect? 'I wasn't fooled by that nonsense about a diary,' she continued, a little recklessly. 'And I don't suppose Poppy will be if she takes time to think about it. So what is it? What are you hiding from?' The beautiful face of the girl in the photograph flashed on to her mind's eye. 'What happened to your wife, Chay?'

His face went white beneath the tan. Whether with anger or shock she couldn't tell, but instinctively she held her breath, waiting for the explosion. It never came.

'Maria. . .is dead.'

The painful words fell into a shocked silence so sudden, so complete, that she heard a petal fall from the bunch of yellow daisies she and Tom had picked and put in a jug on the kitchen table.

Sophie drew in a long shuddering breath. 'I'm sorry,' she whispered. 'That was unforgivable of me.'

'You keep doing unforgivable things, Sophie,' he rasped, the hard planes of his cheeks, the fierce hook of his broken nose so close that she could hardly breathe. She lowered her lashes, to block out the pitiless expression.

'You. . .you just seem to bring out the worst in me,' she whispered.

'Do I?' He hooked her chin with his hand, lifted her face to his unsparing scrutiny. It seemed to last forever. 'I wonder what the best is like?'

Defensive, prickly, too aware that his fingers at her throat were making her tremble, she retaliated. 'You're not about to find out.' Still he probed, searched her face, and she panicked. 'Of course, if you let me keep your photographs it would help,' she said, deliberately provoking.

'Would it? In that case I'll have to live with the worst.' And he dropped his hand, turning away, missing her surge of relief as she leaned weakly back against the sink. When he spoke again his tone was once more harsh. 'You'd better come down to the stables with me to fetch Tom; he wants to show you his pony.'

It took a moment to pull her wits together and he glanced impatiently from the doorway. 'I'm coming,' she said quickly.

He led the way out of the kitchen and across the garden and then held open the gate to a narrow path that ran between old drystone walls down the hill towards a group of buildings.

Walking alongside him on the narrow path, his arm brushing against her with every step, was a nightmare. He was so. . .physical. She tried to drop back, but he put his hand on her shoulder, easing her in front of him to give her more room, and he left it there. The nervous tingles from the unintentional contact were suddenly in danger of becoming a solid warm glow.

Sophie fought it. With each step she reminded herself of his insults, every cutting remark, the casual touch of his hands, of his lips used to emphasise his complete mastery over her. She was his prisoner, she reminded herself. And somewhere out there was Nigel, waiting for her to 'kiss and tell'. Already she had enough for Nigel to have a field-day if he continued to demand her co-operation in return for information about her sister. . . She glanced at the man beside her, and felt a deep pit of cold misery in her stomach.

Tom's delighted face, his small hands tugging her away to admire his golden-coated pony, came as a blessed relief. 'She's lovely, Tom. What's her name?'

'Melita. It means honey,' he told her.

'The old Roman name for Malta? How pretty.'

'I call her Melly.'

Sophie rubbed the pony's nose. 'Can you ride her yet?'

'I can ride anything,' he said proudly.

Startled, she turned to Chay. 'Tom's only had Melly a few days,' he said, coming up to them and offering the pony a knob of sugar on the flat of his hand. 'She's a birthday present from his grandmother.' He gave some sugar to Tom, and, taking her arm, led her along the yard to introduce her to the other horses.

'You have a mother?' she murmured in mocking disbelief, as she made a fuss of a gentle-mouthed grey mare.

'You thought, perhaps, that I sprang full-grown from dragon's teeth?'

'I don't think anything,' she said, preferring to keep her thoughts to herself. 'But I know you are quite prepared to keep me here against my will.'

'I'm glad you realise that. Although, as a prison, this

has much to commend it.' His gesture invited her to look around. Tom was laughing as his pony butted him with her nose, wanting more of the sugar he had in his hand. Twany could be heard, singing tunelessly as he worked in the tack-room. Around them a warm, flower-scented evening drew in.

'"The isle is full of noises, Sounds and sweet airs, that give delight, and hurt not. . ."?' Sophie quoted softly. Then she turned to him. 'But it's still a prison, Chay. No matter whether you are locked up, or simply bound to a place by memories.' She forced herself to face him, confront the hard line of his mouth, his shaded eyes. 'I'm sorry I asked about your wife, Chay. You must have loved her very much.'

He didn't answer. He didn't need to. The brief expression of pain that crossed his face was all the answer she needed.

Tom raced up. 'Will you ride with us tomorrow, Sophie?' he begged. 'Please? She could ride Rowan, Papa.'

'I. . .' Words failed her. What could she say to the child?

Chay's hand reached over her head to stroke the beast's neck. 'Do you ride?' he asked abruptly.

'Yes,' she said. 'But it's. . .it's been a while.'

'Yes!' Tom punched the air. Then rushed off to tell Twany.

Chay turned back to the bay. 'We go out very early,' he said. 'We won't wait for you.'

'Aren't you afraid I'll bolt for it?'

His eyes gleamed dangerously. 'You could try,' he offered.

'Why are you keeping me here? Why is it so important?' He didn't answer. 'Please, Chay, let me go.' And instinctively she laid a hand upon his arm.

His face hardened. 'It will take more than a pair of bright eyes to move me, Sophie. I warned you.'

For a moment their eyes held. Then Tom's insistent clamour for her attention broke through, and she let him pull her away to meet Rowan. And when she looked again Chay was striding away across the concrete yard.

So much for her determination to get away. Well, tomorrow was another day. She'd think of something. She had to. And with that promise to herself she surrendered to Tom's enthusiasm.

'When is your birthday, Tom?' she asked, as they walked up the path together half an hour later.

'On Sunday,' he said. 'Do you really think Papa might let me have a party?'

'Why don't you ask him?'

Tom pulled a doubtful face. 'If you asked him for me,' he suggested, 'he might say yes.' He tucked his hand trustingly in hers. 'He likes you.'

Startled, she glanced down at the boy. 'What makes you think that?'

'He ducked you in the pool,' Tom said confidentially. 'You only do that to people you really like.'

She choked back her laughter at this child's-eye-view of friendship. Then she remembered. She had ducked Chay, too.

Sophie was showing Tom the way to make waterspouts in the bath when his shrieks of laughter brought Chay to see what all the excitement was about. His arrival coincided with a particularly tremendous whoosh of water, which erupted over the edge of the bath to splatter a pair of hand-made shoes and well-cut trousers.

'What the devil. . .?'

Before she could stop him, Tom shouted, 'Look, Papa!' and copied her.

Sophie leapt to her feet. 'I'm sorry——'

Chay was staring down at the bath, watching Tom's game. 'Matt and I used to do that. I'd forgotten.'

'Matt?'

'My brother.' He glanced at her. 'We used to compete to see who could make the biggest spouts. The mess we made. . .' He shrugged. 'Matt and I used to compete at everything.' His gaze returned to the child in the bath. 'Stupid.'

'Is it? I used to compete with my sister. Without much success.'

'Used to?' His eyes met hers in sharp query, and she remembered that his brother was dead. 'Not now?'

'No. Not now,' she said, a little shakily. 'We grew up.'

'That was clever of you. Matt never quite got over the fact that he was a year younger than me, the need to prove himself. I suppose I should have let him win occasionally.'

'He would have known,' she said. She had always known, on those rare occasions than Jennie had taken pity on her. 'And it's far worse.'

'How reassuring.' She stared at him. He was angry. What on earth had she said? 'I'm going to change.' He paused. 'If you need anything tonight, Twany lives in the cottage behind the stables.'

A reminder that she was being watched? 'I'll be fine,' she said abruptly. She turned to the boy in the bath. 'Come on, Tom. The water's getting cold. Time to get out.'

'Ask him now, Sophie!' Tom demanded in a loud whisper.

'No, Tom, not now,' she shushed him. Now was not a good time.

But it was too late; he had heard. 'Ask me what?' Chay demanded, turning in the doorway.

Sophie, wrapping Tom in a towel, kept her eyes firmly on the boy. 'Tom seems to think you'll be more likely to agree if I ask you if he can have a birthday party,' she said quickly. Then, because this seemed to imply some criticism, she added, 'I can't think why. I'm sure you'll let him have one.'

There was a long moment of silence and she finally looked up, unaware how her eyes were pleading for the child. Chay regarded her intently, the slightest frown creasing his brow. Then he turned to Tom. 'This was your own idea?'

'Yes,' he said. Then, under his father's searching gaze, he faltered. 'Not exactly.' Chay's glance swivelled back to Sophie, and she flinched at the frostbitten chill that accused her. But Tom hadn't finished. 'Dr Paul said I should have a party, and invite Elena and Michael and little Paul and. . .'

For a moment Chay's eyes continued to challenge Sophie, and for a moment she met him head-on. Then he pulled a face and turned back to Tom. No apology. Well, what did she expect?

'All right,' he said, holding up a hand to halt the excited flow. 'I get the picture. So, you want a party for your birthday?' The child nodded, almost holding his breath. 'What kind of party?'

'One like Uncle Matt had. Grandma told me about it. With cowboys and Indians and a barbecue,' he said, hopping from one leg to the other as he began to believe it was going to be all right. 'On the beach.' He began to rattle off a list of the most desirable food, who should be invited and what games they would play, oblivious to the brief spasm of anguish that crossed his father's face. 'Can I, Papa? Please?'

Chay tucked down until his eyes were level with

Tom's. 'A party means a lot of work. Who's going to arrange all this?'

'Sophie will,' Tom said confidently. He turned and looked up at her. 'You will, Sophie, won't you?'

Chay raised his eyes to meet hers and she was surprised to discover that a glint of amusement had replaced the anger. 'No problem, then. If Sophie is prepared to organise it, Tom, of course you can have a party,' he said. 'But she must decide.'

'But that's not——' Fair. It wasn't fair. But he already knew that. That was what he found so amusing. Because Tom had taken her agreement for granted.

'Yes!' he cried, punching the air, abandoning his towel as he danced about the bathroom. 'Yes! A party! Thank you, Sophie! Thank you, Papa!'

'But it can't be Sunday,' he warned. 'We'll have it on Saturday.'

Tom didn't care. He was having a party. Over-whelmed by the child's excitement, Sophie turned helplessly to Chay as he straightened. 'But I can't,' she said.

'Can't you?' Chay regarded her with an expression that would have provoked a saint. 'You tell him,' he said. Then he turned and walked away.

Sophie took one look at Tom's ecstatic face and knew she couldn't do it. Between them they had her trapped, and she suddenly discovered that there was more than one way to be held prisoner. A fact, she was sure, that Chay was quite well aware of.

'Come on, Tom,' she said, with a trace of a sigh. 'Let's get you into bed.'

She left him compiling a list of friends who must be invited to his birthday party and went downstairs in search of Chay. She found him in the drawing-room. He had changed into a cream linen suit, with a deep blue shirt that seemed to reflect into his eyes, turning their depths from Arctic to Mediterranean, making it very hard to remember how angry she was. He glanced up from the drinks table.

'Would you like something?' he offered.

'A gin and tonic, please,' she said, with feeling. 'That was a bit below the belt, Chay.'

'Oh, quite a long way below,' he agreed, handing her a glass, quite unperturbed by the admission. 'But not quite as low as you rifling through my desk.'

Sophie blushed. 'How did you know?'

'I didn't.' He raised his glass. 'But I do now.'

'Oh!'

'You saw Maria's photograph.' It wasn't a question.

'I was looking for my passport and car keys.' She sipped nervously at her drink. 'She was. . .very beautiful.'

'Yes. She was certainly that.' His eyes had gone blank. He put his glass down with a snap. 'I suppose you saw the manuscript as well. Did you read it?'

'No.'

'I wish you had been as restrained when you decided to spill the beans to Poppy.'

'Since I'm so much trouble, perhaps you should reconsider keeping me here,' she suggested hopefully.

'And disappoint Tom?'

She took a deep breath. 'In that case, Chay,' she said, 'I freely confess to helping myself to some of your notepaper to write to my neighbour.' She produced the letter she had written. 'Would you post it for me? She'll worry if I don't let her know that I've been delayed.'

'Delayed?' He took the letter from her and glanced at the address.' When he looked up his face was lined with suspicion. 'What reason have you given for the. . . delay?'

'I didn't give any reasons. But she looks after my flat, feeds my cat. . .'

'Really? Your cat?' He was deeply sceptical. ' "Don't forget to feed Tiddles, and by the way could you send the enclosed to the *Sunday*——?" '

'No!'

'Perhaps you'd care to tell me why I should believe you?'

'No, thank you,' she resolutely declined his offer. 'I don't care to be called a liar.'

'Maybe you could convince me that you're not?'

'With pleasure. Please don't be squeamish, Chay. Just open the letter and read it for yourself,' she instructed coldly. 'I realise that it's not quite in the rifling-through-desk class of prying. But you're pretty good at the handbag variety, so reading other people's mail shouldn't prove so very difficult.' Her grey eyes sparked anger, and for a moment they seemed to hang on the edge. . .

'Papa?'

Chay swung around. 'What are you doing out of bed, Tom?' he snapped.

The boy was clutching a sheet of paper and a pencil. 'I just wanted to ask Sophie. . .

'Ask Sophie what?'

'Chay!' She crossed to the boy and put her arm around him. 'What is it?' she asked gently.

'I just wanted to ask you,' he half whispered. 'Would your friend like to come to my party?'

Sophie went white. 'Friend?' Chay repeated, his voice dangerously soft. 'What friend, Tom?'

Reassured by his father's gentle tone, Tom relaxed. 'He came yesterday. . .when you were out.'

'Did he?' His eyes met Sophie's over the child's head. 'What was his name?' The question wasn't addressed to Tom.

'It was Nigel,' she said.

'Nigel. Of course. Put him on your list, Tom. I'd very much like to meet. . .Nigel.'

Tom's face creased in concentration. 'How do you spell that?'

'Sophie will tell you later.' He crossed the room and steered Tom through the door. 'Go back to bed now.'

Still concentrating hard, the boy wandered back up the stairs. For a long time after he had gone there was silence.

'Did you think I could just disappear and no one would worry about me?' Sophie finally demanded, unable to bear it a moment longer.

'Why did he assume you would be here?'

'Where else would I be? He was waiting for me to get home. When I didn't turn up he phoned my hotel. I wasn't there either.'

'So? Why didn't you leave with him?'

Because he wouldn't take me. He wants me to stay and have an affair with you and tell him all about it so that he can put it in some sordid magazine. What would he do if she said that? She shuddered. 'Don't you think I wanted to? You have my passport.'

'You could have got a temporary travel document from the High Commission.'

'And my camera.'

'It must be insured.'

'I couldn't have left Tom,' she said a little desperately. 'I didn't know about Twany. . .'

'He'll be back, then?'

She stiffened at the thought of Nigel waiting on Sunday evening. 'No,' she said quickly. 'Why should he bother? I didn't do the job——'

'Damn you!' He thrust the letter into his pocket. 'I ought to have thrown you out, battered and bruised as you were.'

'Then why didn't you?'

'I don't know!' They glared at one another with a deep and mutual antipathy. Then he took a step towards her. 'Yes, I do,' he said, his voice like velvet ripping as he grasped her shoulders and dragged her towards him, his mouth descending in a hard, bruising kiss.

It was as if he hated himself for being unable to resist her. As if he was punishing her for being irresistible. The surprise, the shock of it stunned her. And by the time she realised that she ought to be struggling, making some serious move to stop him, it was very nearly too late.

His hands had slipped from her shoulders to her waist, drawing her into treacherously seductive contact with his thighs, his loins. Her body was already beginning to dissolve, seduced by the warm scent of his skin, melting against him until the soft curves of her body were pressed hard against his body, and she was dangerously close to forgetting that she detested him. Close to forgetting what he had done to her. Close, but not totally lost to sanity. In a moment of blinding anger at his arrogant assumption that he could kiss her without so much as a by-your-leave, and casually reduce her to mindless jelly, she swung her right foot and kicked him, very hard, on the shin.

For a moment the tightening of his grip was the only indication that he had felt anything. Then, with a shuddering sigh, he released her abruptly and stepped back, looking down at his leg as if he couldn't quite believe what had happened. When he looked up his eyes were leaden. 'If you weren't enjoying yourself, Sophie, you only had to say,' he said.

'Enjoying. . .' Hardly able to believe her ears, she exploded. 'Let me tell you that I've enjoyed a visit to the dentist more,' she lied. 'And, as for telling you anything, I ask you to recall that my mouth was otherwise engaged!'

'So it was.' His cool fingers touched her bee-stung mouth, hot and throbbing from his cavalier treatment. 'But for future reference, Sophie, if you simply stop kissing someone back, they usually get the message. There's no need for violence.'

She hadn't! She hadn't kissed him back! How dared he suggest that she had? 'Haven't you got an appointment you're anxious to keep?' she reminded him sharply. 'I'm sure Poppy Curzon will be far more appreciative of your caveman tactics.'

'You may be right.' His voice took on a dangerous edge. 'I'll let you know in the morning.' With that he turned and walked from the room, and a moment later the front door closed somewhat forcefully, making her jump.

For a long breathless moment she stood there, hardly able to believe her ears. Hardly able to believe the sharp bile of jealousy that stung at her throat. 'Poppy Curzon is welcome to you,' she called after him, a little desperately. The hollow echo that came reverberating back to her ears that Poppy Curzon had got him was not a comfort.

She fled to the study. If the key opened the door to the second floor she would be able to lay her escape plans. But when she wrenched the drawer open, the key had gone.

'Sophie!' There was a sickening jolt as her fall was abruptly halted. 'Sophie, wake up.'

She tried to speak, but the fear, the horror of it clammed her mouth, and nothing would come out. Her heart was pounding horribly and she still couldn't believe that she was alive, that Chay was holding her close, rocking her gently, his arms about her and her cheek pressed against the smooth dark silk of his dressing-gown. 'Wake up, now.' His voice was insistent. 'You're safe.'

Safe. She lifted her head and stared up at him. 'It was a dream, wasn't it?'

'More like a nightmare, to judge by the amount of noise you were making,' he said softly.

She was trembling with the sickening sensation that still clutched at her. 'I was falling and falling. . .' She shuddered. 'It was horrible.'

'Do you often have nightmares?'

'Not like that.' Not real, screaming nightmares. Only endless exhausting dreams in which she searched hopelessly for her sister. She shuddered again. 'Never like that.'

He held her away from him and looked at her. 'Come on. Downstairs. I'll warm you some milk.'

Something in his eyes alerted her to the dangerous intimacy of being held by him like this, on her bed in the middle of the night. 'No.' She drew back a little. 'I'll be all right,' she said, with an attempt at brightness, then spoiled the effect by shivering convulsively. Still, somewhere in the dark recesses of her mind, she was plunging down that endless cliff-face.

'The minute you close your eyes, it'll start all over again,' he warned her. 'Believe me. I know,' he added with conviction. He looked around, took her wrap from behind the door and held it out for her. 'You'll have to wake up properly before you can go back to sleep.'

No need to throw back the quilt, she noticed dimly. It had fallen to the floor in her agitation, leaving her covered only by her brief two-piece sleepsuit, an oyster satin camisole and matching French knickers that left precious little to the imagination. She swung her legs to the floor and dived into the wrap, tying it firmly around her.

'I'm sorry that I disturbed you,' she muttered, keeping her eyes firmly diverted from the short silk dressing-gown tied carelessly about his waist, under which she was fairly certain he was naked.

'I wasn't asleep.' He placed his hand firmly at her back and propelled her from the room and down the stairs. 'Come on.' She glanced at him as she opened the kitchen door.

'Why can't you sleep?'

He took a carton of milk from the refrigerator and poured it into a saucepan and set it to heat. 'I said that I wasn't asleep, not that I couldn't.'

'But. . .it's three o'clock in the morning.' Then bright colour spread across her cheeks. 'Oh!' She reached hurriedly for a mug to cover her confusion. Poppy had clearly welcomed him with open arms.

He took the mug from her. 'I posted your letter.'

'Then you read it?'

He didn't answer. 'You didn't write to your parents. Won't they worry too?' he asked, carefully pouring out the milk and handing it to her.

She sipped, not wanting to discuss her relationship with her parents. 'I don't live at home. They don't know where I am from day to day.'

'You mentioned a sister? What about her?'

'Jennie.' She felt suddenly hollow with longing. 'We're identical twins.'

'Identical. . . Lord help us, there are two of you?'

'I'm afraid so.' For just a moment her eyes responded to the unexpected smile. Then they clouded. 'At least, we *were* identical.'

'Were?'

'I haven't seen Jennie for nearly seven years. She ran away from home when she was seventeen.'

'Ran away?' He was clearly shocked. Angry, almost. 'Why?'

Her lips tightened at his disapproval. What could he possibly know of such things, shut away in his private world? 'It's a common enough story,' she told him, defences slamming up, but too late. 'She got involved with a man my parents disapproved of. Then when she became pregnant he left her to face the music alone.'

'But your parents? Were they so harsh?' he demanded, and she glanced up to find herself the object of a pair of deeply questing eyes. It seemed oddly important to him.

'No. They were never harsh with her.' On the contrary. The only thing they had ever tried to deny her had driven her away. 'They loved Jennie. They would have done anything for her. That's why she ran. She knew how badly she had behaved,' she replied, quickly dropping her lids to disguise the sharp sting of tears glistening in her eyes. She had seen her parents age while they had privately grieved for their beautiful daughter who, rather than bear their imagined reproach, had taken her wounded pride and disappeared without a trace. And she had been unable to comfort them. The mirror image of their lost child, they couldn't stand to have her near them. And soon afterwards she too had left.

Now she had been given a chance to reunite them. All it had needed was a photograph of Chay Buchanan and she had blown it. Except that Nigel had given her another chance. If she could get a little gossip—a scrap of dirt. . . And there *was* something. She knew it. Tied up in the story of a dead wife, a motherless child and a writer who couldn't stand publicity.

She stared into the mug. Why else was she here? His prisoner? Sitting in this silent, night-time kitchen, drinking warm milk and recovering from a nightmare with a man who she knew she should loathe? But didn't. No matter how hard she tried. She stood up abruptly and crossed to the sink to rinse her mug. Well, she would just have to try harder. For Jennie's sake.

'Leave it,' he instructed, coming behind her and taking it. For a moment his long, strong fingers entwined with hers, a gentle gesture that for once appeared to offer no threat. She glanced up at him over her shoulder, about to protest that she was quite capable of doing it herself, but as their eyes met the words died in her throat. His look was fathoms deep and for a moment neither of them moved.

'I think I'd better go back to bed,' she said quickly, and wondered if that breathless little sound had really come from her. 'Thank you. . .for coming to. . .' She hesitated, unable to think of a word that would exactly cover the circumstances.

'To what?'

'To help,' she offered, with a little lift of the chin.

'Any time, Sophie. In fact, it's getting to be quite a habit.'

'A habit!' She repeated her words out loud as she lay in her bed. Anyone would think she was her own personal disaster area.

Despite his instruction to sleep, for a long time Sophie lay wakeful in the dark, forcing herself to remember just what had driven her over the edge of that cliff in a boiling red haze of rage. Making herself hate him.

CHAPTER SEVEN

CHAY's hand on her shoulder brought Sophie instantly awake, and she opened her eyes to find his dark tousled head above her. 'It's time to get up,' he said abruptly.

The light was pearl-soft. It was still very early and she was certain it was only a moment since she had closed her eyes. She groaned, remembering Tom's eagerness that she ride with him. 'What time is it?'

'You don't want to know that.'

'It's that early?'

'It'll be worth it,' he said crisply, as if he too regretted the closeness of their late-night tryst; as if he had also spent the intervening hours reminding himself just what had brought them together.

She struggled to sit up. 'Is that a promise?' she asked, smothering a yawn.

'You have my absolute guarantee. But you have just five minutes to get ready if you want to catch the sunrise from the ridge.'

'Five minutes?' She regarded him with rather less than amusement. 'As long as that? I could be ready for a party in five minutes.'

'Now, that I would pay to see,' he said, as she swung her feet to the floor, then Sophie blushed wide awake as she realised that she was freely offering him more of an eyeful than was entirely sensible in the circumstances. She made a grab for the cover and quickly hauled it up to her chin.

'What about Tom?' she asked sharply. 'Is he up?'

'He's downstairs having breakfast. We'll see you down at the stables. In five minutes.'

The second the door closed behind him she dashed to the bathroom to splash her face with cold water to finish the job of waking up. Then, pulling a soft cream shirt and a comfortable pair of dark red trousers from the wardrobe, she dressed quickly. It had not been an idle boast when she had said she could be ready for anything in five minutes. She had spent a year as a junior photographer on a provincial newspaper, where she had rapidly learned that if you didn't move fast, you didn't get your picture.

Chay straightened from adjusting Tom's stirrups as she hurried into the stable-yard and turned away to fetch a hard hat for her. 'Here.' He jammed it on her head. 'If you come off, it's like hitting concrete.' He fastened the hat beneath her chin, apparently unaware that his fingers were an exquisite torture against her neck. Or maybe he wasn't. Something seemed to happen to her skin whenever he touched it. It seemed to spark under his touch, come alive. Something he could hardly fail to be aware of. So much for her middle-of-the-night determination to keep a safe yard of distance between them.

The moment he had finished she turned away to make a fuss of Rowan, using the excuse of getting acquainted with the horse to cover the need to get her breathing back under control.

'Come on, Sophie, up you get,' he said impatiently, and she turned and placed her foot in his linked hands. He threw her up into the saddle, then adjusted the stirrups for her. She gathered in the reins and murmured a few crooning words in Rowan's ear as she walked her around the yard. Chay gave her a long hard look, then, apparently satisfied that she knew what she was doing, he mounted the huge bay gelding. 'Lead on, Tom,' he said.

Tom trotted confidently off, and Sophie watched

with considerable admiration. 'I thought he only got Melly a day or two ago?' she asked.

'She's not his first pony. His grandmother put him on a Shetland as soon as he could stand. Her own career as a three-day-eventer was cut short by an accident, but she's determined to have a Buchanan in the Olympic team. Since Matt and I refused to co-operate, she's turned her attention to Tom.'

'With some success, apparently.'

'We'll see. I was pretty keen until I reached my teens, but once I bought my first motorbike. . .' He shrugged.

She glanced at him, trying to imagine what he must have looked like astride a bike in close-fitting black leathers. Dangerous. 'And Matt?' she asked quickly.

'Once Matt discovered that girls love to be around horses he did spend an awful lot of time at the stables.' He grinned unexpectedly. 'But I'm afraid not very much of it was on a horse.'

'What. . .? Oh!'

He laughed as she blushed, then reached across and caught her arm. 'There, look.' As they crested the ridge and came alongside Tom the sun was rising, dripping gold, from the fairy-tale blue of the sea. They sat and watched in silence as the dark rocks and barren landscape turned to butter and honey about them.

'I think,' she murmured at last, 'that was the most beautiful sunrise I've ever seen.' But then everything seemed more focused since she had met Chay Buchanan. New-washed and crystal-bright.

The bay moved restlessly and they began to move on, walking the horses along the ridgeway path. 'You say that as if you'd seen the sun rise a hundred times. Do you make a habit of getting up before dawn?' Chay asked.

'I've been up before dawn working every day since I

came to Malta. It goes with the job. Sunrises over power stations, over sea-fronts, over municipal buildings, hotels—especially hotels, because there are fewer people about. I even took a photograph of that new hotel your company built. . .' Even as the words left her mouth she knew she had made a mistake.

'You have been busy,' he said, with just a touch of acid. 'What a pity you couldn't bring your camera with you today. You could have added "Sunrise over Chay Buchanan" to complete your portfolio.' Underlying the even tone there was steel in his voice, and suddenly the beauty of the morning turned to ashes.

'There's not enough light for a portrait,' she responded miserably. 'I hate using flash for faces.'

'I'm sure you could have forced yourself.'

'Whether I could have or not is surely all rather academic? You are not about to sit still while I take a photograph of you, at sunrise or any other time. Are you?'

'No, I'm not. But I very much doubt that you've forgotten why you're here. You're just biding your time, hoping that I will.'

He turned the bay gelding on to a path already taken by Tom, who hadn't been interested enough in the sunrise to linger. 'Stay close,' he warned, as he spurred the horse into a brisk canter.

Sophie almost laughed out loud. Did he really think she was crazy enough to try and escape on horseback? The hills were mined with old rabbit-warrens. One careless footstep and he would be forced to come to her aid yet again. Twice was more than enough.

She followed at a sedate trot, unwilling to risk life and limb on the unknown path, but as she approached a fork in the track Chay was waiting for her. Perfectly still, horse and man as one, looking out to sea. Only a playful breeze whipped up a lock of dark hair and winnowed the bay's mane to betray that the pair were not some lost heroic statue. Then he turned and the illusion evaporated.

'If you want me close, you'll have to slow down,' she said, trotting up alongside him.

'I thought you could ride,' he said witheringly. But he kept his impatient mount at walking pace as they waded, knee-deep at times, in acres of narcissus and euphorbia and blue borage. The next hour passed, it seemed to Sophie, with the speed of light, as he pointed out landmarks, including another tower, abandoned and crumbling, on a distant headland, built, he told her, by the knights to guard against the marauding galleys of their enemies.

Tom, who had trotted ahead most of the way, had dismounted and was waiting impatiently for them at the cliff-top path.

When he saw him, Chay swore softly and, tossing his reins to Sophie, swung from the saddle and strode across to the boy.

'Come away from there,' he commanded.

'But I wanted to show Sophie,' he said, his high voice carrying to her on the breeze. 'I wanted to tell her that this is where you and Uncle Matt used to race one another up the cliff. See,' he said. 'It's almost *exactly* where she was stuck.' And he pointed, too excited to see the shock whiten his father's face. He turned away from the edge and ran across to Sophie. 'Uncle Matt and Papa used to race each other up the cliff-face at the beginning of every summer holidays. Grandma told me. Come and look.' He tugged at her hand.

Grandma, Sophie thought privately, as she slipped from the saddle, must have been mad. The boy clearly couldn't wait to try it for himself. 'They must have been a lot older than you,' she observed, forcing her voice to remain calm, even though her entire body seemed to be trembling at the thought of him climbing down that dreadful rockface.

'Papa was ten and Uncle Matt was nine,' he said proudly.

'You've a few years before you try, then,' she said, trying to keep her voice a great deal calmer than she was feeling at the thought of his small, infinitely fragile body being battered against those rocks. 'Even Uncle Matt waited until he was nine,' she reminded him.

But his face was set in a dangerously truculent expression at the thought of waiting. 'I'm going to do it before then,' he said, with determination.

Sophie glanced across at Chay, who was rigid with shock as he stared at the boy. 'I think you'd better go back to the stables, Tom,' she said quickly. 'Twany will help you with Melly.' She gave him a leg up and watched for a moment as he trotted down the hill. Then she tethered the two horses to a nearby bush and walked across to Chay.

'I had no idea he knew. She must have told him when she was over here for Easter. It explains the sudden interest. . .' He sank on to a rock. 'I cannot believe that my mother could be so stupid. To fill his head with such rubbish.'

'He seems to set a lot of store by what his Uncle Matt did,' Sophie said carefully, as she lowered herself beside him.

'My mother is always telling Tom stories about the things Matt used to get up to, and heaven knows there's plenty to tell. But this. . .' He turned to her. 'How could she?'

'Because she missed him.' Her parents talked about Jennie all the time. Not how clever she was, or how pretty, but the crazy things she had done. The endless times they had been called to school to listen to the

Head's complaints about her wildness. The hours they had waited for the police to find them when Jennie had insisted they must prove themselves by spending the night in a deserted house. . . As if, by recalling the times when it had all turned out happily, they might make it happen again. She shook the thought away. 'What happened to him, Chay?'

'He. . .fell.'

'Fell?' She stared at him in growing horror as she followed his blank stare. 'Down there?'

His face was bleak as he stared out at the sea. 'It was the best part of seven years ago. The twenty-seventh of October.'

'What was he doing on the cliff?' she asked. 'The pair of you must surely have grown out of such craziness by then?'

'Must we?' he replied tersely. Then, realising that this was hardly an explanation, he shrugged. 'We'd been coming to Malta for the summer holidays for as long as I can remember. Dad was in the Navy, based here in Malta at one time. He bought a long lease on the tower and did it up as a holiday base. "Doing the cliff" became a part of the holiday. A nightmare to overcome before you could enjoy the weeks of freedom.'

'I don't understand. . .'

'You can get to the bottom of the cliff from the beach, if you climb over a few rocks and don't mind getting a bit wet. There's a cave there and one day we'd been exploring it. When it was time to go back Matt challenged me to climb out. I told him he was mad, but Matt said I was just scared, and set off on his own. I was older, responsible for him, so I couldn't let him go on his own.' His mouth tightened. 'And I was damned if I was going to let him beat me.' He glanced at her with a little start, almost as if he had forgotten she was there and he was talking to himself. 'I should have done, of course. Then it would all have been over.'

'And he would have crowed all summer,' she said, her warm grey eyes deep with understanding

'It shouldn't have mattered, Sophie.'

'When you're ten years old, Chay, you don't know that.'

He stared at her with something like surprise that she should understand. 'I suppose not. Anyway, that was the start of it. Stupid, dangerous, intensely competitive. Looking back, I'm amazed that neither of us had been killed, or at the very least seriously hurt, before.'

'Why didn't your parents stop you?' Sophie asked in amazement.

'Father died when I was nine, in a car accident, and Mother didn't know we were doing it. At least, not at first, and when she found out she just laughed. It proved we were strong and gutsy. She liked that. Matt took his dare-devil madness from her. And, anyway, it had become a sort of ritual, the first thing we did when we came back every year.'

'But surely you weren't *still* doing it?' she asked. The very thought of a world-renowned novelist risking his life in such a manner was surreal.

'No. I hadn't been to Malta in three or four years. But Matt was living here then. Running a wind-surfing club in summer, painting in the winter.' He glanced across at her. 'Those panels in the bedroom are his.'

'They are very beautiful,' she said quietly.

He searched her face, saw that she meant it and nodded. 'I'd won some literary prize that year and the whole world wanted me. I'd been doing the lecture circuit—the States, Australia, the Far East. I don't know how many thousands of miles I covered. I wrote to ask Matt if I could come for a couple of months before starting the new book.' He caught her questioning look and shrugged. 'A courtesy. We bought the lease jointly from Mother when she decided the tower was too much to cope with, but it was Matt's home. When I arrived he was in a really stupid mood. On a sort of high. I should have recognised the symptoms; he was always like that when he had a secret.' He paused. 'I'd been travelling for the best part of twenty-four hours and all I wanted was to crash out, but Matt had other ideas. I had hardly stepped over the threshold before he threw down the challenge to "do the cliff".

'I told him to forget it. Neither of us had climbed the thing in five years, and I was certainly in no shape to attempt it. But he wouldn't let it rest. He said I wouldn't do it because I knew he could beat me. I told him to consider it a fact.'

Sophie felt her heart turn over with pity. She knew what it was like to be the one always following in her brilliant sister's footsteps. 'He must have been very jealous of you,' she said, with feeling.

'I don't think I had realised how much until then. The stupid thing was that I had always envied him his ability to paint. I had offered to arrange an exhibition. . .but he reckoned his pictures would only sell as curiosities because he was my brother. He was wrong.'

He was quiet for a long time and Sophie said nothing, remembering her own dogged determination to copy everything her sister did, and Jennie cruelly leading her into dangers she had been ill-equipped to deal with. She had broken her leg the year they were sixteen, putting her horse to an impossibly high fence that Jennie had cleared with ease. She had spent months with her leg in plaster, coming to terms with the truth that it could just as easily have been her neck. She had grown up that summer, and when her sister had gone on to play new and even more dangerous games she had finally been able to resist the temptation to play follow-my-leader. But she had always blamed herself for not being there when her sister had needed her.

'Did you climb it with him?' she asked eventually, to blot out unhappy thoughts of her own.

He too seemed to come back from a long distance inside his head. 'No. The fact that I simply didn't care was like waving a red rag in front of a bull. He was determined to show me. And he was good. He was fit from wind-surfing all summer. The only exercise I'd had was flapping my mouth. Then, just before the ledge, he seemed to get stuck, and shouted for me to come and give him a hand.' Chay's skin was a sickly grey. 'I. . .I thought he was just fooling. Trying to get me on to the cliff-face so that he could race on and beat me. By the time I realised and tried to reach him it was too late. I just wasn't fast enough. . .'

He stood up abruptly and crossed to the edge, and stared down into the abyss. Feeling slightly sick, Sophie watched him. Then, to her relief, he turned away and walked back to the horses and freed the reins. She felt bitter shame at the horror he must have felt when he saw her perched upon the ledge. She wanted to say how sorry she was, but his expression did not invite the unburdening of her own guilt.

But there was something. 'Chay?' she said, as they made their way down the hill.

'What is it?'

'Does Tom know how. . .?' She stopped as something clicked in her brain.

'How Matt died?' he finished for her. 'No,' he said, then, as he saw her brow furrowed in deep concentration, he frowned. 'I'll tell him what happened when he's old enough to understand.'

'He's very headstrong. I'm not sure you've time to let him grow up. I believe you should tell him as soon as possible,' she advised.

'Do you? And do you suggest I include the part where I was too stupid to see that Matt was in trouble until it was too late to help?' he demanded harshly.

Her heart almost broke for him. Impulsively she reached across to touch his hand. 'Don't blame yourself for what happened. Matt knew the risk.' So had Jennie. The words jumped into her brain. Jennie had chosen to live dangerously. She could come home any time she wanted to. All it took was courage.

'Matt never considered the risk in anything,' he said coldly. Then he turned to her, and she flinched at the chill in his eyes. 'And I seem to be developing the same careless habit. The longer I keep you here, the more you learn about me, my family.'

'Then perhaps you should let me go right now.'

'No. After next weekend it won't matter. You'll stay until then.'

She was still washing up the breakfast things when there was a ring at the doorbell.

Chay answered it and came back with an attractive woman, somewhere in her late thirties. 'Here you are, Gian, this is Sophie,' Chay introduced her. 'You can see for yourself that I'm not working her to death.'

'Chay!' Gian protested. 'I never said——'

'Gian is Paul Manduca's wife, Sophie. I believe he's sent her to check up on me.'

'What utter nonsense,' she retorted, taking Sophie's hastily wiped hand. 'How are you? Quite recovered from your fall, I hope?' Sophie was aware that Chay was extracting a certain sardonic amusement from the way Gian was sizing her up, trying to work out precisely what their relationship was.

'I'm fine now, thank you,' Sophie reassured the woman. 'I could leave any time,' she added pointedly.

'But I understood that you were staying for a while?'

'You understood correctly, Gian,' Chay intervened smoothly.

'I'm so glad. Theresa is wonderful, of course, but getting on. She was Maria's nurse, you know.' She looked quickly at Chay, clearly afraid that she had said something indiscreet. But there was no reaction beyond a slight tightening of his jaw that only the closest watcher would have detected. 'Tom needs someone younger around him. And that's the reason for my call.' She turned to Chay. 'I do wish you would get a telephone installed, Chay, it would make invitations so much easier.'

Chay's expression suggested that he was not impressed by this argument. 'You can always call me at my office.'

'But you're not at your office, Chay,' she pointed out, and turned back to Sophie. 'I'm taking the children out this afternoon for a treat before the school holidays end, and I wondered if you and Tom would like to join us? I know how busy Chay always is. At least——' she glanced a little shyly at him '—he is usually busy. But since he's not working today, maybe you have something else planned?' She arched a dark questioning brow.

'No, nothing at all.' Sophie studiously avoided Chay's eyes, certain they would contain a warning. 'And I'm sure Tom would love to have some other children to play with,' she said. 'Where are you thinking of going?'

'Nothing too exciting. A boat trip round the harbour, perhaps, and then ices in Sliema.'

'If you'd like a boat trip, Gian, why don't you let me take you out? I'm sure we could find somewhere more entertaining than a tourist trip around the habour,' Chay intervened.

Gian turned to him in surprise. 'Oh, but, Chay, the children love it, and besides, you will be so bored with just women and children for company,' she protested.

'Nonsense. I can't think of any company more charming. Sophie will make us a picnic and we'll go over to Comino and swim in the lagoon. What do you say, Sophie?'

She chose to ignore his infuriatingly smug expression at having checked any opportunity to stray from his control with such ease. 'That sounds like fun,' she agreed. 'I haven't had a chance to swim in the blue lagoon.' She smiled with her teeth. 'Only take photographs.'

'You have a camera?' Gian asked with interest. 'Will you bring it and take some photographs of the children for us?' She pulled a face. 'I'm hopeless. I always manage to cut off the important bits whenever I try.'

'Sophie's camera is out of action, Gian.'

'Oh, what a pity,' Gian said, then brightened. 'It doesn't matter, I'll bring mine along.'

Aware of Chay's eyes narrowing dangerously, Sophie quickly moved on to the subject of the picnic. 'Now, is there anything your children don't like to eat?' she asked.

'Very little,' Gian assured her with feeling, and, after a few moments discussing arrangements for the afternoon, she left.

'Don't get any smart ideas about taking a photograph of me or Tom,' Chay warned as Sophie returned to the kitchen, having seen the other woman to her car.

'I'm fresh out of smart ideas,' she snapped, 'or I wouldn't be here.'

'Maybe. But, just in case, I shall take the films to have them developed.'

'Whatever you say,' she agreed sweetly. 'I'm sure Gian will appreciate the gesture.' Then, rather more tartly, she added, 'I do hope you're getting a good discount for bulk.' She didn't wait for his reply, but turned her attention to the preparation of the picnic, slamming the food angrily upon the table.

'Are you cross with me, Sophie?' Tom asked.

She had been so wound up with temper that she hadn't noticed Tom's huge eyes. 'Oh, Tom. No, darling.' She put her arm around him and hugged him. 'Come and help me get the picnic ready.' And a few minutes later she breathed a huge sigh of relief as she heard the front door close behind Chay as he left for the yacht club to fetch the boat.

Chay was already down at the boat, packing away the food when Gian arrived with her children just after two o'clock, and she was not alone.

'Sophie, this is Cesare. My little brother. He flew in this morning so I brought him along. I hope you don't mind.'

Gian's brother was hardly little. He didn't quite have the stature or maturity of Chay, but he had the 'knock 'em dead' good looks of so many young Italian men. And he clearly knew it. He immediately stepped forward and took Sophie's hand very tenderly in his.

'Sophie,' he murmured, dripping Latin charm. 'What a beautiful name.'

Sophie caught her lower lip between her teeth in an effort to stifle a giggle. 'Of course I don't mind, Gian,' she said. But she wondered what Chay's reaction would be.

'I thought he would be company for Chay,' Gian added, looking around. 'Where is he?'

'Down at the boat. We'd better join him.'

Tom led the way, leaping down steps that had been hewn from the living rock to the small jetty that lay adjacent to a delightfully sheltered curve of beach nestling beneath the tower. Gian followed, leading her youngest by the hand, and Cesare insisted upon taking Sophie's arm and helping her down.

As he swung the children aboard, Chay's impassive gaze followed them along the jetty and Sophie profoundly wished that Cesare would stop treating her like a piece of precious china.

'Cesare,' Chay acknowledged the man briefly. 'Good to see you. Will you get the rope?'

'Scusi. . .' he murmured, as with the utmost reluctance he surrendered her hand to go to the front of the boat.

Chay hadn't given any indication as to the type of boat he owned, but if Sophie had had the time to wonder about it, she would have assumed something sleek and expensive, rather like the car he had driven away in earlier in the day. Certainly not the workmanlike vessel that was tied up alongside the jetty. A decommissioned Navy patrol boat, it hardly came into the usual category of rich men's toys.

'Not quite what you were expecting?' he asked, apparently able to read her mind with disconcerting ease and amused at what he found there.

'On the contrary,' she snapped back. 'It's fast and dangerous. Exactly like its owner.'

He held out his hand to help her and she had little choice but to lean briefly on him as she jumped down, but as she tried to withdraw her fingers his hand closed fast around them. 'I'm very glad you realise that, Sophie Nash,' he murmured, so softly that only she could hear. 'It would be a mistake to underestimate me. Or to think you have found a champion.' His eyes strayed to the figure impatiently holding the rope at the fore.

She raised her brows a fraction. She hadn't thought of Cesare as a champion. He caught her look. 'I'm not fooled by those innocent grey eyes of yours, Sophie. But Cesare might be. He doesn't know you the way I do.'

'You don't know me, Chay.'

'I'll be the judge of that. Help Gian to fasten these, will you?' he said, thrusting a pile of orange lifejackets at her, and retired to the wheelhouse. 'Let her go, Cesare,' he called.

Gian's children, slightly in awe of Chay, were quiet on the journey, but the moment they were set free to splash in the warm, turquoise-blue water they forgot their shyness and the noise-level rose dramatically.

The children swam for a while in the brilliant water, only Gian's little two-year-old needing armbands. When they had had enough they flopped on to the beach, and Gian produced sun-block and proceeded to cover her children with it. Sophie followed suit, rubbing some of her own on to Tom's shoulders, despite his squirming protestations that he didn't like it.

'Be still, Tom,' Sophie warned him. 'You don't want to burn.'

'It's goopy,' Tom answered, pulling a face. 'You don't have cream on your back.'

'Of course I do,' she replied firmly.

Cesare dropped to his knees beside her. 'May I do this for you?' he said. 'Your skin is so fair. You must be careful not to burn.'

About to say that she had covered herself with sun-block before leaving the house, she caught Chay's warning look.

'Thank you, Cesare,' she said, handing him the bottle with a smile. 'If you could just rub a little on my back.' And she lifted the heavy weight of her hair and twisted it and held it to her crown, her arms provocatively raised.

Gian called, and Tom took his chance to escape and play with the other children, leaving her to suffer the tender ministrations of Cesare, under Chay's menacing eye.

'The straps, *cara*. . .' he murmured apologetically, as he smoothed the cream into her shoulders. 'They are. . .in the way.' She wondered just how many times he had used that helpless little boy technique to ease down a bathing suit that was 'in the way'.

'It's all right,' she said quickly.

'Nonsense,' Chay intervened, throwing a dark shadow between herself and the sun. 'You must protect yourself properly. Here. Give it to me.' Cesare hesitated for a moment, then reluctantly surrendered the sun-block to the imperious hand. 'Your sister needs a little help,' he said, and Cesare was effectively dismissed. He turned and walked stiffly away and Sophie felt rather sorry for him.

'That was unkind,' Sophie chided.

'No, it wasn't. You were being unkind.' And she gasped as he jerked down the soft wide straps of her swimsuit to leave her shoulders quite naked. Then his long, sensitive fingers began to smooth the cool cream into the nape of her neck.

For the past four days, whenever she had been in his company, she had been aware of her body in a way that was new and rather frightening. It was as if the air between them was a conductor, carrying a tiny current of electricity from him to charge her skin and make it tingle.

Now his touch, gentle as a butterfly's kiss, concentrated that charge, and her eyes closed tight and her hands curled into clenched little fists as she fought back the urgent need to complain when his hands moved away from their teasing caress of the skin at her nape. Then the flat of his palm stroked a broad path across her shoulders, before sliding down her back to coat her warm skin with the cream, and she was unable to prevent a gentle sigh escaping her lips.

'Back done,' he said, and she twisted around on the warm sand to face him.

'Thank you,' she offered, a little unsteadily, reaching for her cream.

But he refused to surrender it. 'I haven't finished.' She watched, mesmerised, as he tipped the cream on to his fingers. Then he reached out, and in one fluid movement smoothed it into her throat and down the gentle rise of her breasts until the top of her swimsuit brought him to a halt. For a moment she thought he wouldn't stop there, would simply push the soft fabric away to reveal the tight buds thrusting eagerly against her suit. And the warmth she felt was nothing to do with the sun. It came from deep inside her, forcing her to acknowledge that she wanted him to do that more than anything else in the world.

'Chay.' She murmured his name, closing her eyes, quite lost to shame. It was madness to let him touch her like this. But a quite delightful madness.

'Now it's my turn,' he said, and her eyes snapped wide open as the derisory edge to his voice brought her back from the brink. . .

'You don't need sun-block,' she said quickly, her voice not quite her own. 'You're too dark to burn.'

'It doesn't do to be careless,' he reminded her softly, taking her hand and squeezing cream into the palm. 'Shoulders first, I think, don't you? Make a thorough job of it—I want Cesare to be quite sure that you're unavailable.'

And he presented her with his straight, well-muscled

back and waited. It was agony. She wanted to touch him, stroke him, smooth her hands over his skin. But she was angry too. After a moment he turned his head.

'A man could burn while you're thinking about it,' he said.

'Is that so?' She slapped the cream on to his back, taking some satisfaction from making him jump for a change, rubbing vigorously in all directions, determined not to let her mind know what her hands were thinking as they plied his warm skin and felt the muscle-packed flesh contract beneath her fingers. But his skin was like warm silk, and her hand gradually slowed to a gentle caress as a delicious languor seemed to seep through her body. 'Can I have some more cream?' she asked. Then looked up, to find herself being regarded with disconcerting intensity.

'I think you've had quite enough for a public place,' he said, rising to his feet and dropping the bottle beside her. Then he walked into the water. Angrily she tugged the straps of her costume back into place, glaring at him as he sliced vigorously through the water. Then, realising what he had said, horrified at her own lack of self-control, she looked around, expecting to be the object of a row of dark, accusing eyes.

CHAPTER EIGHT

THE beach was deserted. Sophie leapt to her feet in a sudden panic. Where on earth had everyone disappeared to? Then she caught a glimpse of Gian and Cesare, their hands full of ice-cream cones, as, Pied Piper-like, they made their way down to the cove with an eager band of children at their heels.

She hurried to help. 'I'm sorry, Gian,' she said. 'I would have come with you if you'd said. . .'

'You were busy. And Cesare helped,' she said, handing out the cones to the children and warning them not to drop them in the sand. She glanced at the figure in the water. 'Could you eat two? I'm afraid that Chay's will have run to liquid by the time he's. . . cooled off,' she continued innocently.

As good as her word, Gian had brought along her camera and a couple of films. Sophie took a number of shots of the children paddling and playing a game of French cricket that Chay organised. Cesare kept his distance, restricting himself to long, passionate glances when he thought Chay wasn't looking.

As they settled down for tea she began to snap away at them to use up the remainder of the second roll. Tom turned to Chay to offer him an apple. As she focused on the boy Chay leaned into the shot. It was so natural, so charming a scene, that she had taken it before she had time to consider the wisdom of defying him. For a moment she held her breath, but he hadn't noticed, and she quickly moved the camera on to a safer target. But he had not forgotten his warning and when they were packing up Chay picked up the films.

'Give them to me,' Gian said firmly, scooping them from his hand before he could prevent her. 'I have to go into town tomorrow. It only takes a day to get them developed, you know. I'll get you copies of any that you want.'

For just a moment Chay hesitated, but he made no objection, simply shrugged. 'Fine. Bring them over when you come to the party on Saturday. We'll have a look then.'

'How are the preparations going?' she asked.

'I've barely started,' Sophie confessed. 'I'll have to make the cake tomorrow.'

Gian grinned sympathetically. 'Shall I take Tom home with me?' she offered. 'He can spend the day with us tomorrow and give you a clear run at it. You can come over in the evening to collect him and have supper with us.'

'I know he'd love to,' Sophie said, but doubted that Chay would let his little gaoler out of her sight.

She was wrong. 'Sounds like a good idea, if it's not too much for you, Gian?'

'I won't notice another one,' she laughed. 'Cesare can help. And Paul's home tomorrow. He's got a long weekend.'

'Then tell him to save Saturday to give me a hand, will you? He has more experience of dealing with vast quantities of children than I have.'

'How many are you expecting?'

'Hundreds,' Chay said.

'Sixteen,' Sophie amended. 'His entire class at school, apparently. And your children, of course.'

'Then we'll both come early and give you a hand,' Gian promised.

'Won't you bring Cesare?' she asked, unable to resist annoying Chay. The younger man's eyes brightened at this encouragement.

'I have to return to duty, Saturday night,' he murmured. 'But perhaps dinner, this evening. . .?'

She shook her head quickly, hoping that Chay hadn't heard.

After they had all gone it suddenly seemed very quiet. It made Sophie nervous. She had suggested that Tom was an inadequate chaperon. But when he was there she felt. . .safer. But after her reaction when Chay had covered her with the sun-block. . .

'I'm going to take the boat back to the marina and pick up the car,' Chay said, as she was clearing away the picnic debris. 'You'd better come with me.'

'What's this? Parole?'

'I'll feel safer with you under my eye. I'm certainly not leaving you here to keep an assignation with Cesare.'

'I haven't. . .'

He made a dismissive gesture. 'I saw that little whispered interchange before they left. What did you arrange?'

'Nothing!'

'No? You're very edgy.'

'How kind of you to notice. What a pity you are less astute about the reason.'

His forehead creased in a frown. 'It makes no difference. Cesare will think of some excuse to return.'

She glared at him. 'I have to organise dinner.'

'We'll eat out,' he snapped. 'Can you be ready in half an hour?' He held up a hand before she could protest. 'My apologies. I forgot, temporarily, that in five minutes you can be ready for anything.'

'But not twice in one day.' And she stormed up to her room to stand under a cool shower until her skin tingled and she had regained control of her temper. Although as she dried herself she acknowledged with a certain wryness that the touch of one man had more to do with the way her body glowed than the effects of the sun and the needle-sharp shower together.

She dropped the towel and turned to the mirror, lifting her hand hesitantly to her breast. She drew her fingers lightly across the slight swell of her cleavage, wondering what it would be like to be crushed naked against his chest, to be made love to by a man like Chay Buchanan. Gian had seen Chay's response to Cesare and misunderstood. She had thought that by whisking Tom away for the night she was conspiring to aid romance. Offering two adults who desired each other the perfect end to the perfect day. And it would have been. She knew that. If only it were that simple.

How pleased Nigel would be if he knew how well his perverted little plan was going. The thought sickened her. Because between the nightmare, when she had woken in his arms, and this moment, something had happened. She didn't quite know what. Only that one perfect night with Chay Buchanan would almost certainly break her heart.

She shook her head and, realising with a shock how the time was flying by, grabbed her hair-drier.

She made it with a minute to spare, flying down the stairs, only to come to an abrupt halt two steps up as she saw that he was waiting for her, staring somewhere into space, his hands thrust deep into the pockets of his trousers. He turned as he heard her, and paused for just a moment. And, just for a moment, the dangerous thrill as she caught the widening of his eyes was worth the effort she had made.

She had applied the merest touch of make-up to skin already golden from days in the sun; to eyes made startlingly large with a touch of shadow and a whisper of mascara; to a full mouth that now smiled with a lip-gloss echoing the vivid pink in the print of her full-skirted sundress, its fitted bodice crossing her back in a pair of lattice straps. She had tied her hair back with a scarf and a white linen blazer hung from one hand.

His expression was quickly cloaked. 'You barely made it,' he said, without comment on her appearance.

But she didn't need the words. She had seen his eyes. And, as they made their way down to the jetty, she remembered the shocking kiss that neither of them had wanted. . .and that neither of them had been quite able to resist.

Chay jumped down into the boat, then turned to lift her in, holding her for a moment, suspended in his arms. Sophie, already vulnerable to this man's deadly attraction, felt her lips soften and part under the strong tug of desire. He must know, must feel the wild beating of her pulse as he held her.

The temptation to melt into his arms and take him with her was almost unbearable. Then Nigel's smug smile intervened. This was what he wanted. And afterwards he would want chapter and verse. She pushed herself away and stepped back, breathing a little heavily but infinitely safter on her own feet. 'I think I'll stay out here for a while,' she said quickly.

'It'll be chilly once we're moving,' he objected abruptly, and, taking her arm, led the way to the wheelhouse.

They covered the distance to Sliema at a seemingly breathless rate of knots, while Chay explained the radar and the radio with a briskness that she could not help but envy. Her own feelings were much harder to control. Perched on a high stool beside him, she found her eyes constantly wandering from the instruments to dwell instead on the strong line of his jaw, the passionate curve of his mouth.

He had kissed her. Thrilled her. But she suspected that those angry kisses were simply a foretaste of the pleasure that he might bestow in return for total surrender. He turned and caught her look.

'You're not paying attention,' he said, a little fiercely.

'I. . .I'm sorry.'

'Not half as sorry as you're going to be if you keep looking at me like that.'

'Chay,' she begged, her eyes wide.

'Sophie.' He mimicked her cruelly.

She shot out of her seat to drag in great lungfuls of fresh air, and by the time he had slipped the boat into its berth she was feeling steadier. But he wasn't about to let the matter drop.

'Do you want to tell me about it?' he demanded, as they made their way along the decking to the shore, passing row upon row of expensive and beautiful yachts and powerboats.

'I don't understand.'

'Yes, you do. You're not a child. You're flashing out unmistakable signals. Good God, I could have undressed you on the beach this afternoon and you wouldn't have cared if the Royal Marine Band had been playing a tune while I did it.'

Colour stained her cheeks, but, unable to deny it, she kept her eyes fixed ahead of her, unable to meet his, although she knew he was looking at her with a slightly perplexed expression.

'I don't mean to be a tease. Truly.' Her colour deepened. 'I'm not normally quite so. . .excitable. I'm afraid it's you, Chay.' It was a painful admission.

They had reached his car. He said nothing while he unlocked it and helped her in. But his fingers didn't linger on her arm. The sun had gone and it would soon be dark, but it was stifling inside the car. He lowered the windows then turned to her.

'But?' He refused to let it drop. 'With you there always seems to be a "but".'

'Of course there's a "but". Do you expect me to fall into your bed?'

'Have I asked you to?' His jaw tightened convulsively, and she shook her head. 'But you wish I would?'

Was it that simple for him? 'Wouldn't Poppy object?'

'Poppy?'

'It was three o'clock when you came home last night.'

'Was it?' His eyes gleamed dangerously in the near darkness.

'Well, you hadn't been to bed. . .'

'No,' he agreed. 'I hadn't.' He reached forward and started the engine, reversing the sleek dark shape of the Lotus Esprit out of its parking space and heading towards the town, where the shops had opened for the evening and the streets were filling with people out to enjoy a walk along the promenade.

'Chay,' she said suddenly, relieved to have something, anything, to break the awkward silence. 'Can you take me to a toyshop?'

He threw her an exasperated glance. 'A toyshop?'

'I'd like to get Tom a present for his birthday.'

'You don't have to——'

'I would like to.' Then she bit her lip. 'But. . .'

'But?' he repeated, dangerously.

'I'm afraid you'll have to lend me the money, until you give me back my bag.'

His face darkened, but he executed a sharp turn and drove up into the town, braking sharply in front of a store. It didn't take long to find exactly what she was looking for. A pair of cap-firing six-guns in a holster.

'What do you think?' she asked.

'I think. . .that he'll love them.' He looked around. 'Theresa left some money for Tom to choose something

for himself, but I think I'll get that stetson to go with
the guns.'

'What have you bought him?' she asked.

'He needed new tack for Melly.'

'Oh,' she said, as she waited for him to pay for her
purchases.

'Oh, what?' he demanded, then followed her eye
and saw the cowboy outfit hanging on a stand. 'You
think he should have something to unwrap on the big
day?' She didn't answer. 'We'll take that, too,' he told
the assistant.

'Thank you,' she said, as he stowed the packages in
the car.

He looked up and met her eyes across the roof of
the car. 'Well, now that my son is about to achieve his
wildest dreams, do you think we could do something
about mine?' He smiled slightly as a slow flush crept
across Sophie's cheeks. 'I was actually thinking about
dinner,' he murmured.

Overcome by confusion, she ducked into the car.
'Where are we going?'

'The Barracuda, at St Julian's Bay.'

'Oh, yes, I know it.

'Have you been there?' She shook her head; she
hadn't, although she had passed the spot frequently.
The bay was always full of *dghajsa*, the colourful boats
painted with the eye of Osiris to ward off the evil eye,
but now the sea was dark, only visible because of the
reflection of lights from the buildings that piled almost
on top of one another at the water's edge.

They parked a little way from the restaurant, and
when Chay took her hand to help her out of the car he
did not surrender it, but kept it tucked in his, and
Sophie didn't dare pull away.

The restaurant was perched precariously on a sharp
bend, hanging out over the harbour with steps that led

directly down into the sea like a smuggler's haunt.
'This is lovely,' Sophie exclaimed as she took in the
warm, intimate atmosphere, the only lighting the glow
from candles at the small tables.

'Two martinis please, George, and a table looking
out over the harbour.'

George swept them to a table by the window, quickly
whisking away the 'Reserved' sign and placing it on
another near by. He brought their drinks and a menu,
and lingered to discuss the choice of food and wine
with Chay. Sophie sipped her drink and stared out at
the lights of the shipping on the horizon, leaving Chay
to choose for her. 'You're not allergic to seafood are
you, Sophie?' he asked. She shook her head and he
ordered for them both.

She felt odd. Light-headed. Maybe it was too much
sun, but she didn't think so. She felt drawn by his eyes
upon her and turned to face him. Her heart turned
over, like a puppy rolling on to its back to have its
tummy tickled. No, it definitely wasn't too much sun.

'Tell me about your family,' he said, twisting his
glass between his long fingers. 'You've told me about
Jennie, but what about your parents?'

'My father is an art teacher at a comprehensive
school a few miles from our home, my mother works
part-time as a secretary. We're very ordinary people.'

'No boyfriend?'

'No one special.'

'No?' There was an edge to his voice. 'What about
the journalist you wanted the photograph for? I
thought you said that he was "very special".'

She recalled her angry declaration that first night of
her captivity. 'Nigel is. . .' Quite suddenly she wanted
to spill out the whole truth. Unburden herself. But if
she told him what had really happened when Nigel
came to the tower he would never believe that she

wasn't up to her eyes in something too nasty for words, and she wouldn't blame him. 'I can't explain.'

'You don't have to explain anything to me, Sophie. I'm the last person to pry into someone else's business,' he said. But she could almost hear the shutters slamming down.

'No. . .' she protested, but he had already turned away from her as George arrived with dishes piled with huge prawns sautéed in their shells.

And what was the point of protesting that he had misunderstood? She could never tell him. She took a large gulp of her martini. It bit like fire at the back of her throat and she gasped. By the time she had recovered the prawns had been served, and she was able to devote her full attention to the task of dismembering them. Perhaps, after all, it was better if he thought she had someone else. Safer.

'The prawns are delicious,' she said at last, in an attempt to break the uncomfortable silence.

'Have you finished?'

She glanced at her plate, surprised to find a pile of debris. She had hardly noticed that she was eating. 'Yes, thank you.'

His glance brought George to clear away. 'So,' he said briskly. 'You'd better tell me what's happening tomorrow.'

And they spent the rest of the meal discussing the arrangements for Tom's beanfeast.

It was odd, she thought, as they drove home in silence, the haunting strains of Sinatra in September mood filling the gap in the conversation, but when Chay had withdrawn from her, the uncomfortable need he had woken in her had seemed to fade. She risked a sideways glance at the hard profile, dark against the dim lights from the dashboard. Could it be that it wasn't just her? That the charge of desire was a two-way circuit and, when he had misunderstood about Nigel, he had somehow broken the connection? It was all very confusing.

He drew up outside the tower and opened the door for her. 'I'll go and put the car away.'

'Do you want coffee?' she asked.

He shook his head. 'No, thanks.' His voice did not encourage her to linger.

'Then I'll see you in the morning.'

But she was in no hurry for bed. Despite her long day she knew she wouldn't sleep. She was still sitting at her dressing-table, brushing her hair, when there was a light tap at the door.

'Sophie?' Chay's voice was muffled through the heavy timber.

'Hold on,' she called, and flew to wrap herself in her flimsy gown before turning the key in the lock and opening the door.

'Was that to keep me out, or you in?' he asked. She didn't answer. She didn't know what had prompted her to turn the key in the lock.

'What do you want?' she demanded.

He thrust her camera bag at her. 'I want you to go. Now.'

'Go?' She stared uncomprehendingly at the bag, then raised her eyes to his. 'That's it?'

'Isn't that enough?'

'No. It's not nearly enough. You keep me here for days against my will, then choose to throw me out in the middle of the night without so much as an apology?'

His eyes darkened slightly, he took a step forward and a frisson of excitment bubbled in her blood. 'An apology?' he demanded. 'What, precisely, should I apologise for?'

Her pulse picked up a beat. This was better. For the last two hours, while he had been polite but withdrawn, she had felt as flat as punched dough. Now suddenly she felt alive again. 'Give me half an hour and I'll write a list,' she offered.

'Don't bother.'

'I won't!'

For a moment they stood facing each other a little breathlessly. 'You'd better pack your things and go before I change my mind.' He turned and began to walk away.

'Right now?' she enquired disbelievingly.

He was back at her side in a single stride, her arm firmly grasped in his hand. 'Damn you, Sophie, but you play dangerous games.'

For a moment she stared at his hand, then quite deliberately raised her eyes to hold his glance. 'Do I?' The question was rhetorical. She knew she was playing with fire, but she couldn't help herself. 'I'm glad to have my freedom, Chay, but it's a little late to do anything about it right now.'

'There are plenty of hotels.'

'Dozens! I should know! But if you want me to leave right this minute, I have to tell you that you still have my suitcase under lock and key!'

An explosive rush of air expelled between his teeth was a warning that she had gone too far. 'Then let's get it. I wouldn't want anything to keep you.' He caught her hand and hauled her after him, up the stairs to the second floor. He reached up and took the key from above the ledge.

'That's what happened to the key,' she said, the words startled from her.

'You didn't expect me to leave it about after you admitted snooping?'

'That was the first place I looked,' she said furiously, then stepped over the threshold. Unlike the floor below there were no dividing walls. It was just one massive room. An artist's studio. Sleeping and work-space in one. Left just as it had been the last time it had been used, a half finished canvas was still propped against an easel. A portrait of a girl. Brushes and paints were heaped anyhow on a work-table. 'This was Matt's room,' she said.

She picked up the photographs of Maria from among the debris. It was the one that had been in Chay's desk.

'The door is locked to keep Tom out. He broke the glass in that photograph and cut himself a few months ago.'

'I see.' She replaced the frame very carefully. 'Will you ever tell him?'

His eyes narrowed, dangerously. 'Tell him?'

She lifted her chin very slightly. 'Will you ever tell Tom that Matt is his father?'

'It was this morning, wasn't it?' he said slowly. 'When we were out riding? I saw something in your face and I had an idea then that I'd said too much.'

'It took me a while to figure it out, Chay, but the dates didn't add up. You didn't arrive in Malta until late in October. Tom was born in April.'

'He could have been premature.'

'You buried your brother, comforted your mother, rushed back, wooed and won Maria and produced a son all within seven months? I said you were fast, Chay. But even you would be hard-pressed to achieve that schedule.'

'Haven't you overlooked the fact that Maria might already have been part of my life?'

'Have I?' she asked. 'I don't think so. You had been away from the island for four years.' Her eyes returned to the photograph of Maria. She could hardly have been more than eighteen or nineteen years old. 'I think Maria would still have been in school then.'

'Did I really tell you all that?' Sophie didn't answer. She didn't really think he wanted her to.

'I wouldn't ever betray you, Chay.' She glanced at him. 'I don't suppose you have any reason to believe that. But it's true, none the less.'

'I don't think you would do anything to hurt Tom,' he said carefully.

'I wouldn't do anything to hurt either of you,' she said, without hesitation. And then with a jolt realised that she meant exactly that. No matter what it cost her.

For a moment he stared at her, then nodded, as if accepting that she meant it. 'You know so much, you might as well know it all.' He swept a pile of papers from a sofa to make room for them both. 'I suppose I should have the lot cleared out,' he said, looking around.

'I do understand.' Her mother had kept Jennie's room as a shrine. 'But from what you've told me about Matt, I think he would find it rather. . .'

'Silly?' he provided, as she struggled for some word that wouldn't offend. 'You're right, of course. He'd laugh his boots off that anyone should take him so seriously.' He lowered himself beside her. 'He never took anything that seriously.'

'Not even Maria?' she asked. 'She was the secret, wasn't she?'

'You remember everything, don't you?'

'Everything.' Everything connected with Chay Buchanan. She thought she would remember this week for the rest of her life in brilliant rainbow-bright detail.

'After the funeral I came back here to clear up the loose ends. I intended to sell the lease on the tower, try and forget what had happened. But the day I came back Maria arrived, distraught, on the doorstep. It took a long time to get the whole story from her.'

Sophie remembered his interest in Jennie and began to understand a little. 'Had her family turned her out?'

'Oh, no. Quite the reverse. She had escaped— climbed down a drainpipe, apparently.' He smiled slightly. 'She must have had considerable practice during her assignations with Matt, since she was already betrothed to a man her family had carefully chosen for her. They are old people. A noble family, from the Mdina.' Then his face grew grim again. 'They had only one answer for the sort of disgrace she had brought to them. She had been told she would be kept out of sight until her baby was delivered and then she would be sent away, to the convent.'

'I've seen it. At least the outside.' Grim walls, bars. The guide had told her that the only way out for the nuns was in a coffin. And that was a concession only granted as recently as twenty years ago. Before that the nuns had even been buried in a cemetery within the convent grounds. She shuddered. 'So you let her stay.'

'Yes, I let her stay. But that wasn't enough. Maria thought it would be, that I could protect her. It wasn't that simple. And her brothers were at the door within the hour, demanding that I hand her over.' He laid a finger along his nose. 'A memorable encounter.' He shrugged awkwardly. 'I told them the child she was carrying was mine and that we were going to be married. I don't think they believed me, but they gave me a week. If we weren't married by then, they would be back.'

'Not long.'

'No, but I didn't need to be pushed. I was afraid they might still return mob-handed in the night to try to reclaim her, and without a passport I couldn't even get her out of the country. So we were married within three days by the British High Commissioner. It was the only way I could be certain that Matt's child wouldn't just disappear to be adopted by some unknown family.' He sat forward, staring at his hands. 'He was a Buchanan, entitled to everything that Matt had, that I could give him. When Tom was born it was like getting a small piece of my brother returned to me.' He looked at her then. 'A kind of forgiveness.'

CHAPTER NINE

'You didn't tell anyone?'

Chay shook his head. 'My mother had to know. But Maria's family had sufficient influence to keep any mention of the family name out of the newspapers, so it wasn't picked up by the British nationals. You do see? I couldn't take the risk that they would take Tom. But once my name was on the birth certificate, he was mine——'

'Yes, I understand.' She covered his hand with her own. 'Truly.' But her heart bled too for Maria, a young girl who had married a stranger to protect her child.

'Why did you stay here afterwards?' she asked. 'I would have thought——'

'Don't you think I wanted to go?' he turned on her angrily. 'I never wanted to set foot in this place again. It was Maria. She refused to leave. She stayed up here in Matt's room day and night. . . I should have known then that it could only end in disaster. But I threw myself into research for my next book and hoped that once the child was born she would snap out of it.

'Just after Tom was born I had to go to London for the launch of a book I had finished the year before. The publishers had arranged the usual round of chat-shows and interviews, and to tell the truth I was the last person in the world Maria wanted about her. Matt and I weren't twins, like you and Jennie, but we were very alike. She must have found it hard to take. I hoped that, if I left, she might begin to recover her spirits, take some interest in the baby.' He let out a low, soft breath. 'Theresa had come a few months

before Tom was born—she had looked after Maria as
a child—and Paul promised to keep an eye on her. . .
I thought she would be all right.'

'Paul knows?'

'It's a little difficult to keep something like that from
a doctor. And he knew Matt.'

'What happened, Chay?'

He sat back and stared up at the ceiling. 'Publicity
happened.' He closed his eyes. 'I hadn't told Poppy
that I had married. I didn't quite trust her not to use
wedding-bells for a little extra hype, and I wasn't in a
position to produce the blushing bride for the obligatory photographs. In the event, of course, I was
presented as the literary world's eligible bachelor, a
girl thrust on my arm whenever there was a camera
pointed in my direction. Maria must have seen the
photographs in the papers. Her family certainly had.'

'But surely Paul——'

'If Paul had known what was happening he might
have been able to help. But Gian's mother had been
taken desperately ill and they had rushed off to
Florence to be with her.' He paused painfully. 'Maria
swallowed a handful of paracetamol. She didn't mean
to kill herself. . .it was a cry for help. But no one
heard.'

'Oh, Chay. How pitiful.'

'It was a couple of days before Theresa realised there
was something wrong. The symptoms take longer than
sleeping pills but are just as deadly. I flew straight
back, but by then it was already too late to do much
more than pray. She made me promise to stay at the
tower, Matt's home. She wanted Tom to know he was
Maltese, to learn to speak her language. And she
wanted me to try and reconcile her family to the
boy. . .' His voice cracked on the words, and as he

turned to her she took him in her arms and held him, her own cheeks wet against his shirt-front.

It was a long time before he held her away from him. 'Sophie——'

'It's all right, Chay. No matter what happens, I'll never betray your trust. Never.' She held his head between her hands. 'Believe me.'

His eyes held hers. 'That was the reason I couldn't let you go. Maria's family pride was frozen stiff with the disgrace. And how they hated me staying here. They wanted the whole thing swept under the carpet. They even sent a lawyer, threatening all kinds of problems if I didn't take the boy and leave the island.'

'Dear God. What did they do?'

'Nothing I couldn't handle.' But his face tightened at the memory. 'He was their grandchild, and for Maria I was determined they would never be allowed to ignore him or forget him. I took him to the cathedral every Sunday because I knew they would be there. And I knew, that first day, when Maria's mother saw him, that I had one friend. Theresa brought a letter from her. Be patient, she said. Be quiet. And I have been very quiet. Nothing to cause a ripple of publicity of any kind.'

'So you stopped writing and became a respectable businessman instead.'

'I tried to stop writing. I quickly realised that was impossible, but I told Poppy that I had burned myself out. The bills didn't stop coming in, though. I was halfway to qualifying as an architect when my first book was published. The tourist industry was booming, so property development seemed the obvious choice. And every time Maria's father saw my logo it served as a reminder that I wasn't going to go away.'

'He's had plenty to remind him. I've seen your boards everywhere.'

'Have you?' His look was long, assessing.

'I found a business card. . . When Poppy mentioned your business. . .'

'It hardly matters. You know everything else.'

'Not quite. What is going to happen on Sunday? You said it wouldn't matter after Sunday.'

'Maria's father has finally relented. A heart-attack has apparently given him a glimpse of his own mortality. On Sunday, Sophie, after the most delicate negotiations with his lawyers, Maria's father is going to receive his grandson.' He raised one shoulder slightly. 'You came blundering into that, threatening all kinds of mayhem. I couldn't take the risk.'

There had never been any risk. But it hardly seemed to matter now. 'You've sacrificed so much——'

'No. I gave Maria my promise. I would do it twice over if necessary.'

'Thank you for telling me. Your trust. . .is a precious gift.' Sophie reached up and kissed him lightly on the mouth. For a moment nothing happened. Then with a groan he gathered her into his arms and he kissed her. There was nothing of the practised flirt or the arrogant predator about his embrace. It was simply a man holding a woman, kissing her because that was what he wanted to do more than anything else in the world. And Sophie responded unreservedly, with a delight that shimmered through her.

'Sophie. . .' he murmured. His breath was soft on her eyelashes and her arms curled about his neck like a silk scarf and drew him down to her. For one hectic, rollercoaster moment, as he kissed her with a fierce, almost angry intensity, she thought she would die of happiness.

Then without warning he broke away, and, ignoring her soft cry of loss, held her at arm's length, as if she represented some mortal danger. And, as he stared at her, it seemed to Sophie that her fate hung in the balance.

He stood up and turned away. 'Go to bed, Sophie. Now.'

'Chay. . .?' Her voice quivered with the shock of his rejection. They had been on the edge of something so beautiful, so thrilling. . .his dismissal was like a blow. But his back remained turned resolutely towards her and after a moment she turned and stumbled down the stairs.

Sophie was about to start Tom's birthday cake when the doorbell rang the following morning.

'Sophie,' Poppy smiled, swept into the hall without waiting to be invited, and stepped past her.

'Chay's out,' Sophie informed the woman's back. When she had crawled miserably from her bed that morning, just after dawn, there had been no sign of him.

There was the minutest pause. 'Mmm. I know.' Poppy turned with a delicately teasing laugh that must have taken hours of practice to perfect and quite set Sophie's teeth on edge. 'I've. . .er. . .just left him,' she said, managing to load the words with hidden meaning. A burning blush betrayed Sophie. It was barely eight o'clock. Chay hadn't left very early this morning. He had left very late last night. 'I've called to collect his manuscript.' She regarded Sophie with a touch of amusement. 'He told me where it is,' she said. 'Don't let me keep you from your chores.'

Sophie turned on her heel. It was none of her business, she reminded herself as she returned to the kitchen, what Chay got up to with Poppy, or if he had decided to go ahead with publication of his book now that everything was going to be settled with Tom's grandfather. Although after waiting so long it seemed a little careless. . .

But last night she had been so sure that *she* was the one he had wanted to hold in his arms. . . She cracked the eggs into a bowl and began to beat them ferociously, not sure whether it was Chay or Poppy she wanted to reduce to batter.

She jumped a little while later, as the door banged after Poppy, then sagged against the work-top, unable to support herself any longer, and let the bitter tears fall.

Half an hour later she had pulled herself together and was beating sugar and butter to cream when she sensed Chay's presence. The mixer had drowned out the noise of his arrival. And even as she refused to acknowledge him he leaned over her shoulder and hooked his finger through the mixture. 'Mmm, chocolate.'

'Don't do that,' she warned tetchily.

'Or?'

She turned and looked up over her shoulder. 'Or I shall have to slap your wrist,' she threatened, a little shaken by the unexpected closeness of a mouth bracketed by the deeply carved lines of a smile. He must have been home for a while because he had showered, and moisture still clung to the thick mop of dark hair. And, having finally gained her full attention, he dropped a kiss tasting of cake mixture on her mouth.

'Why don't you try? he invited. Her heart gave a painful little gasp and, apparently satisfied, he moved to the table and picked up a list. 'Are you in a desperate hurry for any of this, because I'll be a while?'

And she could imagine just what would take the time. 'Don't rush back,' she advised coldly. 'But, if you can *spare the time*, there is something you can do for me.'

'Oh? What's that?' His voice had lost some of its warmth, the message was getting through.

She kept her eyes on the mixture she was beating. 'Book me a flight home for Sunday. As early in the day as possible.' She couldn't stand the long, empty silence that folllowed this request. 'I have to deliver the photographs to Island Holidays at the beginning of the week,' she rushed on. 'And then I have a job booked in——'

'Liverpool. You said. You're not the only one with a retentive memory.' She turned, pleading silently for him to understand, but his eyes had shut her out. 'And I imagine that you can't wait to get home and file your story. It must merit quite a bonus.'

Wrong. The bonus was to have been for something else entirely. 'I'm not a journalist,' she said flatly.

'But your "very special" friend Nigel is.'

I won't tell him! Never! But the words remained locked in her head, and she was still rooted furiously to the spot when the front door banged shut behind him. It didn't matter, she told herself. Eventually he would know that she hadn't betrayed him.

So what? that cruel inner voice taunted her. Last night had meant nothing. He had held her close and kissed her simply because she had been there, to listen while he poured out his grief and guilt; if he had swept her into his bed it might just have been perfect. But he had gone to Poppy instead, and any delay in leaving would simply prolong the agony.

And on Sunday evening Nigel would be coming for his pound of flesh. She was determined to be gone long before then.

Chay returned early in the afternoon and dumped the shopping on the kitchen table, along with the flight confirmation and a courier bag with her films. He curtly declined her offer of a late lunch and departed for the beach with Twany to begin building the barbeque. The fact that he had apparently got the message did little to restore her spirits.

He returned late in the afternoon, took a beer from the fridge and offered her one. She took it gratefully. She normally hated drinking anything from a can, but Chay had simply ripped the ring-pull off his and tipped it up, to drink long and deep, and she followed suit, too hot from a day spent over a cooker to care about such niceties.

'Have you checked your films?' he asked, leaning back against the table.

'They'll wait until I get home. I'll need my light-box to choose the best. I suppose you've taken out. . .?'

'I've taken out the personal ones. They're very good.'

'Consider them a contribution to your family album,' she snapped, and his face darkened. 'I'm sorry,' she said, quickly. 'After what you told me last night. . . that was tactless.'

'After last night I thought we were well beyond the point where the word tact would have a place in our relationship.' He threw the can in the bin. 'I clearly misread the signals.' He turned, the muscles in his neck corded with tension. 'Or did you spend the long night hours dreaming about Nigel? Or perhaps the handsome Cesare?'

'No!'

'Then doubtless you've had time to do your sums and realise how much your story is worth.' She was too angry to answer. 'You'd better go and get ready,' he said abruptly. 'We're due at Gian and Paul's in half an hour.'

She stiffened. 'I think I'd prefer to stay here.'

'Then think again, lady. They're expecting you.'

She fought back the urge to defy him. He looked fit to drag her there. 'If you insist.'

'In this particular case, I'm afraid I do.'

'Meaning?' she demanded, and regretted it the moment the word was out of her mouth.

He lunged forward and seized her arm. 'Meaning, Sophie Nash, that the next time you flash "come to bed" out of those big grey eyes of yours, don't expect me to act the gentleman if you should change your mind at the last minute.'

'Gentleman!' She almost exploded.

'Good God, do you think it was easy to send you away last night?' His fingers were biting into her arm as he held her pinned against him. Her breathing was ragged and she was held by a pair of eyes that generated enough electricity to power the national grid. 'But you are a very unwilling guest in my house, Sophie. Taking you to my bed would have been in the worst possible taste, don't you think?'

She knew that he was a hair's breadth from kissing her, and she mustn't allow that to happen. Ever again. She wrenched herself free. 'Especially when there's a more than willing reserve!'

'What the hell is that supposed to mean?' His dark brows drew together.

'Oh, don't be bashful, Chay. When Poppy dropped by she certainly wasn't——'

'Poppy was here?'

'She came to pick up your manuscript.'

'So. That was——' He broke off. 'Did you see her take anything?'

'No. I didn't stick around. I don't find her company that appealing.'

He pushed her through to the study and swung back a large painting to reveal a safe. Her searching had been pointless. She hadn't even thought of a safe. 'There!' He threw the pile of notepads on to the desk.

'I don't understand.'

'Poppy, thanks to you, is convinced I have a book just waiting to be published. In fact there are three. A trilogy. But even you didn't know that. So this morning I had a message from her husband, saying he was interested in leasing a berth at the new marina and could he meet me there. And while I was conveniently out of the way Poppy called, hoping to find a manuscript. But she could hardly expect you to stand by while she ransacked the study. So she made sure you wouldn't hang around. The only way she was certain would work.'

Poppy was married? 'She didn't——'

'No. She didn't get anything. No thanks to you.'

'I'm sorry.'

'Go and change, Sophie. We're going to be late as it is.'

In normal circumstances it would have been a delightful evening. Paul and Gian were welcoming; Cesare was on his best behaviour. His light-hearted charm was a million miles away from Chay's withdrawn, slightly dark mood and when he held out a glass of wine and raised his brows at the vacant chair beside her, Sophie's smile was welcoming.

He had clearly come to the conclusion that she and Chay had had a row and set out to amuse her, telling her about his job as a pilot with a commercial airline.

'I come to London sometimes,' he told her. 'May I call you?'

She hesitated. He was a pleasant companion, but without the glowering presence of Chay to restrain his ardour. . . 'I have some pretty friends,' she countered. 'I'm sure they'd love to meet you.'

'Give me your number quickly, *cara*. . .' he said with a soft laugh.

'She's not on the telephone.' Chay took Sophie's arm and jerked her to her feet. 'It's time to go. Tom's nearly out on his feet.'

And it was only Tom's presence in the car that prevented her from telling him exactly what she thought of him. The child curled up in her lap and by the time they were home was fast asleep. Chay took him from her and carried him off to bed, curtly declining any help.

Feeling slightly lost, she gathered up her films and went upstairs, thinking that she might begin to pack. But she didn't have her suitcase, and by the time she fetched it from upstairs she was too tired to do anything other than fall into bed.

Gian and Paul were the first to arrive with their brood the following afternoon and Paul immediately departed for the beach to help Chay. After that the children arrived thick and fast. Gian looked over their heads. 'How many did you say there are supposed to be? We'd better keep count in case we lose one or two.'

'Sixteen from school, your three and Tom. Twenty.' They had a quick count-up and led them down to the beach.

All the children had made an effort to come as cowboys and cowgirls and even some of the girls had guns. Led by Tom, they fired their caps off furiously, until the sound ricocheted around the cliff and the air was filled with the sharp scent of the explosive. For ten minutes they were allowed to let off steam in a gunfight that would have done justice to the OK Corral. Then Sophie began to organise games while Chay and Paul started the barbecue.

At about four the men began to cook, while Sophie

and Gian took the children into the sea to cool off. It seemed forever before Chay banged on a tin plate with a huge wooden spoon and they could hand them over to be fed. Sophie sank gratefully on to the sand and closed her eyes for a few minutes.

Despite a series of disturbed nights, sleep had eluded her as she had tried to order her thoughts through the long night. It had almost been a relief to get up as the dawn broke to ice Tom's cake.

Breakfast had been all excitement, with Tom opening his presents, then Chay had taken him down to the stables to get him out from under her feet. There had barely been time for a quick lunch before Gian and Paul had arrived. But at least there hadn't been time for any awkward silences.

'I hope you're not asleep.' Chay's voice seemed to come from a long way off, but she lifted a hand in a half-hearted way. She wasn't asleep, she wanted to say, but it was too much effort. 'You do know how dangerous it is to fall asleep in the sun?' he persisted. Why wouldn't he go away? 'Sophie?' She forced one eye open to convince him and was just in time to see the water coming, but far too late to avoid it. It hit her, icy cold, in the stomach, and she came up with a yell. 'I'm so glad that you're not asleep.'

He had been in the sea, presumably to cool off after the cooking, and water was running down the broad expanse of his chest, dripping from the tousled mop of dark hair, and somewhere in the ocean depths of his eyes, he was laughing.

Sophie saw a dangerous shade of red that brought her up from the sand in one fluid movement, and she flung herself at him. He stood his ground for a second, as if transfixed, then he turned and ran, urged on by the delighted children.

His long legs quickly out-distanced her but she

pounded after him in mindless determination, following him behind a group of rocks that took them out of sight of the party. Then she stopped. He had disappeared. There was a small cave that had been gouged from the cliff-wall by the constant wearing motion of the sea and she stepped towards it.

'Chay?' she called uncertainly. Then she shrieked as he grabbed her from behind and pushed her into the cave. 'Let go of me!' she demanded as he turned her, caught her with one arm about the waist and held her fast.

'But you've caught me,' he protested, without much regard for the truth. 'The question is, Miss Sophie Nash, what are you going to do with me?'

'Nothing! Let me go, Chay. I'm soaked!'

'So you are.' A wicked smile lifted the corners of his mouth as he regarded the T-shirt, thrown over her swimsuit to protect her skin, which now clung wetly to her body, offering no hiding place for embarrassingly prominent nipples that seemed to peak in almost automatic response to his merest touch. Now, inches from his bronzed torso clad only in his tormentingly brief swimsuit, her body almost groaned with longing for him. As if he heard, he tightened his grip, drawing her closer, so that the rough hair on his legs grazed her soft thighs, her tell-tale breasts were pressed against his chest, and her abdomen. . . She gasped as she realised just what was pressed against her abdomen, the shock bringing some semblance of control to her disordered senses.

'Chay. . .the children. . .'

'The children are occupied. However, I could be persuaded, for the payment of a small forfeit—a kiss, I believe, is traditional. . .?'

It wasn't fair. He shouldn't do this to her. She wanted to be strong, but held like this, pressed against the unyielding strength of his body, escape was the last thing on her mind. And his eyes, more blue than green, as if reflecting the flawless sky, told her that he knew exactly what she wanted. 'I thought I had captured you. . .'

'Possession, Sophie, is nine-tenths of the law,' he reminded her, and her lips parted on a little breath of excitement, her lids fluttering down as his mouth descended with agonising slowness. His lips touched the delicate hollow of her cheek, sending a delicious tingle rippling through her skin to every part of her body, and for a moment she remained perfectly still, waiting, knowing that this was just a prelude. . . To nothing. She opened her eyes.

'You've had your forfeit, Sophie. Don't be greedy.' He turned her round and gave her a little push. 'Hadn't you better go back and give Gian a hand?'

Tom hurtled up to her as she stumbled back along the beach to rejoin the others. 'Are we going to have the cake now?' he asked.

'Not on the beach. You can blow out your candles and cut the cake when everyone comes later to collect your friends. Have you all had enough to eat?'

'Sure thing!'

Sophie managed a convincing smile at his attempt at a cowboy accent. 'Well, then, we'd better get on with the sandcastle competition, pardner,' she said, diverting her eyes firmly away from the spot where Chay was tugging on a pair of shorts.

She organised everyone with spades and set them to work. Gian smiled as she dropped down beside her.

'Well? Did you give that naughty boy what he deserved?' she asked.

'What? Oh, Chay. Sure, I beat him to a pulp,' she said, imitating Tom.

'Is that what they're calling it now?' Sophie looked

up sharply, but it was nothing but the mildest teasing. She sighed. She was the one who felt she had been pulped.

'That was the most exhausting afternoon I have ever spent.' Chay closed the door behind the last of their guests. After a spectacular firework display, made especially by Twany for Tom's birthday, Tom had cut his cake and handed it round to the children while Chay and Sophie had offered something more substantial to their parents.

Now he put his hands on her shoulders and looked down into her face. 'Thank you for today, Sophie. Tom had a great time.' He smiled. 'I rather think I did too.'

She had made a point of keeping her distance from him since he had made a fool of her on the beach. Now he was too close, and she was much too vulnerable. 'Where is Tom?' she asked rather briskly, moving away.

He dropped his hands and looked around. 'He was here a minute ago.' They found him asleep on the sofa in front of the fireplace, his gun still clutched in a grubby hand. Chay stood over him for a moment. 'I'll take him up to bed. Why don't you make us both a drink?' he said, scooping up the sleeping child.

She poured him a Scotch and herself a glass of wine, then fetched a tray and began to gather up the glasses and plates. She was carrying it through to the kitchen when Chay came down the stairs.

'Did he wake up?'

'No. I took off most of his things and tucked him in. I'm afraid he's rather grubby and he hasn't brushed his teeth.'

'I don't suppose they will drop out overnight. Can you open this door, please? Your drink is in the drawing-room.'

'I'll fetch it and come and give you a hand.'

'There's no need.' She was tetchy. He was too masculine, too desirable. She wanted him too much, and since she couldn't have him, she didn't want him near her. Not if he was going to tease her, poke fun at the desire he knew tormented her, as he had done on the beach.

'I'll be the judge of that.' He took the tray from her and put it on the draining-board. 'This is my house, Sophie, even though you seem to have turned it on its head from the moment you arrived.'

'You made me stay,' she reminded him, a stubborn tilt to her chin as she turned on the taps and let hot water run into the sink.

'Well, you have your flight booked tomorrow. There's apparently nothing more to keep you.'

'Great.' She dumped a pile of plates in the sink and began to wash them, heaping them on the draining-board with a noisy clatter.

Chay began to dry them and stack them neatly. 'You will take a little more care with the glasses, won't you?' he asked, as she reached for a crystal tumbler. She swished it around the suds with restrained violence and set it to drain with excessive care. As she reached for the next he caught her wrist. 'I couldn't care less about the glasses, Sophie, but wouldn't want you to cut yourself.' Tears sprang unbidden to her eyes and she bit her lip, trying desperately not to let them fall. 'Sophie?'

She blinked furiously. 'Yes?' she croaked, her throat tight, her voice hoarse.

'What is it?' He turned her to face him, but she refused to look up. 'What's the matter? You're like a prickly pear this evening.'

'Green and spiky,' she hiccuped as she blinked back the tears and faced him. 'Well, thanks.'

'Just spiky.' He brushed the tears away with his thumbs. 'Is it because I didn't kiss you this afternoon?'

Damn him! Why did he always see straight through her? Worse, why did he have to say it out loud? It was bad enough that he knew, without him insisting she admit it. 'You did kiss me.' She managed a whisper.

'Not quite the way either of us intended. You must surely have realised——?'

'Must I? Why don't you run it by me, Chay?' she invited. All her desires were apparently hanging out for the world and his wife to see. It would adjust the balance, soothe her pride, if instead of that superior know-it-all smirk just this once he had to admit his own arousal. 'Tell me how it was for you.'

His face was gratifyingly grave. 'For me, Sophie? It was like this. If I had kissed you, I don't believe anything could ever have stopped me until I had tasted every last part of you. And then made love to you until we were both exhausted.'

'Oh!' The sound came in a little rush of breath. Whatever she had expected, it hadn't been that.

'Not quite the time or place, was it? Now, shall we finish washing the glasses? Or had you something else in mind?'

'Oh, er, yes. . .the glasses.' She turned back to the sink and stared at the crystal. 'At least. . . I'm sorry. I don't think I can,' she said, as her legs began to tremble.

'You did ask,' he reminded her, and then with a muffled oath he swept her into his arms and carried her into the drawing-room, to the sofa set four-square before the fireplace. 'This is ridiculous, Sophie,' he murmured into her hair.

She didn't want it to be ridiculous. She wanted to bury her face in the warmth of his neck and let him hold her and never let her go. But she resisted the urge, held herself away from him. 'Is it? You were the one who insisted upon playing the gentleman.'

'I had to.'

'Even if it was what I wanted?'

'Even then,' he said.

She took a little heart from the hoarseness of his voice, and peeped up at him from beneath long lashes. 'Maybe I could persuade you to change your mind.' He caught his breath as a delicate flush coloured her cheekbones.

'Sophie. . .' he warned her. 'What on earth am I going to do with you?'

Her blush deepened. 'I was rather hoping you knew, Chay,' she whispered into his neck. 'I've done the theory, but I never could. . .quite get through the practical.'

There was a pause. 'And you carry a packet of condoms with you in case the opportunity. . .er. . . arises to take a re-test?'

CHAPTER TEN

FOR a moment his words didn't quite penetrate the warm, comfortable haze generated by Chay's arms wrapped about her. When it did, when the implication of what he had said finally broke through the rosy glow, cruelly shredding it, Sophie erupted from his arms, and he made no move to hold her.

They had come a long way in a few short days, but this was the most brutal reminder of the true status of their relationship. That when he had first brought her to the tower he had searched her bags to find out who she was, knew things about her that no other man had ever come close to touching. And because of that he thought she was lying to him.

When her shaky legs had put ten feet between them she finally managed to speak. 'I might be a twenty-three-year-old virgin, Chay Buchanan, but that doesn't make me stupid. My sister——' her voice almost cracked with the hurt of his disbelief '—my twin sister, was an unmarried mother by the time she was seventeen. It was like looking into a mirror. . . The resulting mess left a lasting impression on me. I have no intention. . .' She saw the beginning of a smile across his lips. 'It's not funny!' she said angrily.

He was beside her in a stride, his strong arms around her preventing further retreat. 'I agree, my love. It's not in the least bit funny. It's just. . .' He tilted her face up to his, forced her to look at him. 'Tell me, how long have you been carrying that packet about with you?'

'Ever since. . .' She flushed crimson and her hands

171

flew to her hot cheeks. 'Do you think they've passed their "sell by" date?'

'I really don't think I'd be prepared to risk it,' he said, with the utmost seriousness.

'I. . . I didn't think.'

He finally allowed himself to smile. 'Do you know, Sophie, that is one of the things I most love about you? You just jump in with both feet. I begin to believe that you are congenitally incapable of deception.' He drew her against his chest briefly, and buried his face in her hair.

You'd better tell him, Sophie, her little voice prompted. Right now. But she ignored it. There was plenty of time for explanations. She needed this moment, just to be held by him.

After a while, when she didn't say anything, he held her away from him and looked down into her face. 'Sophie Nash, do you know that you could break a man's heart? Just by looking at him like that?'

'I. . .I would never want to break yours, Chay. I would never want to hurt you in any way.' For a brief dizzy moment he kissed her, then he tore himself away.

'I'll go and open a bottle of champagne,' he said, a little raggedly. 'We've got a few things to discuss.'

'No, don't go. . .' she murmured, reaching for him in a sudden panic at the thought of him leaving her on her own. 'I must tell you. . .'

He drew in a sharp breath. 'If you don't let me go right now, Sophie, I swear you'll suffer the same fate as your sister.'

'I. . .I'm not seventeen any more, Chay.'

He swore softly. 'You're playing with fire, Sophie. I'm not made of wood.'

'Chay. . .' she protested—but to an empty doorway. 'This is ridiculous,' she finished, but talking to herself. But wonderfully ridiculous. She curled up in an armchair and laid her cheek against its broad arm, and hugged the thought to herself.

As she lay against the old worn leather, a bright packet of prints on a low table in the direct line of her sight intruded on her thoughts. They had been brought over by Gian and left for them to look at. She reached almost automatically for it and began to flip through the pictures. Quite ordinary snapshots in the main part, of their day on the beach, until she came to the photograph of Chay and Tom grinning over a bright red apple. She smiled. It was a real winner; she had known it would be the moment she had taken it. Then, as if a goose had walked over her grave, she shivered. If he saw it he would think she had done it deliberately. That she had planned it. . . She pushed it into her shorts-pocket as she heard him coming back.

She turned, forcing a smile to her lips, certain her guilt must be written clear for him to see. Then the photograph was wiped from her mind as she saw the second man, grinning broadly in ghastly contrast to the hard-edged danger of Chay's expression, as they crossed the endless expanse of the room and came towards her. Nigel. For a moment the room swam. It couldn't be him. It was Saturday, she wanted to scream. She had another day before Nigel came to demand her happiness in exchange for Jennie's. Time to explain, time to tell Chay everything. But there was no more time.

She saw the anger glitter in Chay's eyes and knew that nothing she could say would ever put things right. 'You have a visitor, Sophie.' Chay's voice was like a splinter in her heart. 'The cavalry has arrived to rescue you, apparently.' He stared at her as if he was seeing a stranger. 'Just a fraction too soon.'

'I didn't hear the door. . .' she said stupidly.

'That's because your friend was flashing his headlights across the road in the expectation that you would notice him. That was the signal you arranged when he called?' he asked, with deadly scorn.

She leapt to her feet. 'Chay, this isn't. . . I didn't——'

But Nigel interrupted, making a liar of her. 'Sorry if I interrupted something special, sweetheart, but my deadline has been moved up. I couldn't wait until tomorrow.'

'I've nothing for you, Nigel,' she said dully.

'We had a deal. . .' Nigel warned. 'Remember Jennie. . .'

'A deal?' Chay regarded the man with distaste. 'I'm afraid if you want the photographs, they have already been destroyed.'

But Nigel didn't care what Chay thought of him. He was used to people looking at him as if he was something nasty they had trodden in. 'I know,' he said smugly, and ran his hand up her arm. 'She told me when I called.'

'No. . .' Sophie moaned softly at the innuendo he had managed to insinuate into those innocent words.

'But after a few days tucked up with you she guaranteed that she could provide me with something far more interesting.'

Chay's eyes were flint, all the colour gone from them. 'That was your deal? How unfortunate for you both that I didn't seize the many opportunities thrown in my path.' He stared at Sophie. 'Don't be too hard on her. She really did try.' Chay, his face all black and white shadows in the lamplight, took a step towards him. 'But you had better take the. . .lady. . .home now. I'm sure she has more than enough to excite your readers.'

Nigel, edging back towards the door, was no longer smiling quite so confidently.

Sophie swung back to Chay, determined to convince him that this was none of her doing. 'Chay, listen to me. . .'

His eyes were riveted to her face. Leaden eyes, in which contempt for them both was written clear. 'I think,' he said, ignoring her plea, his voice hard and cold as black marble, 'that the sooner you both leave my home, the better.'

'Come on, Sophie,' Nigel coaxed.

'Are you still here?' Chay's eyes finally released her as he made a sudden move in Nigel's direction.

Realising that he was in imminent danger of being pitched bodily through the door, Nigel hastily backed off. 'I'll wait in the car while you get your things,' he threw at Sophie. Then he fled.

She tried to move—to go to Chay, tell him, make him understand that she hadn't wanted to be a part of Nigel's sordid little plot to uncover his secrets. But nothing seemed to work. Her legs, her arms, her tongue were all made of wood. And her brain seized up beneath the glacial expression that forbade any attempt at explanation. Was it only fifteen minutes since he had held her? Kissed her?

'I'm truly sorry that I didn't understand how badly you wanted me to take you to bed, Sophie, to put the final touch to your. . .story.' His voice sliced through her heart like a knife. 'Especially when you offered yourself with such flattering frequency, even to the point of tempting me with the special prize of your virginity. I really must try to be less. . .'

'Noble?' she said quietly.

'Gullible.'

A sob broke from her lips and she turned and ran, passing the abandoned champagne and glasses standing on the hall table, up the stairs to her room. She flung her clothes into the case, bundling them up with no attempt to fold them. He had said she could break his heart. Well, he had just broken hers, not trusting her, not giving her a chance to explain. And why on earth should he believe her? Trust her? She had, after all, been part of a plot. . . But she hadn't realised. . . How could she have known that she would fall in love?

She banged the case shut and took one last look around. It felt like the end of something, but how could that be so? Nothing had started. Only love, and that apparently didn't need time. She fought back the longing to take a last glance at Tom. Instead she walked down the stairs and through the hall, eyes straight ahead, to where Chay was waiting grey-faced at the front door. He caught her arm and she stopped, but refused to look at him. 'Why?' he demanded.

For a moment, for just a moment, she thought she had a chance, that she could explain why. But deep down she knew it wouldn't make any difference. Nothing could. It would simply prolong the agony of parting. 'It was just a job,' she said.

He abruptly released her, and as she stepped through the door and out into the night it was slammed behind her and the lock was turned.

The sound of rain woke her. It was days since she had returned to London. Days in which the rain had sounded a constant background to the ringing of the telephone that she left unanswered. She jumped as it began again, and she glanced at the clock. Seven-thirty. He knew she would be gone by eight. Work. Any sort of work, to keep her mind busy so she wouldn't have to think. She lifted the receiver, cut off the call and left it off the hook, then swung her feet out of bed, shivering in the chill of a spring that in London refused to blossom.

She made tea and poured cereal into a bowl, though

she knew she couldn't eat. The doorbell rang. It would
be Sarah from next door, checking up on her. Worrying
about her. But it wasn't Sarah, it was Nigel, his foot in
the door before she could slam it. He pushed his way
in.

'Go away. I have nothing to say to you.'

He took an envelope from his pocket, holding it
under her eyes so that she was forced to look at it. 'I
went to see Jennie last night,' he said. 'She's got this
flu that's going round. Looks pretty poorly. They go
through these places like. . . Well, you know. I expect
the kid will get it soon.'

'How can you?' she demanded bitterly. 'How can
you be so. . .evil?'

'Evil? That's a bit strong, Sophie. All I want in
return for her address is everything you know about
Chay Buchanan. He said you knew plenty.'

'Nothing that I'm prepared to talk to you about.'

'Pity. Your sister——'

'My sister is a grown woman, Nigel. She can come
home any time she wants. It's taken this for me to
realise that.' She took a step towards him. 'But the
truth is, Nigel, that I don't believe you know where my
sister is. I poured my heart out to you because it was
my birthday and hers, and I had had a glass too much
wine at a party. And miraculously, it seemed, through
your contacts, you found her. Just a little *too* miraculously. Because there was just a little favour you
wanted for the information. Since I was going to Malta
anyway. Something else I had mentioned at the party.'
She took another step towards him. 'And I so much
wanted to believe you that I would have done anything.
You knew that, didn't you? It's the stock-in-trade of
people like you.'

His eyes hardened and he gripped the envelope

between his fingers, holding it out as he tore it to shreds. 'You'll never know now, will you?'

The pieces fluttered to the carpet. She knew. Until that moment she hadn't truly been certain. But while there had been a chance he could have used the information he would never have thrown it away.

'You don't understand, do you, Nigel?' She looked him in the face. 'Even if I had believed you, it would have made no difference.' Then she picked up the pieces, all quite blank, walked into the kitchen and dropped them in the bin.

But she had been right, and for a moment a mixture of pain and relief flooded through her, making her weak. She had promised Chay. In the quiet darkness of the tower, when he had told her about Maria and Matt, she had promised that she would never betray him. Even for her sister.

And the agony of letting Jennie go had somehow cleared her mind. The more she thought, the more she had been sure. She wiped away a tear, suddenly feeling a little better. Chay had said, with some justification, that she jumped in with both feet. That was what had got her into this mess in the first place. But not this time. This time she had done the right thing.

She went back into the living-room and looked around, but Nigel had gone. She walked across to the door and closed it behind him, thankful that she need never see or speak to him again.

Sophie walked across to the bedside table to replace the receiver on the telephone and glanced at her clock. There was plenty of time for a shower to wash the stench of the man away. Then she frowned, and knelt on the floor to look beneath the bed in case it had fallen. But it hadn't fallen. It wasn't there. Her beautiful photograph of Chay and Tom. The photograph that she had found in the pocket of her shorts after the nightmare journey home. The photograph that she had stood beside her bed in a little silver frame. It was gone.

Nigel.

She flew to the phone to call the police. The frame was antique. She would have him arrested for theft. Then she stopped. There was no time for that. She had to warn Chay, and there was only one way to do it.

The tower stood as she had seen it that first morning when she had come looking for him, the butter-coloured stone a little more dusty, the flush of spring flowers already past their best. It was time for the hardier geraniums and oleanders to soften its stark lines.

As she stood before the great front door her head-long rush back to the island to warn Chay seemed foolhardy in the extreme. He might shut the door in her face, refuse to speak to her. But she had to try.

She raised her hand to the antique dolphin knocker, but before she could announce her presence the door was flung open and Theresa, white-faced, gave a little scream.

'Miss Sophie! *Dio grazzi*!' Then she looked around. 'Where is Mr Chay?'

'Isn't he here?'

Theresa's eyes rolled. 'No, he is——' She stopped. 'You must come. Help me,' she said breathlessly. Then retreated into her own language.

'Theresa!' The sharp tone in Sophie's voice shocked the woman into silence. 'Tell me! What is the matter?' The woman pointed to the cliff, then buried her face in her apron. Sophie followed the gesture, a slight frown creasing her forehead. Then, with a sudden unease that fastened itself around her heart and wouldn't let go, she grabbed Theresa's arm. 'Is it Chay? Is he on the cliff?' Theresa began to wail pitifully, shaking her head, and suddenly Sophie knew. 'Oh, no. Please, God, no.' The words were wrenched from her. 'Where is Chay?'

'Gone. . . He's gone. . .' Her eyes were rolling, and it was obvious the woman was beyond sense. Kicking off her high-heeled shoes, Sophie began to run. Down the path to the beach, along by the cave and then over the rocks, taking care not to slip. The thought that Tom needed her help, that there was no one else, made her slow when all she wanted to do was race.

She caught her breath as she saw him. About thirty feet up and very still, his face chalk-white. He looked so small.

'Tom' she called, very gently, very evenly. 'I'm coming up to you. Just hold on.'

He didn't move, didn't speak. He was clearly too frightened even to move his head. She looked for a way to get to him and then, with a swift prayer to whatever saint looked after fools and little children, she grasped the handhold that offered itself so invitingly. But she was not a dare-devil boy. Nothing would have tempted her on to the cliff-face again. Only love.

It was a slow and painful climb for unaccustomed limbs, but she had learned her lesson the last time. If she tried to rush she would never make it. And, for Tom's sake, she had to make it. Foot by foot she moved towards him. It wasn't a difficult climb if you didn't look down or think about the drop. Or Matt Buchanan falling to his death as his brother tried to reach him.

Tom began to wail just before she reached him. A long thin sound that cut her to the heart and lent a desperate speed to her hands and feet. Then she was beside him. 'Hi, pardner,' she said softly. His face began to crack, but she didn't want him to cry. He would have to participate in his own rescue or they were both in trouble, and she quickly moved her body over Tom's, so that he would feel her at his back, protecting him, and almost at once he seemed to relax a little. 'Shall we see if we can get on to the ledge?' she suggested, and after a long moment he nodded, once.

Her first thought had been to take him back down. At least the drop reduced with every step. But, having climbed so far, she was certain that neither of them would make it, and the ledge was only a few feet further on. For a moment she glanced up, half hoping to see Chay's familiar face, the strong hand extended to help. Then she gritted her teeth. No one was going to help them.

She felt for a handhold and found a likely lump of rock. It held firm and she pulled herself up, and showed Tom where to put his hands. It worked, and, confidence restored a little, he allowed her to help him until he was perched on the ledge and he, at least, was safe.

For a moment she remained where she was, aching, sore and deeply frightened, but she knew she would have to make the effort to join the boy on the ledge before her own strength gave out. She reached for a rocky protrusion, an ideal handhold from which to pull herself up, but as she shifted her weight it gave way. Clawing momentarily at space, her heartbeat rattling in panic, sweat standing out in beads on her forehead and upper lip, she knew she was going to die.

Then her clutching fingers found something solid and stuck fast. Tom lunged to help her. 'Get back,' she yelled sharply. As she saw the pinched white face leaning above her, she swallowed and tried to smile. 'Sorry, Tom. I'll be fine. Just sit right back, away from the ledge. I'll just have a little rest.' She tried to ignore the sweat gathering under her fingers and the pain in her chest. The sense of *déjà vu* was almost overhwelming. 'Chay,' she whispered fervently, but this time Chay wasn't there to rescue her.

'Can I offer you a hand, Sophie Nash?' She jerked out of a half-faint. She was beginning to imagine things as her need for him conjured the words from her brain. Yet the gentle voice had sounded so real that she was unable to stop herself glancing up to the cliff-top, but there was no one there. She glanced at Tom, cowering back on the ledge. At least he was safe, she thought. She had done that for Chay. That was all that mattered, and she laid her forehead against the rock.

Then Chay was there beside her, his arm was around her, and she was being propelled upwards on to the ledge beside the boy.

'Chay?' She stared into the grim white mask of his face. 'Where did you come from? Theresa said——'

He indicated the top of the cliff a few yards above them. 'Shall we adjourn the inquest until you're both safe?' he interrupted abruptly. 'Sit there and don't move. I'll come back for you.'

Then he made Tom stand and slowly, carefully, coaxed him to climb the rest of the way. To Sophie it was agony, watching as the two of them covered the distance, Chay's calm voice indicating the best route and Tom, confidence recovering fast, putting his hands and feet where he was told, unaware of the hand at his back ready to grasp him. Why on earth didn't he just carry him up? Dump him over the edge and make sure he was safe?

Finally it was done, and she let out a long, slow shuddering breath and felt all the tension slide out of her body.

'Now it's your turn, Sophie Nash.' And there was no doubt from his expression that it had been a mistake to return. He was still angry with her. Very angry.

'I can manage,' she said stubbornly, as he ordered her to put her arms about his neck.

'Can you?' he said sharply. 'I don't think so.' Then, his voice a little gentler, 'Perhaps you should let me help.' And her heart began to beat a little faster.

'Despite the undoubted provocation?'

'Despite everything. Come on, Sophie, let's go home.' And together they climbed to the top. He made no effort to disguise his help. Her ego was long beyond the need of such protection. His hand was there behind her all the way. Steadying, comforting, reassuring. Then he was hauling her over the ledge.

Tom was waiting. Theresa too, crouched over the boy, crying, wiping her eyes with her apron, her arms cradling him, rocking him. But when Tom saw Sophie he broke away.

'You've come back, Sophie,' he said, flinging himself at her, all terror apparently forgotten. 'Will you stay now? You won't go away again?'

'Tom!' Chay's voice was sharp. 'Haven't you got something to say to Sophie?'

Tom's face fell. 'I. . . I'm sorry, Sophie.'

'Are you?' She gathered him in and hugged him. 'I do understand,' she whispered. 'It was a challenge. Something you had to do.' His dark eyes looked at her uncertainly, and then she knew why Chay had made the boy climb the last few yards himself. 'But now it's done,' she said. 'You've climbed the cliff like Uncle Matt and Papa and you'll never have to do it again.' She saw the flicker of relief touch the child's eyes before he threw his arms about her neck, and she felt the little body tremble against her.

Then Chay picked him up and held him close for a moment, before handing him over to Theresa. 'Take him back to the cottage, Theresa, and stick him in the bath,' he recommended. 'Then give him something to eat. He must be hungry.' He ruffled the boy's hair. 'Go on, Tom. We'll come down and see you later.'

'Why is he going to the cottage?'

'All his things are there. I arranged for him to stay down with Theresa and Twany while I was in London.'

She stared at him. 'But you're not in London.'

'No,' he said. 'I'm not.'

'Chay——' she began. 'I know you're still angry——'

'Angry? Of course I'm angry.' She stepped back as if slapped, and he swore. 'Oh, Sophie,' he said fiercely, catching her and pulling her close against his chest to bury his face in her hair. 'I'm not angry with you. You risked your life to save Tom. It wasn't as if you didn't know. . .' He gave a long, painful shudder. 'I'm angry with myself for not realising how serious he was. You did warn me.' He straightened, held her at arm's length and finally managed a lop-sided smile. 'We really must stop meeting like this.'

'Twice is more than enough,' she agreed, her heart-rate racketing dangerously out of control.

'At least I don't have to carry you this time.' He put his arm around her shoulder. 'Or do I?' He frowned. 'You're trembling.'

'I'm s-s-sorry.' And then her teeth were rattling and she was shivering and her legs were like rubber. He swore and swung her up into his arms. 'Come on. I think we could both do with a large brandy.'

She peeped up at him from under a curtain of long thick lashes and took the biggest risk of her life. Far worse than climbing the cliff, the consequences of misjudgement just as final. 'You promised me champagne. . .once.'

He stood her, very carefully, on the living-room floor, and turned her into his arms. 'So I did. You shall have bottles of the stuff. You can bath in it if you want to, but not right now. Right now there's someone you have to meet.'

He turned her round, and for a moment she didn't understand. A young fair-haired woman stepped towards her, oddly familiar and yet. . . 'Hello, Sophie.'

'Jennie?' Sophie took an uncertain step forward. Then she flew to her, hugging her, crying and laughing all at once. 'Oh, Jennie.' Then she saw the smaller, younger Jennie, hiding shyly behind her mother.

'This is Kate.'

Sophie bent down. 'Hello, Kate. I'm your Aunt Sophie.'

The child touched her face. 'You're just like my mummy.'

'Yes, darling. Exactly like.'

'Come on, Kate. Mummy and Sophie have a lot to talk about.' Chay took the child's hand. 'We'll go and find Tom and he can show you his pony. He might even let you sit on her.'

It was a long time later, hours in reality, years in words, before they finally stopped talking and went to look for Chay and Kate and Tom. The three of them were in the cottage having supper, and Theresa waved them into seats and produced two more plates.

'Chay. . .'

'Later, Sophie. We'll talk later.' When we're on our own, his eyes promised, and her face grew warm.

'But I don't understand. Why did you bring Jennie here?'

'Because when I took her to your flat, your next-door neighbour told me you had rushed off to Malta on some emergency. This was the contact address she had. So we followed you.' He frowned. 'Why. . .?'

But Sophie had already leapt to her feet. 'Oh, lord,

I forgot. . .in all the excitement. Nigel stole a photograph of you and Tom from my flat. . .'

'When?'

'This morning. . .'

He didn't waste time asking what photograph or when she had taken it. 'Excuse us, Jennie.' He rose and took her arm. 'Tell me,' he demanded as he strode with her back up to the tower, and a little breathlessly she explained what had happened.

There was a newly installed telephone on the desk in his study and he punched in a number.

'Poppy? Chay Buchanan. Don't talk, just listen. I want you to call the editor of *Celebrity*. He's going to be offered a photograph of me with Tom by someone called Nigel Phillips. It's stolen. Tell him if they use it he'll be charged as an accessory.' He listened for a moment. 'Well, just in case he's prepared to take the risk, you'd better issue a press release. You can announce a new Chay Buchanan novel for the autumn list. The first part of a trilogy——' He broke off as there was a burst of excitement from the receiver. 'Yes, yes. You'll have the manuscript by courier. And you can also mention that I'm getting married.' He glanced at Sophie as she made a choked sound. 'You've met the bride.' He grinned at her. 'Yes, it's Mary Poppins. When? Well, I've got the licence in my pocket, so don't bother to ring back, because we'll be on our honeymoon.' He took Sophie's hand and pulled her closer. 'Where?' He laughed softly. 'My dear Poppy, that information is classified.' He pressed the cut-off button and put the receiver on his desk.

'Chay. . .' Sophie protested, a little breathlessly. 'You can't. . . You mustn't. All that publicity. . . It'll destroy everything you've worked for. . .'

'No, my love. Did you doubt for a moment that once

his grandfather had met Tom he could fail to love him?'

'It went well?'

'The first few minutes were a bit sticky. Then. . . Well, you know Tom.' He captured her chin and tilted it until she was completely at his mercy. 'And you know me. I warned you once that I was prepared to keep you here for as long as I had to.'

'Imprisoned at the top of your tower?' she asked, a little shakily.

'If necessary. I'm going to ask you a question. I'd like the answer to be yes.'

'But I have to explain.'

'No, you don't. You said that you would never do anything to hurt Tom or me. "Believe me," you said. I should never have doubted you. Can you forgive me?'

'There's nothing to——'

'I want to hear you say yes. Can you forgive me?'

'Yes, Chay,' she said.

'Convince me,' he insisted, pulling her into his arms.

Slowly, a little shyly, she raised her hands to cradle his face and stood on tiptoe to kiss him. It was so sweet, so wonderful, like rain after a drought. 'Is that convincing enough?' she asked at last, a little breathlessly.

'We'll come back to that one.' He took her hands. 'I'll tell you at length, when I've less important things on my mind, just how I found Jennie. But with friends who have access to the right computers——'

'How on earth did you know that was what it was all about?'

'Something he said. *Remember Jennie.* I checked up on Phillips. He's done this sort of thing before. A very nasty piece of work.'

'He said he had found her in one of those awful bed and breakfast places. . .'

'He lied.'

'Yes. I was very stupid to have ever believed him.'

'No, darling. You were vulnerable. People who care are always at the mercy of the unscrupulous. But we shouldn't be too hard on him.'

'Why not?' she demanded indignantly.

'Because without him we would have never met. And I would never have been able to ask you to marry me. Will you marry me?'

'This is where you want me to say yes?' she asked, her voice breaking a little.

'You're catching on, my darling.'

'Am I?' She slid her arms around his neck and a little smile played about her mouth. 'Convince me, Chay.'

And it was some time later before she was able to gaze up into that fierce, proud, wonderful face. For a moment the whole world held its breath and waited. 'Yes, Chay,' she said. 'Yes, please.'

Modern Romance™
...seduction and
passion guaranteed

Tender Romance™
...love affairs that
last a lifetime

Sensual Romance™
...sassy, sexy and
seductive

Sizzling Romance™
...sultry days and
steamy nights

Medical Romance™
...medical drama on
the pulse

Historical Romance™
...rich, vivid and
passionate

29 new titles every month.

*With all kinds of Romance for
every kind of mood...*

MILLS & BOON®

Makes any time special™

MAT3

Coming Home

Scandal drove David away
Now love will draw him home . . .

PENNY JORDAN

Published 21st September